*For Bobbie Simms, who had a part
in this book from the beginning, with thanks*

Prologue

I was the son my father never had, the child who would follow his dreams of an America expanding westward to the Pacific Ocean. And I was the parent that my husband longed for, the one who gave him the love, acceptance, and respectability he needed. I was a daughter and a wife, conscious always of the proper role of a woman . . . and always chafing against it. And yet I was myself—only I learned that lesson almost too late in life.

My father was Thomas Hart Benton, for forty years a United States senator from Missouri, one who fought for westward expansion and who fought equally hard against slavery, to the final destruction of his political career. He was a man of towering strength who brought me up in his shadow, wanting me to be both the helpmate he missed in my invalid mother and, still, the dainty, beautiful daughter he thought all men should have.

My husband was John Charles Frémont, explorer, topographer, soldier of fortune, presidential candidate, senator, governor, mining king, and, sometimes, bankrupt failure, court-martialed soldier, disgraced businessman—a man whose whole life was shadowed by the fact of his illegitimacy. That I loved him passionately has never been in doubt, nor that he loved me equally. But ours was a rocky relationship, with him away more than he was at home, filled with dreams and visions of what could be, while I coped too often with what really was. Our marriage was a series of good-byes—sometimes he returned to me in glorious triumph, but there were also days of dark disgrace. I saw two of my infant children die, watched my husband flirt with the temptation of a lover—a temptation I myself once put firmly behind me for his sake—and suffered a devastating estrangement from the father who had taught me all I knew—all this for the man I'd impulsively eloped with at the age of seventeen.

Without my father and my husband, the course of American history would be vastly different—less dramatic, I believe, and less triumphant. Westward expansion, even the crossing of the continent with the railroad, would have come without them but perhaps not so soon nor so effectively. The world should not judge such men as it does ordinary mortals . . . and yet it judges them more harshly. When I think of the part they had in the course of history, I like to believe that I, too, had a hand in the shaping of our country's history. I know I was of inestimable help to my father and, perhaps more important, I shaped the life of my husband. I was a good wife and a good mother to our children . . . but my life went beyond those roles, and I was not typical of my time, more's the pity.

John died nine days ago in New York—we were apart more than we were together these last years, but I still needed him, still hoped he would settle down here in California. His death, so sudden and so shocking, has forced me to look at myself . . . and at our life together. It is time to figure it all out, to untangle the raveled skeins of love and need, power and control, greed and good that went into our lives. I can only bring it all back to life in writing, as I brought vitality to the written reports of John's expeditions all those years ago. Lily, the daughter who has protected me all her life, tries to discourage me, saying my memoirs will be too sad, so I often write secretly, even furtively, when she is busy with her chores. But the story is not sad, really, and tell it I must, lest the world forever misunderstand Father, John . . . and, most of all, me.

JESSIE
A Novel

JUDY ALTER

TWODOT®

GUILFORD, CONNECTICUT
HELENA, MONTANA

A · TWODOT® · BOOK

An imprint of The Rowman & Littlefield Publishing Group, Inc.
4501 Forbes Blvd., Ste. 200
Lanham, MD 20706
www.rowman.com

Distributed by NATIONAL BOOK NETWORK

British Library Cataloguing in Publication Information available

Library of Congress Cataloging-in-Publication Data

Names: Alter, Judy, 1938– author.
Title: Jessie : a novel / Judy Alter.
Description: Guilford, Connecticut : TwoDot, [2021] | Summary: "An Old West
   novel highlighting the life of Jessie Benton Frémont"— Provided by
   publisher.
Identifiers: LCCN 2020043880 (print) | LCCN 2020043881 (ebook) | ISBN
   9781493052653 (paper ; alk. paper) | ISBN 9781493052660 (electronic)
Subjects: LCSH: Frémont, Jessie Benton, 1824–1902—Fiction. | Frémont,
   John Charles, 1813–1890—Marriage—Fiction. | Politicians'
   spouses—Fiction. | Women pioneers—Fiction. | GSAFD: Biographical
   fiction. | Historical fiction. | Western stories.
Classification: LCC PS3551.L765 J47 2021 (print) | LCC PS3551.L765
   (ebook) | DDC 813/.54—dc23
LC record available at https://lccn.loc.gov/2020043880
LC ebook record available at https://lccn.loc.gov/2020043881

∞™ The paper used in this publication meets the minimum requirements of American National
Standard for Information Sciences—Permanence of Paper for Printed Library Materials, ANSI/NISO
Z39.48-1992.

Chapter One

"Miss English's Seminary!" I exploded. "That's for spoiled rich girls without any brains in their heads."

We were in my father's library. No matter which Washington boardinghouse we lived in—and there were several—Father always had his own private room, where he worked surrounded by his law books and exploration journals and maps—always maps, on every surface, rolled and stood in the corners, a few prize ones hanging on the walls. Now Father sat at his desk, the top rolled back and the pigeonholes exploding with notes, letters, and the clutter of his daily life. A vial of ink and a quill lay carelessly on the desk. Father had never yet adjusted to pen points and much preferred to use his penknife to sharpen a quill when he began to compose the lengthy speeches for which he was noted in Congress.

He was a big man—more than six feet tall—with heavy features that spoke of strength and eyes that looked directly at you, as he did now at me. Father's hair was already white, though he was only in his early fifties, and I thought he looked like the king of the jungle, like the lions in the book I'd just read. Father seemed to have the same strength and power . . . and I knew even then that he had the power to send me to boarding school.

Still, I would not be talked out of protesting, just because of Father's stern look. I was used to that. I sat at the smaller desk that he had fixed for me years earlier and where I'd spent more hours than could be counted, every one of them happy. A girl's school was the last place I wanted to go. I belonged at my father's side, where I'd been since I was three.

"Your mother and I have talked about it," Father said, his voice bringing me back to reality and the dreaded thought of Miss English's Female Seminary. "You're young . . . and we don't think you're ready for marriage. . . ."

"Marriage!" I exploded again. "Father, I'm only fifteen. Of course I'm not ready for marriage. And who would I marry? The only men I meet here are politicians . . . and they are old."

"Thank you, Jessie," he said, chuckling and smoothing the rumpled cravat he wore and tugging at his linsey waistcoat. "I know I'm old, and so are my colleagues.

But there have been one or two men who have . . . ah . . . admired your skills as a hostess. . . ." He paused, as though deciding not to cloak his words, and then, running a hand through his hair, he said, "You know so much about politics that some would find you not only attractive but a boon to their careers."

"You taught me," I said forthrightly.

"I know, I know"—he shook his head—"and I'm proud of your capabilities. But now I want you to learn the things that . . . well, the things every young girl should know."

"Liza?" I asked. My sister, two years older than I, was my temperamental opposite, content where I was curious, docile where I was angry.

"Your sister will go with you. She is much more . . . compliant . . . about this matter."

"I'm sure," I said bitterly.

"Now, your mother is waiting for you." He dismissed me.

I turned and left the room, mustering all the dignity I could to keep from crying, and headed up the stairs to my invalid mother's room.

Mother lay on the fainting couch, in the darkened bedroom where she spent most of her days. Today she was wearing a soft mauve wrapper with a pale-green cashmere shawl pulled around her shoulders against the cold, though a fire burned strongly in her fireplace. The dark-green blanket over her legs lay almost flat to the couch, so thin was she. But her face brightened when I walked into the room, and the smile brought just a bit of color to her paleness. Mother was as fair as Father was dark—Liza and our younger brother, Randolph, took after her, while Father's dark hair and coloring were given to me. Sometimes I thought it was as though we were two separate families—Father and I together by looks and temperament and interests, with Mother, Liza, and Randolph joined in the same way. My littlest sisters—Sarah and Susie—had yet to declare themselves in the matter of looks, but I secretly hoped they, too, would favor Mother, leaving me, in a sense, Father's only child.

I was never clear why my mother was an invalid. In my early years she was more active around the house, though she never partook of the society that Washington offered. Still, when we were little, she was more a part of our daily life. I can yet see her sitting by Father's desk in the evening, her hands busy with knitting or embroidery while Father worked. Between them there was a companionable silence.

But as we grew into our teen years, Mother grew less and less a part of the household, though she continued, from her bedroom, to exert a firm control over the running of the house and the affairs of her children. She had good days and bad, though I never heard of a specific ailment. Sometimes I thought she had given up on life—perhaps because of the death of my younger brother, James, at the age of

four from consumption, or maybe, I sometimes supposed, because she found Father's rigorous dedication to government too tiring. At any rate, she had no interest in his speeches, his passion for westward expansion, his devotion to Andrew Jackson; and I, who cared so much about these things at an early age, wondered how she could put them from her mind. It never seemed to occur to Father that she should be other than she was. They obviously loved each other, but I knew there was something of a minor key—just slightly dissonant—about the relationship between my mother and father. As I grew older, I knew it was not a relationship after which I would pattern my own married life.

"I've been waiting for you, dear," she said now, reaching out a thin hand.

"I know, Mother. Father told me. How are you today?" With an effort I kept the anger out of my voice. Father had cautioned me often enough about upsetting Mother.

"I'm fine, thank you, Jessie. Your father has told you about the school?"

I took the hand that was still stretched toward me. "I'm not happy about it, Mother. I . . . I belong with Father, helping him."

"No, Jessie," she said, her voice firmer than usual. "Your father's business is a thing apart from us. It is men's business, and you are a lady . . . a well-born lady. I pray that someday you will be mistress of a large home . . . something like Cherry Grove. . . ." Her eyes took on that faraway look they always did when she talked of her childhood home in Virginia, where an enormous, graceful house, set in a mountain valley, was surrounded by apple and peach orchards and meadows where cattle grazed. I was always restless and impatient at Cherry Grove, longing for the bustle of the capital, but Liza much preferred it to Washington. And Mother, I sensed, would have given almost anything to be living at Cherry Grove.

I sat with her a few minutes longer, making desultory conversation. When she dozed at last, I slipped out of the room for the privacy of my own bedroom, where I could give in to the anger building inside of me. Boarding school indeed!

Strangely, there were no guests that evening for dinner. Often Mother would come down for the evening meal if it were just family, but I guess that night the rigor of telling me I was going to boarding school had been too much for her. She remained in her room.

"Tonight," Father said, when we were all gathered at the table at five o'clock, "we will discuss Hamlet. Eliza . . . Jessie . . . Randolph, I believe you have all three read the play."

While we mumbled, "Yessir," Sarah and Susie were quick to chorus, "We haven't. We don't know about it."

"Listen, and you shall learn," Father said patiently, and the little girls obediently fell silent. "Randolph, what was Hamlet's most outstanding characteristic?"

Randolph thought a moment, and then he said, falteringly, "He made a botch of everything."

"Splendid," Father boomed. "That he did."

"He ... he had a chance to do something great, and he, well, he thought too much." Liza's opinion was tentatively offered, but it, too, met with Father's approval.

My sister looked pretty tonight, wearing a lavender muslin dress with an embroidered collar, and it struck me that she always looked softer and more delicate than I did. More, I thought, like Mother. My dress was muslin too, but it was darker—a shade of green—and I had not added the dainty touch of the collar.

"He had," I said, "no one who believed in him. I don't think it is possible for people to achieve great success unless others believe in them."

Father looked startled for a moment. "You may be right, Jessie. And I am lucky to have all of you." His voice included all of us, but his eyes rested on me.

The discussion continued over roast beef and potatoes, wandering into the nature of Polonius and, finally, the presence of evil in mankind—as evidenced by Gertrude. But I listened with only half my attention, for my mind was occupied with my own importance to Father as the one who believed in him enough to make his success possible.

Late that night as I lay curled under a pile of blankets—Father insisted we sleep with the windows open for the sake of our health—my mind still boiled with resistance to boarding school.

I was convinced Father needed me to believe in him—and how could I do that from the distance of school? But worse yet, how would I myself survive school and its isolation? What would I do if I weren't privy to Father's speeches and plans, caught in the whirlwind of politics, attuned, as I was accustomed, to the various winds of change that blew through the capital?

I looked resentfully at Liza, who slept peacefully next to me as though her life were not about to change dramatically.

In a way, my duties as my father's assistant had begun in late 1828, while he was working hard to get Andrew Jackson elected to the presidency. I was three at the time. Liza and I had new purple capes to show off, and we had headed directly for Father's library once Mama fastened the clasps for us. As I danced down the stairs, in my imagination I could already hear Father's boom of pleasure as "his girls," as he called us, pirouetted before him.

To my dismay the library was empty. Already I was fascinated by this room. I adored my father—and his library seemed to hold the secrets of his existence. Fre-

quently, I peeked around the door to watch him covering page after page with his bold, sprawling handwriting.

Liza would whisper, "Father will scold you for bothering him," and I would reply confidently, "No, he won't. He'll smile at us." And he usually did.

So when I found the library empty this day, my disappointment soon turned to intrigue. It was my turn to act like Father. I spotted a stack of foolscap on the desk and, near it, some red and blue chalks. Nothing would do but that I help Father with his writing, so I licked the chalk and began making my own marks on the paper, right over his.

"Jessie!" Liza whispered in horror, ready to run for the door.

"Write to Father, Liza," I said as I made marks as bold as his all over the paper.

"I can't. . . . I'm afraid he'll be angry."

"Father doesn't get angry at us," I told her, and pretty soon she was making tentative light marks on another sheet of the foolscap.

I was wrong about Father's anger. By the time he found us, we had thoroughly dirtied our new capes with chalk and, worse, had ruined the pages of a speech he'd planned to deliver in the Senate the next day.

His voice was like thunder. "Who did this?" he demanded, though it was plain for all to see who had done it.

Eliza began to cry, but I went to stand in front of Father and ask, "Do you really want to know?"

He stared at me, the edges of his mouth quivering as though he were trying hard to hold on to his anger. "Yes, I want to know," he said, his voice still loud and terrible.

"A little girl that says 'Hurrah for Jackson,'" I told him.

Father stood frozen a moment, while I held my breath and, behind me, Liza sobbed in anticipation of a spanking.

The spanking never came. Father began to chuckle, and then he had to sit down to roar and slap his knee. When he finally had gently, his anger gone, "That was the speech I am to deliver tomorrow. The only copy."

"Father," I said, "you can say it by heart." He nodded. "Yes, Jessie, I probably can."

Soon after, a small table and chairs appeared in his library. "So you can practice writing and helping me," he said. Ostensibly the table and chairs were for both Liza and me, but Liza preferred other pursuits.

Andrew Jackson was elected, of course, and I became a regular visitor at the White House, tagging along behind Father as he went to see the president almost daily on national business. Father had told the president the story of the ruined speech, and it gave me a place in the old man's heart. He was the saddest man I ever knew. Father and I would find him in a rocking chair, staring absently out the window, his shoulders sunk in despair. More than once we found him with his head buried in his hands. Then Father would back quietly out and start in again, making a lot of noise so Mr. Jackson had time to compose himself.

While he and Father talked, the president would sit in his rocker, with me on a stool beside him, and stroke my hair. Sometimes he would get so involved in what he was saying that he would twist my hair, hard, but I learned to squinch my eyes—he couldn't see my face—and bear it.

"Father," I asked one day as we walked the dirt streets of the city, heading home, "why is Mr. Jackson so sad?"

"His wife died, just before he was elected president," Father said, "and he's lonely. That's why he likes you to sit by him."

"I think he should come live at our house," I declared, swinging my parasol. "That old White House is cold." Even though it was a warm spring day, I shivered.

Papa chuckled. "Yes, it is cold," he said. "But you bring the sunshine into it. Maybe one day you'll live there."

"Yes," I said confidently, "I will." And it became a goal of mine.

Father often took me when he went to the Senate for its regular sessions. I would be deposited in the Congressional Library where the librarian, a Mr. Meehan, would bring one book after another for my delight. I was too young to read them, of course, but he always brought books with lovely illustrations, and I studied everything from the birds of Mr. Audubon to French engravings and reproductions of works from the Louvre. The French works were somehow my favorites, and it was a joke later that I was an unofficial member of the Senate's Library Purchasing Committee. They consulted me whenever they were considering a French work.

I loved growing up in Washington, though Liza always complained about dirt and smells—she would have, given her choice, lived at Cherry Grove, with Mother's family. And I, given my choice, would have remained free to wander the streets of Washington with Father, rather than be cooped up in a seminary.

———

For one who had been tutored at home with her sisters, one cousin, and one brother, Miss English's was a shock. There were nearly 150 pupils, if you counted the day students, who twice outnumbered the boarders. Unfortunately, I was to be a boarder.

"It will do you good, Jessie," Father said, "to be around other girls your age. You are too much with adults."

"I like adults," I protested.

There was no budging Father. "You might like the other girls, too."

I was to room with Liza, which was small comfort, since she instantly thought Miss English's the most wonderful place she had been in all her life and rushed about making friends with girls who giggled and talked a lot about how important their fathers were—this one was a senator and that one an ambassador and so it went. At least Liza could keep up on that score, for her father was the famous Senator Thomas Hart Benton from Missouri. I told her to repeat it often and loudly.

The studies were no problem for me—I was already fluent in Spanish, because Father worked with documents of Spanish explorers in the Southwest. If any subject gave me pause, it was mathematics—I never liked figures and never wanted to bother with them, a malady that would haunt me all my life. But mostly I found the studies boring—geography, for instance, dealt with the lands of Asia, which had no immediate meaning for me. I was thoroughly versed in the geography of the American West, and I knew why it was important. And I knew, from Father, the history of the major European countries and the British Isles—and what that history meant to us in America. I saw no sense in looking at maps and memorizing the location of countries and capital cities, if no one told me why they mattered.

In our free time—recess periods, they were called—we were to benefit from the outdoor air when the weather was at all cooperative. That meant that groups of girls stood around on the lawn surrounding the school, gathered into tight little knots of gossip and shrill laughter. I ignored them, preferring to walk rapidly around the perimeter of the lawn. Father's lessons on healthy living had not been lost on me.

Once in one of my walks I came upon a classmate sitting alone on a bench. Where I might have expected her to look lonely, she looked somehow content and self-contained. She was one of the prettiest girls in the school—I'd seen her before and noticed that she was taller than most of us. Her hair was very blond, and her light complexion matched it. But the thing that really made you look twice at Harriet Wilson was the look of laughter in her eyes. She enjoyed life.

"Why are you here?" I asked. "Don't you want to join the others?" My head nodded vaguely toward a group of five or six girls, with Liza at the center. They were busily engaged in talk, though frequently one could see a hand move to smooth a hairdo, adjust a sash. They were not indifferent to their appearance.

"Not really," said this girl, who was far prettier than the other hundred and more girls in the school. "I never feel really a part of things," she said.

Curiously, I asked, "Why ever not?"

"My father is not anybody important," she said. "He's a government clerk. It makes the teachers . . . and sometimes the girls . . . look at me differently." The words sounded as though she bore a stigma, but her voice was light with laughter. It didn't bother her terribly.

I laughed with her. "My father is a senator, but it doesn't mean that I'm any smarter . . . or as smart as you . . . in class."

She flashed me a smile. "That's not the point, at least not to Miss English. Your father is important. I know he is Senator Benton from Missouri. The teachers know it too—they are anxious to call on you."

I thought a minute. It was true that if my hand was raised, I was likely to be called upon, no matter how many other hands waved in the air. I had to admit I often raised my hand, just to relieve the boredom of the classroom.

"And they don't call on you?" I was curious, incredulous.

"Not very often," she said. "I'm here on charity and there's not much of it here."

It was the beginning of a friendship, one that blossomed strangely enough in the branches of a mulberry tree outside my room. It was the only place where Harriet and I could go and talk with privacy, away from the prying eyes and sharply tuned ears of Liza and her gaggle of friends. We talked of our dreams, but they weren't dreams of the other girls—I spoke passionately of my father's work and my desire to be part of all that happened in government, my belief—absorbed from my father—that America's destiny lay westward.

"I have no such lofty ambitions." Harriet laughed, with a deep-toned laugh much more genuine than the high-pitched giggles of Liza and her friends. "I plan to marry a very rich man, make him happy . . . and thereby make myself happy."

I was scandalized. "You do?"

"Of course. Why not?"

"What if you don't fall in love with a rich man?"

"What is love?" she asked. "I will make myself love a rich man, but never a poor one."

I was so startled I nearly fell out of the tree.

We were discovered one night, very late, sitting up there, by Miss Fredericks—a flighty French teacher—who heard Harriet's laughter pealing down from the tree. Looking up from her window, she must have spotted my white muslin gown—it was late spring by then, and we wore the coolest nightclothes possible.

"It's a ghost!" Miss Fredericks shrieked, bringing three other teachers running to her bedroom window.

"It's no ghost," Miss James, the math teacher, said dryly. "It's two misbehaving girls, and we shall change their ways immediately." It was the end of our sessions in the mulberry tree. Harriet and I were called before Miss English and strongly reprimanded, with a warning that we had neither one paid enough attention to our studies.

Miss English was a severe lady who took herself very seriously and dressed always in black, which matched her very black hair—I suspected she used some sort of dye on it to keep it from having any streak of gray, though she must have been forty at least. But there was never the hint of a smile about her face or, more telling, about her eyes, and she tended to peer at us as though she were nearsighted. Usually she used a lorgnette, which gave her a decidedly haughty appearance . . . and made me dislike her even more.

"If this situation continues," Miss English intoned, looking at us through the lorgnette, so solemn that I wanted to burst into laughter, "we shall have to inform your parents. You, Miss Wilson, are perilously close to being expelled."

"And me?" I asked. If Harriet was in trouble, why was I not in equal peril for the same offense?

"We would, of course, talk to the senator," Miss English said, firmly closing the discussion.

Later Harriet laughed, but I was indignant. "It would not be fair to expel Harriet and merely scold me," I said to Father later, having told him the whole story the first chance I got.

"But it hasn't happened, Jessie," he said. "Fight only the battles in front of you . . . don't look for new ones. And, Jessie, stay out of trees." His voice was stern, but his eyes danced.

"I can't believe you told him," Liza said. "Weren't you afraid?"

"Of what?" I asked scornfully. "I *wanted* Miss English to expel me!"

Liza gasped in horror.

———

The matter of the May Queen brought my discontent with Miss English—and my friendship with Harriet—to a head. Long before time for the election—every girl in the school voted—I began an impassioned campaign to win that honor for Harriet. She was, I reasoned, the prettiest girl in the school, and she should therefore be the queen. She was also, I was convinced, the friendliest and most pleasant.

It was not hard for me to convince the other girls to vote for Harriet. I was, after all, Senator Benton's daughter. I went from girl to girl in the school, using all the tact and cleverness I could muster to convince them that Harriet must be the Queen of the May.

"You really think Harriet ought to be the May Queen, Jessie?" asked Genevieve Appleby, a plain girl, with hair neither blond nor brown.

"Yes," I said firmly, "I really do. She's the prettiest girl in the school." With what I thought was great cleverness, I added, "She's far prettier than me . . . and sometimes I'm jealous. But she's so nice."

"Oh, yes, she is," breathed my willing victim.

"Can we be in the court?" asked Virginia Drew, another of our classmates, a passingly pretty girl with red hair but without the innate charm that Harriet possessed.

"Of course we can," I assured her, my fingers crossed behind my back.

At long last the day arrived when the election results would be announced. The entire school was called together—all the students and the teachers. I had personally canvassed enough of the girls to be sure that Harriet was the winner, so as we sat in the assembly, I reached out to clasp her hand in a sign of victory.

She smiled at me, pleased at the prospect of her honor. "Jessie, I'm . . . well, I'm grateful. And my father . . . he's your slave for life, he's so excited about this."

I nodded wisely and turned my attention to the podium, where Miss English was announcing, "The Queen of the May this year will be . . . Faith Bywaters!"

Faith Bywaters! Instinctively I leaped from my seat, crying, "Miss English, I'd like a recount of the votes. I'm almost certain that Harriet Wilson had the majority."

Miss English turned that supercilious lorgnette on me. "Miss Benton," she said very formally, "you are out of order."

"But, Miss English, I protest the results of this election." Being in order was not something Father had taught me about. "I demand an explanation."

Miss Susanna Bigelow, the history teacher, rose from her seat and in a tremulous voice suggested, "Miss English, I don't believe Miss Benton is feeling well."

"I'm perfectly fine," I said, whirling on her.

"Miss Benton," came the command from the podium, "you will accompany Miss Bigelow to the nurse's office. I'm quite sure you will benefit from a dose of senna."

Senna! That hateful, bitter purgative that made you sick when you weren't! I looked at Miss Bigelow, and then down at Harriet, whose eyes for the first time since I'd known her had lost their laughter, and then finally up to Miss English. She stood ramrod straight, staring directly at me as though daring me to challenge her authority. My only source of justice was Father . . . and he was nowhere near. I was beaten. Resentfully, I followed Miss Bigelow.

The senna made me so sick that I stayed in my room for two days, with Harriet hovering over me and wringing her hands. "Jessie," she kept repeating, "I am so sorry. It was all my fault."

"Nonsense," I said weakly, "it was my own fault. But Miss English is wrong."

"She said," Harriet told me, "that I had sufficient votes to win but that the faculty disqualified me because I was not attentive enough to my studies."

"Balderdash!" I exploded, and then had to hold my aching head. When the spasm passed, I said more calmly, "The faculty disqualified you because your father is a clerk."

Her familiar laughter came back. "I think you're right. But I'm sorry that you had to suffer for it."

"No," I said, "I suffered from my own stubborn nature. Father says I remind him of Don Quixote, charging at windmills."

What Father actually said, when he heard about the incident, was that I must learn to be philosophical about my defeats. It was not a lesson I learned quickly or easily, just as I did not learn to limit my battles to those right in front of me.

～

The immediate result of the May Queen fiasco, as Father called it, was that Harriet's parents withdrew her from school, and I was left without the confidante who had become so important to my survival in an alien atmosphere.

"It's not fair!" I stormed to Father, who simply replied, "You should have thought ahead to the consequences of your action."

I ignored that, claiming loudly, "I will not go back to that school!"

Father simply returned to his work. I, of course, went back to the school.

School dragged on another month after Harriet left, and I managed to pass my courses, but without distinction. I, who could discuss the known geography of the American West without looking at a map, was found deficient in geography of the world and only passable in math. The faculty agreed—grudgingly, I thought—that I excelled in written expression.

"Who," I wanted to demand of them, "do you think has been writing Senator Benton's speeches . . . well, at least transcribing them . . . for the last five years?" Of course I excelled at written expression. I had been taught by a master.

At commencement exercises Liza bemoaned the end of the school year. "Summer," she said dramatically, "will be so dull! What shall we do?"

"Probably go to Cherry Grove, just as we do every other summer," I said impatiently, wishing we could, instead, stay in Washington.

"Oh," she said with relief, "that's right. It's a Cherry Grove summer."

We watched the girls in the final form parade across the stage in their white gowns, and we listened to the valedictorian—a strange, passive girl with poor eyesight but lots of family money—deliver a stilted and unintelligible talk on moral responsibility. I vowed I would never be one of that simpering group of girls who called themselves "Miss English graduates."

～

This was, indeed, one of our summers at Cherry Grove. We alternated. Some summers we went to St. Louis—Father's legislative and legal home—and every other summer we went to Cherry Grove, Mother's spiritual home. For me the summer dragged by. Father made only two trips to Virginia, claiming that legislative business kept him tied to Washington, though I thought he simply preferred the hectic pace of the capital to the bucolic life of the plantation.

My southern cousins—all ten of them—were the only bright spots in the whole summer. My special favorite among them was Sally McDowell from Lexington, Kentucky, a few years older but a close friend since she had boarded with us and studied with our tutor, some four or five years earlier. I'd found in her a girl with the spirit that Liza seemed to lack. Sally was far from sharing my passion for government, but she was active, daring, and certainly not above an adventure. But this summer Sally was, as she put it, "fixing to be married," though the wedding would not take place for another year. His name was Francis Thomas.

"He's from Maryland," she breathed to me in barely concealed excitement. "He plans to enter government."

"A politician?" I asked archly.

Sally's tone betrayed slight indignation. "Yes," she said deliberately, "he means to run for office. He feels it is his duty to serve the country which has been so good to him."

"Do your parents like him?" I asked, wondering why I seemed determined to anger my favorite cousin. I knew without asking that Francis Thomas was old—at least forty. Too old to marry Sally!

"Oh, yes," she said enthusiastically, politics forgotten for the time being. "They like him because he loves me. He can't bear for me to go anywhere without him."

That sounded bothersome to me, but then, I knew little of love and did not expect to for some time. Still, I was interested, even intrigued, by Sally's absorption in this man. She had nothing else on her mind, if her talk was any indication, and she counted the days until their December wedding.

"I am only sorry I can't be here in December," I said politely. Her face registered a kind of instant regret, as though that were what she thought she ought to feel. "Oh, can't you come from Washington?"

"I will ask Father," I promised, "but I doubt he can get away. And you know how hard the trip is on Mother."

"Poor Aunt Elizabeth," she said sympathetically.

I never met Francis Thomas the whole long summer, and I wondered that Sally could be so in love with a man so distant that he couldn't come once from Maryland to Virginia to see his betrothed in a three-month period. I was beginning to develop definite ideas of the nature of romance.

"Trifling poor fellow, that he be," I heard Aunt Jasmine, the family cook, mutter one day, and I believed she must be right. Sally was fixing to marry a trifling poor fellow.

Marriage was on my mind, for when I returned to Washington in time for the fall opening of school, it was to the news that Miss Harriet Wilson would marry Count Bodisco, the Russian ambassador, in the spring.

Count Bodisco was well known to me, though he would never have recognized me should we have met. Still, I had seen him riding through town in his barouche, which glittered with brass and varnish and was pulled by four prancing long-tailed black horses. In his huge Georgetown house, he had once given a children's Christmas party so showy that it was yet the talk of the city. Liza and I, being young then and the ages of his visiting nephews, had been privileged to attend.

"Look at the fires," Liza said, her breath half held in amazement as our carriage approached the house high on a hill.

I was as awed as she. Beacons of light flared from either side of the doorway, and in an open square in front of the house great bonfires burned, as though to ward off the cold winter night. Inside the house was a fairyland of lights and flowers and refreshments, the likes of which Liza and I had never seen, living as we did with a father who believed the plain and good life—open windows at night, high-top shoes, and lots of vegetables—led to health.

Tables were covered with toys, games, picture books, and stacks of little satin bags with "bonbons" in gilt letters—the bags were for us to take home. And there were dolls, and dainty fans, and bolts of pretty ribbons—everything a child could dream of.

The count greeted each of us ... and therein lay a future shock. At that well-remembered Christmas party I thought no more of him than that he was a funny little old man, short, with a wrinkled face and great wispy sideburns and beard. He looked to me sort of like a miniature version of Father Time. He was then so remote from my life that I thought no more about his appearance, which was, truth be told, ugly.

But when it was announced that he would marry Harriet, I became more immediately concerned. And I was then, of course, some ten or more years older and much better, I thought, able to judge his rightness as a potential husband.

From my point of view he failed utterly. He was well over sixty—and Harriet barely sixteen—and he was short and ugly. No matter that he was rich, drove fine horses, and lived in a house so grand it was almost a castle. He was ugly.

"Jessie," Mother said one evening when I went in to visit her, "you have been asked to be a bridesmaid in the wedding of a certain Harriet Wilson to Count Bodisco. Do you know this Harriet?"

Mother had been kept in ignorance of the May Queen fiasco because, as Father said, it would just upset her. She would have seen it as another of my causes.

"Yes, Mother, I know Harriet. She was at Miss English's." Then I blurted out, "Why would a girl my age marry old Count Bodisco? He's ugly."

Mother gave me a reproving look. "He is a very wealthy man and, I presume, a very generous one," she said as though that settled it. "You must have several new gowns for all the festivities—surely a silk or two. It will mean a lot of work." She sounded tired, but her eyes gleamed. Mother liked the idea of fancy clothes . . . and so, I must confess, did I. At fifteen I was still wearing the muslin and chintz considered proper for young girls and had never yet had a silk dress. The possibility of silk almost made it all right that Harriet was marrying an ugly old man.

I didn't tell Mother that Harriet's father was a government clerk and that the family had too little money and too many children. It would have somehow demeaned Harriet in my mind to give voice to that. But I was sure Mother had caught the heart of the matter—Harriet was marrying an ugly old man so that she, and perhaps even her family, would no longer be poor. For days I walked around with that bit of conjectured knowledge, and it did little for my state of happiness. Poor Harriet, was all I could think.

It was to be a proper wedding in every detail—fine gowns for the young brides-maids, lavish cakes and wine, flowers everywhere, and, of course, protocol.

I was happily at work in Father's library one cold Saturday afternoon in January when Count Bodisco called on him. On weekends Father often let Liza and me come home from school, and when I was home, I was privileged to continue my earlier habit of writing down his speeches as he paced the room, composing them as he walked. He would later take my copy and laboriously add details here and there, rewriting a hundred times, before returning it to me for a finished product.

Father had long been in the habit of allowing me to stay when he had visitors—his reasoning was that I learned from listening. So I made no move to leave when the count was ushered in.

"Ah, Jessie, one of my darling girl's bridesmaids," the count said, and I had the feeling that he was frowning at the heavy wool skirt and plain white shirtwaist I wore. No doubt he wanted me dressed fancier for his wedding parties.

"Good afternoon, sir," I said, rising just slightly and giving him my hand.

"Sir," he said, turning to my father, "I'm much concerned over doing things right at this wedding. The groomsmen . . . well, that's troubling me. I've asked Henry Fox and James Buchanan to be of the party, but which one should be given the place of honor?"

Mr. Fox was the English ambassador, while Mr. Buchanan had been our ambassador to Russia. I knew that in the count's view it was a question of recognizing not just the men but their countries. Would he give precedence to England or America?

The two men stood by the window, staring out at the cold gray day as they pondered the diplomatic problem. I stared at the contrast between them. Father not only towered over the short count, but he outdid him in bulk. The count was one of those men thick about the middle but with spindly legs—at present they were stuck into heavy black Wellington boots, giving the appearance of huge feet tacked on to the little legs. He had removed a felt hat when he came in, leaving his hair going in rather wild directions. It was thin hair, lank and lying limply on his head, with sideburns that met to become a straggling mustache above teeth that stuck out rather far. His face was wrinkled, and his eyes seemed to water a bit as they sometimes do in people of a certain age. He was uglier than I remembered.

Beside him, Father, with his firm mouth and direct way of looking at you with a clear eye, seemed to represent safety and security.

I knew little about what were delicately called "marriage relations." Mother would never have brought herself to talk about such things with me, and Father's idea of a progressive education did not extend that far. But I knew how our barn cats reproduced, and I knew, from gossip at Miss English's if nothing else, that some kind of similar physical closeness was involved in marriage between men and women. Sitting there that afternoon, looking at the count, it dawned on me that Harriet would have "marriage relations" with this man. If I ever thought about such relations for myself—and what girl didn't fantasize?—my love was tall, dark, handsome, and, of course, young—just enough older than myself, as I took it as true that husbands should be slightly older than their wives. But not over forty years! The whole idea was repulsive to me, and I blushed furiously, grateful that their heads were still turned to the outside.

"I think you can arrange the matter," Father was saying. "Instead of having the bridesmaids on one side and the groomsmen on the other, why not mix them? A maid and a man next to the bride, and another pair next to the groom."

Trust Father to come up with an innovative solution. The count was effusive in his thanks, grateful to be rescued from a diplomatic dilemma. And so it was decided that I would stand with Mr. James Buchanan next to the bride. Mr. Fox, with Harriet's sister, would stand next to the count.

Finally the great day came, after much preparation. I had spent hours standing for an imported English dressmaker—"Try not to wiggle, Miss Benton," and "Please, Miss Benton, the shoulders straighter"—while she built my dress of white figured satin with blond lace about the neck and sleeves. The skirt was plaited all around, with long points in the front and the back cutting the fullness away to a slim waist. The sleeves were full, with the lace falling over the elbows and flowing from the modestly cut neckline. With this stately dress we wore wreaths of soft white roses, carried fans of ivory and white feathers, and bouquets of white camellias. I felt deliciously sophisticated and adult.

"Harriet, get away from the window! You must not let the guests see you before the wedding." Her mother, a small woman obviously overwhelmed by the opulence, pulled nervously at Harriet's sleeves.

"Bother," Harriet said, laughing. "They can't see me, and I'm curious about the people." She was dressed like a Russian bride, in heavy satin with silver lace and a red coronet, studded with diamonds, on her head. A full-length train of silver lace fell from the coronet, sparkling like drops of water caught in the early-morning light.

"You'll meet them soon enough," I warned her. "All Washington is curious about you, and they'll come calling the day after the wedding."

"Really?" she said. "What fun! Look at that grand carriage—why, it's President Van Buren. Just think, the president of the United States at my wedding."

"He's not at your wedding," her mother said, suddenly showing an unexpected spark of wit. "He's at the count's wedding."

Blissfully happy, from all appearances, Harriet took everything as humorous and laughed aloud at her mother's comment. Then she was back to peeking out the window, commenting on this grand carriage and that as they rolled up the long driveway to the house where the wedding was to be held. If I was still worried about her "marriage relations"—and I was—nothing seemed to faze Harriet.

By the time we were allowed to descend for the ceremony, the house and piazzas were overflowing with people—men in full-dress uniforms of the army and navy, women in fancy silks. When the doors to the parlor were rolled back to reveal the wedding party—each of us placed by Bodisco exactly where he wanted us to stand—the crowd let out a collective murmur of appreciation. The ceremony went off without a hitch, though I suppose all were as nervous as I was.

After the ceremony the wedding party descended into carriages to travel to the count's home for breakfast. The wedding carriage, the count's glittering barouche with matched black horses, was so grandly decorated with silk rosettes that Harriet later confessed to me she felt like a Russian princess, not the daughter of a clerk in the American government.

I said nothing, for all this grandeur had not erased from my mind the thought that she was paying too high a price for wealth. I wanted to demand, "Do you love him?" Then I remembered her words way back and Miss English's: "I will make myself love a rich man . . . but never a poor one."

Breakfast was followed by dinner, with an enforced rest for the bridesmaids in between. Exhausted, we slept on sofas and tried not to muss our finery.

State dinners were nothing new to me—hadn't I served as Father's hostess for more than one a year now, and wasn't I a frequent guest at the White House? Yet this was the first dinner where I was a major participant, so to speak, acting independently as myself instead of as Father's daughter. Sitting opposite the wedding couple, next to Mr. Buchanan, I caught Father's eye from far across the room, and his nod told me that I was acquitting myself well. But the dinner was as long as it was stately, and I was glad when the day of festivities ended.

At home I fell exhausted into my bed, my only thought that I would never marry a foreigner who demanded such pageantry of a wedding. I was through with society and the roles it forced women to play.

CHAPTER TWO

"THERE," I SAID TRIUMPHANTLY, "NOW I LOOK MORE LIKE RANDOLPH ... MORE like the son you wanted me to be."

I shall never forget the look of horror on my father's face as he turned and saw me standing in the door of his library, scissors still in my hand, my hair cut to shoulder length. Indeed, save that his was gray, our haircuts were remarkably similar.

The famous Thomas Benton was momentarily speechless. When he again could find his voice, he demanded, "Jessie! What have you done?"

"Cut my hair," I said calmly, "so that I won't have to go back to Miss English's." I had not looked in a mirror after attacking myself with the scissors, so I wasn't sure how bad I looked. From the expression on Father's face, it must have been pretty bad.

But that was not what bothered Father. "The son I wanted?" he asked.

"Even Mother says you hoped I would be a boy," I said, "and you've raised me like a son, taught me the things a son would know, even taken me quail hunting. But now you're trying to change me suddenly by sending me to Miss English's. I don't even know who I am."

"Who you are?" he echoed.

I had loosed the tirade and my confusion came pelting out. "Who am I? Your assistant? A gossipy seminary student? Somebody's future wife?" With that last question I gave away the real cause behind my bizarre hair-cutting act and my terrible, deep unhappiness.

Harriet Wilson's marriage had rocked all my understanding of the life that lay ahead of me, planting the undeniable suspicion that I would be expected to make a proper marriage in which love—whatever that was—had no part. Granted, I didn't believe Father would ever make me marry someone as old and ugly as Count Bodisco, although James Buchanan had become a frequent caller at our house and often wanted to talk politics with me instead of Father. But what I wanted in life was to be Father's assistant, to go on as I had before this awful seminary business and before Harriet's wedding.

Senator Thomas Benton missed the point entirely. "Jessie," he said sternly, "you must quiet that rebellious nature of yours. It is unbecoming in a woman."

But all right in a man? I wanted to ask. For once prudence kept my mouth shut. "You will return to Miss English's tomorrow," he decreed, and I knew there would be no reprieve.

Mother was distraught over my hair, which only made Father angrier than ever at me. It was one of those rare nights when Mother felt well enough to come to the dinner table. Father always suspended his dinnertime intellectual exercises when Mother was present. To us children it meant that we would not be quizzed on Shakespeare or Sir Isaac Newton's discovery of gravity or the significance of the Lewis and Clark journey, the latter being a particularly favorite topic of his.

When Mother was present, we talked of the weather, our accomplishments, the food, and, often, Cherry Grove. Tonight, unfortunately, the topic was my disgrace.

"Your lovely hair," she moaned. "It had those red highlights that reminded me of your father when he was young." She looked at Father, who merely smiled at her and laughed.

"You told me," he recalled, "that you would never marry a red-headed man . . . or a Democrat."

"I almost waited until you were gray," she said serenely—Father had courted her for six or seven long years before she agreed to marry him—"and I couldn't do anything about the other. But now I am partial to red hair . . . and, I suppose, to Democrats."

"I still have a good bit of hair," I pointed out rather petulantly, "and it's still the same color."

She turned her head away, as though she could not bear to look at me. "You look like a boy," she said.

"I think Jessie looks pretty," Sarah said loyally, only to be shushed by a look from Father. I had pulled my hair back to the nape of my neck and secured it with a false hairpiece, so that I had a semblance of propriety, but great wisps of hair, now too short to be caught up, kept pulling loose and dangling about my face, giving me an untidy look, at best.

Dinner was so uncomfortable that Mother fled to her room before the sweets were served, and even Miss English's began to look the better choice to me.

The girls at school were not kind. The episode of the senna tea had made me an outsider, considered slightly unusual, and my haircut only confirmed it. My moment of social glory in Harriet's wedding, which had given me great prestige among students and faculty alike, was forgotten in light of my newest departure from social acceptability.

I was miserable. Fortunately, the term was soon over and I had a summer reprieve.

The summer of 1840 was a St. Louis summer. Father had to campaign, for he would stand for reelection in the fall, and even Mother was going to undertake the two-week trip to St. Louis, though Father worried constantly that it would be too hard on her. He of necessity had to make the trip to see the people who had voted him into office for nearly thirty years now.

Though Liza pouted and would have asked, if she'd not been so timid, to be sent to Cherry Grove instead of St. Louis, I was in a state of high excitement about the trip. I loved Washington, and it was my heart's home, but St. Louis, with its sense of adventure and frontier, was a close second. Even as a little child, my anticipation would rise on the stage trip across the Allegheny Mountains to the Ohio River. We took steamboats to Louisville, where we dutifully stopped to visit relatives, while I danced in impatience to be on. Then it was New Orleans, and back up the muddy Mississippi to St. Louis.

I loved the steamboats, though Mother was always exhausted and hated the trip. Father spent all of his time in the gentlemen's club, which was filled with smoke and spittoons. Still, Father found there the men he needed to talk to. Mother could have spent the days in the ladies' cabin visiting with other ladies whose husbands were with Father, but she generally preferred the privacy of her stateroom. I myself liked the dining room, where the tables were laid with heavy white linen and we were waited on by white-coated Negro men whose only aim in life, it seemed to me, was to bring me one sweet delicacy after another. Meals began with two kinds of soup and were followed with fish, roast, all manner of cold dishes, and more desserts than my mind could conjure. By the time we arrived in St. Louis, I was always thoroughly spoiled and imperious, used to giving orders, and it took Father a day or so to "beat that attitude out of me," as he liked to say.

St. Louis was home to me, almost as much as Washington. This year I was particularly glad to be there, for no one in St. Louis would give an instant's thought to my shorn locks.

The house Father had built long before he married Mother was of two stories, with long galleries running its length on both floors and screened from the public by locust trees. Father set up his office on the lower gallery, preferring always to be outdoors. Visitors would begin to come by early in the day to talk of politics and government, of Indians and westward expansion.

Gradually, Father and I mended the rift caused by my haircutting. There was no open reconciliation, but he began to allow me to sit quietly on the gallery when General Clark came by to discuss Indian affairs—he was in charge of them for the entire region, and I was awestruck to actually meet and listen to the famous explorer from the Lewis and Clark expedition—or when old Mr. Dent came to recall perilous times he and Father had shared—he used to get mixed up and call me "Mrs. Benton," and I never had the heart to correct him.

Colonel Garnier, an exiled Spanish gentleman who had fought with Wellington in Spain, came by daily, and both Father and I listened to his stories. Colonel Garnier was particularly pleased that I was fluent in Spanish.

"She must know the language of Mexico," Father said to the colonel. "Our nation's future lies that way."

"She reminds me of my sister," answered the colonel. "That is why I call her Rosita."

Sometimes Judge Lawless, who had fought with the French at Waterloo, would join us, and the two old soldiers would relive the battles of their youth. I'd be sent running for large maps, which were unrolled on the tables, and then the battles were fought with pins—beeswax heads for the Spanish troops, red wax for the English, and for the French, black.

Even Mother, who often had her chaise moved onto the second floor gallery, had callers. Some neighbors, who were very French and spoke heavily accented English, would bring her fruit and flowers from their carefully cultivated gardens, and Sister Elizabeth from the hospital came almost daily. Mother always sent her back with a basket of things for the hospital—sometimes food, sometimes soap, or toilet water for the female patients. I would hear Sister Elizabeth say *"Permittez, ma soeur"* and Mother, in her schoolgirl-perfect French, would reply *"Bonjour, ma soeur."*

It made me happy to think that we spoke French upstairs and Spanish down.

As summers always do, this one ended too quickly, and we were back on the steamboats down the Mississippi to New Orleans, up the Ohio to Louisville and then Wheeling, and then by stage home to Washington. At the end of that trip lay the inescapable Miss English's Female Seminary. By now, at least, my hair had grown back to a respectable length.

—∼

That fall Father began to talk excitedly of the explorations of Joseph Nicolas Nicollet, a French explorer who had surveyed the upper Mississippi and then the upper Missouri and who was now preparing a huge map of his findings.

Father described the mapmaking process in detail, crowing with glee because the map would show tiny details—where a cliff rose out of the earth, where a stream branched into two tributaries. "Why, even you and I could follow it to Oregon, if only the map went that far," he told me triumphantly one evening when he'd come to the school to visit.

I wasn't sure I wanted to go to Oregon, bur Father paid no attention. He was as wound up as when he gave one of his notoriously long speeches in the Senate.

"They've got to go farther," he said. "They've got to map what lies between the Mississippi and the Rocky Mountains . . . and then they have to push on to the Pacific. America must settle those lands . . . and we can't settle them until we know what lies there."

"And what does lie there?" I asked.

"Grasslands, I'm sure of it. The high plains are grasslands, not that Great American Desert the army keeps reporting. Nicollet has a bright young assistant—chap named Frémont—and I've been talking to him. He's as excited about all this as I am. We're going to get that expedition together, one way or another."

A flash of jealousy went through me. I wanted Father to talk to me, not some young man with a French name. "It sounds exciting, Father," was all I said.

Liza, being in her last year of formal schooling, was allowed to spend more weekends at home than I—the irony was not lost on me that she, who loved the school, was there less often than I, who loathed it—but from both her and Father, on his regular visits to me at school, I began to hear more about this Frémont person. He apparently had become a frequent visitor at our home, and Liza was quite taken with him.

I met him only once that fall, when Father brought him to a school concert where Liza was playing. Father introduced him with some pride as "that young explorer I told you about. He's going to map the road to Oregon."

John Charles Frémont had two things in common with the awful Count Bodisco. He was short and he was older, though not by as many as forty years. In fact, he was eleven years older than I and not much taller. I thought him no more than sixty-four inches at best. But after that first moment I never again thought of John's height or lack of it, because he had a certain self-possession that made him loom as tall as Father in my mind. He was tanned, with the look of a man who shared Father's passion for the outdoors—he had, after all, recently returned from a topographical expedition to the West—and he had deep-blue eyes that seemed to look right through me when he took my hand and bowed gallantly over it.

"Jessie, I've been looking forward to meeting you. Your father speaks highly of your capabilities."

Blushing, I thanked him and told him that Father spoke equally highly of him.

"We must be wonderful people," he said, smiling.

I wish I could say that something about John Charles Frémont, some romantic instinct, struck me at that first meeting, that I was forever after in love with him—stories since have woven such a romantic web about our first meeting. But it is not the truth. I thought him charming—perhaps a bit too charming—and I thought him extremely patient to flatter Father so by coming to his daughter's musicale.

But what struck me most was that outdoors quality he possessed, the self-assurance of a man who enjoyed the outdoors and would never be confined in a parlor. I had grown up under the tutelage of a man who was convinced that the healthy outdoor life had saved him from the consumption that had killed his brothers, and I naturally looked askance at any man content to sit indoors.

And when Frémont spoke of the lands he had seen—surely just the edge of the American West—his eyes glowed with excitement. "We saw land no white man yet has seen," he told me with fire, "not even Lewis and Clark. And there is more, much more land to be discovered. *I* want to find it."

I was not my father's daughter for nothing. I admired the passion, the determination, though it was admittedly self-serving. John Charles Frémont, I sensed, did not necessarily want to discover the West for the good of the United States—he wanted it for his own greater glory, and all the better that it served his country. Who could blame him?

We sat through Liza's piano playing, technically proficient but spiritually lacking. I looked at Frémont from time to time to see if he noticed but could detect no sign. He was attentive and properly polite, his eyes intent, his body perfectly still, while I had a bad case of the fidgets.

The interminable musicale ended, and Father and Mr. Frémont stayed only long enough to be polite, flattering Liza about her performance. Then they were gone, and we were back in the schoolgirl routine.

I thought no more about the lieutenant. He went back to his maps, and I to my endurance of school. The Christmas holidays—and the end of the term—were fast approaching, and my whole attention was focused on persuading Father that I had had enough of school.

I pressed my campaign over the holidays. Father had moved us just recently into the three-story brick house he had built on C Street in the capital. After years of making do in a series of Washington boardinghouses—where the conversation was always brilliant, the food good, but the sense of permanence and home lacking—Father had felt settled enough in his senatorial career to build a home. It was a magnificent house—dark mahogany paneling everywhere, Mother's antique furniture, long stored elsewhere, now on proud display, the walls covered with portraits of members of Mother's McDowell ancestors. The Benton side of our family had no history illustrious enough to leave a legacy of portraits. No, the sense of tradition came from Mother's side of the family, but Father brought to this new house his own sense of energy, his library, which surely outdid that at Miss English's and was probably, I thought, as large as the newly begun Congressional Library. But most of all, Father brought his vitality to this new house, which fairly buzzed with life and purpose.

I loved it from the first moment I walked through the front door, and I was more determined than ever not to be sent back to boarding school.

"Father, I've brought your coffee." It was early in the morning—before six a.m.—the hour when I knew Father began his day. For years, as a child, I'd met him in his library at that hour, and now I knew it was the time he would be most driven by sentiment, most susceptible to my pleas.

He was already at work at his desk, the early-morning dark broken by the light of the candelabrum he had invented—four spermaceti candles fixed in front of a large white blotting paper, which reflected their light. Father was so intent on what he was writing that I had to knock gently before he looked up.

"Jessie!" His face brightened with pleasure. "I do miss you when you're away. Pour me some of that fine coffee you're carrying."

It was coffee liberally dosed with chicory, a taste he'd long ago acquired from Mother. I poured it, still steaming, into a huge cup and handed it to him.

"You have not told me about your work for some time, Father," I said.

The smile on his face bespoke his pleasure in sharing his work with me, though the news was almost grim. "It's a trying time for this country, Jessie. The slavery issue has not been laid to rest"—South Carolina had threatened some nine years earlier to withdraw from the Union if slavery was made an issue—"and I foresee it breaking this country apart."

"Missouri is a slave state," I murmured. "You could own slaves yourself if you'd a mind."

"I've no mind for that," he said vehemently. "When we preach democracy, we must put it into action. No man should own another man."

Amen, I silently agreed.

"But we move ahead on other issues," he continued, "the things that Jackson and I worked for—education for everyone, the abolishment of the poll tax—all those things have come to pass. We will make this a country for all people, not just the rich."

"And the American West?" I asked. Unbidden, Lieutenant Frémont leaped into my mind, though neither Father nor I had mentioned him. Suddenly, though, I could see that handsome, rugged explorer's face before my eyes with such clarity that it startled me.

"We're still working on the next expedition," Father said. "Nicollet wants to lead it, though I'm not certain his health is good enough. You'll see Frémont again while you're home for the holidays. He is here often."

Of course, I recalled that both Father and Liza had mentioned that Frémont was often at the family dinner table. Liza's interest in him was, to say the least, far removed from Father's.

"I think," my plain sister had said hesitantly, "that he may be . . . well, you know. . . ."

"No, Liza, I don't know," I'd replied impatiently.

"Oh, Jessie!" she said in exasperation, and never did tell me what it was that I didn't know. I guessed, of course, that she hoped Lieutenant Frémont was interested in her. Even more, I supposed, she was most interested in him. Instinctively I knew that Liza was the wrong person for this explorer—she had not the sense of daring to match his. Besides, she was much taller than he.

Momentarily distracted with thoughts of Lieutenant Frémont, I returned my attention to Father. He was still talking about westward expansion and "Fifty-four forty or fight"—he believed the Columbia River could never be the northern boundary of the United States, that it had to be set at the fifty-fourth parallel—and I sat as patiently as I could, itching though I was to bring up the subject of my schooling.

When at last my opportunity came, I lived up to Father's critical assessment of me as Don Quixote. Rather than working tactfully toward the moment, I leaped in with both feet, unfortunately, in my mouth.

Father's reaction should have been no surprise to me. "Leave the school? Of course you can't. Liza will finish her work this spring, and that leaves you another year. Absolutely not!"

Desperately I said, "Father, didn't you tell me part of the reason I had to go off to school was so that I would not entertain . . . ah, unsuitable suitors? Like Harriet Wilson did."

"The Bodisco marriage," he said loftily, "is quite a satisfactory one, I understand. Both parties are happy, and there is a blessed event expected."

That bit of news shook me just a little, reviving my uncertainties about Harriet's marriage. Obviously, if a blessed event was expected, the marriage had been consummated. The thought gave me a momentary shudder.

"That is beside the point," I said. "If Count Bodisco had courted me, you'd have been livid with anger."

He nodded his head warily, knowing he could do nothing but agree with me and yet not sure what trap I was leading him into.

"The point is, Father, he did not court me. And no one else has. I will be perfectly safe . . . and virtuous . . . here at home with you and Mother. And I do not need the studies at Miss English's."

"And what," he asked, "makes you think you don't need them?"

"Well, I've been correcting the French teacher all fall—oh, don't worry, I've been tactful. And once when I asked about studying the things that are important today— the issues that absorb your attention, like slavery and westward expansion—I was told that it was more fitting for us to study the ancient Greeks and Romans. Fiddle!"

I'd been calculating when I pointed out that a classical education had little to do with what Father thought was important, and I saw him start a little when I said that, as though my arrow had hit home. I followed with the final barb.

"I'm tired of learning to pour tea. I've known how to do that since I can remember."

He smiled ruefully. "You can pour a fine cup of coffee, I'll speak to that."

Boldly, I pushed my case. "And you'll speak to my leaving school?"

He was not to be caught so easily. "No, miss, I will not. School is your mother's fondest wish for you, and her word is law with me."

"May I tell her you will accept if she will?"

"No," he said, his firmness returning, "you may not even go that far. Now, pick up that quill and let me dictate this speech to you. It goes better that way than if I try to write it myself." He shuffled the papers on his desk, as though frustrated by them, and I obediently took a sheet of foolscap and sat with my pen poised.

I had not given up hope.

Perhaps it was cheating, even outright dishonesty—the thought has long worried me since—but I caught Mother on a day when she felt too weak to argue, too weak for disagreement. Her state also made her sensible of the advantages of having me home to be Father's companion.

"If you are insistent," she said, waving a thin arm in the air as though disassociating herself from the question.

"May I tell Father that I have your permission?"

"Yes, yes, you may tell him. Jessie, what is to become of you?"

Then she put a hand to her head and said faintly, "I'll worry about it later. Would you bring me some tea, please?"

"Of course, Mother." I nearly flew on wings to the kitchen to get the tea.

Within days notice was sent to Miss English that I would not be returning and that a family servant would call for my belongings.

"You got your way, didn't you?" Liza asked angrily.

"You don't have to go back either," I said, "but you want to."

"Yes," she said, "I do. And I'll make a better marriage than you because I've finished at Miss English's."

I wanted to laugh aloud and point out to her that marriage or the prospect of it had nothing to do with my leaving the school. But Liza never understood my relationship with Father, and it was too late to try to tell her.

———

Lieutenant Frémont was at our house two or three times during the holiday, and I had several conversations with him—conversations that I thought he deliberately sought.

"It is a pleasure to see you here, Jessie," he said, bowing once again over my hand in his courtly manner. "I'm told the house lacks a certain sparkle when you're not present."

I hoped my laugh did not sound as self-conscious as I felt when I said, "Nonsense. Father may sometimes lack for a hostess, but . . ."

"One who understands the issues of which we men talk," he said smoothly, his eyes never leaving mine.

My gaze locked into those eyes, and I replied, "I am as interested in the progress of this nation as my father is . . . and as dedicated to certain causes."

"The exploration of the West?"

Was he laughing at me? "Yes, of course," I replied hastily.

"Jessie!" Father's voice boomed out. "Don't be monopolizing Mr. Frémont's time. There are several people here tonight I want him to meet."

Father had gathered six or eight politicians—most of them men of significant influence in the government—for an evening around the fireplace. We had given them a sumptuous meal—gallantine of turkey, creamed oysters on toast, lima beans, watermelon pickles (carried by coach all the way from Cherry Grove), and a whiskey bread pudding. Now they were enjoying after-dinner glasses of port, the entire company gathered around the fireplace in the upstairs parlor.

Lieutenant Frémont had stopped me in the hallway outside the parlor, and it was evident that we were having a conversation tête-à-tête rather than joining the group.

"I am sorry, Father," I said with all the brightness I could muster. "Lieutenant Frémont has been talking to me of exploration . . . a favorite subject of mine," I added with a droll note in my voice.

"Of course," Father boomed, though his voice, I thought, lacked its usual heartiness.

The conversation that evening was not on such earthshaking matters as slavery or westward expansion but revolved around the forthcoming inauguration of Mr. William Henry Harrison. "He is a farmer," said one, while another countered, "So have been many of our presidents. And this one has been in the Congress."

"And a governor and minister to . . . what country was that?" The discussion of Mr. Harrison's qualifications rolled around my head, while I sat and—unobtrusively, I hoped—watched Lieutenant Frémont. Every few minutes I would catch him flashing me a look that hinted at some shared secret . . . and somehow that look went right to the bone.

"I see," Liza said indignantly as we prepared for sleep that night, "that you are much taken with John Frémont."

"I only talked to him briefly," I protested. "I don't know if I am taken with him or not. Are you?"

"Of course not," she said indignantly, flouncing away from me.

Ah, Liza, I thought, *you are, and you don't know what to do about it. And I don't know what to tell you.*

It was far easier for me to analyze Liza's reactions to the handsome explorer than my own. I found, after that fateful night, that his face appeared to me at odd hours during the day and, sometimes, during restless and wakeful nights. I was not certain why he intrigued me, except that somehow, deep down, I felt we shared a sense of mission—the mission of westward expansion that Father had given to me before I was old enough to realize it. *Destiny,* I thought, *has brought this man into my life.*

Destiny, of course, did not translate into love, and with the examples of my parents and Harriet Wilson Bodisco before me, I was very much concerned about love, trying to puzzle out for myself—with absolutely no confidants—what it was, how I would recognize it.

Meantime, I tried to remain calm and collected when the lieutenant was in the midst of our family circle, which he often was after Liza returned to school and I stayed behind. I succeeded in being poised about half the time, or so it seemed to me.

"Aren't you the calm one?" he said with a laugh one night, again catching me in the hallway outside the parlor. "What would you say if I told you I've determined to marry you?" Those blue eyes were fixed on mine with a penetration so strong as to be mesmerizing.

"I would say you are being impertinent," I replied, my light tone hiding the rapid beating of my heart. "Come, the others are waiting for us."

Our hallway conversations grew more frequent—always brief, usually light—except when he made comments about marrying me, which he did occasionally—and always deliberately. I began to anticipate them with pleasure, and I kept seeing his face before me at odd moments. I was glad Liza was away at school.

Of course, the night came when he kissed me. The party had preceded us upstairs, and as I turned to mount the stairs, he laid a restraining hand on my arm.

"Jessie? A moment, please."

"Yes?" That pounding heart again. I was sure the breast of my woolen shirtwaist must be vibrating strongly enough to betray me as I turned toward him.

"I must tell you," he said seriously, "that I am in love with you. My comment about marrying you . . . it was not frivolous. I . . . I knew from the first moment that you would be special in my life. You had . . . the effect of a rare picture, that quality of sense and feeling and beauty."

Too taken aback to say anything, I simply stared at him. And he, with no hesitation, moved his mouth toward mine. It was a gentle, sweet kiss, one full of promise but strangely lacking in passion, if I could even have recognized passion at that point in my life. Still, I felt a burning on my lips long after he had taken his away.

"We . . . we must join the others," I said, more flustered than I could ever recall being.

"Yes, of course," was his smooth reply. To my further discomfort he looked greatly amused.

If John's kiss was inevitable, so was Father's anger. The anti-John campaign, however, began slowly enough.

"Jessie," Father said one morning when I joined him early, as was once again my habit, "you've been showing partiality to Lieutenant Frémont lately. I . . . well, girl, I don't think it looks proper."

"There is nothing improper about it, Father. We are always with your guests."

"Yes, yes," he said as he fiddled uncomfortably with the inkwell on his desk, "but you are also too often off by yourselves. Even James Buchanan commented on it the other night."

"Mr. Buchanan," I said archly, "needs a wife to keep him from meddling in other people's affairs."

In most circumstances Father would have laughed at my boldness, but he was too distressed this time to see any humor. "That," he said, "is not the function of wives."

"What is?" I countered.

"Promoting their husbands' careers," he said, with no hesitation.

I wanted to ask how Mother rated, then, but kept my quiet instead. The conversation had wandered from Father's initial concern, and I was willing to let him lead it where he would. He led it right back to Lieutenant Frémont.

"I wish you to pay less attention to him. I do not want Lieutenant Frémont courting you."

"He isn't courting me!" I replied quickly, though I could feel a blush giving away my own suspicion that he was, indeed, courting. "Besides, you think he shows a great deal of promise. You're ready to turn the next major expedition over to him if Monsieur Nicollet is unable to lead it."

"Giving him an expedition and giving him my daughter are two different things," Father said dryly. "He is an army man, with no family background that we know of, no money to speak of, and very few prospects for the kind of future I expect for you."

Something inside me stiffened at Father's words. He didn't know it, but *mon père* had just strengthened the lieutenant's case.

Without waiting for me to reply, he said, "I never issue orders to you, Jessie, and I hesitate to do so now. But I wish you to pay less attention to Frémont. He'll still get his expedition."

"Of course, Father," I said, though my heart was rebellious. What, I wanted to ask, about the order to go to Miss English's? That question, however, was not politic and could well have landed me back at the dreaded seminary. I realized I must tread carefully.

I couldn't have avoided John Frémont if I had wanted to, although clearly I didn't want to. At Father's gatherings he continued to seek me out, showing a rare talent for finding me away from the crowd—lingering to give the maid a suggestion about brandies, pausing to check my hair in the mirror before following the crowd to the upstairs parlor. My attitude stiffened a little in spite of myself, because I knew Father was watching like a hawk.

Once when Father saw me talking to John, he beckoned across the room, motioning me toward him.

"Excuse me. My father apparently needs me," I said, leaving John with a studied look on his face, as though he were puzzling out the situation.

"Yes, Father?" I asked, my voice indicating, I hoped, that whatever the ostensible cause of the interruption, I knew what lay behind it.

"Your mother needs you, I think, Jessie. She's had a difficult day."

"Of course," I said obediently, and left for Mother's room, where I found her sitting in a chair knitting, looking stronger than she had for days.

"Father said you sent for me?"

A slightly puzzled look crossed her face, but then she quickly said, "Yes, dear, I did. I . . . well, I wanted some company."

Mother rarely chose my company. Liza's ways were more soothing to her, and she hated listening to my ideas on politics and government. Such subjects were, in her view, beyond a woman's interests, which should be bound by her family.

"Mother," I said directly, "you have guessed that Father sent me up here to keep me from conversing with Lieutenant Frémont."

Her look said plainly that I had hit upon the truth. "We . . . we don't feel he is an appropriate match for you," she said, her belief in her own conviction giving her strength.

"I wasn't marrying him, Mother. I was merely talking to him."

To myself I added, *But I may very well marry him, whether you and Father like it or not.*

John was gone by the time I returned to the parlor.

The next day a messenger delivered a handwritten note:

Have I offended you or your family? I would like to talk to you privately. If possible, meet me in front of Nicollet's studio at four o'clock this afternoon.
With utmost respect,
John Charles Frémont

The very secrecy of it thrilled me to the core. I felt a woman, no longer a girl. Of course I would meet him, if I had to lie to Father and sneak away from Mother to do it.

He was pacing the street when I arrived, deliberately a little late. "I thought you might not come," he said anxiously. "Can we walk a bit?"

"Of course."

He tucked my hand into his arm possessively, and I lacked the strength or will to remove it. For some minutes we walked in silence, while I burned impatiently to know what he wanted to say. Occasionally, when I glanced at him, I saw a faraway look in his eyes, as though he were plotting his next expedition. In a way, he was.

"I have noticed a difference in your father," he said at length.

"He still professes interest in our maps and another expedition, but he is . . . well . . . less cordial. Have I offended him?"

As was my way, I took the direct approach. "Yes," I said, "you and I both have. He thinks we are too interested in each other."

He shook his head sadly. "I suspected as much. If I have offended you, Jessie . . ."

I whirled to face him, standing still to stare at him. "Oh, no, John"—it was the first time I had used his given name to his face, though I'd repeated it a thousand times in my mind—"you have . . . you have made me happy."

His face split into a grin. "I am so glad," he said. "You see, from the first night—the musicale at that awful women's school—I was captivated by you. I want to marry you, Jessie Benton."

With the feeling that events were moving too fast and that I was being carried along on a tide, I was speechless. But I was also thrilled. He was everything I wanted in a husband, and the thought that he had chosen me seemed so good that I was afraid I might wake from a dream any minute.

For a long minute we stood thus on a Washington street, staring at each other while passersby detoured around us with tolerant smiles, and then John put his arms around me and kissed me soundly, not the soft and gentle kiss he had earlier stolen in the house on C Street, but a strong, possessive kiss that sent a flutter coursing through my belly.

It was, of course, a shameful public display, and I pulled quickly away—well, almost.

"I am sorry," he said at once. "I had no right."

"It is all right," I said, taking his arm again, "but we best continue to walk."

Before my very eyes his elation turned to gloom. "There is the matter of your father," he said. "He does not think I am worthy."

"No," I protested, "that's not it. I . . . I am not certain what the problem is, though Father might never approve of any man I wanted to marry." It was only a small lie, I told myself, since in a way Father really did not think him worthy, and yet I could not bear to say that to this man whom I now loved with all my heart.

"You will continue to be welcome at our home," I told him. "I know Father that well. We shall simply have to pay less attention to each other."

"That," he said, grinning again, "is exactly the opposite of my intentions."

"Perhaps," I said boldly, "we could meet like this from time to time."

"Perhaps we could," he said.

And we did. We began a clandestine romance that was conducted all spring on the streets of the capital city. My arm securely clutched in John's, I wandered up one muddy street and down another. Of course, we met people who knew us—mostly who knew me—and, of course, the word got back to Father. But not until after the funeral for President Harrison, which was an amazing and wonderful day for me.

Poor Mr. Harrison, whose wife never wanted him in the White House anyway, died less than a month after his inauguration in March of 1841. The funeral procession was scheduled for April 4, and since it would not be easily visible from our house, John arranged to have the Benton family observe it from Mr. Nicollet's studio, which overlooked Pennsylvania Avenue and the approach to the Capitol. It was, he explained to Father, a courtesy to Mother, so that she could see the procession without exerting herself. Father had no graceful choice but to accept the invitation with pleasure, although he himself was an official mourner and would not join us. However, my Grandmother McDowell, who was visiting from Cherry Grove, would be with us.

April 4 was a cold, gray day, but John had built a fire in the fireplace and filled the studio with pots of geraniums—in honor of my mother and grandmother, he told everyone. A serving table was laden with cakes and delicacies, and comfortable chairs were drawn up to the windows for the ladies to view. John himself wore his dress uniform, "in reverence to Mr. Harrison," he explained. The workroom—and the worker—had been truly transformed.

Dimly, from the outside, we could hear the dirge and the tramp of horses, but inside all was cheerful. When the fire was roaring and his guests were settled with cakes and ices and their attention riveted on the parade in front of them, John drew me around the drape that sectioned off a portion of the workroom.

"Jessie," he said urgently, "I can wait no longer. Will you promise to marry me?"

"Yes, John, I will." There was no hesitation in my answer, and it was followed by another of those kisses that left me breathless and stumbling for words. I know that when we returned to the group, my face shone as red as the cherry ice John served, but all eyes were out the window and no one noticed.

Thus a funeral turned out to be the happiest day of my life to date. It was followed by disaster.

Father had always been somewhat suspicious of the funeral party, as I called it in my mind, but his suspicion turned to certainty when someone—or maybe several people—told of seeing John and me together on the street, more than once. Father, however, was a clever politician. He said nothing to me, and I had no inkling of disaster until John sent me another note.

Dearest Jessie,
I have been ordered on an immediate expedition. I must see you at once. Would
Mrs. Crittendon lend us her parlor?
*   With adoration, John*

Maria Crittendon, the wife of a lawyer with whom Father was associated, had intuitively known of the romance John and I shared, and she, instead of frowning, had given her blessing—secretly, of course. Once she had caught me in a private moment and whispered, "I believe in romance. If I can help, let me know."

Now she could indeed help, but would she? Was it too bold a deed to ask of her?

Not at all, the lady assured me, and it was arranged that John and I would meet there at four o'clock the next afternoon.

"Papa Joe Nicollet is frantic," John told me, clutching my hand in his as we sat on the horsehair sofa in the Crittendon parlor. "He says he cannot complete the maps without me, and it is folly to send me off on a trumped-up expedition."

"Trumped up?" I echoed.

"He and I both believe that your father prevailed upon the secretary of war to organize this expedition, not for the national good, but to get me away from you."

"Mr. Poinsett would do that?" I asked incredulously.

"He is your father's good friend," John said. "The expedition is an opportunity for me—the chance to lead an expedition myself—but it still rankles."

"I shall miss you," I began tentatively.

"You best." He laughed. "And I hope you will wait for me. The expedition is neither dangerous nor long. I shall be back in Washington in six months."

Six months! I felt faint, but John grabbed my arm strongly. "If we love each other . . ."

"Yes," I whispered, "I will wait with happiness. *Le bon temps viendra.*"

"Yes, my darling," he whispered into my hair, "the good times are coming."

A tactful cough from Maria Crittendon signaled that we had enjoyed all the privacy we should. Knowing I would not see him for six months, I kissed him once more, boldly, my passion learning to meet his demanding strength.

I did not see John again before he left, but within days I had been given another set of circumstances to think about.

"You and Liza will go to Lexington for Sally McDowell's wedding," Mother announced. "I will stay here, and so will the younger children." The truth was, of course, that Mother did not feel up to the trip. Still, she had not lost her authority.

"You must go to the Alum Springs before the wedding to remove the tan from your skins," she said. "You look like savages."

Liza and I were thus both disconcerted about our appearance and filled with dread about the hot water of the springs. It did not bode well for the summer. Mother's other caution to me cut far deeper.

"Be sure to be nice to your cousin Preston," she said. "He is a fine young man, who will make some lucky young woman a reliable husband."

The translation, of course, was that I should aspire to be that lucky young woman. But was reliability all I sought in a mate? I hardly thought so.

"Yes, Mother," I murmured. "I have always been fond of Preston, and I shall be on the watch for suitable lucky young girls."

She closed her eyes and reached for the cold rag kept near her for easing her headaches.

John was off in the West, where the future had no boundaries. I was being sent to the South, where tradition held us all to the past. But I could neither protest nor resist. I went to Virginia.

CHAPTER THREE

LIZA AND I, APPROPRIATELY CHAPERONED, TOOK TRAINS PART OF THE WAY TO LEX-ington and then bumped along in private carriages until at last we arrived at that city surrounded by the Blue Ridge Mountains. It was the home of the Virginia Military Institute, and Anne Smith's Academy for ladies of wealth, and Washington and Lee University. To me, however, it was simply not Washington.

Other carriages arrived simultaneously, full of our various aunts and their children and nurses and maids. We were a house party of over thirty by the time we had all gathered, but none of the aunts seemed the least bothered by the confusion nor the massive preparations required. Life in the McDowell household went smoothly on, as though Aunt Susanna had long been used to feeding and organizing an army of hungry relatives.

My aunt and Sally's mother, Susanna McDowell, was one of my favorite people and one of the reasons I was glad to be in Lexington. She, in turn, was openly glad to have Liza and me part of the wedding group. "I have so enjoyed your letters, Jessie," she said—I wrote to her regularly as a schoolgirl—"but I only wish your dear mother could have made the trip."

"Mother was just not strong enough," I told her, only repeating what she already knew.

"I do hope," she said, peering at me, "that her . . . ah . . . weakness has not been inherited. You look perfectly healthy, but there is . . . about the eyes . . ." Aunt Susanna was Mother's sister, and she understood Mother's illness better than I was able. But I resented her suggestion that I might have inherited Mother's "condition."

"Just a little tired, Aunt," I assured her. "I will rest longer tonight and be fine in the morning."

Though I rushed to the mirror to examine my eyes, and did find them a trifle puffy, I knew it was not fatigue but wanting—and maybe a dose of rebellious anger—that had dimmed my appearance. I wrote daily to John but could, of course, receive no reply. By then both John and I knew better than to correspond openly. So I was left to wonder how and where he was. Sometimes I traced an imaginary route on one of Father's maps that I had folded—heaven help me if he found that out!—and put in a valise. But I was most uncertain of where John was . . . and how he was and whether or not he thought of me.

If Aunt Susanna was a comfort to me, my Grandmother McDowell was a joy. She was then in her eighty-ninth year and in failing health but full of contentment for the life she had lived, though it sometimes sounded harrowing to me as she regaled us with stories of her youth.

"My mother . . . your great-grandmother," she said dramatically, "carried to her grave a long cut on her forehead from a knife thrown by an Indian in the British service. When she was tired or upset, the scar would turn red and swell . . . she called it her King George's mark."

She told a fascinating story of the English officer who came to our great-grandmother's house and demanded to be fed. When he was served peas that were very green in color—mint or lettuce or something had been added to them—he accused her of trying to poison him. Calmly, the hostess called her youngest child to her and fed her several spoonfuls of the peas. "You may feel safe now, gentlemen," she is supposed to have said. "Whoever eats at my table, invited or not, has my best care. My husband, my young sons, my brothers, are all in the rebel army, and I pray for their success and your defeat, but you will get no harm from me."

They ate their peas and went on their way. Listening to Grandmother tell the story, I was thrilled to think of the people from whom I was descended. They had done something important for their country—and that thought, of course, sent my mind reeling back to John and his current service in the army.

———

"Jessie, wait until you meet Francis," Sally gushed. "He's a perfect gentleman." Her blond curls cascaded around her face, giving her a schoolgirl look that was strangely inappropriate for a girl about to marry a man of forty or more.

"I can hardly wait," I murmured, though in truth, after one day, I was already bored with the wedding festivities. Besides, I remembered Aunt Jasmine's description of him as a "trifling poor fellow."

Days in Lexington were long, though we went gaily to one pre-nuptial party after another. Liza enjoyed it thoroughly, but every party was a trial as far as I was concerned, partly because it was difficult to get there. Lexington was not like Washington, where everything was in walking distance—nothing here was close to anything else, and all of it was separated by steep ridges. We took carriages everywhere, and they frequently had to have the wheels blocked as they descended one incline after another, lest the carriage fly down the hill ahead of the horses.

People came from the countryside around to attend these parties, for the McDowells were well known in Lexington. Some guests arrived in country carryalls and others in fine carriages. The ladies wore low-cut dresses of silk, dresses that Mother would never have allowed on me—high-cut dresses had not yet become fashionable for women—and they threw wonderful plaid capes over their shoulders for warmth against the spring chill. I felt woefully childish in my high-necked dresses.

But the worst of these parties was that I reminded everyone of a long-dead cousin, "poor, dear Eliza" who had been married to "poor Charles." Both poor souls had died unexpectedly, at young ages, leaving orphan children, and though those children were now grown, their parents were far from forgotten. Unfortunately, I resembled the late Eliza, though as more than one aunt said in a whisper loud enough to be heard, "Jessie's nose is not nearly so delicate."

The children of Eliza and Charles were present for the wedding, the eldest being the cousin named Preston, whom Mother had strongly recommended to my consideration. He was down from West Point, and though the aunts did not comment on it as much as I feared, it was clear that Preston and I resembled each other as closely as twins.

◆

"Jessie! Want to see me scratch my ear with my elbow?" Preston was as bored and out of patience with the formalities as I was.

"Certainly," I said with more enthusiasm than I had shown for most of what went on around me.

He bent double and very nearly had his elbow in his ear with a little patience. "I've been practicing," he explained proudly when I complimented him.

"Good," I said dryly. "Everyone needs a talent."

"And a little amusement," he said, sinking down on the end of the chaise next to me. "I'm about stifled with this wedding."

"So am I," I said offhandedly. Actually I was consumed with longing instead of stifled with boredom, but the end result of both emotions was about the same. Either one of us would have done anything to bring excitement to the day.

The much-talked-of Francis Thomas did nothing to brighten the days. He was tall, thin, and nervous, given to fluttering about in a manner that I would have found unpleasant in a woman, let alone a man. He positively hovered over Sally, his yellowish complexion turning slightly pink when he looked at her. Was it joy, anger, or jealousy? I was never able to decide.

Liza thought him a fine figure of a man and openly pined for such a man for herself. I was silently scornful.

"Ah, yes," he said on meeting us, "Senator Benton's daughters. I . . . know your father by reputation."

Liza smirked and simpered but said nothing. I was not silent. "How kind of you," I murmured, thinking how Father would laugh at my diplomacy. Mr. Thomas had been far from complimenting Father with that veiled reference, and I knew it. But neither did I give him the satisfaction of thinking I had ever heard of him before he decided to marry my cousin.

I could hardly bear it when Sally asked later if I did not think he was wonderful.

"Oh, indeed," I said, but the irony was lost on her.

"Jessie! I've found a place to escape." Preston said this in a whisper, then turned quickly away with a motion behind his back for me to follow him.

A rainy day was keeping us confined to the house, and our older relatives had taken over the parlor to listen as a young cousin—whom I thought foppish—filled them with tales of his European tour. We were clearly not wanted, though I wondered when, if ever, we would be considered adults. Still, I didn't want to spend the day in that parlor.

"This way," Preston said conspiratorially, and we mounted the steps to the attic, where it was cool—open windows let in a cross breeze—and quiet. "I hate the way they talk about us as though we weren't there," he said.

"I don't suppose they realize," I answered, "but they are very cruel. What was your mother's nose like?"

He laughed aloud. "More delicate than yours," he said, mimicking the aunt's tone. But then he turned serious. "We do look alike, you know, as though we had shared parents."

"Maybe. But you are too thin for a Benton. You obviously belong to the McDowell side of the family."

He shrugged ruefully and began idly playing with the clasp on a trunk near him. With a loud snap it gave, and a slight push of his hand popped the lid up. Inside, carefully laid in layers of paper, were astonishing clothes—old army uniforms, beautiful gowns for women, delicate laces and striking feathers, all manner of fine things.

"Whatever . . . ?" Preston wondered aloud.

"You've found the family closet," I said. "Maybe some of the clothes even belonged to your parents."

That gave him a funny twist for a moment, and without another word he began to dig through the clothes, though I noted the care with which he moved one thing aside to find what was beneath it. Fishing out an army uniform, he held it up against himself, as though trying it for size.

"Far too large," I said from my spot on an adjacent trunk. "The jacket is twice as big around as you."

"You're right. I'm too thin," he said with a sigh.

"Here, let me try." It was not without some embarrassment that I found that the army uniform came closer to fitting me than it did Preston. "What else is in there?" I asked.

He pulled out a garment of satin covered by unbleached silk lace. "Here . . . I bet it's Aunt Susanna's wedding dress."

It was Empire in style, the waist almost up to the arms and not a pleat or a gore in the skirt to indicate the waist, except for a narrow band, which ran to a bow in the back.

"I've heard that Uncle William McDowell brought it from Paris," I said, reaching to touch the delicate fabric.

There is no way to account for what happened next, but within minutes we found ourselves dressed—Preston in the wedding dress and me in the army uniform. Looking at each other, we laughed aloud, the happiest I'd been since arriving in Lexington.

"Let's go downstairs and show off," I said boldly.

Preston paled at the thought. "We can't . . . I mean, it would make them angry. . . ."

"Nonsense," I said. "They will see the good humor in it."

I was wrong again, though at first that wasn't apparent. When we walked into the parlor where Cousin Edward McDowell was still holding forth about Europe, there were gasps of . . . well, I thought they were delight. "Eliza's dress!" . . . "It must be Charles's uniform" . . . "How striking they look!"

But then they discovered that we had, as it were, switched costumes, that the girl cousin wore the army uniform and the boy cousin the wedding dress. Surprise turned to horror, and we watched helplessly as the relatives turned angrily from us. With Preston pulling on my arm, we retreated to the attic and our own outfits.

Much later Aunt Susanna asked whatever I had been thinking of. "Nothing," I answered truthfully. "They were lovely clothes, but the uniform fit me better than it did Preston . . . and we just dressed up."

My beloved aunt was angry at me. "I would not be upset, Jessie, with your dressing up. But it is unsuitable for a young woman to dress as a man. . . . There is . . . there is no excuse. It will make people think you wish yourself a man." She shuddered at the thought, and it took all her strength to ask, belatedly, "Do you?"

"Of course not, Aunt," I answered quickly. "I would not be other than I am for anything." And within my mind a quick refrain sang, "I would not be other than John's love and Father's daughter," but I dared not say that to Aunt Susanna.

"I shall not," she said stiffly, "inform your mother of this incident. It would only distress her needlessly, but it goes without saying that I expect exemplary behavior from you from now on. You must act like a lady."

There it was again, that prescription about ladylike behavior. I wanted badly to argue, to repeat that we had merely been dressing up to relieve the boredom of a rainy day, and what did it matter who wore what costume? With difficulty I kept my silence.

Mother, I thought, might not ever mention Preston to me as a suitable prospect for marriage if she knew of today's incident. It was a dark irony and of little comfort.

Late that night, curled in bed, I whispered the story to John, as though he were next to me, and I was gratified that he roared with laughter. Or at least I thought he did.

⁓

Sally and Francis were married in a ceremony held in the bride's home, with only their families present, though between the two of them, that amounted to a goodly number of people. Sally wore clothes made by family servants, and the bride's cake had been lovingly made by women who had cooked for the McDowells since before Sally was born. It was decorated with wreaths of ivy and geranium leaves carefully sculpted of candied rind of watermelon. The most touching moment of the entire festivities came when the old butler who had served generations of McDowells brought the cake in to "Miss Sally." Two young servants had to hold his arm and guide him, lest he wobble so as to drop the cake. But at last—while we waited breathlessly—he placed the cake in front of Sally with a flourish, and her gasp of thanks brought joy to the old man's face. So too did the drop of whiskey given him by Sally's father after his successful completion of his mission.

Francis Thomas sat throughout this charade with a strange and unemotional expression on his pale face, his eyes staring covertly from under hooded lids at first one guest and then the other, as though he were taking stock of the assembled company.

Sally, I wondered, how can you? And then John would appear unbidden in my vision, with his healthy good looks that spoke of a vigorous outdoor life, and his self-confident smile, and I would know how lucky I was to have met him. The contrast between John and Sally's new husband did not even bear discussing.

⁓

Father greeted me with fury when I returned home.

"Obviously," I said, facing his anger, "you have heard from Aunt Susanna. She told me she would not upset Mother."

"She has not," he boomed, "upset your mother, but she has written me, simply out of concern for you. She does not think . . ." He paused as though to consider his words. "She does not think you have a proper vision of your role as a woman."

"I think," I said dryly, "I am getting a better and better vision each day, but it is not an encouraging one."

"Jessie, Jessie," he said, real emotion straining his voice, "you have so much to contribute. You have been such a great help to me and will continue to be, I hope. You can be a help to any man . . . but you must do it as a lady."

"It is a lesson I trust I have learned," I said with unusual submission, "and I will certainly plan to be of help to the man I marry." My words were deliberate, and Father took them that way, with a sudden flash of expression across his face.

"Well," he said with bluff heartiness, "that's a long way in the future."

I bit my tongue to keep from asking, "And how soon is Lieutenant Frémont expected back?"

⚊ ⚊

One day I begged leave from my duties in Father's library to go for a walk. The day, I explained, was so fine that I could not confine myself to the indoors.

"Of course, Jessie," Father said heartily. "I'll just work on my notes for this speech."

Hurrying away from the house on C Street, I felt more than a twinge of guilt. My destination was Monsieur Nicollet's studio, and my object was news of John. His "Papa Joe" would tell me the latest word, I was sure.

Mr. Nicollet greeted me warmly. "Miss Jessie, it is a pleasure to have you in my studio." His words were tinged with a Gallic accent, and he bent over my extended hand in the French manner. I thought him utterly charming. "What brings you to my studio? Ah, I know . . . of course . . . you want to know what I have heard from John."

He began to laugh at his own cleverness, but the laughter ended in a fit of coughing, and I remembered that the ostensible reason John was given charge of the expedition that summer was that Papa Joe's health would not permit him to travel. Papa Joe had been indignant at the time.

When he had regained his composure, I said, "You are right, of course. That is exactly what I want to know."

"I will keep you in suspense a few moments more," he said, "while I prepare tea. Here, please make yourself comfortable." Gallantly, he held a chair for me at a round table that was placed at the windows—I wondered if it was still there from John's rearranging of the furniture for the funeral cortege, all those months before.

Mr. Nicollet—I could not call him Papa Joe to his face, though in my mind he forever bore that affectionate name, and my French was not good enough for me to attempt "Monsieur" without stammering—bustled about in the small kitchen and soon appeared with two delicate cups of English china and a pot of steaming tea. Though the day was hot, the tea was delicious and relaxing.

"Now," he said, when at last we had settled at the table, "you want to know. I hear from John that he has mapped the Des Moines River—what he was sent to do. He has established its course from the mouth, up to the Raccoon Forks, about two hundred miles, and he has sketched the major topographical features. Very thorough, that young man is."

I beamed in pleasure at this praise for my lover. "He has been working hard," I said, somewhat inanely.

"Ah, yes, but they have had some recreation. He writes me of hunting deer and wild turkey in the woods."

"And he is well?" I asked, a faint tremor of anxiety going through my body. Surely, if he was not well, Papa Joe would have said so by now.

"He is in fine health . . . and he expects to be back in the capital city by August. He is . . . he is a very responsible young man, but I tell you nothing you do not already know."

"I am pleased to hear it from you, sir," I said, and meant it sincerely. Surely if John made a smashing success of this expedition, Father would look on him differently.

It was not to be so. Father heard that John had returned even before I did, and he made two quick announcements to me. The first was that John had successfully completed the mission he was sent on—that Des Moines River again, a river I was beginning to resent!—and the second was that I was not to see him.

"Neither elsewhere, unchaperoned, nor in this house," Father thundered.

"Why?" I countered.

"Your mother and I agree that he is not a suitable match for you," he said formally. Then, with some exasperation, "Jessie, we've had this discussion before. He's poor as a church mouse, with no formal training for the army and therefore no prospects. . . . He simply cannot offer you the life you were meant to lead."

"He has had magnificent training from Mr. Nicollet," I responded angrily, "training that makes his future as an explorer seem bright indeed." Even before I finished speaking, the look on Father's face told me that I had erred by defending John.

He glowered and said, "Jessie, I have told you my wishes."

"And I have heard them," I said, a phrase that I thought had the singular beauty of not committing me to comply with those wishes.

I knew that John would not dare seek me out or even write me a letter. Papa Joe Nicollet would have told him the climate of the Benton household, and John was nobody's fool. He would wait for me to make the first move. It was symptomatic of how comfortable I felt about our love that I felt no hesitation in making that move. I went again to the Nicollet studio, this time sneaking away when Father was engaged with business in the Capitol Building.

John was there, pacing anxiously and wondering how to get in touch with me, as Papa Joe told me later. I stood briefly in the doorway looking at him. The outdoor life had toughened him, giving him a hardy manliness that was, to my eyes, irresistible. His blond hair was bleached and his complexion darkened, both by the sun. But it was the way he held himself—strong and sure—that most impressed me.

There was no pretense of propriety. John simple opened his arms, and I walked into them.

"Jessie," he murmured, stroking my hair, "I have missed you more than words can tell . . . and the fact that I could not write to you, could not hear from you . . ." His voice drifted away in a whispered anguish.

"Shhh!" I put a finger on his lips. "We are together now, and we shall not be parted again." Young as I was, I am sure I did not realize what boundaries I had crossed, what common standards of courtship and manners I had left behind by being so open about my emotions. "Ah, Jessie," he murmured, "I hope you are right." And because Mr. Nicollet had tactfully left us alone, John kissed me full on the mouth, hard enough to cause that strange twisting sensation in my stomach. For a moment I went weak at the knees with wanting more.

Then, to myself, I vowed to see that my pledge was faithful. We would never be parted again. It was the most foolish pledge I ever made in my life . . . and one that I wished over and over I could have kept.

Mother and Father within due time heard that I had been seeing John surreptitiously. To my surprise Father did not openly confront me about my disobedience. I suspect he saw the inevitable handwriting on the wall. For once he turned the handling of his rebellious daughter over to his invalid wife.

Mother, not the politician that Father was, was nonetheless equally cunning and clever. She bided her time, passing only pleasantries with me on my daily visits to her room, for several weeks after John returned. Then one day, perhaps because she was feeling stronger than usual, she brought up the subject almost abruptly.

"You have been seeing Lieutenant Frémont," she said, though there was more resignation than accusation in her voice.

"Yes, Mother, I have," I said. One of the lessons I learned early was that lying was not only immoral, it often proved impractical.

"Your father has asked you not to see him." Those pale blue eyes stared directly at me, making it hard for me to return her look directly. I reasoned, however, that if I did not defend my love, I was not worthy of it . . . or him.

"I could not abide by Father's wishes," I said, reaching for her hand as though the gesture would bind us together. "I . . . my tie to John is stronger."

"Stronger than your tie to the father who has raised you and who has counted you his most important aide?" Her voice held no hint of resentment that I had taken the role that should have been hers. Indeed, I sensed a slight panic that I might desert Father, leaving her to bear the burden of being his supporter.

"Yes, Mother," I said. "Parental ties are strong, but when we meet the person with whom we are intended to spend our lives . . . our soul mate, if you will . . ."

"Poppycock!" she said, her voice showing more strength and exasperation than I had heard in months. "You are too young—only sixteen—to make such a decision. You have no idea who you are meant to spend your life with. And marriage decisions are not made for such flighty reasons. . . . You need to think of his ability to provide you with security, the comforts of life."

She grew impassioned as she gave what was for her a long speech.

"Look," she said, ". . . at how well your father has provided for me and for you children."

I drew a deep breath. "It took you seven years to marry Father. Did you not have the same strong feeling for him that I have for John?"

Mother turned her head away, and I was mortified that my arrow had hit home so closely. "Mother," I said, taking that limp hand in mine again and noticing how pale her skin was against my own healthy tone, "I would not hurt you, and I know that you love Father. But you must understand that what John and I share is different."

"We ask you," she said woodenly, as though repeating a fixed speech, "to wait one year before you reach any decision."

I was nearly knocked off my feet by this slight indication of possibility, this hint that someday approval might come our way. "May I see John in that interval?" I asked.

"Only in our home, at large dinner parties," she said. "He will continue to be invited. But you may not see him under other circumstances."

I stared out the window. There was no answer, no way to explain how long a year was, how difficult their request. What I also knew was that I could not explain to them the burning in the pit of my stomach whenever John kissed me. Whether or not my parents would understand that eluded me completely, but I had the sense—and the schoolgirl propriety—not to mention it.

In the end I avoided giving Mother a promise. It was a promise I could not make, though I was reluctant to disobey her. I left her room with a kiss and a whispered "I love you, Mother."

I knew I would never give in to the year's separation forced on us. John and I continued to meet, but now secretly, and the furtive nature of our romance gave it added spark. Ah, the forbidden fruit! Mornings, beginning very early, I worked with

Father in his library, and then, after the midday meal, I always took my exercise—a long walk on which I accidentally happened to meet John.

"Jessie, I think I shall accompany you today," Father said. "We haven't walked through Washington together for a long time. Remember the walks we used to have when you were little?"

"Of course I remember, Father," I said, hoping to calm the rapid beating of my heart. If Father was to find out I was meeting John . . . the consequences seemed too terrible to ponder.

"I remember," he went on, "the first time you saw the slave market, and you were so horrified at those poor people in chains."

"I still am," I replied.

"So am I, so am I. I guess that came to mind because this damnable slavery issue is everywhere . . . and it's going to split this country, mark my words." Then, brightening, he said, "Come, we won't walk anywhere near the slave market. Where would you like to go?" Anywhere but the public gardens near the White House, I said to myself, knowing that was where John awaited me. Aloud I said, "Have you been to Mr. Nicollet's studio lately to check on the maps of Lieutenant Frémont's latest expedition?" It was a bold move.

"Jessie," Father said in exasperation, "is this an excuse to see the lieutenant?"

"No, Father, it truly is not. I know how interested you are in these explorations, and the studio is just the right distance for a fine walk." My reasoning was twofold: John would not be there, which would make the visit acceptable to Father, and when John did return, Papa Joe would report that I had visited with my father. John would then understand why I had not met him.

As we walked, Father and I talked of borders and boundaries, of England's belief that the Columbia River must be the northern boundary of the United States while Father held out for a line more to the north, which would include rich timber and farming lands yet to be settled.

"And Mexico, Jessie," he said, "we're bound to have trouble there, but California must be made a part of the United States. There is no sense in a country not stretching to its own natural borders, and this country will go from ocean to ocean."

I knew he had spoken at length on this subject in the Senate just the day before—so long that at least half the senators departed during his speech, he reported—and I felt a surge of pride in his strong beliefs, his commitment to what was right for his country. In spite of my anxiety over missing John, I was enjoying once again being my father's close companion.

Mr. Nicollet greeted us effusively, though I saw a flash of confusion in his eyes when we were first admitted to the studio. I managed to respond to it with a strong smile, and he responded with that most Gallic of gestures—a slight shrug.

The visit was a success. Father was most impressed with the maps that were under way and with John's work, which completed the earlier work Mr. Nicollet had done on the upper Des Moines. With Mr. Nicollet's running commentary Father leafed through John's sketchbooks, commenting on the thoroughness of detail in them.

I watched over his shoulder, thrilled to be seeing John's hand at work, as it were.

"Tell the lieutenant that Jessie and I are sorry to have missed him," Father said as we left, unaware of his own irony, "and give him my compliments on a job well done."

"I will do that, sir," Papa Joe said, giving me a quick smile that told me he would say even more than Father had asked him to.

John and I had a good laugh about the incident the next day, when he confessed that he had been nearly undone with concern waiting for me. "I thought you were ill . . . or that you had met an accident walking here. A thousand possibilities, all of them bad, went through my mind. . . . Oh, my darling, I could not bear it if anything happened to you."

My finger to his lips silenced his concern, but in a few minutes he said, "Jessie, we cannot go on like this. How long must we meet in secret and feel guilty because we love each other?"

"A year," I said, knowing in my heart that we would not—could not—wait the year.

I waited, half in anticipation and half in dread, for word of our meetings to get back to Father. Sooner or later someone would recognize us in the public gardens— the place we most frequently met—and mention it. But if anyone told him, Father chose not to mention it to me.

On rainy days we met in Maria Crittendon's parlor. That good lady was my guardian angel—friend, confidante, and adviser all in one charming and gracious person, who tactfully disappeared from the parlor for a few minutes each time we were there. She never left us long enough to compromise my honor, but she gave us the privacy needed for a stolen kiss or two, a pledge of love.

John was still an occasional guest at our home. Father had lost none of his enthusiasm for westward exploration, but he seemed to have lost some of that feeling for John himself. He was civil but distant, and John was included only when Mr. Nicollet came. "Courtesy to Nicollet," I heard Father grumble to Mother once. "Can't invite him without his aide."

When John was present, we carefully avoided each other, though I know Father saw the looks we exchanged across the dinner table or during the long talks in the parlor afterward. Sometimes they were looks of love and longing, and sometimes they spoke more of amusement. It made us smile to think of the wonderful secret we shared. Most evenings I was so busy with my duties as hostess that it was not hard for me to keep my mind off the handsome lieutenant sitting at the other end of the dinner table—Father always sat him there, as though to distance him from me.

In September, John began to act distracted and nervous. On our walks in the public gardens, he was moody, silent for long spells of time. My questioning brought no satisfactory answer except "I have something on my mind." He began, to my careful eye, to lose that look of health that he had brought back from his expedition.

One day he was almost distraught beyond words. We met in Maria's parlor, as the weather had turned too breezy and cool to be comfortable outside. Indeed, Father had questioned the wisdom of my going for a walk, and I, desperately concerned about John's agitated state, had nearly flown out the door of the house over Father's protests.

Now I sat in a stiff horsehair-stuffed chair, watching as John paced in front of the fireplace where Maria had lit a small fire to warm the room. He took three steps one way, then turned and took three the other way, his hands always clasped behind his back, his brow furrowed in concern.

"Jessie, this cannot go on . . ." he began.

"I know," I interrupted. "A year is too long. I shall speak to Father."

"No, Jessie, hear me out, please. That is not what I mean." There was a terrible desperation in his voice, a kind of begging.

"What is it that you mean?" I asked, now fearful to hear the answer.

Of a sudden he was on his knees before me, clasping my hands in his and looking at me with the most pitiful expression I had ever seen. Fleetingly, I wondered what had become of that strong outdoorsman.

"There is . . . there is a terrible secret in my past," he began, while I waited with bated breath. "My parents . . ." He seemed unable to go on.

I knew, of course, something of his family. He had been raised in Charleston. His mother's family had been planters in Virginia, but his father was a Frenchman—hence the last name—who had given French lessons and ballroom instruction. The family had been poor, and John's mother had taken in boarders to help provide for John and two other children. The father had died when John was quite young, and he had been fortunate to find a sponsor who saw to it that he advanced in school. I had long thought that John's fierce pride and his determination to succeed could be traced to the poverty of his childhood. Indeed, I had once assured Father that I knew John would provide for me appropriately because he had once been poor and was determined never to be so again.

"What about your parents?" I asked gently, somewhat relieved that the terrible secret was theirs and not John's. For just a moment the possibility of another marriage, another wife, had flashed through my mind.

47

"They were not married when I was born," he said slowly and deliberately, hesitating over each word. "I am a bastard." He almost spat the last word.

Stunned, I stared at him. Did he think this would change my love for him? How could he even imagine such inconstancy on my part, such faithlessness? And yet I could not laugh at him, for it was obviously something he took seriously.

"Did they love each other?" I asked.

He nodded, and the story came tumbling out. His mother's family, fallen on hard times, had sent her to live with a sister in Richmond when she was but ten or twelve, and the sister had married her off to an elderly widower when she was seventeen—just my age.

"She never talked of it," John said, "and I don't know the details, only that he was sixty or more when she married him, and that they were married for twelve years but had no children."

"And then?" I prompted.

"And then she met my father and fell in love with him. They . . . they had an affair, and my mother's husband divorced her. It was a scandal . . . a terrible scandal, and they left Richmond for Savannah."

"But, John, they loved each other and they loved you. And it was wrong for her to be married against her will to an old man. Surely there is some higher law . . ."

"But your father is right, Jessie. I cannot bring you an honorable name."

"It is honorable because it is your name," I said. "And no one today knows your family's story. It will be . . . our secret."

I was the one who initiated the slow kiss of longing that time.

John held me woodenly at first, still wrapped in misery, but I kissed away his doubts. Too soon we heard Maria's tactful cough in the doorway.

———

In early October, President Tyler gave a ball in honor of the prince of Joinville, son of King Louis Philippe of France. Mother had been planning my appearance at the ball all summer. It would be, she said, my coming out into Washington society as a young woman of marriageable age.

I was to wear a Paris gown that had belonged to Sally McDowell—now Sally Thomas. Indeed, Liza and I had brought it carefully back from Richmond after the wedding. I spent many hours corseted into that *peau de soie* gown while the dressmaker fitted it here and there under Mother's watchful eye.

"Jessie, dear, you don't seem excited about this ball," Mother complained. "It . . . it marks a milestone in your life. I remember my own first grand ball. . . ." And she was off into a hazy reminiscence of grand days in Richmond.

I wanted to tell her I might be more eager if I knew that I could arrive at the White House on John's arm.

I went, instead, on Father's arm, and Liza took his other arm. The arrangement made me feel still the little girl, rather than the young woman ready for society that Mother had promised me I now was.

Senator Buchanan, as courtly as ever, was the first to ask me to dance. "You look lovely tonight, Miss Jessie," he said, having added the "Miss" to my name, I guess, in recognition of my new status as an adult.

"Thank you, sir," I replied, concentrating on the waltz rather than on my partner.

"You will soon be receiving suitors, I imagine."

Was there something in his voice that cautioned me? "Oh, I doubt that, Mr. Buchanan. Father will never find anyone he thinks good enough for me." I tried to laugh lightly.

He fixed an intense stare on me. "Perhaps you will one day have to defy your father."

I expressed the proper indignation, but inwardly I thought, *If only you knew . . . !*

— ∼ —

Liza was asked to dance three times by a young lawyer and was bloomingly happy, especially since Father seemed to approve of the man wholeheartedly. I watched them with the sour feeling of jealousy creeping up from my stomach.

John was at the ball, of course, as one of Washington's most interesting and eligible young bachelors and also one of its leading army officers. He approached as Father and I stood, glasses of fruit punch in our hands.

"Senator. Jessie." He nodded his head at Father and bowed to me as he greeted us. Then, "Senator, may I have the honor of the next dance with your daughter?"

Caught in public, with this senator and that congressman and his wife standing next to him, Father could do little but mutter, "Of course." Oblivious of his stare, John and I lost ourselves in the dance and the music, the joy of being—however formally and properly—in each other's arms. My feet fairly flew, and I doubt I have ever since danced as well and with as much abandonment as I did that night.

Father still looked glum when John returned me to him, with a courtly bow, and departed to dance with Maria Crittendon. I followed them with my eyes, which must have shown what was in my heart.

"Come," Father said. "It's time for us to leave. Your mother will want a full report before she will sleep tonight."

— ∼ —

I married John Charles Frémont the next day.

CHAPTER FOUR

IT WAS NOT THE WEDDING A GIRL DREAMS OF. JOHN AND I WERE MARRIED October 19, 1841, in the parlor of Maria Crittendon's home, by Father Van Horsleigh of the Catholic Church. Father Horsleigh's presence pleased John, for he had been raised a Catholic, but would have even further enraged Father had he known. Maria was our only witness, and I wore the tartan-plaid gingham dress I'd been working in that morning, with a cashmere shawl thrown over my shoulders because of the chill. To have even dressed in a Sunday silk would have aroused suspicion in the Benton household, and I thought that what I wore mattered little in the long run. I was seventeen years and five months of age. John was twenty-nine.

John wore his army uniform, which only made him the more handsome, and I thought him on the losing end of this bargain. I got a handsome army officer, full of dignity and pride, and he got only a scrivener wearing a gingham dress.

Maria had lit the small fire in the parlor and filled the room with pots of dried ferns, a modest attempt to add a festive air. She had also baked a wonderful tea cake and after the ceremony served us tea and cake and brandy to warm our souls—or perhaps fortify them against the inevitable storm that would brew when our marriage became public knowledge.

The words are similar in any religion, and I can yet hear Father Horsleigh intoning, "Do you, John Charles, take this woman to be your lawfully wedded wife . . . ?" Fearing that my knees would buckle, I grasped John's arm fervently. The father tactfully left out the part about "Who gives this woman?" thereby saving all of us, particularly Maria, a difficult moment.

This was not a spur-of-the-moment wedding, planned in frustration during our exhilarating waltz the night before. Indeed, we had been planning it for over a month. We felt sure that at the end of the prescribed year, Father would have another injunction to serve, another stumbling block to put before us. If John were able to make a miraculous discovery or accomplish some other brilliant advance in the name of the United States, Father would look more kindly on our union, but we could not count on that. Nor could we count on winning parental approval.

"We'll be too old to have children if we wait for your father's word," John once lamented with a laugh.

I thought it only half a joke.

But after John's confession about his illegitimacy, I saw the need more clearly than ever for us to marry in haste. Only by marrying this terribly insecure man could I restore his self-confidence, make of him the whole man he must be to accomplish the great things that lay ahead of him.

"We shall elope," I said one afternoon in late September.

"Elope?" he yelped, so loudly that I was sure every passerby for miles heard him.

"Elope," I whispered.

Given a moment to adjust, he took to the idea wholeheartedly, and we began to plan. First we enlisted Maria's willing help, though I cautioned her that my father would be furious at her. She shrugged at that and implied he was often furious at people and got over it.

"The senator"—I meant her husband this time, not my father—"will be displeased. He will be afraid it will make an enemy of my father for him."

"I am not afraid of that," she said with a knowing smile. "But I will not invite him to the wedding."

John went to several ministers before he found one who would agree to perform the secret ceremony. Most were, with good reason, afraid of Father and of the publicity. They would, they said, be pleased to marry us at a traditional public ceremony, but they would have nothing to do with secrecy.

"I have friends in Baltimore," John said, "who would find a priest. . . ."

"That won't be necessary," Maria interrupted. "I know a priest here in Washington."

And that was how Father Horsleigh came to pronounce us man and wife. "You may kiss the bride," he said gently, and John wrapped me in his arms. For the first time our embrace was passionate and sanctioned, but it was so prolonged that once again I heard that tactful cough of Maria's.

Father Horsleigh left as soon as his duties were performed, as though he were nervous about discovery. We thanked him profusely and assured him of our complete silence. It struck me as funny that he said "Bless you, my children" as he left.

After we visited with Maria in a most civilized fashion, John and I kissed goodbye demurely at her doorstep and went our separate ways.

Father was waiting for me when I returned home. "Jessie!" he bellowed from his library. "Come here!"

With faint heart I mounted the stairs. "Yes, Father?"

"Where have you been?" he demanded. "I've got a speech on California nearly done, and I need you to listen to it."

Relief flooded over me, nearly making me giddy. "I'm sorry I've been so long, Father. I stopped to visit Maria Crittendon." It wasn't even a white lie.

"That silly woman," he muttered, and once again I thought *if only you knew . . . !*

Life went back into its routine, though for me there was always a difference—that secret, wholly satisfying knowledge that I was Mrs. John Charles Frémont. Being uninitiated in such matters, I could not wholly understand John's anxiousness to consummate our union. But I did know about the fire in my stomach caused by his kisses.

"John," I asked one afternoon, "have you . . . have you ever . . . ?" I blushed and could go no further.

"Have I ever made love to a woman?" he asked dryly.

"Uh . . . yes . . . I guess that's what I wanted to know."

He laughed aloud, a great, uproarious laughter that came from deep within him. Finally he calmed enough to inquire, "Are you asking out of jealousy . . . or to be sure I'll know what I'm doing?" Embarrassment nearly overcame me, and, resisting an urge to slap him soundly, I turned away.

He reached a gentle arm for my shoulder and said softly, "I . . . I'd like to tell you about it, Jessie, though it's not a story I'm particularly proud of."

He was seventeen and a student at Charleston College when he fell passionately—his word—in love with a dark-haired girl named Cecilia. She was from a large French family, and John began to neglect his studies to spend long days with Cecilia and her brothers. Charleston was still surrounded by wild and tangled woods where they could hunt. Some days they took a sailboat down the bay to the islands to fish, and on truly exciting days they went beyond the bar and far out to sea. "Those were the days that first taught me to love the outdoors," he said. "In a way, Cecilia was responsible for my becoming an explorer."

Jealousy flashed through me.

"The college gave me a warning . . . something about habitual irregularity and incorrigible neglect . . . but nothing stopped me from spending every waking moment with Cecilia. They warned me that I had disappointed my family and friends, that I would be disgraced, but none of it mattered. Cecilia and her family were all the world to me, even her angry old grandmother, who used to yell at me in French—which I understood just well enough to know that she was not being complimentary." He chuckled at the memory.

"What happened to Cecilia?" I asked, breathless.

He shrugged. "The faculty at the college were right. Eventually, I tired of her, and I began to hate the bad reputation I had earned for myself. I, as they say, 'came to myself and began to study.'"

"You tired of her?" I nearly screeched, and now it was John's turn to put a silencing finger to my lips. I brushed it away to demand, "And will you tire of me?"

He laughed again. "Of course not, Jessie. I was but seventeen, and now I am twenty-nine. I know my course . . . and you are at the center of it."

How lucky I am, I thought, *to have the love of a man who is so sure and who has already sown his wild oats.* Aloud I said, "I am jealous of Cecilia."

"If we can *ever* behave like regular married folk, I assure you there'll be no cause for your jealousy, my darling."

We intended to keep the marriage secret for the prescribed year, but such was our naïveté that we failed to realize that once a marriage is recorded, it becomes a matter of public record. And once it was public, the gossip began. It was only a matter of time until word reached Father, and we lived in dread of an eventual explosion of anger.

Inevitably, the strain began to show on both of us. John was sometimes short of temper, even with me, though he was always profuse in his apologies and declarations of love afterward. Still, most days he saw no end to the limbo in which we lived.

For my part the strain made me occasionally inattentive to Father's business, something that had never happened before. He was completely puzzled when, copying a speech, I omitted an entire page or, searching out a book from his library, I stood staring out the window motionless. "The book, Jessie?" he would ask impatiently.

But the strangest of all the signs of our difficulty appeared on my face—a rash at the corner of my mouth. The skin grew coarse and reddened, making it appear that my mouth was lopsided, pulled down and to the side. I began to hate looking in the mirror, and I was afraid John would no longer want to share those stolen kisses. Though the redness was fairly well contained, I was fearful it would spread to cover half my face.

Mother was so perceptive that it alarmed me. "Reminds me of your great-grandmother," she said. "You'll remember that her scar turned red and swollen when she was upset. Perhaps you have your own King George's mark." She stared thoughtfully at me, an unspoken question lying between us.

"I cannot imagine whatever I would be upset about," I lied, and then cursed myself for not having seized the opportunity to take Papa Joe's advice and confess the whole truth. I would rather at that point have told Mother than Father.

It was Mother, not Father, who first heard the news. On one of her better days Mother was in the parlor, wrapped in a shawl but talking brightly with Mrs. Poinsett, wife of the secretary of war who had sent John on that trumped-up expedition. Though I knew Mrs. Poinsett shared my parents' disapproval of my "fascination" for John, I thought little of finding her in the parlor. She and Mother were close friends, and Mrs. Poinsett was among the few Washington women Mother saw frequently. When I passed by the parlor a time or two, they seemed to be chatting amiably over tea, and their light voices followed me into Father's library, where I was doing some research for him while he was on an extended trip, planning to go from Kentucky to St. Louis.

But then the voices fell, and a hush seemed to settle over the house. At first, occupied with my work, I paid no attention, but gradually the changed atmosphere became apparent to me. Within minutes I heard the guest leaving, and almost immediately Mother's voice summoned me into the parlor.

She sat like stone in her chair, chin in the air, eyes out the window. "You have married that lieutenant," she said, forming her words slowly and deliberately, as though the statement were painful for her.

"Yes, Mother, I have," I replied, suddenly determined to make my stand and defend both my marriage and my husband.

"He is no gentleman," she said, now nearly spitting out the words, "to have taken advantage of a girl your age."

"I am the one who suggested we elope," I said boldly. "I had to persuade him."

"Jessie! No girl suggests an elopement!" Finally she turned to look at me. If she expected to see me weeping or repentant, she was disappointed, for I stood proudly before her.

"Mother," I said, "I love John Charles Frémont, and we shall have a magnificent life together. . . . He will make you and Father proud. If Father weren't so stubborn, he would see. . . ."

"That's enough, Jessie. You will not criticize your father when he acts in your best interests."

"But I know my best interests better than he does," I said, working desperately to keep a pleading tone out of my voice. "I only ask that you give John a chance."

"What other choice do we have?" she asked bitterly. "Your marriage is apparently already the talk of Washington. . . . Your father and I are the last to know. The entire government will be watching to see how we react."

"And how will you?" I asked.

"I will send for your father immediately," was her only reply. Father was angrier than even I had anticipated, much angrier than he had been the time I whacked off my hair, and long gone were the days when I could charm him out of his anger, as I had done as a child. He was stunned that I would directly disobey him, and his anger made him stonily silent in my presence. We passed not even the merest of civilities for the first twenty-four hours that he was home, twenty-four hours in which I did not leave the house, though I managed to send a message to John. Too stubborn to beg and too determined to recant, I matched his silence, though I continued my work on his various projects and speeches.

Late the afternoon after he returned home, Father summoned John to his library. Rushing to beat Micah, the butler, when I heard the knocker on the front door raised, I opened the door to see my husband—how the words echoed in my heart—pale but determined looking, wearing his army uniform, as he always did on what he saw as important occasions. He gave me a thin, tight smile—but no kiss—and we both approached Father's library.

"Jessie, I asked to see Lieutenant Frémont," Father said icily. "Not you."

"We are married, Father, and you must see both of us or neither."

Father was not used to being crossed by anyone, let alone his rebellious daughter. His face turned so red that for a moment I worried about apoplexy. John's face, by contrast, was ashen white, for even he was a little taken aback by my boldness.

"Sir," John began, his voice a trifle tremulous, "we would not have angered you . . . or disobeyed your wishes . . ."

"If they had been reasonable wishes," I said.

John held up a hand in my direction as though to quiet me, and I realized that he was telling me he was the man—the head of our household, as it were, though we had no household—and I should let him do the speaking.

"I'm sorry," I murmured, and my apology startled Father almost as much as my rebellion had. How could I explain to him that I intended to be a proper wife to John, not the unsuitably rebellious woman that he often feared I would be?

"We meant no disrespect, sir," John said. "I would not cause you any grief or embarrassment . . . and I would do anything to protect Jessie. But I must have her with me as my wife."

"And I must be with him," I said, taking his arm.

Father shot me a look and then said angrily, "If you must both be together, go and do so. But you will not be together in this house." Now it was my turn to be stunned. Father was sending me away. Never in my wildest imagination did I think that his anger would carry to that extreme. I clasped John's arm tighter for support, and he put a comforting hand over mine.

"Very well," he said formally, "Jessie and I will leave immediately. I will send word when we have settled, so that you will not have to worry about your daughter."

"I'm done worrying," Father said. "She has literally made her own bed. . . ."

I fled before he could see the tears forming in my eyes.

I struggled to maintain my composure during my farewell with my brother and sisters—Liza, Randolph, Sarah, and Susie—the little girls, too young to understand, thought I was off on a great adventure.

"Will you write to us, Jessie?"

"Of course, my darlings, I will write you long letters and tell you of wonderful adventures."

"We will miss you," Sarah said solemnly, while Susie bobbled her head in agreement.

Stooping to catch them both in my arms, I murmured, "And I will miss you ever so much."

Randolph, being older, knew that things were not as they should be, though he didn't know the full story and was too proud to ask.

When he formally held out his hand, I took it in one of mine and tousled his hair with the other. "You must behave," I said, and he promised.

Liza was cool, angry because I had brought turmoil to the household, jealous a little—I think—of my boldness and the new life waiting for me, puzzled because she could never see herself taking such a step. "I . . . I wish you happiness, Jessie." She held herself aloof until I put my arms around her.

"Thank you, Liza. I shall miss you more than you know." Then, brushing away a tear, I smiled. "But I won't miss the seminary. I am glad to have school behind me. You must represent the Bentons there."

Liza, always in her element at the school, would stay there until she was thirty, I thought, if someone didn't marry her.

My farewell with my mother was tearful and hard on both of us. She had retreated to her bedroom again after Mrs. Poinsett's visit and had not emerged since. When I went to tell her I was leaving, she lay on the chaise, a robe over her, and I thought again how frail she looked.

"Jessie? Your father . . . ?"

"He is angrier than either you or I thought he would be, Mother," I said, kneeling beside her lounge. "John and I are leaving."

"Leaving?" She sat up in alarm. "Leaving for where?"

"I don't know, but I will write as soon as I do. Father does not want us here."

With a moan she fell back on the chaise and covered her eyes with her hands. She was silent so long that I worried, but then she said, "I will talk to him. I was angry with you, Jessie, but never this angry. I cannot bear for the two of you to be . . . estranged."

"I can bear it, Mother, only because I must, because my love for John takes precedence. And I'm not sure that talking to Father will have any effect."

"I must try," she said, and determination gave her voice some of the firmness it had been lacking.

Amid hugs and tears we babbled about our love for each other and how soon we would be together again. As I turned to leave, she held out her hand for mine and whispered, "Give my regards to the lieutenant. And, Jessie, make him a good wife."

I promised, both aloud to her and silently to myself.

We fled Washington, going to Baltimore, where Papa Joe Nicollet was then in ill health and being cared for by the clergy at St. John's College. John had other friends in that city, and it seemed a logical place—indeed, the only place—for us to go. We spent our first married night—our honeymoon, as it were—in a small and not very grand hotel. I had necessarily left home with only a few belongings—one small satchel—and so looked suspicious to the desk clerk. Or at least I thought that was the way he looked at me. I could hardly explain that, yes, I was married, but that I had just run away from home and my wardrobe would follow me when I knew where to have it sent.

We were shown a small room with dingy wallpaper, dark woodwork in need of polish, an iron bedstead that appeared to sag in the middle, three straight chairs scarred by use, and a chest of drawers with a torn lace runner across the top.

"Jessie?" John's voice was full of question.

"Yes," I replied, fighting to keep back the tears. Sudden visions flashed through my mind—the grand wedding I should have had, with everyone who was anyone in Washington dancing to my happiness, the honeymoon in a classic small hotel in New York City or perhaps somewhere in Virginia, and the tour of Virginia to introduce my relatives to my new husband. Instead, here I was in Baltimore, and my relatives would hear soon enough of my disgrace. There would be no festive parties. What had I done?

"Jessie, I am sorry. I . . . I'm not worthy of you, and now I've ruined. . . . Well, you should have champagne and oysters and . . ." He chuckled just a bit. "We'll be lucky to get chops and a half pint of beer here."

And then I saw him again—John Charles Frémont, the man I loved, the man who was haunted by his unworthiness, the man I must always convince that he stood head and shoulders above the crowd, in spite of his small stature. Now he stood before me with an expression that called to mind the young boy whose schoolmates had just called him a bastard. I held out my arms, and he came to me. I clung to his neck, and he nearly lifted me off my feet, so intense was his kiss. We forgot the chops and half pint.

It would be lovely to say that John and I were physically matched from our first lovemaking, that it was a union of passion and fire, but such is not the case. I was a tentative lover, shy and uncertain, and John did indeed "know what he was doing," as he had put it—but Cecilia must have known too. John had little understanding of my uncertainties, my tentative responses, and when he was satisfied, lying content with his head on my breast, I was left full of doubts, feeling keyed up.

"It will get better for you, too," he murmured sleepily, which I found cold comfort.

57

I lay awake in that cold hotel room for hours, as John snored gently at my side, convincing myself that I had done the right thing, that I would never look back in doubt. Together, John and I were going to do something . . . well, something great. At last, content, I curled my arms around my husband and slept. The next thing I knew, sunlight was streaming in the dirty window, making the room bleaker than ever by contrast.

We never got oysters and champagne in Baltimore, but we were well entertained by several of John's friends, all of whom wanted to offer their congratulations and advice, which ranged from confronting Father to moving permanently to New Orleans or some far city and starting life anew.

"I'm afraid you don't understand Jessie," John told one earnest young man. "She is part of Washington. I think she would wither anywhere else. She has to be part of all that goes on in our capital." His words struck a chord of fear in me. What if Father never took us back? What if we were cut off from the Washington I knew?

It would not only be disaster for me, it would be the end of John's army career, a career that now looked so promising.

Papa Joe Nicollet was not much more encouraging. "Such matters never stay secret," he cautioned. "You should have been open and forthright about it. Now you appear to have been sneaky."

"We *have* been sneaky," John said miserably. "There is no way Senator Benton will look kindly upon our marriage now."

"Perhaps you are right," Papa Joe said with his characteristic shrug, "but I doubt it. He is too fond of his daughter, and too interested in the West to be permanently angry with you. You, my friend, are in the right place at the right time." And then another coughing fit overtook him.

—◦—

I wrote Harriet Bodisco—now the mother of a young baby—with our address, and she replied not only with congratulations but with a copy of the announcement of our wedding that Father had placed in the newspaper: "On the nineteenth in this city, by the Reverend Mr. Van Horsleigh, Miss Jessie Ann Benton, second daughter of Colonel Benton, to Mr. J. C. Frémont of the United States Army."

John was indignant. "The man's name must always come first!

I smiled grimly. "I told Mother I was the one who suggested we elope, and I am quite sure Father sees it as my wedding. You . . . in some senses you were just a victim of my headstrong foolishness."

He smiled then, "A willing victim."

In spite of its dinginess, the small hotel room was where we spent most of our hours, and, not surprisingly, we spent them in bed, learning to match each other as lovers. John was right—it did get better as I relaxed and learned to express my love for him with a touch here, a stroke there, and to take the pleasure he gave me. By the end of a week I was as eager as he, sometimes suggesting we decline a dinner invitation or retire early when the party was still animated around us.

"Jessie!" he said with mock reproval one night as I lay in his arms, as sated as he. "This is what your father would not have you know. This is the joy that he would have kept from us."

I had already pondered that, wondering as most brides must do about my parents' physical relationship. Though my father undoubtedly could have been described as lusty, I could not imagine my frail mother responding to him the way I already did to John. Still, it was hard to reconcile her supposed passivity with the production of six children. And yet I was sure theirs was not a union like ours—indeed, few were. We were not only blessed but singled out. Our physical passion was, to me, just one more sign that we were meant to be together for some extraordinary purpose, some calling beyond that of ordinary men and women.

———

After a week, still thoroughly entranced with each other, we were bored with Baltimore, and I was longing for Washington.

"You must go back to work," I told John.

"If we return, you will be subject to all kinds of stares and looks, and people will talk behind your back. I will not let that happen to you. I'll . . . I'll resign my commission and find work here in Baltimore." His voice faltered on the last.

"I hate Baltimore!" I cried passionately, and then was ashamed of myself for such an outburst.

John smiled. "I know you do, but . . ."

"We will go back and hold our heads up," I said. "If we are proud, nothing can hurt us." What I didn't add was that Washington—a city prone to gossip—would talk as much about John as they would me. By now some curious souls would have done their research into his background and unearthed his illegitimacy and the scandalous story of his mother and her broken marriage vows. I knew only too well that these stories were going to haunt John forever, and the sooner we faced them, the less power they would have over us. "Yes," I said, "we must go proudly back to Washington."

He shook his head in disbelief, but that was just what we did. We returned to Washington by coach the next day and settled ourselves in one of the boardinghouses where my family had lived when I was young. I sent a note assuring Mother that I was well and asking her to have my wardrobe sent from the house on C Street to Mrs. Porter's.

Her reply was brief: "Your father is distraught and barely able to work, but he remains stubborn. I am at a loss. We all miss you. May God bless you, my daughter."

Contrary to John's fears about gossip, we were greeted as celebrities. Papa Joe, recovered and back in Washington, was overjoyed, of course, to have both of us back and relieved to have his assistant return to the maps then in progress. But others greeted us cordially, even offered their congratulations, and a few—the most bold—expressed their sorrow over the rift in our family.

"Your father is a good man," Count Bodisco told me when I called at their home, at Harriet's invitation, "and he will see the error of his ways. You wait . . . he will make you both welcome in his home."

"I hope so, sir," I said sincerely, "but he is also a stubborn man."

The count chuckled. "We men . . . we are all stubborn. Now, tell me, do you not think my bride is beautiful?"

As beautiful as you are ugly I thought to myself as I smiled and agreed with him.

The heir apparent of the family was a chubby, darling little boy of six months who—fortunately—favored his mother in both coloring and looks. Harriet had indeed blossomed with motherhood, and she seemed to adore the count, which still puzzled me and made me bless my own fortune all the more.

That winter President Tyler gave a New Year's reception at the White House, and John and I determined to go—at least, I determined and John acquiesced.

"It will do no good for us to sneak in unnoticed," I told him. "We must arrive. . . . Can we borrow a coach?"

While John was pondering, Papa Joe broke in, "Hassler will lend you his, I am sure of it."

Frederick Hassler was director of the US Coast Survey and one of those who had early on offered us his congratulations. But he owned the biggest and ugliest coach in all of Washington, so large that some called it the "ark."

"Oh, no." John laughed. "Then we really would be conspicuous."

It took only a minute for me to see the way clear. "It's perfect," I said. "Please, John, send a message and ask Mr. Hassler if he would be so kind. . . ."

"Jessie, have you lost your good sense?"

"Please, John, just trust me." And he did.

We arrived at the White House while there was still a crowd milling around outside, waiting to enter. All heads turned as the ark rolled heavily to a stop at the front gate.

"Here we go," I said to John.

I had worn my best velvet gown, navy blue with a narrow hooped skirt. My bonnet had bright yellow ostrich feathers, and for once I was every bit the equal to John's grandness in his uniform.

I heard a gasp or two as John alighted and turned to hold his hand out for me. Then, my hand firmly locked in his arm, we made our way through the crowd, smiling at those we knew. The day was warm for January, with a bright sun. To me, that sun shone brightest on the two of us, making us the center of attention.

We were greeted like celebrities rather than outcasts. President Tyler and his niece, Priscilla, were openly glad to see me, and I even drew a smile from John Calhoun. Count Bodisco and Harriet were pleased that we made a public appearance, and Maria Crittendon drew me aside to congratulate us.

"Your father is here," she said with a smile. "He has not talked to me since your wedding."

"Nor," I said unhappily, "to me. Perhaps today is the day. Mother writes that he is miserable."

"So I've heard," Maria said, "and I am sorry for that. I would not have . . ."

"Maria," I assured her, "you did the absolute right thing by letting us marry in your home. I am gloriously happy . . . and when Father comes around, everything will be perfect."

The rooms of the White House were jammed with people, and so noisy, you could barely talk—a steady buzz of chatter competed with the Marine Band, which played bravely, though few paid attention to their efforts. Finally, though, I spotted Father across the Blue Room, deep in conversation with Senator Dickerson of New Jersey—a man who thought exploration of the Rockies useless because the land was suited for little but an Indian reserve. I smiled at the earnestness with which Father was trying to convert the narrow-minded senator. Father was his usual self—his clothes slightly rumpled, his white hair full and undisciplined—but there was an animated look on his face as he waved his hands, talked at length, and never gave Senator Dickerson a chance to say a word.

My arm still linked in his, John and I made our way across the room, though I admit that my husband, usually so poised in a crowd, was a little hesitant. Too soon for him, we approached Father.

"Senator Dickerson," I said graciously, "have you met my husband? Lieutenant Frémont can tell you much about the Rockies. He hopes to lead an expedition there soon." And then, turning to Father, I asked, "Don't you think John could help you convince the senator of the importance of exploration?"

Senator Dickerson looked as if he would escape if only he could see a way, and even Father was a little stunned. He recovered quickly, though, to say, "Of course, Jessie. Just the man to help me here."

And the two of them were off in a fast dialogue about the importance of the American West. Phrases such as "fifty-four forty" and "Oregon Trail" flew through their conversation. Senator Dickerson was overwhelmed.

When the senator finally made good his escape, I laid my hand on Father's arm. "I have missed you," I said, having to shout to make myself heard over the noise instead of whispering the words softly as I would have wished.

He stared hard at me, then at John, then turned his gaze back to me. "I have missed you, too, Jessie. Perhaps we should talk."

"John and I could join you for dinner tonight," I said.

He nodded. "That would please your mother."

And you? I wanted to ask, but I didn't want to embarrass him.

"We'll be at the house at five o'clock," I said.

And so we gathered at the Benton dining table in the house on C Street. Dinner was pleasant—civil, but strained. Mother sat at her end of the table, looking pale but happy, and Father at his end scowled to hide what I hoped was pleasure. When the blessing was asked, little Sarah in a quavering voice added, "Thank you, God, for sending Jessie and . . . uh . . . Lieutenant Frémont home."

I could barely keep the tears back, and I thought I even saw Father blink rapidly.

John was carefully polite and correct, his usual demeanor of self-confidence hiding the insecurity that I now knew lay beneath his every movement. I perhaps tried too hard to be cheerful, prattling inanely about the president's reception and the dresses the various women wore. Even John looked askance at me, as though to ask if I would not be quiet for a moment.

Somehow, though, we managed through dessert—a delicious chocolate silk-bread pudding, which Mathilde, our longtime housekeeper, had made especially because it was my favorite.

"John, Jessie, I would see you in my parlor," Father said, rising from the table to hold Mother's chair. "We will join your mother in the parlor shortly."

Now what? I wondered. Were we to be reviled again, punished further? John shot me a quick look, then stiffened his backbone and followed Father. After a hug from Mother, I too followed, making my steps as bold as possible.

"I . . . well . . . I think it best," Father began, and then had to blow his nose, clear his throat, and begin over again. "I think you should take up residence in this house."

John opened his mouth to protest, but my hand on his arm silenced him. We waited for Father to continue.

"It will be economical for you, and, John . . . well, we have matters to discuss. It's time to think about the next exploration west . . . and, well, dammit all, I miss you, Jessie."

Laughing, I went to hug him and was rewarded with a bear hug by that most undemonstrative of men. "John?" I asked, and when he nodded affirmatively, I assured Father that we should be delighted to reside on C Street.

Immediately, Father began to talk directly to John, and I became an interested listener. "I had hoped Nicollet would lead an expedition to map what lies between the Missouri River and the Pacific," he said, "but it is apparent his health will never again permit him to lead a major expedition. I intend to recommend appropriation of thirty thousand dollars for the expedition, with you named to lead it."

Had John been a lesser man, he might have fainted at this announcement. In five minutes we had had a double dose of news, more than we could ever have hoped for. Even I felt faint.

Father was chairman of the Senate Committee on Military Affairs, which oversaw funds for the Topographical Corps, so there was little doubt that he would be able to secure passage of his appropriation. The Senate surely recognized the urgency of this exploration, and Father knew how to avoid opposition, how even to convince Mr. Tyler that exploration was of the utmost importance and would not lead to war, as Tyler feared.

Father's eyes—and those of many of his colleagues at the time—were on both Oregon and California. Oregon, that vast unknown territory to the northwest, was shared by England and the United States. But England, with its Hudson's Bay Trading Company, clearly had the upper hand. We had but a few missionaries in the area, and Father believed that it was crucial to get settlers into the Northwest. He often said the land would belong to whatever nation settled it first—and Father was determined that the United States would be that nation.

He was equally adamant about California, which seemed a paradise of sunshine and vegetation from the little I had heard of it. Father truly believed that the United States must stretch its empire from coast to coast. War with Mexico? He shrugged off Tyler's concerns. Settlers in Texas, having shed the control of Mexico through their unlikely but successful revolution, were now demanding annexation to the United States. And none of that led to war with Mexico. If the Texans succeeded, could California be far behind? Like Oregon, it needed but settlement by men—and women—from our country. And had not the first group of pioneers reached California the past fall, nearly perishing because of their ignorance of the route? Father believed that more must venture west to settle that land, but if they were to do so, they needed a map to follow. I believed in Father's dream with all my heart . . . and I saw John as the man—indeed, the only man—who could make those dreams into reality. It thrilled me to think of his place in history.

Life on C Street took on a rhythm of its own for a brief period. We lived in two rooms near the back of the house—a parlor and a bedroom, both with a view of the gardens. But most of our hours were spent in Father's library, where John was busy preparing for his expedition—Father had secured financing for a four-month expedition to the Rockies—and I worked as his assistant, just as I had been Father's. First we had to write the report on the Des Moines River survey, a diversionary tactic that had not, after all, prevented our marriage. Once the report was written—a dry and clear-cut account of rivers and rocks, vegetation and rainfall—we turned our attention to the new expedition.

John left on May 1, 1842, taking with him my brother, Randolph.

"The experience will do him good," Father said.

He was, I knew, hiding his fear that Randolph, then a mere fourteen years old, was lazy and self-indulgent.

Randolph viewed the expedition as a great adventure and made no secret of his excitement. "You'll see, Jess. I'll get an Indian or two," he crowed, and I could only fervently hope not.

I was pregnant with our first child, but some instinct kept me from telling John. I think it was because he was so excited about his expedition that I knew a baby could never compete. Better, I thought, to wait until he came home, when the birth would be almost upon us and the expedition behind us.

CHAPTER FIVE

PARTING WAS HARD, MAKE NO MISTAKE ABOUT THAT. I MAY HAVE BEEN A BRIDE, married only seven stormy months, but I had grown accustomed to having John Charles Frémont in my life every waking moment—and in my bed at night. Now it was entirely possible, even likely, that I would not hear from him until he returned in the fall. Oh, if he happened to meet a trader who was going to a post where he could deliver a letter . . . but the route was uncertain, and I would have to content myself that no news was good news. I tossed and turned in our bed many a night, reaching out a hand to touch the spot where John should have been and talking aloud to him, as though to comfort myself. Lost in the space of the Great American Desert, he had no way of knowing my loneliness. And I had no way of knowing if he missed me. My only consolation was that he would be home for the November birth of his first son, an event that would, I thought, make our happiness complete.

John Charles Frémont II made his presence known early, quickening at less than four months. By the sixth month he was what my mother delicately called an active baby. I was bruised and sore, unable to rest without the interruption of those busy feet and hands, incapable of finding a comfortable position whether sitting, standing, or lying down.

"He will have his father's spirit," I said to my mother more than once, "and I am grateful for that." In my mind I was envisioning a young man of perhaps twenty, slightly taller than his father but with the same piercing blue eyes and blond good looks. I saw him graduating from West Point—the honor that had eluded his father—and then following in his father's footsteps for a glorious career with the army.

"Girls," my mother said, "are sometimes surprisingly active."

"This is no girl," I assured her. "This is John's son."

⁘

Summer was particularly hot in Washington that year, adding to my discomfort. Without realizing it, I fell into a pattern almost as listless as my mother's way of life. Before John's departure I had been swept up in the preparations for the trip, busy from morning to night taking his dictation, watching as he and an envious Papa Joe mapped out the routes to be taken, making endless lists of supplies to be ordered. But when he was gone, all activity ceased. It was as though I hung in suspended animation, without the will or the inclination to do more than eat—lightly at that—and sleep. The days until November stretched endlessly before me.

Father summoned me to his library one stifling summer day.

Even he sat in shirtsleeves, dignity having come second to a meager attempt at comfort.

Wiping his brow with a massive handkerchief, he said with uncharacteristic humility, "I need your help, Jessie."

"My help?" I asked vaguely.

His look was sharp and penetrating. "Your help," he said, that brief flash of humility almost replaced by impatience. "We must learn all we can about Mexico— it's taking up my every waking moment—and, well, the next source I want to explore is Bernal Diaz's work on the conquest of New Spain."

"And my part?" I asked.

"It is in Spanish," he said, handing me a volume titled *Conquista de la Nueva España*. "I want you to translate it."

I looked slowly at my father as I began to understand his motives. He could not possibly need a verbatim translation of this fairly thick volume, but he thought to engage me in his business again, to give me something—besides John's absence—on which to fasten my thoughts.

"I suppose," I said tartly, "you need it yesterday."

He harrumphed and then said, "Not quite that quickly. But as soon as you can do it."

And so, once again, I was Father's companion and assistant, sharing his library in the morning hours. He would bring home bits of gossip about Washington affairs— who was siding with the president on what, who had been seen conversing with a certain senator from Mississippi or a legislator from Alabama—"There's trouble brewing over slavery, Jessie, mark my words"—or even what senatorial wife was said to be out of patience with her husband. Father always looked a little sheepish when he brought me outright gossip, and sometimes he would apologize for himself by saying, "It's not anything I pay attention to, but I thought you might be interested."

"Oh, I am," I assured him.

"I saw Mrs. Crittendon today," he said once. "She looks well."

"Yes," I said carefully, "I believe she is. Did you speak?"

"I nodded," he said, as though I should understand that was all that could be expected of him.

Gradually the gulf between us lessened, and we went back to our old relationship, with Father relying on my judgment. I welcomed the challenge gladly. Occasionally I thought to worry that things would change again—for the worse?—when John returned, and that perhaps, even probably, Father would not have welcomed me back as his assistant if John had not been away.

Father's relationship to John, I saw, was very complicated. He desperately needed my husband's skills as an explorer for that grand vision of westward expansion, and he knew that no one could serve that cause as well, but he almost as desperately resented John's marriage to his daughter. As long as John was gone, Father could feel almost victorious over the expedition he led and could, at the same time, convince himself that John didn't exist—at least as far as I was concerned.

Meanwhile I watched the post like a hawk, but no news from John arrived. My longing for him did not diminish as the days passed, though I had expected I should gradually build up a protective shell against loneliness. Instead my wanting of him—physically and emotionally—was sometimes so sharp a pain that it woke me at night, and I would lie and wonder what he was doing and if he felt the same sharp pain. In a quite selfish way, I hoped so. And then John Charles Frémont II would make his presence known—a flutter in my belly—and I would be reminded that I need not worry. John and I were bound together for all time to come by our love for each other and by the child that grew inside me.

"Jessie, you best go to your mother," Father said early one morning in July. "She's in great pain, another of her headaches, but worse than usual."

"Of course, Father." I ran to Mother's bedroom, only to find her moaning in her bed, almost twisting from pain.

"Mother?" I asked softly.

"My head," she whispered. "It feels like it will explode . . . and I wish it would."

Quickly I got a wet cloth and put it on her forehead, thinking to ease the pain some, but she moaned again and let me know, almost by sign language, that the cloth only intensified the pain. I tried to give her a spoonful of the medicine the doctor had left on his last visit—vile-smelling stuff that was, I suspected, not much more than a tonic. Propped up by my arm, she raised her head enough to touch her tongue to the spoon, then fell back against the pillow, unable to take the medicine.

Truly alarmed by now, I called Liza to watch over her and went immediately to Father. "She is worse than I have ever seen her," I said. "How long has she been this way?"

"Since the middle of the night," he said, shaking his head in despair. "She would not let me waken you. She thinks it will get better."

"I think it is getting worse," I said.

"You're right," Father agreed wearily. "I've sent for Dr. Scott." Even while I uttered "Good," I was thinking to myself that Dr. Scott was getting old and feeble enough that I had little confidence in his abilities. He was, after all, the one who had prescribed the apparently useless tonic that Mother had been taking for some time now—without good result. But Mother's medical care was a matter about which I could not question Father's judgment—and Father generally relied on Mother's trust in her physician.

Dr. Scott arrived about an hour later, carrying his black bag, and making "tsk, tsk" noises as Mother's symptoms were described to him. He was a man of sixty or more, with venerable gray hair and beard and a voice that had begun to quake a little, which did not further inspire confidence in me. "She must be bled," he announced. "Shouldn't you see her first?" I asked, aghast. Bleeding was standard medical treatment, and yet the very thought appalled me. None of us in the Benton household had—praise the Lord!—ever had the need to subject ourselves to this treatment, and some corner of my mind was whispering—no, shouting—that it was wrong for Mother. "I shall see her when I perform the operation," he said, his voice delivering a reprimand to me for being so impertinent as to question him. "I have the necessary lancets in my bag. Please be prepared with clean sheets and a bucket."

Mother, weak as she was, greeted the doctor gratefully and agreed immediately to his pronouncement that she must be bled. "I knew it," she whispered. "Please proceed."

Fighting nausea every second, I forced myself to hold Mother's other hand and comfort her as the doctor slashed across a vein in her right arm and held it above the bucket Mathilde had brought. The blood dripped slowly—where had I ever read about people being stabbed and blood flowing from them? I wished in this case it would flow, but it did not—it dripped, and Dr. Scott, seeming to know the quantity he wanted, watched patiently. I said soothing words to Mother, but she was like stone, cold and without response.

The doctor left soon after bandaging the wound he had created, and he instructed us to give her no food nor drink. He would, he said, return the next day.

Mother was no better the next day. Perhaps the headache had lessened a slight bit, or maybe she was just too weak to let us know.

"She must be bled again," Dr. Scott pronounced.

"No," Father said, more loudly than he meant. "She is too weak. She cannot stand another treatment."

Mother surprised all of us by saying, "Please, Thomas, let the doctor do his business. He knows best." Her voice was softer than a whisper, husky in the manner of a person who cannot breathe clearly.

The doctor gave Father a triumphant look and began his procedure. Once again I comforted Mother, but I found it no easier the second time and thought, briefly, that she, being weak nearly to the point of losing consciousness, had much the easier part of this business.

"She is getting worse," Father stormed at me that night, "and the doctor insists on bleeding her. I . . . I am just not sure. . . ."

"Neither am I," I said. "Certainly it is not helping her. She cannot raise her head from the pillow now, and she feels like stone to me, cold no matter how hot the day."

"She believes in the bleeding," he said miserably, "and she wants the treatments to continue. . . ."

The treatments—and our agony—continued for eight long days. Then, one afternoon after the doctor had left, while I was sitting by Mother's bedside, she suddenly stiffened as though in a convulsion, then fell limp in the bed.

"Mother!" I cried frantically, and against all my better judgment began to shake her, my act born out of a desperation to get some response. I got none. "Mother!" I must have screamed over and over, because Father came running into the room.

"Jessie?"

"She . . . she . . . I don't know, but she won't . . . can't answer me." I was nearly sobbing by then. "Is she . . . is she dead, Father?"

He bent his head to her chest, then straightened and put a gentle hand on her neck. "No, but she is unconscious. I'll send someone for the doctor."

"He'll no doubt bleed her again," I said bitterly, but Father was already on the way to the kitchen to send a boy for Dr. Scott.

The message was sent back that Dr. Scott was not well and could not come.

"How can he do that?" I raved. "How can he just ignore a patient, especially one as ill as Mother?"

"Shh, Jessie," Father said, his voice calming me. "There is a new doctor tending to some of the Senate. I'll send for him."

While we waited, I sat at Mother's bedside and held that fragile, lifeless hand in mine, talking to her all the while about how important she was to me, how she must get well, she must not die. I had had my differences with Mother, not only over matters involving me—Miss English's academy and my marriage sprang to mind—but over her treatment of Father. I'd never criticized her, but a corner of me thought Mother lacking in spirit for hiding in her bedroom when she should have been in Father's library. She should have been the one to transcribe his speeches and translate his Spanish texts. For my own part I was grateful that she did not take this opportunity from me, but I still thought she was not enthusiastic enough about Father's work, and I had long ago vowed that my role as a wife would be in contrast to the model with which I had been raised.

But still, for all my doubts about her, she was my mother, and the thought that I might lose her made me frantic. Thus it was that I found myself crooning to an unconscious woman and wishing desperately for the new doctor's arrival.

"She may die," the new doctor said. His name was Thurston, and he was perhaps thirty years old, if you gave him the benefit of a year or two. "She is in extremely critical condition . . . so weakened by all that bleeding."

"The doctor said it was necessary," I replied haltingly.

"It is never necessary," he said firmly, "and in some cases proves fatal. We must give her nourishment. . . . Have a rich chicken broth prepared."

"But she cannot drink it," I said.

"We will drip it ever so carefully down her throat," the doctor said, taking off his coat and rolling up his sleeves. "Go now, have it prepared."

In any other situation I would have resented his abrupt orders—and might have told him so—but concern for Mother had subdued that characteristic independence of mine, and I fled to the kitchen.

We did just as he said—dripped chicken broth into Mother's mouth, kept her as comfortable as possible, fanning the flies away constantly, wrapping her in sheets to retain her body warmth no matter how hot the day. We did this for three long days, making it well over a week that Mother's illness had brought everything else in the household to a halt; the doctor seemed to be there morning, noon, and evening, leaving only to see other patients who could not spare him.

On the third day, in the evening, Mother awoke. I was the first to see that she had opened her eyes, and the sight filled me with such happiness that I wanted to shout with glee. Instead, I managed to ask softly, "Mother? Can you hear me?"

She struggled to speak, her mouth seeming to have difficulty forming words. When a sound finally came out, it was a deep, hollow, almost unintelligible noise. Only because I listened so hard could I tell that she had said, "Jessie?"

"Yes, Mother, I am here."

"Good," she whispered, only it sounded like a voice from the bottom of a well. Then she was asleep again.

When Dr. Thurston heard my report, he said without hesitation, "She has had a stroke. We are lucky she is alive."

From that moment on Mother required constant care. Mathilde shared the responsibility with me, and we spent our days coaxing Mother to take a little broth, or a bit of thin gruel. I once suggested that she might eat more if we gave her more appetizing fare, like the succulent fresh strawberries the rest of us were enjoying, but the doctor squashed that idea, and she was stuck with broth.

Mathilde and I bathed her body—so frail and lifeless it seemed!—and fanned her constantly, to keep the summer pests away. I brushed her hair and often fixed it with a pretty ribbon, knowing how she valued her appearance, but she seemed to pay no mind. Or perhaps, I thought grimly, she had no mind to pay. When she was awake, her eyes had a wide, blank look about them and, sometimes, the look of one who is struck with terror. What was going through her mind in those periods, I never knew.

Father, absolutely crushed by her deterioration, could barely stand to be in the bedroom with her, though he maintained a cheerful facade, making falsely hearty statements about how well she looked. *Why,* I wanted to ask, *don't you just tell her you love her?* But that seemed beyond him. He visited once a day like clockwork, a duty he had imposed upon himself. After five minutes of talking to Mother in his booming voice, he would flee the room . . . and I would see her visibly relax.

"I cannot bear to see her like this," he told me in a rare moment of confidence. "She was the prettiest girl I ever saw . . . and I . . . I have done this to her."

No, Father, I wanted to say, *you haven't. In a way, she has done this to herself.* But Father and I, close as we were, did not share such intimacies.

In early September, with poorly hidden relief, Father announced that he had been called to St. Louis and would be gone a month.

"You'll leave Mother?" I asked.

He shook his head sadly and lied to me with his first statement. "I don't want to . . . but it's crucial that I go west right now. There are fences to be mended locally in St. Louis, if I am to keep my constituents happy." He paused a moment and put a huge arm around my shoulders. "I know I'm leaving her in good hands, Jessie." So my isolation and my desperation grew worse, for now I was alone. Oh, Liza was there, but she was little help to me in general and none at all in caring for Mother, whose appearance frightened her. "I don't see, Jessie," she said to me almost daily, "how you can be so good at taking care of Mother. It frightens me so to see her."

"You would do it if I weren't here," I told her, but I wasn't sure I believed it. I did believe, as Father had taught me, that we do what we have to in this world. But I suspected that there were some, like Liza, who might never learn that lesson. Liza was then being courted by a young lawyer named William Carey Jones. I thought him bright and personable and wouldn't have resented him at all if Liza hadn't been so wrapped up in her romance that she was unable to see anything else, including the crisis in her family.

Randolph was, of course, away with John—strange that I did not worry about him as I did about John—but Sarah and Susie occupied much of my attention and concern. They were young enough not to know that other children had mothers who did not lie abed all day, mothers who were up and about, taking part in their households. Those two darling young girls were missing the only kind of mother they knew . . . and they were devastated.

"Why doesn't Mama hug me anymore, Jessie?" Susan asked, while Sarah, being slightly the older, said with quavering authority, "She is sick, Susan."

"Will she ever get better?"

I knew then why Father told me white lies about Mother and his reaction to her illness. "Of course she'll get better, my darling," I lied.

Through all those long days I wrote faithfully to John, letters that I doubted he would ever see but by their very writing gave me the comfort of his company. Without fear of censure I wrote of my doubts about Mother, my insight into Father's reaction, my anger at Liza, my worry over the younger children . . . and from those unanswered pages, always faithfully sent west by post, I received a reply full of John's love. Or at least I thought I sensed the reply he never sent.

By mid-October, when Father returned, I was exhausted, thin as a rail except for the watermelon that seemed to protrude from my middle. The day after his return Father looked closely at me and exclaimed with absolute amazement, "Jessie! You are too pale and too thin for a woman in your delicate condition. Are you all right?"

It was as though a dam had burst. All it took was one word of concern, and all my fatigue and despair poured out. I was tired, desperately tired, from caring for Mother and translating what bits of the Díaz manuscript I could while Mathilde took the watch. And I was frantic that I had heard not one word from John. Of late, when I lay alone in my bed, I could no longer conjure up John's comforting presence and the reassurance of his love brought on by those sharp kicks in my belly. Instead, I imagined all kinds of threats and perils, from landslides and fearsome storms to hostile Indians and treacherous scouts. I became convinced I would never see John again, that he would never return to greet his son.

When Father asked his simple question, I dissolved into tears and soon found myself wrapped in his arms. My father held me in his tentative embrace and made the most comforting noises he could, muttering, "There, there, it will be all right."

He saw to it that I was put to bed, and I stayed there for four days, waited on hand and foot and fed that same damn broth Mother was getting. But I returned to my duties refreshed, and Father announced it was time to assign a servant to Mother's full-time care so that I could be relieved. After that I visited her two or three times daily but no longer took responsibility for her care . . . and my own health improved greatly.

"Jessie, you are looking well." Maria Crittendon had come to call, the first visit she'd dared since my marriage. Father had, of course, forbidden her presence in the house, and she had not come while he was away—out of a sense of honor, she said. She would not violate his wishes behind his back. I declined to point out to her that she had already done that a year ago and such nicety on her part was too late from Father's point of view.

It was kind of her to say that I looked well, when I knew indeed that I looked as if I had swallowed a watermelon seed that had come to fruit. My pregnancy was so obvious that I could no longer appear in public and was confined to the house—not that I had been out in public much in recent months, anyway. Still, there is something about knowing that you can go if you want . . . and now propriety forbade my venturing forth.

I also knew that once one looked beyond my belly—as I did every day when I looked in the mirror—there were dark circles under my eyes and a paleness to my face that did not speak of radiant health. I had seen some women—I even remembered Mother's appearance when Susan was expected—who seemed to grow prettier with pregnancy. I was not one of them.

Worst of all, I had once again developed the red rash at the corner of my mouth. I called it my King George's mark, remembering the story about my great-grandmother. I looked, I sometimes thought, a little like an Indian captive who had been tattooed before being rescued. I was so conscious of the red, raw mark that I frequently talked with my hand over my mouth—disconcerting, I am sure, for those who tried to converse with me.

"Your father sent for me," Maria said. "He said you need your friends, and he hoped I would be the first among them."

We had, of course, exchanged notes and letters over the months, but I had not seen Maria, because of Father's anger, since John and I had returned to the house on C Street.

"Maria, you are good to come. I am fine . . . though I have had a difficult summer."

"You have not heard from John?"

"No, but I am sure it is impossible for him to write." Actually I was not sure about that at all, and it had begun to occur to me that surely, by now, he could have found a scout or a trapper who was going somewhere near civilization and who would post a letter for him. My worry was turning to anger at John, but I was not ready to share that, even with Maria.

October dragged on, a seemingly endless month. I thought that nothing would ever get better—Mother's health would never improve, John Charles II might take up permanent residence in my belly and never test the outside world, and, worst of all, John would never come home.

———⌒———

Then, magically, when October was almost gone, John did come home, appearing at the doorstep one morning at 6:00 a.m., unshaven, wrinkled, smelling like a barnyard, and thoroughly triumphant.

"I have done it, Jessie," he cried, swinging me off my feet and into the air. "I have been to the Rocky Mountains, and I have planted a flag on the highest peak. That mountain will forever after be Frémont's Peak." He was jubilant, indeed nearly incoherent with the excitement of telling it all to me.

I said nothing but grabbed his head and drew his mouth to mine, greeting him with a kiss that spoke of all my longing and loneliness and need of the past few months.

Suddenly he seemed to see me for the first time. "You are going to have a child!" he exclaimed wonderingly.

"Yes," I said, "almost any day now."

"Why didn't you tell me before I went away . . . or in all those wonderful letters?"

I bowed my head. "I wasn't sure at first," I lied, "and then . . . I didn't want you to worry."

"Oh, my brave Jessie!" he said, clasping me to him.

But then the subject changed, and he was off into tales of the expedition, overwhelmed by his anxiety to tell me every detail within five minutes. "It's not desert, Jessie," he crowed. "It's green . . . grass and rivers like you've never seen. . . . We had a scout . . . you'll never believe my fortune . . . the best scout in the West . . . name is Kit Carson."

"Kit Carson!" I exploded, laughing because I thought it sounded a made-up name.

For just a second John was offended. Then he was off again, telling me the wonders of Kit Carson, who had lived his life on the frontier and was already, by his early thirties, a guide, hunter, and trapper of legend. "He has covered the whole West," John exclaimed, "lived with the Nez Perce, wintered with Jim Bridger on the Yellowstone, been down Mary's River, and knows the Three Forks country of the upper Missouri. . . . He is the most capable westerner I know."

In conversation it came out that this paragon of virtue described by my husband could neither read nor write and that his speech was at best unlettered, a mixture of the Scottish-Irish tongue of Tennessee, where he had been born, and the patois of the West, where he had lived all his life and carved out his reputation.

"I am sure he was helpful to you . . ." I began lamely. "It is fortunate you met him." I could not fathom John's attraction to such a wild man.

"Fortunate?" John exclaimed. "Without him there would have been no expedition. And there will not be another without him. I trust him absolutely."

I reserved judgment, it being beyond my comprehension to imagine my lettered and cultured John having such faith in a mountain man. The only name I recognized in all of John's long exposition was that of Jim Bridger, the trapper who had become famous even in the East. The rest of it, geography that was familiar to John, was a blur in my mind, and I made a vow, then and there, to memorize the rivers and valleys of the West.

"Tell me about Frémont's Peak," I said, and he launched into a description of that mountain—since proved not nearly the highest in the Rockies—and of their ascent of it, a climb that brought them face-to-face with sheer granite walls and compelled them to climb from crevice to crevice.

"It was nothing," John said, "not at all dangerous. But when I finally reached the summit, I realized that another step would have precipitated me into an immense snowfield some five hundred feet below."

I shuddered to think how close he had come to catastrophe. And I shuddered more when he described their trip down the Platte River. "I had determined to chart its course," he said, "but I underestimated the river. It took our rubber rafts and our instruments—guns, ammunition, the sextant, the telescope, and much of our food—but we were able to save all the men, even those who could not swim."

I had known all along that John's glorious adventure was dangerous, and I'd worried about Indians and rivers and storms, but a deep part of me never believed that anything could happen to him. It was written, I believed, that he would come home a hero at the age of twenty-nine. Hearing how close he had come to disaster shocked me to the core. I could only hold him close and thank God for bringing him back to me. Would I ever let him leave again? I knew I had no choice. In my glee to have him home I barely noticed that we didn't that day talk anymore about the baby.

If I was blissful to have my husband home every day—and in my bed every night—Father was beyond himself with pride. All his anger about our marriage and his resentment of John faded before the accomplishment of mapping the route to the South Pass and the Wind River range of mountains. "It is a great thing you have done for this country, son," he said, and I nearly fell off my chair hearing him call John "son."

"Thank you, sir," John said deferentially, and I delighted that he was so politic. "Everywhere I went I heard about western expansion—the Mormon community in Nauvoo, Illinois, the trouble in settlements in Arkansas and Missouri where there have been lynchings, the growth of Chicago and its harbor and lake trade. The West is alive, there's no doubt about it."

"Yes, yes," Father agreed, "and the biggest issue is Oregon. I hear more and more curiosity about that country."

"Yes, sir," John said. "I hope to go there next."

"I'll see to it, yes I will," Father said enthusiastically.

In his first days at home John never once mentioned his son and heir, whose arrival was expected momentarily. As I twisted and turned uncomfortably in my chair, listening while they talked incessantly about the West, I grew more than a little jealous, especially when John Charles II, presumably now a healthy-sized infant, made his presence known by sharp kicks, which caused me to gasp in momentary pain.

"Jessie? You all right?" John would say, and when I nodded, he'd be off about the West again, the baby already dismissed.

John was cavalier about Mother, giving her a warm hug and declaring how delighted he was to see her looking so well. To me he said, "My God, Jessie, she looks awful!"

"You should have seen her three months ago," I replied somewhat bitterly. "She is much improved."

"I cannot believe it. You have had a hard summer, my darling," he said, kissing me on the forehead. But then it was back to the Wind River range and an elaboration of the talents of the wonderful Kit Carson.

Some nights I sneaked away, leaving John and Father deep in conversation while I sought out the comfort of bed for my weary body and confused mind. Neither John nor Father seemed to notice that I had left, and I found that John would come to bed much later, giving me only a brief kiss on the forehead before he dropped off to sleep. There could, of course, be no physical passion between us, given my enlarged condition—it would have been the awkward mating of an elephant and a giraffe—but I would so have welcomed loving strokes and intimate conversation. I got neither, and I learned to feign sleep when he came to bed.

I had expected my brother, Randolph, to return jubilant because of his adventure, yet immediately subdued by his mother's illness. None of that happened. He was sullen and angry that a trip that had started out as a glorious adventure ended, for him, as a boring confinement at Fort Laramie.

"Left me behind, Jessie, that's what he did! Left me at Fort Laramie, along with another lad about my age. We would have been every bit as good as that Kit Carson. . . ."

"I doubt that, Randolph," I said in a placating manner. "Why were you left behind?"

"Indian trouble," he scoffed. "That Jim Bridger, whoever he is, told John that some Indians—Sioux, Blackfeet, and some other tribe . . ."

"The Crow," I supplied, having already learned my lessons well.

"Yeah, the Crow—what does it matter? They're all the same, aren't they? Anyway, all these tribes were on the warpath, so John made me stay behind with Henry Brant. Turned out they didn't have no trouble—"

"Didn't have any trouble," I corrected.

"Yeah, well, you know what I mean. They never saw a mean Indian the whole time, and there I was cooling my heels at that dumb fort."

He had no comment about his mother's illness, except a casual shrug, which intimated that it made little difference in his life. At fifteen Randolph was bored with everything, and I was as concerned about him as Father was. He should, to my mind, have been ecstatic about his opportunities. Instead, like the pessimist who can see only what he does not have, he complained constantly and even whined to Father, who told him sharply to grow up. I applauded silently, even as I feared trouble ahead with Randolph.

Within a week Father had sent him to Virginia to stay with the McDowells, but I feared all the good that would do would be to teach him to drink bourbon like some of his Virginia cousins. James McDowell and I never had gotten along, and I'd heard that he'd said of my marriage that I was headstrong and probably got what I deserved. I'd vowed to show him the greater glory that would be mine, but I didn't relish him as a companion for Randolph. Still, I had more pressing problems on my mind and couldn't devote a lot of time to worrying about Randolph. Perhaps that was what was wrong with the boy—he was not the first item on anybody's list.

"John? Wake up. The baby . . . I think your son is on his way into this world." It was early on the morning of November 15, 1842.

"What? Oh, Jessie . . . are you sure?" Foggily, he rose on his elbows and stared at me.

Impatiently, I said, "If the strength of the pain I just felt is any indication, yes, I'm sure. You must call Mathilde . . . and send for the midwife. But don't wake Father."

The classic story of the about-to-be-father who loses all sense did not apply to John. He was neither excited nor hurried, pulling his pants on slowly and looking for all the world as though he would fall back asleep if I didn't prod him.

"John! Can't you move faster?"

"Is there a hurry?" he asked, and I had to admit that no, there was no hurry. But as another severe pain tore through my belly, I badly wanted the comfort of another woman.

The pain alarmed John, making the whole situation more real to him than it had been as long as I sat there calmly giving him directions. "Jessie! Oh, my poor Jessie! Are you . . . will you be all right? I'll hurry!" And he bolted out the door without waiting for my answer, then ran back in to wrap me in his arms, kiss me tenderly, and whisper, "I love you very much."

Completely happy. I lay back on the bed, only to be wrenched again with pain in a few minutes. By then Mathilde was at my side, wiping my brow with a cool, damp cloth.

"Here, Miss Jessie, take just a sip of this," she coaxed.

I stuck my tongue into straight whiskey and nearly choked on it but managed to get down two or three drops.

"There, there," Mathilde soothed, "that will ease the pain. You be surprised, honey."

Soon I was in a fog, unaware of much around me save the waves of pain that swept over me. The midwife arrived and fashioned rope handles, tied to the bedposts, for me to pull against when the pain was most severe. And she gave me a piece of leather to bite down upon, lest I cry out and, as she put it, "alarm the mister out there." Vaguely I remember Mathilde telling me that Father and John were waiting just outside the chamber and that Mother had not been told. "No use botherin' Mrs. Benton," she said. "Only upset her that she can't be here to help you."

I wasn't sure Mother would even understand, but I was not capable at that moment of dealing with philosophical speculations about my mother's mental condition.

The pains went on until evening, and with each passing hour I felt myself growing more remote, as though removed from what was happening around me and concentrating only on the pain. I heard the words of the midwife—"You're doin' just fine, Mrs. Frémont, just fine"—and felt the comforting hands of Mathilde on my brow, but it almost seemed to be happening to someone else.

Around eight in the evening—so they told me later—the baby thrust its way into the world with a pain so incredibly strong that I fainted. Moments later I revived to the scent of smelling salts only to hear Mathilde say with great pride, "It's a beautiful little girl, Miss Jessie, a beautiful girl child!"

A girl! The baby that was to have been John's son and heir was a girl! All those months I'd been so sure, and now . . . I'd given him a daughter, just as my mother had given Father a daughter when he wanted a son. I turned my head away, lest Mathilde see my tears of frustration.

"Oh, Miss Jessie," she said, "I know's you're happy. Them's tears of joy. Come, take this child in your arms."

I reached out for the bundle that was handed to me. Barely visible beneath all the wrappings was a tiny, perfectly shaped face with blue eyes—no one told me all babies have blue eyes, and I was sure these were the brilliant blue of the child's father—and a soft fuzz of blond hair on her head. She was, as Mathilde assured me, beautiful . . . but what would John say?

John, of course, had never stated any preference for a son. I had merely attributed that longing to him, projecting Father's longings and the values of the world in which I'd been raised. John was, as a matter of fact, pleased with his daughter.

"She is like you, Jessie," he said softly. "She is beautiful."

"No," I answered wearily, "she is like you. She has your coloring. She is . . . I had hoped . . ." With tears streaming down my face I struggled for the words. Then, taking a deep breath, I said clearly, "I wanted to give you a son. All along I thought the baby was John Charles Frémont the second."

He looked startled. "Jessie!" was all he could say.

"Well," I said practically, having recovered my composure somewhat, "girls can't go on expeditions, they can't be explorers, they can't go to West Point . . . they can't do all the things that are important to you."

"Ah," he replied, "but may she grow up with her mother's spirit. You are important to me."

I loved him immensely at that moment, and I felt equally loved. "Wait," he said. "I will be right back." And with a mysterious sense of importance John rushed from the room.

Within minutes he returned carrying a tattered and wind-whipped American flag. "This," he said, "is the flag I planted at the summit of the highest peak in the Rocky Mountains . . . Frémont's Peak. I brought the flag for you . . . I just wasn't sure when to give it to you. Now seems the right time." And with that he spread the flag over me.

Tears running down my face, I stroked the torn fabric, my fingers catching at loose threads and poking through holes. "It is . . . I . . . I have never been so proud of anything," I told him. "I will treasure it always."

"And I," he replied, "will treasure you—and our daughter—always."

"I want to wrap it around her," I told him, and so he went to Mathilde with the flag and instructed her to wrap it around our child. She did so, protesting all the while about its dirty state.

And so our daughter went to sleep her first night on earth wrapped in a torn and dirty flag of her country. She knew little of it, but I knew, and it was more important to me almost than life itself. John had brought me a piece—indeed, the major piece—of his adventure, and we had welcomed our daughter with it.

"*Le bon temps viendra*," John said, echoing what I had always told him. I smiled in agreement and was asleep within seconds.

We called our daughter Elizabeth Benton Frémont, after my mother, but within days her name was Lily. I was only eighteen years old, but I had already lived more than many women of my age.

CHAPTER SIX

"JOHN! ANOTHER NOSEBLEED?"

He sat at the desk that had been set up for him in the sitting room of our private chamber, a large white handkerchief, now stained with bright-red splotches, pressed to his nose. Before him were his notes from the expedition, a penholder, and several pen points, next to a stack of blank foolscap. I saw only the blood. Squeamish about blood ever since Mother's bleedings, I was thoroughly alarmed.

"It's nothing," he said, waving his hand in the air as though to dismiss me. "It will stop shortly."

"Press hard on your nose," I said helpfully. "Perhaps you should lie down . . . maybe on the floor?"

It was John's fifth nosebleed in as many days, and I was sorely tempted to call Dr. Thurston without John's permission. The episodes had begun the day that he announced he must begin work on his report of the expedition. It seemed that whenever he sat down to write, his nose began to bleed. Once he had complained of a headache so severe that he had to retire to bed, and I, still so conscious of Mother, had hovered over him more nervous than I ever was over tiny Lily.

Now John paced the floor, a bloodied white linen pressed to his nose with one hand. Waving the other hand impatiently, he said, "The expedition . . . being outdoors, living my life on horseback . . . it has not fitted me to sit at a desk and write a report. I cannot do it!"

I bit my tongue to keep from quoting Father's wisdom about the folly of saying "I can't . . ."

"I need a secretary," John expostulated, "someone who could write while I dictate."

"There is no money for a secretary," I demurred, knowing that the funds for the expedition were already spent. Tactfully I bypassed the opportunity to point out that part of the condition of his receiving those funds was the presentation of a written report. He had agreed to provide such when he accepted the funds. Neither did I point out to him that Father had never had a secretary—save me, poor substitute that I was.

Suddenly it dawned on me. That was the answer! As I had been Father's secretary, so I could do the same for John. But though the temptation to rush toward this solution was strong, I knew John well enough to know that tact was important—crucial, in fact.

"John . . . I know it's less than ideal, but perhaps I could . . . well, I could make an attempt . . . to be your secretary."

He was aghast. "You? Jessie, what do you know about the West?"

More than you think, I wanted to reply, but I merely shrugged and said softly, "I have written some reports for Father."

That stopped him. He looked startled. "Of course you have. I . . . well, I had forgotten. But Jessie, what of Lily? You have your hands full in caring for her."

In truth Lily took little of my time. I visited her three times daily in the nursery on the third floor of the house—the room where Sarah and Susie had been raised in turn. There I rocked her and sang to her and cooed about how lovely she was, but her day-to-day care rested in the hands of Sophie, a freed Negro that Mathilde had immediately found upon my daughter's birth and who now served as wet nurse. Sophie exhibited a patience with the infant that I never would have been able to show, and the arrangement was working well for all of us—except that I had not much to occupy my time. I had finished translating the *Conquista de la Nueva España* before my confinement, and Father had refrained from giving me any more assignments.

Serving as John's secretary would be the perfect solution to more than one dilemma.

"I don't know, Jessie. . . . What will people say?"

"Fiddle with what people will say," I cried. "We have to get that report written. You do want to go on your second expedition, don't you?"

He was dismayed for just a moment, and then, when he saw the smile on my face, he pulled me to my feet and began to whirl me about the room in a dance of wild abandonment.

"Jessie, Jessie, you are always smarter than I am, always one step ahead of me."

Alarm shot through me. "No," I protested, "I am not at all. You are the one who will do great things. My only hope is to be able to help you."

"Ah, Jessie," he said, "you do, every day, in more ways than you can know."

And so I became John's amanuensis. Father heartily approved the arrangement, removing one lingering doubt from my mind.

"I have no pressing jobs for you now, Jessie," he said. "But, of course, I don't want to give up my rights to your assistance forever."

John spoke up quickly. "I would never rob you of your assistant, sir."

"I know that," Father said, "but we must get this report written. It's . . . it's more important than I can tell you."

But John and I both knew how important it was.

Almost immediately we fell into a working pattern. We worked in the mornings, as I had done with Father, beginning at nine o'clock and working through until Mathilde summoned us for the midday meal about one. To keep up with John, I wrote almost continuously during those four hours, as fast and furious as I could, and often at the end of a session my hand was cramped and sore. While I sat at the desk, scratching with my pen, John paced the room, notes in hand, describing things as though simply talking to me.

"Jessie," he said, "there is no way to make people understand the grandeur of a mammoth herd of buffalo. They simply surpass describing. When we first came upon them, we heard a dull and confused sound from a distance, like a murmuring, but when we came upon that dark mass of living things, not a one of us was unaffected. My heart pounded with the excitement of it. Oh! I wish you could have seen it, Jessie.

"It was early morning, and the herd was feeding. Everywhere they were in motion—here an old bull might be rolling in the dirt, there a pair of young bulls in an obstinate fight sent clouds of dust rising in the air. Indians and buffalo, Jessie, are the poetry and life of the plains."

I wrote it almost exactly as he told it to me.

John had a wonderful sense for the color of the land, and his telling was full of it—the gold of the sunflowers on the Kansas prairie, the red sandstone cliffs of the Platte River, the look of a mountain bathed in fog below and crowned above by the silver of the first rays of morning sunlight.

All of this I wove into his report. When he first looked at a draft, John was startled.

"Should you say that, Jessie? About the silver and gold of the sunlight? In an official report? I thought you would . . . you know . . . stick to the facts."

"There's no reason," I told him, "that facts have to be dull. Your report has plenty of information in it."

And that it did. The report was rich with detail about the fur trade, and traders of the American Fur Company, who, for stacks of buffalo hides, gave the Indians blankets, calico, guns, ammunition, tobacco, and liquor. "It's awful, Jessie. Most Indians would trade their furs, their wives, their lodges, even their horses, for a keg of drink. We have brought ruin to them."

That, too, went into the report. "It must move beyond the location of geographic sites," I told him, "to describe the people of that land—how they live, how they will be affected by westward expansion."

"Badly," he said with a shake of the head.

Sometimes we strayed from the topic at hand. One day, which stands memorable in my mind forever, John was describing the thrill he felt at the summit of Frémont's Peak, when he suddenly stopped and looked at me.

"You know, Jessie, it is because of you that I got to climb a mountain and plant a flag there and have it named for me."

I laughed gently. "Because of me?"

"Because I am married to you," he said honestly. "I was a good aide to Papa Joe, and perhaps I could have gradually climbed whatever ladder of success governs explorers . . . but it would have been years before I was sent on an expedition like this one."

"And what," I asked skeptically, "do I have to do with it?"

"You . . . and your father. Because I married you—Senator Thomas Benton's daughter—I was suddenly . . . how should I say it? . . . prominent in the public eye, in the eye of the senators who approve and finance such expeditions. I owe it all to you."

It was my turn to be solemn. "And is that," I asked, "why you married me?"

He was on his knees in an instant. "Jessie! Don't ever even in jest say that to me. You know it was not! Tell me you know that!"

Lightheartedly, I laughed. "Of course I know, John. I . . . I just wanted to hear what you would say. Any woman would be that vain."

"You are not vain, Jessie, never vain." He held my hands tightly in his and, still on his knees, looked up at me. "Oh, Jessie, I love you more than you can know."

"And I, you," I replied, bending my lips to meet his open, inviting mouth.

There was little more accomplished on the report that morning. The Senate was debating the Oregon issue when John filed his final report. Father's colleague, Senator Linn, had introduced a bill proposing that a series of forts be built along the route to the Rockies and Oregon, that every adult settler should be given 640 acres of land, and that the United States system of justice should apply to our settlers in the Oregon Territory—the British could deal with their own. The bill, directly opposed by President Polk, who favored setting the north limit of the country at the Columbia River, passed the Senate but not the House.

"It's all right, Jessie," Father told me. "We've made our point. They know there are a good number of senators in favor of colonizing Oregon. Someday we'll have thirty or forty thousand rifles beyond the Rockies as our negotiators in that land . . . meantime, John must go there next."

Next? I didn't want to think of John going on another expedition, once again absent from me for months. In working together on the report, we had become soul mates—a trite term I hesitate to use, but there is no other description for our spiritual and emotional bond. The reason, John often told me, that we could write the report so well was that we thought as one. I liked that idea.

Physically, we had also melded ourselves into one after I had recovered from Lily's birth. We often retired after Lily's night feeding, on the pretext that John had reports and maps to study and I had reading to do. Sometimes, as we made our excuses, I saw Father watching us with an inscrutable look. I cannot yet tell if it was amusement or envy or pleasure for us, though I doubt it was the latter.

True to our word, each night we settled ourselves at our respective tasks. But a sideways look from one, a smile of invitation, even a slight gesture would send us running for the bed, nearly stumbling over each other in our haste to be shed of our clothes.

Perhaps it was Cecilia who had taught John everything he knew, but I never resented her. John was a considerate and passionate lover. I have no basis of comparison, having never known another man in all my life, but I have heard talk, and I know that John was one among thousands simply because he thought of me when he made love. He never grabbed for his own pleasure, leaving me to survive as I would.

Instead his hands, his tongue, his voice, urged me on to greater heights, and only when I cried out in satisfaction did he take his own pleasure. Then, exhausted and almost beyond ourselves with joy, we lay together and murmured secrets—the fame his next expedition would bring, the home we would someday have in the West, our wishes for Lily's future. Sometimes, giggling, we talked of such mundane things as what we wanted for breakfast the next morning.

"Shall I rouse Mathilde and tell her you request hotcakes?" I asked, laughing.

"Yes, and do tell her why you look the way you do. Your hair, my dear Jessie, is all over everywhere."

Instinctively, I reached to smooth it.

"Don't. I like it that way. I like knowing why it looks that way." Poor Lily suffered in those days, though I comfort myself that she was too young to recognize our lack of attention. Though I visited her regularly, John saw her only once a day, and then he was little more than an observer. I once accused him of commenting on her behavior in the same way he might have judged a horse racing around the track. He shrugged and said he knew nothing about babies.

When John's report was presented to the Senate, Senator Linn immediately proposed that it be printed for the Congress, with an extra thousand copies made for general distribution to the public. Newspapers across the country printed excerpts, and soon the name of John Charles Frémont was on every tongue.

"Mr. Frémont's book," I told Maria Crittendon, trying to be modest, "is a success beyond our dreams. I hear that young men throughout the East are talking of going west, inspired by what John has written. He is very pleased."

"And so should you be," Maria said, stirring the tea I had given her. "Even John admits that you wrote it, that it is your book."

"Nonsense. I simply took his dictation."

"And turned it into a literary creation," Maria said. "Jessie, it wouldn't be wrong of you to take credit for your part in this."

I know I must have looked startled. "Maria, you know I cannot and will not do that. It is a wife's place to advance her husband in every way, but not to take credit for herself." As I said this, I firmly believed the rightness of my words.

Maria simply gave me a long look and then asked if I'd heard the latest news about James Buchanan. Someone was always trying to link that poor bachelor with this widow or that. I shuddered to think that I, playing a role like that of Harriet Bodisco, might have been a candidate for such a linkage. Briefly, the thought flashed through my mind that with James Buchanan I would never have known the kind of love—and passion—that I knew with John.

"Why are you blushing, Jessie?" Maria asked.

"I'm not blushing," I said indignantly. "It's very warm in here. The fire is too high."

———

John was going to Oregon. As his second expedition moved inexorably closer to us, the prospect filled him with such excitement that he never noticed that my own spirits lagged. Of course, most of the time I pretended enthusiasm as great as his own, and in some ways I did share that optimism.

The settlement of the Oregon valley had long been Father's special dream—in his mind's eye he saw it peopled with American settlers busily occupied in agriculture and the fur trade, and he saw a safe and passable overland trail for these settlers to reach this promised land. In the face of those of narrow vision, who insisted the land beyond the Missouri River was unfit for settlement and the Oregon Territory was not worth the cost of a single exploratory expedition, Father persisted.

But there was no passable trail. Immigrants had so far made their way to Oregon by a tortuous route up the Platte and Sweetwater Rivers to the South Pass, then on through the Green Valley to Fort Bridger and a series of other forts. But beyond the South Pass their trail was marked too frequently by gravestones, skeletons of oxen and mules, even furniture discarded in desperation by those who had attempted the journey before. Those on the overland trail suffered from thirst, hunger, burning sun, heavy dust, and the constant terror of Indians. They died of exhaustion and illness, their dreams of a bright new land fading before their dimming eyes.

John had been to the South Pass on his first expedition. Now he was to explore and map the trail beyond it, going clear to the Pacific Ocean. It would be a glorious adventure, and I knew it. Still, sometimes I gave vent to my doubts and fears about this expedition.

⌒⌒

"You can't make it any better for those people," I said passionately one night. "You are only exposing yourself to the same dangers that have defeated them."

John's self-confidence was at a high peak. "Ah, but I know how to meet those dangers," he said.

"Still," I persisted stubbornly, "you can't change the weather or make the Indians disappear."

"No," said Father dryly. He had been listening in unusual silence. "But an expedition mounted by the government *will* show an interest in settlement of the lands beyond the South Pass. It will tell the public that the land there is important."

Later, in privacy, John said to me, "It's as though I have no choice in this, Jessie. I couldn't stop what's been set in motion if I tried. My life is caught up in the cause of westward expansion now, and in some ways I'm no more than a puppet."

"You shall be the puppet-hero, then," I said.

"Always to you, I hope, if to no one else," he murmured.

As I gave him physical assurance of love, I fought back the dark shadow of foreboding that crept into my mind too often those days.

⌒⌒

In March of 1843 Father left for St. Louis, going first to Kentucky on business, and John took his mapmaker, Charles Preuss, to New York to buy instruments for the trip. From there they would go by rail and steamboat to St. Louis. I was left to pack up the household, including Mother, and journey to St. Louis by stage. It was a tortuous process, and many times during that journey, as I nursed Mother, reassured Mathilde and Sophie that they were not going to meet Indians, listened to Lily fuss, and jollied Susie and Sarah along, I resented the men in my family, who had gone off willy-nilly on their own affairs, and left me to tend to the family.

We took the National Road to Wheeling, but, as we could make at best twenty-five miles a day, it was a long and grueling journey bouncing along in that stage.

"Mother? Are you uncomfortable?" It was a foolish question, asked only as a means of showing my concern.

"How could I be anything else?" she answered in her still-garbled speech, and I was reassured by that small measure of humor.

"How long till we get there, Jessie?" Susie demanded, while Sarah chimed in, "I'm tired of this coach. It's boring."

I placated them with stories of the West, telling them some of John's adventures in terms they could understand, and their wild imaginations then took them off on pretend journeys, which they found much more exciting than this real one, which seemed endless.

From Wheeling we went by boat, finally reaching St. Louis nearly a fortnight after we'd departed Washington. Mother was perilously tired, I thought, and the young ones were cranky, while I myself felt exhausted.

But all my exhaustion was washed away in one fell swoop when John, who had beaten us to the city, wrapped me in his arms. I surrendered to that blissful feeling of love, protection, comfort—all the things a woman wants in life—only to rouse myself almost instantly with the thought that he would soon be leaving me for months and months.

"What is it, my darling?" he whispered in my ear.

I forgot enthusiasm and glorious adventures and all those things in favor of honesty. "A premonition," I said. "A strong fear, like someone walked over my grave . . . or yours."

Suddenly he was harsh and angry. "Jessie, don't ever say such a thing again. You could . . . you could put a jinx on the expedition." In spite of my own irrational fears, I could not believe he was serious. Fortunately, I did not laugh and managed to say lightly, "La, don't take seriously the fears of a woman in love."

It was the right thing to say, and it smoothed away his fears. But nothing soothed my own.

At the last minute, just days before his departure, John applied to Colonel S. W. Kearny, commanding the Third Military Department near St. Louis, for a small howitzer cannon. "The Indians," he told me in explanation as I wrote the necessary letter, "have been known for treachery and audacious bravery. It would be better to have the protection and not use it than to be without when we needed it. There, Jessie, say that to Kearny, old stick that he is."

"Should I say *that* too?"

He grinned at me with the look of a schoolboy caught making gestures behind the teacher's back. "No, I guess not. But there's not much give in the man."

"He is an old friend," I said. "I have known him since I was a child. He is stern, but he is a good friend, and I have no doubt he will give you whatever you want."

What he wanted included five hundred pounds of ammunition for the cannon and the necessary carriage to drag it along. I had my doubts that John would find it practical to haul a cannon over the Rockies and all the way to Oregon, but I bit my tongue and wrote the letter.

To make sure that John's request didn't get bogged down in the proper channels, which would have delayed the expedition beyond bearing, Father went to see

Kearny. He returned home triumphant. "The colonel has ordered the arsenal to fill your request without waiting for the customary approval of the War Department," he told John. "You may get the howitzer two days from now." He paused and looked thoughtful. "Didn't Jedediah Smith take one of those blasted things and find it more trouble than it was worth?"

John bristled ever so slightly. "Smith never had to face a horde of hostile Indians."

Father was still unconvinced. "Can't imagine that Indians have enough weapons that you'd need a howitzer. But you know best.... Sure you aren't expecting to meet some unfriendly Brits . . . or maybe even a Mexican or two down in California?" One corner of Father's mouth turned up ever so slightly as he said this.

"My instructions are to go to Oregon and back," John said. "California is not on my itinerary. And I am to avoid hostile encounters when at all possible. I do not expect to use the howitzer." But he gave Father a long look that said more than his words.

Father slapped him on the back. "There, now, no need to get huffy. I was just thinking about possibilities. I have great faith in you, John, and if you think you need a howitzer, then you need it."

As soon as John and I were alone, I confronted him. "You do plan to go to California, don't you? In spite of your orders."

He had the look of a schoolboy caught denying a prank. "Of course not, Jessie. That would be foolhardy—it could ruin everything I've worked for."

"It could also," I said thoughtfully, "bring you great honor, if you could bring back a meaningful report on the political climate in California."

"Why, my dear Jessie, you are a schemer! Does that mean you'd approve of a side trip to California?"

"Not at all," I said lightly. "It would keep you away too long." But I knew in my bones that he would cross the Sierras, just the same.

John was taking thirty-nine men on the expedition, many of them seasoned explorers, mapmakers, and hunters. He would take Preuss, the mapmaker who had gone on the first expedition and had proved difficult—"obstinate" was John's word. But John insisted his talents were worth the trouble. Most of the others I never knew or met, but there was one who was almost as much in my thoughts as John himself. His name was Theodore Talbot, and I did meet him when he came from Washington to join John in St. Louis. He was eighteen and looked to be tubercular, though John assured me he was in good health and would "toughen up" as soon as they were on the trail.

"Mrs. Frémont," he said diffidently, "I am pleased to meet you. My mother . . . she sends her regards and asks . . ." He blushed furiously and rushed on. "She asks that you write her occasionally. She's already worried about me."

I took his hand in mine and assured him I would write her faithfully. "She is not the only one who is worried," I said. "We women left behind cannot help but worry, even though I know you'll be as safe traveling with John as you would be home in your own bed." Would that I believed what I was saying to that poor innocent young man! My heart nearly broke when John told me later that Theodore carried a volume of Byron's poetry in his pack.

John left on May 13, anxious to be off and meet Kit Carson at a prearranged point. For me his departure came far too quickly—and not soon enough. I would have delayed it forever if I could—Father had even reminded me that he could easily secure John a comfortable post in Washington that would require no travel—but I knew that John by his very nature had to go on this expedition and probably many more. If I loved him, and if I wanted to link my life with his, then I must endure long absences—and the sooner I got used to them, the better all around. I firmly believed that the rewards of my endurance—a second report more brilliant than the first, fame and glory for John—would justify whatever unhappiness I endured during his absence.

But having told myself all this time and again, I wanted him to be gone. The waiting was almost more unendurable than his absence. If I was to live without him and be miserable for eight months, then I wanted to rush headlong into it and get it over with. Instead, we had more than a month of preparation in St. Louis, a month when the expedition was an everyday presence with us . . . and yet not begun. The experience told on my nerves, and I sometimes wondered if John wouldn't be delighted to be gone, just to escape my tenseness.

Anyone who envisions a romantic last night spent together before a long separation does not know much about explorers and their zeal and knows nothing about John Charles Frémont.

When the last pack was ready, the list of supplies checked one more time, the farewells said to the family, including a session of throwing Lily in the air until she was near sick with excitement, John and I retired to our room. But there was no rush to shed our clothes this night. We almost danced around each other, nervous, ill at ease, uncertain what to say, how to behave.

Our first night together, I thought to myself, was less awkward than this. "We will be just fine, John. You must not give us a thought, but simply get on with your work."

"I know," he muttered, standing at the window, his back toward me. "But I shall miss you." He turned to look at me.

Should I have rushed into his arms? Later I often wished I had done just that, but then the tension and the uncertainty kept me rooted to the spot. "I know you will. And Lily and I shall miss you. But it is only for eight months."

"Yes, that's all." He turned to the window again.

Later we lay, together but separate, in the bed, our few fumbling attempts at lovemaking having come to naught.

"Jessie . . ."

I put my finger to his lips. "I know you love me, and that you are sure of my love. We have no need to demonstrate it every minute. Besides," I added lightly, "you left me *enceinte* the last time you left, and I've no need for a repeat performance of that."

He laughed and reached a gentle hand to stroke my cheek.

"Just hold me, John, hold me tight."

And so we spent the night wrapped in each other's arms, comforted and yet tense, neither of us sleeping at all. We greeted the dawn with relief, and when John marched resolutely away from our St. Louis home, I stood proudly on the veranda and waved until he was out of sight. My smile was brave and almost sincere, and there was not a tear in my eyes. I had learned to be game, because I knew I had to be.

Oh, that's not to say that I didn't give way to tears once he was gone. For two days I wandered around the house in a fog, frequently retiring to my bedroom, where I indulged in smothered sobbing—not wanting anyone to hear, lest the family be upset—and then emerged to visit Mother, play with Lily, or seek out Father, who was mostly gone visiting this constituent and that.

The letter from John's immediate commander, Colonel Albert of the Topographical Bureau, came only a few days after John had left. Among his parting words were instructions to open all mail and forward only what had to do with the expedition. Unconcernedly, I slit the envelope and pulled out this letter addressed to John.

"You are hereby ordered to return to Washington immediately to explain by what authority you requisitioned a cannon for an ostensibly peaceful expedition to gather scientific knowledge. A replacement will be sent to lead the expedition."

The letter fell from my shaking hands. A replacement? Take the expedition away from John? All because of that silly cannon? It was inconceivable to me that John should be bothered by bureaucracy, when he was, to my mind, above such petty things. Following my first impulse, I would have taken the offending letter straight to Father, trusting him to take care of the matter. But Father was away in a far part of the state. And, besides, John and I could not always rely on Father. I knew that I, and I alone, could act to prevent this terrible blow.

It took me almost two hours to come up with a solution, and when I did, it seemed painfully obvious. I would send the message, but I would make sure it reached Kaw's Landing on the Missouri River—the departure point where the men were gathering and seeing to the final assembly of supplies and goods—after John was well away. Meantime, I would send my own message by courier from St. Louis. Basil Lajeunesse was still in St. Louis, tending to an ailing wife; he was to meet John's party at Kaw's Landing.

To his hand I entrusted a message that read, "Only trust me, and *Go.*"

"You can deliver this immediately and send back a reply?" I asked, handing him the sealed envelope.

"Yes, Mrs. Frémont. I need only to get my horse, and I will be gone. I will send back a reply by my brother, who is with the party now and will return to St. Louis."

"It is extremely urgent," I stressed. "I cannot tell you how important haste is." I feared that Colonel Albert had sent a duplicate letter to Kaw's Landing.

"I'm gone, ma'am," he said, and was actually down the veranda steps as he spoke. Within days I had a reply back. "I trust and *Go,*" John wrote.

I felt ennobled—there is no less pretentious word for it—by my part in securing John's mission. Bother the Topographical Bureau! They were men of small imagination and large jealousy, and with my help John had outwitted them.

That sense of purpose carried me through the hot, sticky St. Louis summer, though the days were long and the nights empty. Mother was some better, in spite of the heat, and we shared some of the care of Lily, though the burden fell on Mathilde and Sophie, as usual. Father traveled frequently, but when he was home, I helped him with odds and ends. The term describes my life that summer—odds and ends—a little bit of helping Father, a little bit of caring for Lily, a little bit of visiting with Mother, even a little bit of responsibility for the house, but nothing that engaged my energies.

I saw very few people—two who did come regularly to cheer me were the sons of old friends of the family. Montgomery Blair was a lawyer some ten years older than I, and he had recently been joined in the practice of law by his younger brother, Frank. Their father, Francis P. Blair, was editor of the Washington *Globe*, and we three had known each other since childhood. Beyond the Blairs I saw few people— Father's widowed cousin, Mrs. Brant, and one or two others. I went out only occasionally, mostly to church. Behind all this surface activity my life was in suspended animation, waiting for John.

Still my optimism ran high, fed on visions of John's fame when he returned, and I did not really suffer from loneliness and boredom. In September word came from John—a letter dated late in June from somewhere on the prairie west of the Missouri and delivered by two Indians, reporting that all was well and the expedition was progressing as expected. They were some behind the season's immigrants, who passed them on the trail. "To see all those prairie schooners, my darling," he wrote, "is a thrill beyond words. Your father would not be able to contain himself were he to see all these brave souls heading westward. They do, however, need direction and guidance, and I am grateful for the chance to provide that for them."

We shall be home by the Christmas holidays, my darling, and I shall hold you in my arms once again. Until then, please think of me lovingly and often, for I miss you. With regards to your parents and love, of course, to Lily,
John

The last words were, I knew, automatic, the expected lament of a faraway husband. But they did not reflect John's true state, for he was, I knew, exuberant with excitement. If he planned to be home by Christmas, he had given up California. Intrigued as I was by the possibilities a California expedition opened, I was more pleased at the prospect of having him home soon.

To Theodore Talbot's mother I wrote that the party would be in St. Louis by Christmas and she should have her son home by the New Year, without fail. She should not, I cautioned, worry about her son, for "Mr. Frémont, knowing him to be an only son, is most anxious to bring him home to you in safety." It pleased me to be able to reassure the elderly woman.

In the fall Father returned to Washington, of necessity, and urged that the family accompany him, but I had promised John that we would wait in St. Louis . . . and wait we would.

"Your mother—" Father began, but I interrupted him.

"She is in better health and spirits than I have seen her in some months, Father. I think she should stay with me."

"Perhaps you are right," he said, and I sensed that he was relieved to be free of worry about Mother.

Not two days after he left, Mother collapsed with chills and fever, and I called the doctor. He, bless him, ignored Mother's request that she be bled and suggested that she had an ague, which would pass with care. So I spent days in a darkened room with her, coaxing hot broth into her reluctant mouth, keeping warm blankets wrapped about her, and crooning gently to let her know that she was not alone.

Occasionally, she managed to murmur, "Poor Jessie, you are so good," and I would clasp her hand all the tighter.

At night, when Mathilde sent someone to spell me at my watch, I collapsed into my bed, after a perfunctory hug for Lily. One night she clung to me with great, overwhelming sobs.

"That baby misses her mother," Mathilde said in gentle reproach.

"She's too young to understand I must tend to my mother," I replied wearily. "But she is well cared for, what with you and Sophie."

"Babies don't understand 'well cared for,'" she said. "They understand love and being the center of your world."

The thought startled me. Of course, Lily was not the center of my world, but neither was Mother—nor was Father, though he had once been. John was the reason for my whole existence, and I was marking time with all of them until he returned. Even caring for Mother, which I did with such devotion, was a way of making time pass until Christmas—or whenever John came home.

"I love this child!" I defended myself hotly.

"I don't doubt but what you do, Miss Jessie, but she hasn't been given any show of that love."

Briefly, I was indignant that Mathilde would talk thus to me, and the thought even flitted through my mind that Father got what he deserved by hiring freed Negroes—insolent servants. But I knew that was unworthy and that I resented what Mathilde told me only because I knew it to be true.

"I will have breakfast with my daughter," I said, though I knew I sounded stiff. "Sophie can feed Mother."

And so I began to spend the mornings with Lily. At just over a year, she was enchantingly happy most of the time, walking tentatively from place to place but still not sure enough on her feet to run or climb, and only beginning to make intelligible sounds—which she and Sophie seemed to understand, though I only rarely did. When Sophie responded immediately, I was slightly jealous and had the feeling of a foreigner intruding upon someone's privacy. They spoke a language I did not understand.

Still, Lily and I began to develop our own routines, and I found them satisfying. Breakfast was followed by a session of storytelling—I told her stories about all the presidents and senators I had known, and she, not knowing any better, was fascinated, less by the story than by the sound of my voice. And then sometimes I spun tales of what her father was doing. "He has been to Oregon," I repeated over and over, "and now he's coming home to us." Wanting to believe it was the truth, I spoke with such enthusiasm that Lily usually clapped her hands and giggled in delight.

Mother's health, meanwhile, began to improve again, and I thought the world was looking rosy. John would be home in a little more than a month.

———

In November, my peace suffered a severe setback. Eleven men returned from John's expedition. "Wasn't enough provisions for all the men," Basil Lajeunesse told me—he who had taken my desperate message to John. "My wife," he said, "she is still poorly, else I would be with Lieutenant Frémont."

It worried me that John was without Basil. "Did ... did Mr. Frémont send me any letters?" I was alarmed at the mere mention that provisions had run low. It was beyond comprehension to me that John should suffer while in the wilderness. Innocent that I was, I pictured him always well fed and warmly clothed and housed.

"Yes, ma'am, he did." He pushed a moth-eaten fur cap back and forth on his head with a dirty gloved hand and avoided looking at me. Finally, when I was about to explode with impatience, he said reluctantly, "Lost 'em swimmin' a river. Sure sorry, Mrs. Frémont. But I can tell you, the lieutenant . . . he's fine."

To Mrs. Talbot I wrote, "They had perfect success in all of their undertakings, and by the middle of October Mr. Frémont would have been making his way home. They may be somewhat delayed over our first bright expectations, but they should arrive here in St. Louis early in January."

Christmas was a glum holiday, though I expended every effort to make it bright for Lily's sake.

"She's too young to remember, anyway," Mother said from the chair where she sat wrapped in a shawl.

I wanted to suggest that she could do more to add to the Christmas spirit herself, but I forbore.

We ate duck and dressing, rice pudding and turnips, and spice cake for Christmas dinner, but I had had brighter meals when John and I lived in the boardinghouse. I was relieved that the holiday was behind us.

By the New Year I began to expect John at any moment, in spite of my caution to Mrs. Talbot. I awoke each morning thinking that he might have arrived at night, and I went to bed sure that he would arrive before I awoke again. During the day if I had occasion to leave the house—which I did but rarely, only to go to church or the like—I hurried home to see if he had come while I was gone. Every time I opened the door, I expected to see him seated in the kitchen, with Mathilde feeding him a long-overdue meal.

"Miss Jessie, why're you putting out that meat pie and cheese on that table?" Mathilde stood in the doorway of my room, her hands on her hips and her head cocked inquisitively.

"Mr. Frémont will be hungry when he arrives," I said with as much dignity as I could muster, "and I wouldn't want to wake you."

"That be all right," she said. "Besides, do we know he's coming tonight? Or last night, when you put out roast and spoon bread?"

"He will come some night soon," I said, willing it to be so, "and I shall have this light burning for him."

"Yes, ma'am," she said with a shake of her head.

In January a visit from one of John's loyal St. Louis backers convinced me he would be home in mid-February. Robert Campbell, a merchant who had provided many of the provisions for John's departure the previous May—it seemed ten years earlier!—brought the maps he had studied over and over, trying for his own satisfaction to approximate the route John would take. I wrote to Mrs. Talbot the good news that by March 1 her son would be back at her fireside and assured her that had his health failed again, we would have heard.

By the first of February I was in bed with a sick headache. Visions of my mother and her ailments danced through my pounding head, and as Mathilde brought me cool cloths and warm tea, I wondered if I was doomed to be an invalid like her.

"You're too young to be sick, Jessie," Mother said without much sympathy. "It's worry over that husband of yours, off traipsing around the West when he should be home with you and his child."

He has a name, I wanted to shout—and might have except that it would hurt my head. "He has a greater calling than tending to me," I managed to mutter. It would have been unfair to point out that her husband worried over her a lot but did little in the way of companionship. And I couldn't bring myself to tell her that my vision of John's glory had faded a little. I could no longer see his triumphal return quite as clearly.

By March, with headaches still confining me to my room more often than not, I was forced to write to Mrs. Talbot that it would be April before we saw the expedition return. Word had come in a circuitous way that John's pack animals had not been up to winter travel, and the party had made a safe camp rather than venture across the plains, exposing themselves to blizzards and starvation.

In mid-March my father became the focus of all our concern, and worry over John took a second place in everyone's brain but my own.

Word came that the warship *Princeton* had suffered an explosion during a demonstration of a cannon nicknamed the Peacemaker. President Tyler had arranged this "show" for his guests on a Sunday trip down the Potomac. Among the guests was Mrs. Dolley Madison, who was fortunately uninjured. Others, however, were not so lucky. Secretary of the Navy Thomas Gilmer and Secretary of State Abel Upshur, with whom Father had been talking only minutes before, were killed immediately, along with several others. Many more were injured, including Father, who was knocked unconscious by a piece of the boiler that struck him in the side of the head.

"There was a period of time," he wrote us, "for which I cannot account, but I am on the mend now. Still, I have no hearing in that one ear, and the doctors tell me it may never return."

Mother was determined to fly to Father's side, though her flight by steamboat and coach would be slow. "You must come with me, Jessie," she said, anxiety giving her an imperious tone that was quite unlike the quavering voice of her illness.

"No, Mother. Lily and I must wait here for John."

"John, John!" she said. "Your father has been injured, and we must go to him."

"My husband," I replied, "has been gone far too long on an expedition that was to take only eight months, and I will wait here for him, where I told him I would be. Father is recovering . . . he has said so himself . . . and you are not up to the trip."

She would not hear of it and departed the next day, taking Mathilde with her. Sophie and I were left to run the St. Louis house, care for Lily, and, as always, wait for John.

In April a trading party returned to St. Louis from Fort Laramie with the news that they knew nothing of John's party. "Their arrival shows the country to be in traveling order," I wrote Mrs. Talbot, "and the wise in such matters tell me that Mr. Frémont has either camped immediately at the foot of the mountains on this side, or that very probably he did not cross at all but wintered in Oregon. . . . He will not be here until the middle of May."

In June—John had now been gone over a year—the most I could write to Mrs. Talbot was that a Mr. Glasgow, who had just returned from California, had seen John in November and learned that he planned to winter at Fort Hall, a British trading post on the Snake River. "Our loved ones will have every comfort that fire, food, and shelter can give," I wrote, "and you need be under no apprehension. Mr. Glasgow returned by the southern route, so of course he arrived sooner than our party returning by the Yellowstone. But we know the snows are breaking up in the high regions. . . ." I wished I had more faith in my own comforting words.

Father turned evasive in his letters, too, almost nonchalant about John's protracted absence and yet more concerned than ever about my headaches, Lily's health, and our general well-being. "You must be brave," he wrote, leading me to wonder if he was warning me that disaster lay in wait. Did he know something I did not? I dismissed the idea as paranoia, but still . . . perhaps Father knew that John had tried to reach California, and wasn't telling me the whole truth.

By August I was nearly overtaken with illness—caused by my worry, as even I recognized. Panic, and the headaches that resulted, had become like a fog over which I had no control as it enveloped my very being, giving me no option but to bend before it. Perhaps it was a sign of fading hope that I no longer put out a supper for John nor left a light in the window.

One morning Gabriel, the coachman, claimed to have seen John in the middle of the night, lurking about the house. "Wearing his uniform, Miss Jessie, but thin as a rail he was. He looked up to your room, but it was all dark. And then he jus' walked around the house, outside, two or three times. Then, when I was about to call to him, he vanished . . . just disappeared into thin air."

"Why didn't you call to him immediately?" I asked sharply when the story was reported to me the next morning. I doubted Gabriel's tale, for the poor man was known to take a drink more than occasionally, and I could not fathom that John would have returned and yet not come into the house. Still, it was unsettling. Sophie made it all the more unsettling. "He's dead!" she wailed. "Master Frémont is dead, and Gabriel seen his ghost!"

It took every ounce of my control to silence her. I warned her that Lily was listening fearfully and that I would not have the child alarmed. Indeed, I wished I could order myself not to be alarmed, but try as I might to dismiss Gabriel's vision, I was on edge as Lily and I went about our morning routine.

We were sitting on the veranda, hoping to catch whatever small breeze stirred while I told Lily stories—the same she'd heard over and over again about her father. And then, almost magically, he stood before us—thin and brown, hardened by his experiences, but nonetheless my John. I flew down the steps to his waiting arms, all thought gone from my mind except that he had returned to me.

Behind me Lily wailed in fear.

John may have looked thin, but he had lost none of his strength, for he whirled me around once, kissed me heartily, and then hoisted me into his arms.

"Is your father at home?" he asked.

"No," I told him, "Mother and Father are both in Washington. Lily and I are your welcoming committee."

"Good."

By now Gabriel and Sophie and several others had gathered on the veranda, alerted by my scream of joy. With me still in his arms, John mounted the steps, smiled heartily at them, and said, "See to the child, please." Lily stood alone on the sidewalk, still wailing.

Then he carried me upstairs to our bedroom and slammed the door behind us. We spent the rest of the day in bed.

John's lovemaking was at first rough, demanding, as though I were another territory to be conquered. He was, I told myself as I struggled to match his urgency, still full of the energy of the expedition. But when he lay satisfied and exhausted next to me, he panted, "I showed them, I really showed them, didn't I?"

Lovingly, I murmured an assent, but it alarmed me a little to wonder who "they" were. Somehow I knew he was thinking of the childhood taunts he had suffered, about bastardy. I had thought, perhaps foolishly, that when he confessed that great worry to me, it was obliterated from his consciousness. I saw now—at the advanced age of nineteen—that I was young and foolish to think that such problems are so easily banished. I shivered, partly in foreboding, partly in uncertainty.

He took the shiver as one of pleasure and began to plant gentle nibbling kisses on my neck. "It was all for you, Jessie, all for you. Especially California," he whispered in my ear.

"California? You went to California?" Astonishment brought me bolt upright in bed, regardless of his teasing kisses.

"You knew I would," he said dryly, sitting up next to me and covering himself with the bedclothes. "How could you have doubted it? I had to show them."

I stared at him, his face open and honest and his eyes intent. He really believed that he had to justify, even vindicate, himself, and it came to me that conquering the American West would be John's way of overcoming the stigma of his birth. That was why his destiny lay to the West, why he was the perfect son-in-law for Father, whose vision lay in the same direction. Their needs were totally different, but their goal identical.

He rolled over and wrapped me in his arms again. This time he was the John I knew—tender, gentle, teasing, and loving. I was very glad my parents were in Washington.

"Why," I asked sometime during the afternoon, "didn't you come in when Gabriel saw you last night?"

He chuckled. "I didn't know he saw me. That must have given you a fright. I'm sorry. I was afraid I'd rouse the household . . . and that the uproar might not be good for your mother. I didn't know, of course, that she wasn't here. Believe me, I'd have pounded the door down if I had known."

"What did you do?" I asked incredulously.

"Went to sit in that open grass before Barnum's Hotel. I was simply going to rest on a bench and watch the day break. But a clerk from the hotel came out when he saw a man in uniform . . . and then he recognized me." John blushed modestly and went on, "He insisted I rest in one of their empty rooms until it was a decent hour so that I could arrive at home."

"But it was nearly midday before you got here," I accused.

"I fell so soundly asleep I didn't wake until then," he confessed. "I was rather tired."

Finally, now rather tired myself, I suggested we rise and greet the household.

"Once more," he murmured, "let me feel you against me once more. You've no idea how often I dreamed of this moment, how I ached for you." As he whispered these words in my ear, his hands moved lightly over the length of my body, and I could no more have risen than I could have denied him.

———

Lily was at her supper when we entered the kitchen. At the sight of John she puckered as though she would wail again, but I went quickly to her and gathered her in my arms. "This is your father," I said, taking her toward John.

With her new ability to shape words, she managed something that sounded like "Ghost?" and I knew that Sophie had been talking out of turn. Throwing a severe look at the nursemaid, I said firmly, "No ghost. Your father, Lily. Come, give him a hug."

John was as awkward as she was reticent, but the two managed a sort of a hug. Then John held her at arm's length, as though inspecting her, and managed a hearty, "Well, well . . ." After that he seemed uncertain what to say or do with his daughter, so I took her back.

Gabriel served us supper later that night in Father's dining room, which often held a crowd but had, of late, been all too empty. Now the two of us seemed to fill the room, so overflowing were our spirits.

As soon as John was rested and I could supervise the necessary housekeeping chores involved in leaving a house empty, we left—bag, baggage, servants, and Lily—for Washington.

Father greeted John with enthusiasm and relief. "I am more relieved to see you than you can know," he said. "There was a time I was worried about you. Tell me about California!"

"You knew he went there . . . and you knew something to worry about?" I asked. The chances that John had taken—both physical and political—still rankled me. I expected no less than censure from both official and unofficial sources for having endangered his men. Yet here was my own father, praising that foolhardy venture across the Sierras.

Father was almost apologetic. "It was for your own good, my dear. Word came that John had gone up into the Sierra after winter closed the passes. We heard of storms and rumors of starvation . . . and then nothing. Reports I got were that he had disappeared into thin air."

I looked at John, but he avoided my eyes. Then I turned on my father again. "You should have told *me!*"

"Would you have been happier knowing?"

"Happier," I said, "is not the question. I have a right to know what affects me. I will not be treated like Mother, locked away in a bedroom."

Father's stricken look made me instantly sorry that I had spoken in such haste, and I rushed to his side. He gave me an awkward pat on the shoulder and looked over my head to John, who nodded his support to Father. I felt very much the woman controlled by husband and father, not given credit for sense or stamina . . . or anything.

I nursed my anger over this particular issue for several days, but no one noticed—especially not John and Father, who were busy greeting a steady stream of well-wishers who came to welcome John home. The uncomfortable incident, once passed, was out of their minds. I wished it could leave mine as easily.

Mother was little help, though of course I did not tell her my mean remark about being locked away in a bedroom. Still, she thought it perfectly logical that

Father protected me from worry. "He loves you, Jessie," she said in a voice still thickened from her stroke, "and he doesn't want you to worry."

"I don't see that love must mean putting one in gauze and protecting her from life," I said. But I knew that it was useless to talk to Mother.

It was a difficult homecoming for John. Papa Joe Nicollet had died, alone in a hotel room in Baltimore, while John was away. "He should have gone to California with us and died on the trail," John told me with tears in his eyes. "It would have been a better death."

Senator Linn, who was such a strong supporter of expansionism and of the report of John's first expedition, was also dead, a political blow rather than the personal one that Papa Joe's death had been. But Linn's death had been a personal blow for Father; they were colleagues, often aligned against the conservatives in the Senate who would settle for the existing boundaries and let emigration cease. Senator Linn had been a man of vision, like Father and John.

Still, our house teemed with Father's friends who shared his passions about California and Texas. John had only a passing interest in Texas, his focus on California so intent, but he listened patiently as Father explained that the annexation of Texas meant we would fight an unjust war for the benefit of slaveholders. "Mexico still sees Texas as her own," he expounded, "and they'll fight for it. And there's slavery in Texas—that was one reason they fought so hard to shed themselves of Mexico, when Mexico outlawed slavery." Father also believed that it was illegal and immoral for Texas to claim the land between the Nueces and Rio Grande Rivers, never part of the original province of Texas. "Land greedy, that's what they are, taking another country's land," he declared. Soon after we returned to Washington, Father paralyzed the Senate with a three-day speech protesting Texas's acquisition of land not its own. I heard rumbles from his colleagues for months, but, my loyalty firmly fixed with my father, I refused to take this discontent seriously. It never occurred to me that Father could lose his Senate seat.

When Father got to talking about Oregon, John's eyes brightened—I watched that happen, literally. Every visiting congressman who tried to tell John that Oregon was too far, too hard for people to reach, was met with descriptions of the rich land, the plentiful fur trade, the fishing. Some went away convinced, a few angry that John could not be converted to their way of thinking. And California—everyone who visited heard John rave about that land of eternal summer. And visit they did, day and night, each senator or congressman wanting to propose his own theory of the West and why the United States should or should not be looking toward new lands. George Bancroft was there often, and even crusty old Daniel Webster wanted to hear what John had to say about the West. We had no privacy, and we found the constant turmoil wearing.

"Jessie," John said as he sat before his desk one morning when the house was blessedly empty of visitors, "I cannot get a thing done, because I'm waiting to hear that knock at the door. Someone—who knows who?—will come to interrupt us. We haven't had a morning to ourselves uninterrupted to work on this blasted report."

It was true. The "blasted" report was not even begun, though we'd been in Washington a full three weeks.

Father found the solution—a small house near C Street, with apartments upstairs and down, available for a modest rent. Father paid the rent, and we installed ourselves on the upper floor. Downstairs was Preuss, the mapmaker, who also served as palace guard—no one except Father got by him to disturb our work.

We began each day early. I sat with my pens sharpened and my stack of foolscap ready, and John began by demanding to know where we'd left off the day before. That would spark his memory, and in no time he would be pacing the room, hands clasped behind his back, a wild mixture of scientific fact and human story pouring from his lips so fast that my fingers were hard put to keep up. I always felt that it would have slowed him down if I had asked him to wait for me, so sometimes my notes consisted of weird abbreviations and symbols known only to me. Much later, each day, when John had gone to visit with this senator or that, I rewrote my notes into English that at least I could understand.

Chapter Seven

According to John the excitement began at Kaw's Landing.

"There were twelve hundred or more emigrants there, Jessie, along with fur traders, trappers, and freighters headed down the Santa Fe Trail—and there were more coming in every day. It was the noisiest place you can imagine—teamsters swearing at their animals, roustabouts yelling as they worked, oxen bellowing, the clang of the blacksmith hammer.

"We went about our business as best we could—getting animals shod, loading our carts, buying the last of our supplies. The store there does more business daily than the busiest store in Washington. But then your message came, telling me it was urgent that I leave immediately. I have such faith in you, Jessie, that I left almost instantly, but we had to camp a day or two just out of sight of the village, while riders went back to finish buying supplies and the like. "Finally we left—the best-equipped expedition ever to head west. We had thirty-nine men, including Basil Lajeunesse and Preuss, the cartographer, and we carried the best scientific equipment—a refracting telescope, two pocket chronometers, two sextants, a reflecting circle, barometers, half-a-dozen thermometers and compasses. For provisions we took flour, rice, and sugar. My thought was that we would depend on game for meat.

"At first, from Kaw's Landing, we followed the Santa Fe Trail with the emigrants. I was more aware than ever, Jessie, of the scope and importance of the westward movement in this country, and of the need for someone to step forward and take charge. It's as if all these people are drifting west without knowing where they're going, what they're doing. We need maps, roads, railroads, and most of all, leadership.

"The third or fourth night out we visited with Dr. Marcus Whitman, the missionary. He was . . . ah . . . slightly boring—don't put that in the report, Jess.

"We soon left the trail and followed the northernmost fork of the Kansas River westward. I was determined to find a southern pass over the mountains, one that would make an easier crossing for emigrants and would also provide a railroad crossing in the future. But we were soon in a country so barren that one wonders that it could support any life. The river was wide but only a few inches deep, and we were desperate for water—sometimes we had no choice but to drink the muddy water from buffalo wallows.

"As we pushed on, the land became more broken, and I knew that we were gradually climbing. On July 1 we caught a glimpse of mountains—just a blue mass against the distant sky, but I was inspired by the sight. I stood, Jessie, and watched the sun set behind those far-off mountains, and I felt as though some higher power had put a hand on my shoulder and led me westward. What we were about to do was more important than most men dare to dream.

"On July 4 we were at St. Vrain's Fort, where they celebrated Independence Day in fine fashion, and then we went on to Fort Lancaster, which looks like a farm—hogs, cattle, chickens, turkeys, all foraging on the prairie, and even a large vegetable garden. We kept moving southwest, paralleling the mountains, and on July 9 we caught our first sight of Pike's Peak.

"In this country, as I expected, I met Kit Carson, who gave us the bad news that Mexican decree forbade trading. We were in desperate need of supplies and fresh pack animals but had no way to get them. Carson advised that we return to St. Vrain's while he would go to Bent's Fort for supplies. He was successful, and we started westward again. I separated the party into two groups, sending most of the men and all the heavy baggage toward the usual ford of the Green River. Carson, Preuss, and I, and a few others, determined to cut through the mountains, following the valley of the Cache la Poudre River.

"We found ourselves in the wildest and most beautiful part of the Rockies—towering mountains rose all around us. Sometimes the sides were dark with pine forests; others consisted of no more than sheer precipices, cut over centuries by rivers. On the river bottom we rode through a wilderness of plants, tall spikes waving over our heads. The road became increasingly difficult, though we were lucky enough to kill several buffalo. We stopped a couple of days to dry the meat and then pushed on through dense sagebrush sometimes six feet high. By August 7 it was apparent that our light carriages would not make it through. One afternoon I stood on an outcropping and saw to the north the peaks of the Sweetwater Valley Range. Then and there I determined to abandon my effort to find the South Pass and move on with the expedition.

"No, no, Jessie, it was not a defeat. Perhaps a setback, but not a defeat. I could not risk the entire expedition for one wild search. I had my men and my responsibilities to think of, and I believe I lived up to my duties as a leader. In two days we were on the Oregon Trail, like being on a public road after the rocks and shrubs we'd been struggling through.

"Not that there wasn't evidence of the hardship of the emigrant experience—we passed two fresh graves in two days, one of them a child's. It would have broken your heart, Jessie. On a lighter side, we also ran into a wandering ox, headed east, as though it wanted to return to the safety of its home.

"But we came upon a large camp of emigrants in the valley of a tributary of the Bear River, and you've never seen such a tranquil scene. It almost made me wish I was a poet so that I could capture the beauty of that scene—the landscape dotted with the white canvas covers of the wagons, campfires smoking at each small group of wagons, women cooking, children playing, cattle grazing. It was as settled and safe as Missouri, and it's the way the West is going to be.

"We passed three more large camps, and they each gave me a rousing cheer, Jessie. They know that America is on the march, and I'm the leader.

"We were nearing the Great Salt Lake, and I pushed on, anxious to see that phenomenon that no one has recorded scientifically. The best report on it is the old story about Jim Bridger kneeling to drink, spitting out the water, and yelling, 'Hell, we are on the shores of the Pacific!' I recorded some curiosities—hot springs, red-and-white hills, an extinct volcano—and they are in my notes—but it was the lake that drew me. I suppose I half believed the romantic stories that ran among the men—how a subterranean whirlpool connects the lake to the Pacific, and the like. But I was determined to be accurate and scientific about my exploration.

"My first sight of the lake was breathtaking—it stretched far beyond our vision, with several rocky islands rising out of the waves. I felt as Balboa must have when he discovered the Western Ocean from the heights of the Andes.

"We spent a week there. One day Carson and I paddled out to one of the islands in our India-rubber boat. It was exciting to paddle over that clear, calm water, so blue-green in color, but unfortunately our boat leaked badly and almost wrecked us in the middle of the lake. We spent the night on that island, about two hundred feet above the water, and I did a careful chemical analysis of the water. My notes report on it, along with notes on the botany and animal life.

"We set out northward on September 12, riding steadily and reaching Fort Hall on the Snake River on the eighteenth. We were low on provisions, and the men were terribly hungry. Carson shot some seagulls one day, but they were poor fare, and finally, reluctantly, I gave the men permission to kill a fat young horse that we had gotten from some Snake Indians.

"No, no, Jessie, I could not eat a bite of it. I felt as though a crime had been committed. But the meat did restore the spirits of the men, and though I regret the decision, I believe it was right—my responsibility to my men, you know. Later we bought an antelope from an Indian, and I was able to enjoy a little meat—it did make me feel better.

"At Fort Hall we met up with Fitzpatrick and the rest of our party, and we were able to buy five fat oxen, along with several poor horses. The weather warned us that winter was coming—on September 19 it snowed all day, and on the twenty-first standing water froze hard. After a great deal of thought, I called the men together and released any who were not ready to face a midwinter exploration. I did not minimize the hardships but told them supplies would be short, the weather severe. Eleven men decided to return east; the rest of us left Fort Hall on the twenty-third, moving through the Snake Valley toward the Pacific. But as I left, facing a chill drizzle with the wind driving the rain into our faces, I made up my mind that there should be military settlements at Fort Hall and north of the Great Salt Lake for the protection of settlers and the further settlement of those areas. We must stress that in the report, Jessie—these lands must be settled by Americans. Today, when emigrants finally make it over thirteen hundred miles from Missouri, all they have is the slim protection of a British fort.

"It took a long, hard fortnight to reach the Columbia, but that magnificent river was worth every step of the trek. When we crested the bluff at the edge of the lower Columbia, we could see Mount Hood majestically standing guard over the land. I could scarcely realize that it was almost two hundred miles away. We visited Dr. Whitman's missionary establishment, and I must say that I was slightly relieved that the good doctor was away—don't write that, Jessie!

"We followed the Columbia, which narrows enough as it goes between the great cliffs to make travel difficult. Finally we camped at the Dalles, and I took a side trip to Fort Vancouver, while the others prepared for our trip home. What? Oh, it was then early November. We secured a three-month supply of tallow, flour, and peas, along with cattle to slaughter and enough horses and mules to bring the number of pack animals up to 104. We abandoned the flimsy carts we had worried with thus far.

"Ah, yes, Jessie, I know at this point I could have retraced my steps and returned home, and I would have completed the mission of my expedition. I would also have been home months and months ago. But what kind of explorer would that make me? I knew all along—and shared with your father and Senator Linn—that I would sweep southward to explore the Great Basin between the Rockies and the Sierras. Jedediah Smith crossed it from east to west, but no one has gone from north to south. I had to do it—you understand that, don't you?

"By now I had twenty-five men, it was the dead of winter, and I had no maps of the areas I proposed to explore to find Lake Klamath, Mars Lake, and the Buenaventura River. All I knew were tales of disappearing rivers, scorching deserts, high mountains, and wild savages. But not one of my men blanched at the prospect ... and that is what makes an explorer, Jess, the willingness to take risks, to explore the unknown. If I had returned then, I would be less than the man you married.

"We found Lake Klamath easily—nothing more than a twenty-mile-wide marsh, really, and the area populated by the treacherous Klamath Indians—and then we pushed east. Even though the sun shone brightly, the cold was intense and the snow sometimes four to twelve inches deep. On December 14 we killed a cow—forage was getting thinner and thinner—and on the sixteenth the snow was so crusted that the pack animals constantly cut their legs breaking through it.

"Finally we came out on a ridge overlooking one of the valleys of the Great Basin. More than a thousand feet below we looked into a green prairie country, with a beautiful large lake. There we were in a raging storm, but below us there was no sign of ice, no snow—it was all like summer or spring. We called the place Winter Ridge and Summer Lake.

"Christmas Day found us on the Warner Lake in lower Oregon. We celebrated by discharging the howitzer and some smaller arms and by serving a ration of brandy, sugar, and coffee.

"As we pushed on through the lakes and streams that drain the Sierra Range, I began to be considerably worried that the men were tiring and the equipment failing. We had lost fifteen pack animals—dead, abandoned, or stolen by Indians—and on January 10 we killed the last of the cattle. Finally, on January 13, we reached a large lake filled with salmon trout, and did we have a feast, Jess! We named it Pyramid Lake, and the river feeding it, Truckee.

"Within days, though, the men were hungry and desperate again, the animals footsore, and the country barren, rocky, and difficult. I had to do something, Jessie— we simply could not press on and on, not knowing where we were going. And ever since Missouri I'd . . . well, this thought had been racing through my mind . . . and I determined we would cross the Sierras into California. It was my responsibility to my men. . . . I had to see that they were safe.

"No, no, it wasn't practical to go back to the Truckee Valley, and no, my decision had nothing to do with politics. I was not on a mission to uncover routes of invasion to California nor to determine how Californians felt about the United States. Of course, I did hope to find the Buenaventura, which would lead us to San Francisco Bay. Once my mind was made up, I determined that we should go immediately, and we plunged into the foothills of the Sierras. On January 24 we met an old Washoe Indian who offered to lead us to a good pass in the mountains. As we approached the main chain of the Sierras, the road grew rougher and rougher—finally, on January 29, we were forced to abandon the howitzer. You know how much I regretted that, Jessie, yet I had no choice.

"The Indian began to advise us against continuing. We could not understand his language, so we communicated by signs. But over and over we heard *tahve*, the word for snow. The snow now was three and four feet deep in some places, and the temperature below zero at night. But I assured the Indian my horses were strong.

"I had to work hard to keep the spirits of the men up. Sometimes I gave them an extra ration of brandy, and Carson and I frequently described to them the beautiful valley of the Sacramento, with its rich pastures and abundant game. Less than a hundred miles away, I told them over and over, is a land of summer. My instruments showed that we were seventy miles due east of Captain Sutter's great ranch—what, I ask you, can seventy miles be? Well, Jessie, I learned the answer to that.

"We started up on February 2, and there was an air of foreboding about the whole troop. The old Indian told us that from that point, in summer, the crossing took six or seven days. We had no tallow, no grease, and worst of all, no salt. We had been so long without meat that when one of the men asked, I gave permission to kill a fat dog. No, I could not eat that, any more than I could have eaten the horse earlier.

"As the snow deepened, we began a system of breaking paths, taking turns on the strongest horses until both horse and man were exhausted. On the first day we traveled sixteen miles and reached a height of 6,760 feet—I confess that I was falsely encouraged. The next day we made only seven miles, and the next we were brought to a stop. When we tried to force the horses ahead, they plunged two or three hundred yards and then fell, exhausted, refusing to go farther. We left behind us a trail of abandoned baggage and equipment, and finally we had to camp where we were—on a wooded mountainside, without shelter, in a freezing wind. We built fires, covered the snow with boughs, and made ourselves as comfortable as possible.

"Two more Indians had joined us, and one of them began to harangue us, saying our men and horses would die. If we would go back, he said, he would show us a better pass. From signs and the few words we understood, we knew that he was telling us that even if we made it through the pass, we would not be able to get down the other side because of precipices. The feet of our horses would slip and throw them off the trail. But I would not turn back!

"Next morning our Chinook guide had deserted—taking with him the blanket I had generously thrown about his shoulders the night before. I set most of the men to making sledges, while a few of us undertook a reconnaissance on foot. We found snow anywhere from five to twenty feet, sometimes with an icy crust so slippery that it rendered the horses helpless. But when our small party reached the crest of the range, we found a welcome sight—mountain slopes, mostly densely wooded, descended into a warm green-and-brown valley. With the telescope we could even vaguely follow the dim, dark line of the Sacramento. 'It is just as I saw it fifteen years ago,' Carson said, and I knew then that we were right to press on.

"The glare of the snow was so bright that the men had to tie black kerchiefs over their eyes, and we despaired of ever getting the animals over the summit. The men had packed down the trail by foot, making way for them, but it was not enough until I had the trail packed with pine boughs. It was exhausting work, but no one complained.

"On February 20 we camped at the summit, some thousand miles from the Dalles, where I had first made the decision to pursue this course. We had conquered the Sierras in midwinter—I had done it, Jessie. No one will ever be able to take that victory from me! By boiling water we calculated the elevation at 9,338 feet.

"All that lay before us was the descent, and that pales in comparison to the rigors of the ascent. On the night of the twenty-third we saw fires below us—the Indians in the bay—and on March 6 we reached civilization in the Sacramento Valley. Ah, Jessie, it is an enchanted land, and someday I will build you a wonderful home there—lush green grass, sometimes massed with the gold of the California poppy, sometimes wooded with evergreen and white oak, and then—almost before we knew it—we came to the ranch of Captain Sutter. We were a pitiful bunch when we passed the gates of Sutter's Fort—only thirty-three horses and mules left out of sixty-three, skeleton men leading skeleton horses. Captain Sutter was most generous, the best host that I have ever known, and I hope someday I can repay his many kindnesses to me.

"Who is he? Ah, he's hard to describe, Jess—an explorer, an inventor, a prince in his fiefdom! Comes from Switzerland originally, I believe, but he was the first to see opportunity in California and to work with the Mexican government. He trains and employs Indians, Mexicans, and emigrants. And his property—stables, granaries, storehouses, kitchens, workshops. He's irrigating his fields along the American River, his herds are increasing, his wheat fields are green and lush. His latest scheme is to train young Indian girls to work in a woolen factory he plans.

"Oh, yes, we were treated well—our bodies, our spirits, and our animals restored to health. We dined on salmon and trout, roast ham, venison, bear meat, fresh steaks, salads, many fruits, and good Rhine wine—no more dog stew for my men!

"Most important, Jessie—and I want it made clear in the report that I understood this relationship—he maintains his independence. He sides neither with the Americans, who want to throw off the Mexican domination of the territory, nor with the Mexican government, which is well aware of such scheming. Sutter walks a fine line between the factions, yet each side believes that his loyalty is to them. Properly handled, he could be an invaluable ally for the United States.

"I learned a lot about California, Jessie, and what makes it so tempting—you can buy excellent fertile land for next to nothing, and labor is to be had for food and clothing. You don't need expensive barns and buildings and fences. Anyone could go to California and make a fortune, just as Sutter has—I could, and I will, one day. In fact, five of my men chose to stay behind when we left Sutter's Fort.

"But it is a land of friction. The Californians—mostly descended from Mexican and Spanish men, and often native women—are the landholders, and they live an easy life, waited on by vaqueros—Mexican cowboys, Jessie—and Indian servants. But they resent the Mexicans, whom they call *la otra banda*. There is a great feeling that the time has come for California to throw off the reins of Mexico—I want to be part of that.

"We were there about two weeks, and when we left on March 22, we took with us 130 horses and mules and 30 head of cattle. Sutter even sent along an Indian to manage the animals.

"I meant to go south about five hundred miles, skirting the western base of the Sierras—there's a good pass there—and then on toward Santa Fe by way of the Spanish Trail, though I would turn off the trail before reaching that city and make for the headwaters of the Arkansas River. It's about two thousand miles, much of it desert, but it's new territory, never been explored by an American—I had to do it.

"We reached the Spanish Trail without incident in late April. Water was scarce, as we expected, but we had Mohave Indians carrying large gourds of water, and we had killed three beeves and dried the meat. I had done my best to see that we were prepared.

"But you can never prepare for the unexpected. On the afternoon of the twenty-fourth, two Mexicans burst into our camp—one was an old man, the other a young boy of about eleven. They were exhausted, but they managed to gasp out their story—they had been with a party traveling from Los Angeles when they were overwhelmed by Indians. These two were out guarding the horses, the only reason they escaped. They rode at top speed—it must have been for sixty miles—until their horses gave out, and then they continued on foot. They were overjoyed to find us, and we of course promised to give them aid. We took them back to the springs where they had left the horses, but of course the animals were gone—driven off by Indians. I could not divert my whole expedition, but I didn't object when Carson and another guide offered to go in pursuit. They returned the next day, leading more horses than the Mexicans had ever had and waving scalps from their guns.

"Yes, yes, I agree—it is a horrible practice, and you know full well I would never have countenanced it. Might not even have let Carson go if I'd anticipated . . . but I had no way of knowing. Carson will boast of that adventure for years—seems the two of them attacked an entire Indian camp. But that's another story.

"We continued northeastward across the desert, traveling at night and resting as best we could during the day, when the glare of the sun was merciless. The land was hot, rocky, and brown—nothing grows except prickly cactus, sagebrush, and yucca. Once we had to stop completely because of a gale that blew sand in our faces so violently we could not continue.

"Finally, though, we reached the camping ground where the Mexicans had been beset—it was ominous, Jessie. We found the corpses of the two men of the party, badly mutilated, but no sign of the women—they had been carried off into captivity and the Lord knows what kind of fate. The tiny dog belonging to the young boy had sat faithfully by the corpses and was delighted to have his master back—the boy's name was Pablo. But Pablo was frantic with grief and continually cried, '*Mi madre, mi padre!*' until I could scarce stand it for the hurt. It made me feel much better about what Carson had done.

"By May 3 we had reached a marshy area where there were fresh springs, but our horses were dropping in their tracks for want of grass and from the flinty rocks, which cut their hooves to pieces. When we had to abandon a horse, the men cut off the tail and mane to make saddle girths, but I hated the waste of a good animal.

"The next day was the hardest day since leaving the Sierras—fifty or sixty miles without water. Horse skeletons along the way testified that others had found it hard before us. The sun was like a great demon in the sky, and the yellow sand only sent the light shining back up into our faces, while waves of heat rolled and shimmered in the bright light. We survived on the pulp of a certain cactus—*bisnaga*, b-i-s-n-a-g-a—but it was acid and unpleasant. Even after dark we kept on, always hoping to find water with the next step, even though by then each step was an agony. But just around midnight the wild mules kicked up their heels and began to run, so I knew that we were close to water.

"I decreed that we would take a day's rest, but we had no sooner made camp than we were surrounded by Indians—it was, to me, as though the Lord were testing us every way he could think of! I had the camp ringed with guards, kept the men under arms, had the pasture horses driven up close, and tried to ignore the Indians, who were jabbering close to camp—their tongue was Ute, I believe—and insulting us every way they knew how. It was a standoff, until one old Indian forced his way into camp and began to count our numbers with great glee, pointing to the surrounding hills where there were many more of his kind. Finally Carson could stand no more and yelled at the man in a warning tone. The old thief left, and I let out a sigh of relief.

"We continued up the Rio Virgen, always trailed by the Indians—a disgusting lot they were. If a tired horse stopped, it was hair and bones within minutes. This next part is hard for me to tell, Jess. On May 9—the day is marked in my brain—we camped and I lay down for a rest. I was near the end of my strength, though I would never have let my men know how desperately tired I was. Without my knowledge—or, I should add, my permission—one of my favorite men, a fellow named Tableau, went back for a lame mule. . . . We found the mule's carcass, but we never found Tableau, only signs that he had fought for his life, and then a trail indicating he had been pitched into the river—living or dead, I shall never know. The men would have avenged the death—and I was tempted—but our animals could not survive a battle, and we moved on. But we never saw the Indians again. . . .

"That tragic event marked the end of our hardship. We began to notice the land changing, becoming less formidable, and on May 11 we actually went through a shower of rain. I felt as if we were returning to God's earth as we knew it. On May 12 we reached Las Vegas de Santa Clara, and within days we came in sight of the Wasatch Range. From then on I could not get home swiftly enough. We crossed the Continental Divide at Muddy Pass and were in Bent's Fort by July 1 and Kaw's Landing by July 28. We had come full circle, after fourteen months.

"I put the animals to pasture, to be fattened and readied for the next expedition. I could not bear, Jessie, after all they'd been through to sell them so that they could begin to toil again without any rest. And I won't have to gather as many animals for the next expedition.

"That's it, Jessie. That's the story of my second expedition west."

Chapter Eight

I WAS EXHAUSTED WHEN JOHN FINISHED DICTATING. IT SEEMED TO ME THAT I HAD held my breath in suspense each day as he described snow-blocked passes, raging thirst, hostile Indians. It pained me that I could not share that part of his life, and yet I could not even begin to imagine the hardships he had borne.

His mention of putting the pack animals out to pasture kindled a fire of anxiety that was banked in my mind. That winter was the happiest time I had yet known, because John and I worked together as an inseparable team, and yet always there was that edge of sadness. The closer we moved to completing the report, the closer we also moved to John's departure on his next expedition. His comment forced me to face that fact. I who had spent so much time awaiting his homecoming could hardly relax and enjoy his company, because I was already in dreadful anticipation of his next departure.

But I remembered that dream of California, where we would live as a family and John would travel no more. Maybe on this next trip he would find his dream place, and we could begin to plan our lives there. Almost as soon as the idea passed through my brain, I chided my silly self for believing in fantasies.

Promptly every day at one, after our morning of writing, Mathilde brought Lily and a lunch of cold pressed chicken, biscuits, and fruit. We ate together as a family, though John found it uncomfortable.

"It breaks my concentration," he said. "Why can't we just see the child at night when she is in her nursery?"

"She needs to see more of us, to know we love her," I said, echoing the words Mathilde had much earlier scolded me with. John felt no such scolding, though he did try to enliven our little mealtimes.

"Lily, did I tell you about the steer we met on the trail? Headed the wrong way he was, right back to the Missouri River. Guess he just gave up and wanted to come home."

Lily regarded him with a long but expressionless look, and John gave up his attempt at jollity.

"I don't understand children," he said to me plaintively one day as we took our usual walk after mealtime. Mathilde had taken Lily back to the house for a nap, and this was the hour reserved to us, for the late afternoon and evening at Father's house would be filled with company, as always.

"You have not spent enough time with her," I said patiently.

He was almost petulant as he said, "She prefers her grandfather."

I smiled to myself. "She knows her grandfather better," I said. "You may not give up with that excuse."

And so John tried to cajole his daughter with stories of Indians—peaceable, of course—and wildflowers, honey bears in California, and beavers in Oregon. None of it much impressed her, though she did gradually warm to him and, finally, one day took his hand in hers.

"It's time to go home," she announced. "Will you walk with me?"

John bowed low and told her he would be delighted. I stood with my heart beating in joy as I watched the two of them walk solemnly away from me.

"See, Miss Jessie?" Mathilde said. "All it takes is time . . . we grown people got to give those little ones time."

Usually our afternoon walk was a private and wonderful time. We talked of California often, and John built many a castle in the sky for me, so that some nights that land of plenty raced through my dreams. Other days we talked with great seriousness of the prospects for statehood for California, Oregon, and even Texas.

Some days as we approached the Potomac, we were interrupted by well-wishers. One day stands forever emblazoned in my memory. It was misting rain—damp but not enough to discourage us from our habit. My arm was woven through John's, and my head was bent against the wet so that I did not see the person approaching us until I heard that gushing, "Lieutenant Frémont! What a pleasure to meet you here!"

"Thank you, ah . . . madam," John stammered. "I'm afraid you have the advantage of me."

I looked directly at the woman then. She had far the advantage of me in the arena of looks, with blond hair piled on her head in curls, rather after the manner of Harriet Bodisco, and with cheeks rouged ever so gently—not enough to be obvious but just sufficient to give her high color. If I'd told John she was a rouged woman, he'd have denied it and accused me of jealousy.

"You don't know me," she said, her voice still pitched almost an octave too high, "but I know a great deal about you. I've read all the articles, and I think your explorations are so . . . well, so amazing. . . ."

While I watched in disbelief, John's chest actually swelled a bit, and he, who always stood straight anyway, straightened a bit more. "I am in your debt," he said in a courtly manner, and I feared for a moment that he would bow over her hand. "You are most kind to take notice of my efforts."

I wanted to scream in frustration. Instead I said, "I don't believe I've had the pleasure. . . . I'm Jessie Frémont. Mrs. John Frémont." Her eyes rested briefly on me. "Yes," she said, "I thought that was who you were. You certainly are fortunate to be married to such a brave man." And then her attention was full back on John. I might as well have been a moth in the air.

Even John was now becoming uncomfortable. "Well, uh . . . miss . . . it's certainly good of you to be so interested in my work. . . ."

"Oh," she trilled, "I am, I really am. I hope sometime you can tell me about it at length. You know, of course, where to reach me." And with that she was gone, sashaying—there is no other word for it—down the park pathway.

"Who is she?" I demanded, my tone less gentle than I would have wished.

"I'll be damned if I know," John said, honest perplexity in his eyes. "Isn't that the strangest thing you've ever encountered?"

I took his arm again and propelled us into a walk. "No," I said, "it's not really strange. I think, John, you have to be prepared for women fawning over you."

"Why ever?" he asked incredulously. "Don't they know that I am married to you . . . and madly in love with you, Jessie?"

How, I wondered, could any one man be so incredibly contradictory? He wanted monumental public attention over his expedition, and yet he didn't understand the results of that fame, or notoriety. "I believe I shall let her know about that, if necessary," I said with a smile, and we continued our walk.

But I was leery ever after.

———

The second report, three times as long as the first, was completed and presented to the War Department on March 1, 1845. Two days later it was presented to the Senate, which called for an extra five thousand copies. My old friend James Buchanan, now secretary of state, gave a stirring speech in which he testified to his long interest in John's career and his steadfast commitment to westward expansion. "I call for ten thousand copies," he said, and his measure was soundly voted into effect.

A new phrase—"manifest destiny"—began to creep first into the language of the press and then into the everyday speech of Washington. It was said to have been coined by the editor of the *Democratic Review*, but he never got public credit, for it quickly became the rallying cry of the expansionists. Father adopted it with abandon. While we had worked on the second report, James Polk was elected and inaugurated as president. He was an expansionist, and both Father and John were elated. They saw the future wide and open before them.

"John! Mr. Polk has called for us both to meet him at the White House tomorrow afternoon at two o'clock."

John beamed his pleasure, but I was angry. "Am I not to go?" I asked, wanting to point out that I had ghostwritten the report and that I, as much as the two men who stood before me, believed in expansion and that new concept of manifest destiny.

Father silenced me with a look that told me clearly what I already knew: this was men's business. I had my silent revenge, for they returned from the White House the next day a chastened pair.

"How was the meeting?" I asked innocently.

"Fine, fine," Father said, waving a hand in the air.

But John told the truth. "He thought me young and impulsive, because he wants to buy California from Mexico—he doesn't understand that will never happen. I only wanted to show the importance of exploration so that we will know the lay of the land when the times comes . . . but he didn't want to hear the truth. Our present maps contain more errors than truth, but he chose not to believe that."

"He's afraid of war with Mexico," my father said bluntly.

"And well he should be," I added.

"We will get Texas and California by treaty," Father predicted, "and remain a protector of Mexico. They need friends, not warlike enemies."

Since John was going again to California, I prayed Father was right.

❧

"John," I foolishly asked in one of our rare moments of privacy, "must you go on another expedition? Can you not stay at home and be a husband to me and a father to Lily? Father could find you an appointment in Washington." I hated myself even as I said it, for the words sounded weak and pleading.

Where I might readily have expected him to be angry, he was instead patient.

With a light finger he stroked the length of my arm, raising goose bumps. "I can't," he said simply, "and I have always thought you understood that. It is . . . it is in my nature."

"What is?" I asked. "The need to wander, never to stay in one place?"

"No, not that so much. But the need to explore, to discover, to make my mark in the world in the way that few if any other men can. You understand that."

I nodded, for I did understand that about him. I had known it forever, and I wondered if I would have loved him if he had been different. Probably not. I could not have it both ways—a stay-at-home, devoted husband and one who accomplished grand and glorious things. I would not have traded the latter for the former.

Once published, the second report made John such a hero that we had no private time together before he left. The lady in the park, so overwhelmed with his achievements, proved but a precursor of things to come—men and women alike called at C Street at all hours of the day.

John reveled in the attention. Sometimes I would catch him looking across the room at me, and his look seemed to say, "See, Jessie? I told you . . . I've made up for it. I've done something spectacular."

I, meanwhile, was no longer Senator Benton's daughter. I had become John Charles Frémont's wife. I gloried in the role . . . and quieted the small doubts that sometimes rose in my mind.

—◆—

Father, as chairman of the Senate Military Committee, and his fast friend George Bancroft, secretary of the navy, saw to it that John's orders from the War Department for the third expedition could be loosely interpreted. He was to explore the area of the Great Salt Lake again and then survey the chains of mountains west of the Rockies—the Cascade Range in Oregon and the Sierras in California—looking for passages to the Pacific. In other words, he was to step deliberately beyond the boundaries of the United States. It was, of course, to be a peaceable expedition, but the men John hired were mostly sharpshooters, not mapmakers, and in those evening discussions around the table—discussions I refused to abandon, though Mother had long since retired to her room—hints were dropped here and there about "being prepared" for the "eventuality of war." There was no question this time of the legality of taking a howitzer.

Lily and I would stay in Washington, rather than venture to St. Louis, though I regretted the decision in part. St. Louis would be so much closer to welcome John when he returned home. Still, being in St. Louis, cut adrift, as it were, from most of my friends and family, had made the last wait nearly unbearable, and I thought I should stand up to it better in the house on C Street. The reason I gave aloud was that Mother needed me, and she was no longer able to travel west.

The night before John left, when we should, I thought, have been sharing private and intimate moments, found me in the library, taking John's rapid-fire dictation as he answered letters that had been stacked on his desk for weeks. "I have been pressed by business . . ." he wrote to one, while to another he said, "Things here are very hectic. . . ."

Amen I thought. I was to be left in charge of his correspondence, which would keep me happily occupied but would not near make up for his absence.

Once again, on May 14, 1845, we spent a sleepless and passionless night together, wrapped in each other's arms, occasionally murmuring how we would miss each other, I trying all the while to hide my tears. Once John reached a tender hand to wipe away a tear, but he never uttered acknowledgment of its presence. To have admitted that I was anything less than stalwart and brave might somehow have weakened him for the journey. He preferred to think that we were soldiers in a war together, and I kept up the fantasy.

He left early on the morning of the fifteenth, with Lily, Father, and me standing on the veranda to wave him off as he strode down the street alone, a glorious figure in his full-dress uniform. It would be a month before he left St. Louis, and three months before he left Bent's Fort—the point at which he might really be said to have launched this third expedition—but for my purposes he was gone from our lives in April.

"Daddy come back?" Lily asked.

"Yes, my darling," I assured her. "Daddy will come back as soon as he can."

"Where does he go?" she asked.

"On a great adventure," I told her. "A great adventure."

Father looked at me over her head and gave me one of his crooked smiles, a look that seemed to share the mixture of pride and loneliness that I felt.

That night, alone in my bed, I gave vent to the tears that had been building for weeks. The next morning I arose with eyes swollen and puffy and with a pronounced patch of reddened skin by my mouth. It would stay there for months, and I learned to look around it in the mirror.

———

As we sat at breakfast one morning shortly after John's departure, Father having long gone off to the Capitol and Lily happily prattling in the kitchen with Mathilde, Mother seemed to shudder—not the slight shiver of a chill but the great convulsive shudder that bespeaks illness. Her eyes glazed and became vacant, or so it seemed to me, and she seemed unable to rise. When I went to assist her, she managed to mutter, "My arm . . . so heavy."

Frantic, I called for Mathilde, but by the time she came running from the kitchen, the episode, whatever it was, had passed, and Mother seemed returned to normalcy.

"Mother?" I asked. "Are you perfectly all right?"

"Yes, of course," she said in a snappish tone of voice. And then, "Where's Mother? Doesn't she know I want her?"

I froze, my hand halfway outstretched toward her. Slowly, I said, "Grandmother McDowell is at Cherry Grove, as always." Why, I wondered, would Mother expect her to be in Washington? She rarely came to visit and, indeed, had not written of visiting in over a year, preferring to let the family come to her.

Mother's face contorted as though in grief, and she asked hoarsely, "She's not dead, is she?"

"No, Mother," I said soothingly, "she is just fine. But . . . she is not here."

Her eyes took on a hard look, as though she were terribly displeased, and she rose from her chair. "Well, I must go to her at once. I need my mother."

Mathilde nodded at me and stepped forward. "There, now, missus, you let Mathilde help you up to rest. You need your rest before you go on that long journey."

Mother looked as though that were a new and clever idea. "Yes, of course, Mathilde, you're so right. Jessie would never have thought of that."

I opened my mouth to protest, but Mathilde silenced me with a look and began to help Mother out of the dining room. "We'll just go on and take a little rest," she said soothingly.

When I tried to follow, she motioned me away, and when she found me waiting in the hall outside Mother's room, Mathilde said matter-of-factly, "Just wait. She'll likely be back to herself when she wakes up."

I accomplished nothing that morning, pacing the hall outside Mother's room and leaving only when Mathilde nearly dragged me to the kitchen for coffee.

"Grandma's sick?" Lily asked.

"Yes, darling," I murmured absently, wondering if I should send a message to Father.

"She'll be all right. Mathilde says so."

And true enough, Mother awakened herself. "I have had a bad dream, Jessie," she said. "I was looking for my mother, and you. You wouldn't let me go to her."

Fine, I thought, *I am to be the villain in this madness.*

"My arm," she went on, "it . . . it feels sore and heavy."

It was, of course, another stroke—a tiny one that lasted only an instant—but it warned me that such could happen at any time. I would have to pay constant attention to Mother.

My sense of freedom evaporated, and I knew the vigil for John would again be long.

"You don't know the impatience that rages within me," I wrote to Sally McDowell. "I fear that I do not treat her as gently as I might, but sometimes when she doesn't know where she is, or who Father is, I want to shake her and say, 'Mother, behave yourself.'"

Writing to Sally McDowell was a godsend for me, especially because I could be honest with her about Mother. I did not want to fill my letters to John with such tales of woe, and Father did not want to hear about Mother's illness or episodes. I hardly could be discussing them with the servants or Lily, Randolph was off at Cherry Grove more than he was at home those days, and Liza was in love. "I hope William won't be frightened if Mother does something . . . you know, something foolish," she said one day, and I nearly flew in a rage at her. Then I had to calm myself—she was twenty-three and William was the first real prospect she'd had. But I couldn't ever imagine worrying about John's reaction, so great was my trust in him. I just shook my head over Liza.

"I don't know that I could be so patient," Sally wrote. "You are truly a saint." I was grateful for her faith and glad she wasn't privy to my inner thoughts. She, on the other hand, wrote bittersweet letters. Behind the bright chatter about her daily activities I sensed a growing sadness, and I feared it was true that she had married a "trifling poor fellow." "Francis," she wrote, "is very attentive. He cannot bear for me to talk to another man." I thought that a bad sign.

In late June I read in the newspaper of John's arrival in St. Louis earlier that month. Now he was such a national hero that the newspapers would track him as long as he was in reach of civilization. Somehow that made me feel oddly more distant from him, as though the man I read of were a stranger.

Still, I hung on every word and laughed aloud over a misadventure in St. Louis. He had, it seems, an encounter with mountain men there, or at least with a group of men who wanted to be mountain men and go west with him. According to the *Weekly Reveille* several hundred men gathered to hear of John's expedition—though only a handful could be signed on—and John, to satisfy them, mounted the nearest podium to speak briefly about his plans. That podium, however, was a rickety fence, and even boosted that high above the crowd, he could not be heard. Those in the back began to press forward, pushing mercilessly on those in front until the fence gave way . . . and John and several others went crashing to earth.

"He could have been hurt badly," Father grumbled, "a stampede or something."

"But he wasn't," I said brightly. "It says here that his description of the hardships to be faced discouraged many men."

"Yes, but I'm glad to hear Basil Lajeunesse is with him again," Father said. "I have great confidence in that man."

"So does John," I said, remembering the burly man who had once carried my message to John and, later, brought me news of him when I was desperate. I too had faith in Basil Lajeunesse.

"I imagine Carson's waiting for them at Bent's Fort," Father said, and I added my fervent hope that this was true, since John relied so heavily on Kit Carson.

Even as I read about John, I wrote to him constantly, my letters skirting the things that worried me—his safety, Mother's health—and dwelling instead on the things I thought would be cheering to him. During the summer immediately after he left, I wrote mostly of the praise the second report was receiving. Newspapers across the country counted him a hero, his accomplishments equal to those of Lewis and Clark, and they praised the language of the report, the very human terms in which John had managed to recount his exploration of a wild and uninhabited land.

I could not resist speculating in one letter on his status as a hero. "For you to be so lauded at your young age"—if I was twenty-one, he was about thirty-two, though he had never told me his exact age, which sometimes struck me as strange—"leaves a great puzzle. Whatever can you do next? Will you all our lives have to be going on to ever greater adventures? A part of me hopes so, my darling, for I am so proud of all you do. But there is another part of me that longs for that California home you promised me."

I could almost hear John's voice whispering in my ear that he must make California ours before he could provide a home there for Lily and me. But I never could hear him promise to settle down in that home.

—⁓—

Although it was a hot and sticky summer in Washington, I was amazed at how fast time flew by. Mother continued to be up and down—one evening she wandered in while Father entertained guests, her hair askew and her expression confused, only to seat herself grandly in a chair and say, "Pray continue, gentlemen, do not let me interrupt you."

While I rose in haste to shepherd her back to her room, Father held out a hand to slow me. "Elizabeth," he said kindly, "it's good of you to join us. We will continue."

And then, though his guests squirmed with discomfort, he said, "Now, gentlemen, about this problem with Mexico . . ."

This problem with Mexico was ever on our minds. Since Congress had voted to annex Texas, there was always the possibility that Mexico would declare war to retrieve its errant colony. True, Texas had fought hard to win its independence almost ten years earlier, but Mexico could still consider it merely a rebellious province and act to assert its control. Meantime, we were besieged with rumors—fortifications in Matamoros, armed troops gathering at various points throughout Mexico, guns and fortresses along the border.

Father did not believe in war with Mexico over either California or Texas, but of the tension over the Lone Star territory he said, "At least it diverts attention from California for the time being."

That slight hope soon was dashed too, as rumors came that more troops from Mexico were being sent to California—with British support—to strengthen the government there. "They say," Father said, "that the Americans in California are calling for revolt, and they must be prepared."

"And how will they react to John's arrival?" I asked.

He just shook his head, and I shivered a little in fear. I had to remind myself that I knew—I absolutely knew—that John would return home safely.

My attention was soundly diverted in the fall when Father impatiently called to me one afternoon. "Jessie! Jessie, where are you? I need you right now."

I rushed into his library to find him more disheveled and unhappy than I had seen him, even when Mother was at her worst.

"Father? What is it?"

"It's a great calamity for this family, that's what it is!" he ranted.

"Randolph?" I asked. "Is he all right?" Randolph, still exiled to Cherry Grove, had not mended his wild and reckless ways, and I worried always about his well-being, though I was never sure if he would be thrown from a horse or shot by a jealous husband. At sixteen he was precocious in many ways.

"Randolph?" he thundered. "Who in blazes said anything about Randolph?"

"Father," I said, my voice nearly as loud as his and my temper as short, "calm down and tell me what has you so upset."

"Sally!" he said, his tone indicating clearly that I should have known that—by prescience, I suppose. "That fool she married is taking her to court."

I had only once in my life fainted, in childbirth, but for just a moment there the world seemed to grow fuzzy, and I felt the need to grope quickly for the back of a chair to steady myself. "To court?" I echoed dumbly.

"Never trusted him," Father said, "never thought he had the sense he was born with. But now he's accusing her of . . . of . . ." He could not bring himself to say it.

"Of affairs with other men?" I asked.

"Yes, by damn," he thundered, "among them my good friend Senator Linn, who is no longer on this earth to defend himself."

"Oh, good heaven," was all I could say. Francis Thomas was now governor of Maryland, surely a man of responsibility and judgment. Still, to accuse Senator Linn. . . . Father's good friend and ally in Congress had died while John was on his second expedition. I knew that the senator's reputation was not one of loyalty to his wife—a great, fat woman who ate bonbons constantly and laced herself too tightly, leading to a great indisposition of the spirit. She had accused almost every young woman in Washington of having a flirtation with her husband, and I had often wondered that I myself had escaped such accusation. Sally had been but one among two dozen named by the spiteful Mrs. Linn.

When I ventured that thought to Father, he growled, "It makes no difference. That jealous husband of hers has chosen to make a case of it."

Sally and her father, James McDowell, arrived at our house the next day, he in high anger and she in tears. Her father had gone to Maryland to fetch her home to Virginia, but they had come instead to Washington for Father's counsel. They got, along with his support, his anger.

"The family," he thundered, "will not stand for this. Sally's reputation is above reproach, and there will be no problem proving that the man is a fool . . . a damned fool!"

Cousin James seemed somewhat relieved, and the two men went off for a brandy, leaving me with Sally, who had changed a great deal from the young bride I remembered. Then she had been bright and full of the promise of the future; now there was a great sadness in her eyes and a drawn tightness to her mouth. It was a change that I had not discerned in her letters, in spite of her hints.

"I cannot believe it," she sobbed. "I cannot believe that Francis would do such a thing."

"Did you . . . did you not suspect," I asked delicately, "that his judgment was . . . well, impaired?"

She stopped sobbing long enough to give a wry laugh. "Impaired? Jessie, how tactful you are! That wonderful man I married turned into a mean-spirited, suspicious being who watched every move I made . . . and I made none wrong, I assure you. But this . . . to make a public scandal."

"I am quite sure, Sally, that you gave him no cause," I told her. I remembered that tall, thin, nervous man in ill-fitting clothes whose blank expression and hooded eyes had made me uncomfortable.

Sally and her father stayed with us a fortnight, mostly, I think, to gain courage from our support. In some ways their visit had the opposite effect, for when they returned to Virginia, Francis Thomas began to accuse Father of corrupting his wife by persuading her against him. Father and Cousin James had decided, however, that nothing would clear Sally's reputation except a lawsuit, and they determined to bring that.

We had contrived in every way possible to keep Sally's predicament from Mother. "It would upset her unnecessarily," Father insisted over and over, and so we had told her that Sally and Cousin James were merely visiting on a pleasure trip. To my consternation, when Sally bid her good-bye, Mother said, "It will all come out all right, my dear. That husband of yours is no good. I told him so the other day when he came to call."

Sally looked alarmed, but I knew that Mother was once again mixing reality and the strange fantasy of her mind. What always puzzled me was how accurate she sometimes was about reality.

From then on, until the case was finally settled in her favor in March, I wrote to Sally frequently, hoping to keep her spirits up, and found in her replies that she was bright and determined not to be beaten down. Still, it was an awful thing for a woman to be accused of infidelity, and she bore a stigma.

"I cannot walk out to do ordinary shopping," she wrote, "without people staring and whispering."

I, who could not walk out those days without notice, knew what she felt—only when I walked out, people oohed and aahed because I was married to the famous explorer, not because I was an unfaithful woman. I could not imagine how Sally must have felt . . . but, then, I would not have chosen the husband she did. Maybe, in the end, our lives depended on the choices we made.

In November, Father and Liza and I testified in Sally's behalf. The courtroom was packed, and we were all nervous, but I remember saying in a clear voice that I had always thought Francis Thomas a queer man. The spectators giggled when I quoted Aunt Jasmine about "a trifling poor fellow," and the judge pounded his gavel for order.

In spite of the fact that we were all convincing and that other friends and neighbors testified to the strength of Sally's character, the judge postponed his decision, and we experienced that dissatisfaction that comes from an issue left unresolved.

"It's awful to have such disgrace in our family," Liza moaned.

"Don't worry," I said. "Maybe Mr. Jones will never know you come from a family of sinners."

"Jessie!" she said angrily. "That was not what I was thinking."

But I knew better. Father, lost in his own thoughts, ignored both of us.

The strain of the trial showed on me, and when it was over, I took to my bed for two days with a severe headache. Poor Lily stood at my bedside, asking softly, "Mama sick?" until I realized that I could be following in my own mother's footsteps—or lack of them—and rose from my bed.

"Mama," Lily said, "you have a funny red spot on your face."

I looked in the mirror and saw that my own King George's mark—that red spot at the corner of my mouth—had returned. I would not tell John of it in my letter to him.

President Polk notified Father that he was sending an emissary to California—"It's a secret mission, Jessie," Father said solemnly, repeating an involved story about how this young man, Archibald Gillespie, would travel in disguise through Mexico into California.

"What is his purpose?" I asked.

Father shook his head. "Polk won't say, even to me. But he did say that Gillespie expects to meet John and that we might send a packet of letters if we wished."

I flew on wings of happiness to the library, where I spent several hours penning a long letter. "My darling," I wrote, "it is with joy that I write a letter to be sent by courier—a much more reliable means of delivery than we have had up till now. I know it will be months before you read these lines, but still, knowing they will be carried to you by hand makes you seem so much closer to me." I did not tell Father that I had included in my letter secret references that warned John to be ready for military action. I wanted to write, "Seize the moment, my darling!" but that seemed too blatant, given the strong possibility that my letter could fall into the wrong hands.

Just before the holidays the crisis with Mexico seemed to lift a bit. The government there agreed to entertain an envoy, and President Polk prepared to send off one John Slidell, empowered to offer $5 million for New Mexico, $25 million for California north to the Monterrey area, and another $20 million if the purchase could include land north to San Francisco.

My own spirits soared accordingly. If the United States could buy California—I cared not a fig for New Mexico or even Texas at that point, though I never told Father—John might well become the first governor, by virtue of being in the right place at the right time. And, of course, because he was a hero. Another heady thought, but one I judged it best not to put into writing in my letters to him. Instead I repeated our motto: *Le bon temps viendra.* I knew those good times were indeed coming!

This spirit of optimism carried me through the holidays, which we survived in good stead. Mother did not have any more of her "episodes," and Lily was enchanting with her conviction about Santa Claus and her delight in the modest presents she received—a doll, an orange, and, from Father, a toy soldier that would, he told her, remind her of her own father. She gave him a long look and said clearly, "I remember my father." The very words had a distant sound—as though he were a stranger she vaguely remembered—and I swore that John must spend more time with her.

—◆—

Liza married William Carey Jones in March of 1846. The ceremony was small, owing to Mother's poor health, but it was in our parlor, with President Polk, George Bancroft, James Buchanan, and several other government notables in attendance. Though he and Father were at odds over Mexico, President Polk escorted the bride to the supper table, a great honor for the entire family. Lily carried a basket of rose petals, sent from the hothouses in Virginia at dear cost. That, I thought, was the prettiest thing about the wedding. But I was prejudiced, of course, and I did have to admit that Liza looked lovely in white *peau de soie*. William, in proper tails and gray trousers, looked nothing but ashen and nervous. Afterward there was champagne and a roast-duck dinner and much celebration.

Even Mother managed the festivities well, except for the time she demanded loudly, "What did you say his name was, Jessie? Carrie? Isn't that a woman's name?" I managed to hush her before either the bride or groom heard this impertinence.

At the end of the day—a long one, by anyone's standards—I sank into the comfortable chair in Father's library. "Very different from my own wedding," I mused.

He looked sharply at me. "That was your choice," he said. But then he softened his tone. "No regrets, I trust? Even with your bridegroom a continent away?"

"No regrets," I said firmly. "When I look at Liza . . . or poor Sally . . . I realize what a good choice I made." Liza had, after all, married an unemployed lawyer, while my husband was off seeking glory.

Father grinned. "Modesty, your mother would remind you, modesty. Perhaps Mr. Frémont also made a good choice."

"That he did, of course," I said, rising to kiss the top of his head on my way to bed.

All the hopeful signs about relations between the United States and Mexico had dwindled to nothing by March. The Mexican government refused with finality to receive Slidell as an emissary, and anger at our country ran so high in Mexico that, against Father's opposition, troops were sent to the Rio Grande under the command of Zachary Taylor.

Though I was greatly disturbed by this turn of events, it would have paled to nothing had I but known that even then John and his little band had set themselves against the Mexican government in California, staking out their rebellion for three days on a small elevation called Hawk's Peak in the Galiban Mountains above the Santa Clara Valley and the Salinas plain. Innocently, I still believed that John would be home in May or June, and I waited in happy—well, impatient—anticipation. The second expedition, with its string of false arrival dates, had apparently taught me nothing.

Instead of holding my husband in my arms come May, I read disturbing and frightening news of him in a Mexican newspaper brought to me without comment by James Buchanan when he brought more papers for translation. The newspaper reported on the incident at Galiban, though I was sure it distorted the facts. John had been ordered out of California by Don Jose Castro, the commanding general in California, who had previously welcomed him and offered protection. Instead of leaving John had taken his men to Hawk's Peak and prepared to stand off an attack.

"Stand off an attack!" I exclaimed, but the imperturbable Mr. Buchanan merely shrugged, and Father said only, "We must avoid hostilities."

It appeared to me that it was too late to "avoid hostilities" and that John was already in danger—though the incident was some two months behind by the time I read of it. The Mexicans charged that John was in contact with Thomas Larkin, the American consul at Monterrey, and therefore taking orders from the American government. "He wasn't," Father said, "and that must be understood. Polk expects to buy California peaceably."

Meantime, the Mexicans cheered over their great victory when John retreated after three days.

"Retreated?" I demanded, and Mr. Buchanan solemnly handed me a packet of diplomatic dispatches from Mr. Larkin, in which Larkin successfully persuaded John that American honor was not at stake and that retreat was the prudent course of action. Over that great distance I shared John's frustration as he bowed to the order that war was to be avoided. If John could have conquered California and brought it into the Union with unsuspected swiftness—why, the world would be his! It would be the most important acquisition for our country since the Louisiana Purchase.

I was, of course, comforted to know that John was safe—or had been at the latest dispatch—but it occurred to me that had he been in similar peril during the second expedition, I would never have known. He could literally have fallen off the face of the earth, and I would simply never have heard any more of him. Now that he was a national hero, I was kept more apprised of his movements. Though it caused me some worry, I much preferred the hero's status.

Perhaps because of Galiban—who knows?—John was advanced to lieutenant colonel. I knew of it but had no idea when he himself would hear of the promotion. He would value it less for the honor, I thought, than for the recognition, the proof that an unknown from Charleston who had never attended West Point could rise in the army. With a twist of fear I began to see John as less explorer than soldier.

Anticlimactically, I received a letter from John. Though it was May when it finally reached my hands, the letter had been written in January, well before Galiban. It merely confirmed what we already knew—John was, or had been, in California. He was, he wrote, anxious to be home. The expedition, he said, had been harder than he had expected and, among other things, his hair had turned gray. He would travel north to the Willamette Valley, looking for a better wagon route to Oregon, but then he and his men would turn their horses homeward. "*Le bon temps viendra*," he wrote. By now I knew that those good times would not come in May or in June, and I began to pin my hopes on September.

Try as I might, I could not picture my handsome husband with gray hair. His daguerreotype, sent by his mother, hung over my bed—I called it my guardian angel—and after reading his letter I spent a long time staring at the likeness, trying to superimpose gray hair. But my vision was always riveted to the flag hanging next to it—the one John had brought me from his first trip to California and spread over me in bed just after Lily was born.

"Father," I said one evening as we sat alone in the library, "I think that the newspapers should be told about Galiban. The country deserves to know that John took a stand against the Mexican government."

"No, Jessie," Father said with a determination that startled me.

"We're trying to settle this peaceably, and we can't show public praise for open rebellion . . . even if it was John who rebelled."

"But," I persisted doggedly, "the public should know that he is a hero."

"They already know that," he said wryly. "And you've been telling anyone who will listen. Patience, Jessie! John has done great and good things for his country, and he will be duly recognized and honored. But don't you, as his wife, try to rush things."

I seethed, though whether from impatience or from what I perceived as a reprimand, I wasn't sure. I suspected, though, that Father had in a much more subtle way told me a variation of what Mother babbled in her disorientation: I should be content to be a wife and mother and let John attain glory on his own, without my help.

Never! I vowed. *John and I were an equal partnership.*

When John's action was made public, to great acclaim, neither Father nor I spoke of it to each other. But there was a gulf between us, the first since my marriage to John had almost split the family asunder. This time Father and I both knew the importance of what was at stake, and we treated each other courteously.

In the meantime Mexican troops crossed the Rio Grande, ambushed an American patrol, and killed sixteen men. Cries for war echoed everywhere, and President Polk sought Father's support, though Father was deeply troubled.

"It's not Texas," he told me, "it's Mexican soil. We are the invaders . . . much as I grieve for those sixteen men and their families." When the president himself was unable to convince Father of the rightness of war—how, I wondered, could war ever be right?—he called for help, first from Mr. Buchanan, who had previously believed that California should be urged to declare itself independent, as Texas had done, and then join the Union. Now Buchanan favored war, but he was unable to convince Father, and neither could Mr. Bancroft. Finally Father's old friend Francis Blair came up from Virginia and talked to him in terms of his political career. "If you lose your seat over this, Tom," he warned, "you lose your chance to work for the causes important to you."

And, I added silently to myself, *you lose your chance to support John.*

Finally Father capitulated, though he never overcame his reluctance. Congress declared war on Mexico, and Taylor's troops were rapidly victorious at the battles of Palo Alto and Resaca de la Palma. Father became once again a close confidant of the president, and it was at his suggestion that Mr. Polk sent General Stephen Kearny, an old friend of our family, west to Bent's Fort as the head of what became known as the Army of the West.

Things balance out sometimes. With all United States energy seemingly focused on Mexico, England reached terms with Polk's government, and the territories of

Washington, Oregon, and Idaho became part of the United States, with the forty-ninth parallel as boundary. Manifest destiny had won on one front, but there remained the vexing problem of California. To me it mattered not, except as it involved John.

Shortly after I heard of the standoff at Galiban, another opportunity presented itself to send a letter to John—by courier this time, on the person of a trader named James Magoffin, who was headed for Bent's Fort. In haste I wrote a lengthy letter about my pride in all that he had done—specifically Galiban and the promotion in rank. "Your merit has advanced you in eight years from an unknown second lieutenant to the most talked of and admired lieutenant colonel in the army," I wrote, telling him of the officers who had called at C Street to congratulate him. I hoped desperately that by the time Magoffin reached the fort—August or September—John would soon be there on his way home, but intuitively I knew that John would still be in California and still in danger. I clung to my vision of a triumphal return to Washington.

"Lily," I wrote in closing, "has your report read to her every night in bits, and she is very proud of her father." I didn't add that Lily was uncertain about why her father was away so long.

"My grandfather is here," she had said, as though that solved the need for a father.

◆━━◆

By September we knew that California had been peacefully taken over by American troops in the summer. They had entered Monterrey, raised the flag, and put in place a constitutional government. My heart raced when I first heard that news, for I was sure John expected to be named the first territorial governor.

But hot on the heels of this good news came disturbing rumors about something called the Bear Flag Revolt, with John at the center. Though the details were vague, we learned that John's men had seized the town of Sonoma and raised their flag, which bore an awkwardly drawn grizzly bear. They took a few of the town's leading citizens prisoner, and John soon found himself head of a growing rebel army. But he was outmaneuvered—Mexico and America went to war, and the American navy raised our flag at Monterrey. Still, I told myself, John was the first!

Father felt compelled to write a lengthy speech in which he claimed that John had acted purely out of self-defense. I too repeated loudly the claim that John must have acted out of self-defense or in revenge for some personal insult—look, after all, how Castro had treated him earlier. "Fighting is not his aim," I wrote to one of his botanist friends, "and I am sure he knew nothing of the war." But even as I wrote, I crossed my fingers in the superstitious way of childhood, for I knew that John's aim was personal only insofar as the conquering of California would bring him glory.

Throughout John's third expedition the strangeness of time lapses bothered me. Though I heard news of him much more quickly than I had before, I always had to interpret them in view of the distance between my husband and me, a distance not only of thousands of miles but months of travel. So when I heard of John in, say, July, I knew it would be December before he could reach home, and when I heard of him in October, still in California, I knew that he would be there until spring, because snow had already closed in the mountains. So by the fall of 1846 it was clear that I was in for another winter without my husband—if he had not crossed the Sierras before the snows, he would effectively be there until spring, and I wanted no repetition of his dangerous crossing of the previous expedition. But the waiting grew harder.

Of that long second winter I prefer not to recall much—the weather was grim, Mother was some better but certainly not well, Father was on edge about California and Mexico, and I was impatient. Lily was the only bright spot in my life—Lily and an occasional letter from John, though I had come to realize that his letters were now deliberately misleading—for fear of spies. When even my husband was not telling me the truth, whatever the reason, the world looked none too bright.

In my darkest moments I began to wonder about California senoritas. They were, so everyone said, of flashing eye and few inhibitions. Could John remain loyal to me—could he go without a woman's attention—for two long years? I remembered his frank admissions about Cecilia, admissions that spoke of his physical needs. How were they now being met? I wanted to believe the protestations of love in his letters, but sometimes as I lay achingly alone in my bed, I could not help but doubt.

My King George's mark appeared and disappeared all winter, and Lily never failed to remark its presence.

Spring, they say, brings new hope, and so it did with me. *Surely John will be home soon*, I thought, as I watched the cherry trees bloom and the trees green out gently.

And then in May, spring brought not John but his good friend and trusted companion, Kit Carson. He was as much a surprise as his visit, for I had always envisioned a tall, lean man, hardened by frontier life, invincible and strong even in appearance. Instead Mathilde one morning admitted a man not much taller than John, sunburned to be sure, but otherwise no different looking from many a man on the streets of the city, save that his suit fit him poorly and he looked uncomfortable.

"Mrs. Frémont?" There was a diffidence about his manner, as though he were uncertain around ladies.

But there was no diffidence about me. "Mr. Carson! Come, you must tell me all about John." And with that I swept him into the dining room. The poor man could more easily have defeated an entire Indian tribe—as he was rumored to have done—than he could have withstood my enthusiasm.

Amid apologies for Father's absence in St. Louis—"I know he will regret not being able to greet you"—coffee was served, and then I demanded everything he knew, though I confidently expected to hear that John was the triumphant governor of California and that only duty had kept him from me.

Instead there came, haltingly and with regret, a tale of official power fights and ultimate disgrace for John. I sat silent, my knuckles white, my face grim, as I listened, and I could almost feel the King George's mark creeping onto the corner of my mouth.

It seemed that when General Kearny reached California, he assumed command, though Commodore Stockton of the navy was already in command. John, having originally been ordered to report to Stockton, continued to do so, though trying to be courteous and conciliatory to Kearny. Both John and Stockton felt that Kearny had essentially arrived after the action, after the conquest was complete. Indeed Stockton appointed John governor of California on January 6, but Kearny rescinded the order less than a month later. Eventually orders were received putting Kearny in charge, but he, for some unknown reason, failed to share these orders with John. He made demands—of paperwork and men—without justifying them, and John refused, believing he was acting according to the orders he had been given.

"Kearny has promised to bring John back in chains, Mrs. Frémont," Kit told me miserably. "He's even been heard to threaten him with execution."

I gasped in horror, though the thought of execution was so remote to my mind that I could not even grasp it. But John, who was to return in triumph, coming home in chains! Silently I cursed Father for being in St. Louis when I needed him.

"Mrs. Frémont. Are you all right?"

I shook my head and managed to murmur, "Give me a moment to collect myself, Mr. Carson. I've had a terrible shock, as you can imagine."

"Yes, ma'am."

After a moment my brain stopped whirling, and I knew that once again I had to take matters into my own hands, just as I had when John's expedition had been threatened over that silly howitzer. "We must go to the president," I said.

Carson looked alarmed, then looked quickly down at his rumpled suit. "Me? Go to the president of the United States?"

"Yes," I said firmly, "we will go together."

And so we did, the very next morning. President Polk looked startled to find me in his waiting room, and his visible alarm increased when I explained that Mr. Carson felt impelled to tell him of the situation in California. He acquiesced, but not gracefully, an ostentatious glance at his watch telling us that our time was limited.

I watched the president closely as Carson told him the story, again speaking haltingly and slowly. None of it surprised Mr. Polk. He knew all along! With great difficulty I controlled my anger, my fists clenched so tightly that the nails dug into the palms of my hands.

The most Mr. Polk said was that he hoped the difficulties between the various parties could be resolved without court-martial.

Court-martial, indeed!

———

I fled to St. Louis as soon as Mr. Carson was gone, leaving Mother behind in Mathilde's care, with only the barest of explanations to the few close friends who would miss me. This was news that I could share with no one.

"Jessie, Jessie, they cannot court-martial a man for following orders," Father said. "Calm yourself."

But I could see that he was worried, and even Lily seemed to grow pale and listless under the tension with which we lived. Rumors swirled about us as summer progressed—John was under arrest, John was staying in California, Governor Kearny had conceded his mistakes, Governor Kearny had arrested Commodore Stockton. Each rumor set me afire with renewed fear, and sometimes I would wake in the night, crying out after a bad dream.

Each time Father would be instantly at my bedside, stroking my hair, calming me, reassuring me. We were caught in a vicious cycle—I worried over John, Father worried over me as I grew more pale and thin, and Lily was desperately frightened by things she did not understand.

Then, finally, there was news. "Jessie?" Father's voice was gentle as he approached the chair where I had positioned myself on the veranda to catch any breeze that might stir. "There's word, Jessie."

I leaped to my feet. "What is it?"

He shook his head. "It's not good. John will indeed be placed under arrest. This time it is certain. His troop is traveling with Kearny, and they're expected upriver at Kaw's Landing within the week."

"Then I will go there," I said.

"Jessie, a woman can't travel alone by steamboat. It's . . . no, I cannot permit it." He shook his head. "And I cannot go with you. I have too much here and . . . it's best I not get into the midst of it yet."

I looked sharply at him.

"No, no. I will certainly defend John to the utmost, but it is in his interest right now that I not rush to meet him. You, too, must wait."

But there was no stopping me, and finally Father acquiesced. Hardly aware of the journey and its discomfort, I found myself in the huddle of shacks that was Kaw's

Landing. There I waited four days, alone in a dirty and uncomfortable room, until word spread that John's troop was in sight.

Kearny's troops had arrived the day before, and I had stood silently to one side as they rode by, Kearny himself in the lead, looking angry and determined. I made no move, for I did not wish him to know of my presence. Word was that he had ordered John and his men to keep "a good distance" between them.

Now, though, with John expected, I ran to the street and was in the front of a small line of spectators. I held my breath as they approached, John in the lead. Gone was any thought of triumphal homecoming. This was a man who had been beaten. He was tired, haggard, and though he was thoroughly tanned by the wind and sun, there was a paleness about him. Still he sat erect on his horse, and he issued a firm command to his men to stay in formation until they had passed through the cluster of buildings.

When he was still several hundred yards way, I could wait no longer. "John!"

For just a moment he looked as though he thought he was hearing voices, perhaps having a hallucination. And then he saw me. A quick command, and his men came to a halt. He was off his horse, arms spread wide, running toward me.

As we met in a wild and furious embrace, a great cheer went up from his men.

Chapter Nine

I asked John nothing as we stood by the rail on that long steamboat trip back down the Missouri. John's men knew our need for each other, and after their first hearty greetings, they left us a great circle of privacy. Clutching each other, we watched the muddy water swirl by—that river, with its dark and swift waters was nothing like the quiet blue Potomac—and said little for the first hours, though John would every once in a while turn to stare at me as though to fathom my thoughts. I knew enough not to smile brightly at him—a response he would have at once recognized as artificial—but I tried to hide my fears and show him, through touch and glance, how grateful I was to be with him again. And I tried not to let him know how his gauntness, his sagging posture, his appearance, worried me. He exuded a determined self-control and a kind of endurance, but I saw in his eyes that this demeanor hid a great sadness. What could have happened to the self-confident man I sent off on his third expedition?

His hair had, as he'd written, turned gray. The outer, I decided, reflected the inner—John had aged. Still, I found his new gray locks distinguished, even attractive. More than once I raised a hand to run through his hair, only to drop it quickly as I remembered our lack of absolute privacy.

Gradually, bits of the story began to come out, though I doubted I would ever hear it in its entirety, from beginning to end. The march home, most recent and most humiliating, was foremost in his thoughts.

"All my work, Jessie, all the botanical specimens and the equipment . . . everything important about this trip was left behind. No doubt it's been trashed by now." His tone was bitter—justifiably so, I thought.

"Why ever?" I asked, almost unable to grasp the enormity of this loss. The third report? How would it be written?

He read my mind. "There will be no third report, Jessie. Kearny said it was a military expedition all along, and the equipment was camouflage."

"He can't," I cried indignantly.

John hugged me tighter to him and said resignedly, "He can, my darling, he can. At least I'm free of him for now."

Most of John's volunteers, refusing to serve under Kearny, had been discharged without pay and abandoned in California. Only a pitifully few men had returned with him, and they had, as rumor had told it, been forced to stay well to the rear of Kearny's troops. Once Kearny had even ordered John's men to move their encampment—they were too close, he claimed.

"Was he afraid of you?" I asked.

John looked grim. "He had good reason. There was no sentiment for his life among my men, though I'd never have let them put their words into action."

When I asked about Basil Lajeunesse—having missed him among the men who greeted me—I struck a nerve so raw that John shuddered and turned from me. At length he said simply, "Dead."

"Dead?" I echoed.

"Killed by the Klamath Indians in Oregon, over a year ago now. My God, the time that has passed."

I asked no more about Lajeunesse, but I grieved for the burly man who had been my friend and John's protector.

We watched as the sun sank over the western horizon, though night brought no coolness to the sticky August heat on the river. John showed no inclination to go to the makeshift quarters that had been prepared for me, and I would have bitten off my tongue before I told him how tired I was from standing all day.

"Kearny called me to his tent at Leavenworth," he said. "Read me a formal statement saying I was to consider myself under arrest and proceed to Washington. At least he didn't feel forced to take me there under guard."

"He wouldn't dare," I said. "Father would . . ."

"Jessie," John interrupted me, "your father will defend me, I know that, and I am grateful. But the truth is that I am right, and truth will out. Kearny will be disgraced and I'll be proved right, I swear it."

I clutched his arm all the tighter, convinced to the core by his words and thrilled by his conviction.

We fell into silence again, until I broke it, saying, "Tell me about California."

Wearily, he shook his head. "It's ours," he said. "The British didn't get it, and no matter what Kearny thinks or says, I had something to do with that. And the Californians, they are my friends. They said to me, '*Viva usted seguro, duenna usted seguro.*'"

"Live safe, sleep safe?" I asked.

"Yes. Something that is said only to friends. I brought California to this country in peace and friendship," he said, "and right now that's all that matters."

There was much more I wanted to know, a whole two years' worth of his life to be caught up with, but it would be days, even weeks, before I knew the truth about

Galiban and the Bear Flag Revolt, before I understood the Capitulation of Couenga, before all the spaces and gaps were filled in.

That night, just before I drifted to sleep, John said, "Jessie? I forgot what may be the worst of it. I gave Thomas Larkin three thousand dollars to buy me a tract of land in the hills behind San Francisco. I thought you and I could live looking at the sea . . . a man is always at peace, Jessie, when he can watch the sea."

I knew that was a belief bred into him during a childhood in Charleston. "I would like that," I said, feeling no need to add that I was at peace watching the great Mississippi River. A childhood in St. Louis had done that for me.

"But Larkin somehow bought a wild piece of land up in the mountains, a hundred miles from the sea," he said. "Las Mariposas . . . The Butterflies . . . it's useless. Indians all around . . . a man couldn't live there or raise cattle without getting both himself and the cattle butchered."

Indignantly I sat up. "What will you do?"

"I'll get my money back," he said, "but I'll have to get the rest of this settled first."

I went to sleep twisting that pleasant name over and over on my tongue . . . Las Mariposas . . . The Butterflies.

In St. Louis I expected Father to be at the docks to greet us, offering his support for John. He was nowhere to be seen, but to our amazement a good-sized crowd of well-wishers waited there. Someone blew a bugle, everyone shouted such slogans as "Three Cheers for Frémont" or "California!" and there came a chorus of "Speech, speech!" Perplexed, John looked at me, but I could only shrug. For once in my twenty-three years I was innocent of conniving. I had nothing to do with this reception.

Finally, at the crowd's insistence, John spoke briefly, thanking them for their support. To the shouted questions of "What really happened?" and "Will you stand court-martial?" he merely nodded and said he could not discuss such matters. Again he thanked the crowd and began to shoulder me through the mass of people.

When at last we were settled at home—only to find that Father, in high dudgeon, had departed for Washington, leaving a message that we should come as quickly as we could—John asked, "Jessie? How did these people know?"

"I knows," said Mathilde, still holding Lily in her arms as the child eyed John suspiciously. "The senator, he told me, that general—what's his name? Kearny? He made too much noise all over town about how you'd disobeyed him and he was going to court-martial you. The people know better . . . they know you made California free."

John blushed, and I thought to myself that Kearny had made an enormous mistake. I was more optimistic than ever about John's future, court-martial be damned, as Father would have said.

We stopped barely long enough to gather Lily and Mathilde and to pack the few bags necessary. Lily, still uncertain about the stranger in the midst of her comfortable world, clung to me as we boarded another steamboat for the trip south to New Orleans, but John made valiant efforts to entice her. In those poetic tones he could muster only when he thought his words were not for posterity, he told her about the bumblebee that had landed on his knee as he crossed the Continental Divide.

"I know," she told him solemnly. "Mama read it to me from your lepote."

He turned quickly to me, but I mouthed the word "report" and he understood.

"I am glad she read that to you," he said solemnly. "I want my favorite girl to know what I have done."

Both your girls, I added under my breath.

After that Lily was more at ease with John, though she never quite seemed to adore him as she did her grandfather.

We found that grandfather in his library furiously scribbling on foolscap when we entered the house on C Street. "I've been to see the president," he said. "They've already started a campaign of defamation. We've got to act fast." He was so frantic that I feared he might burst a blood vessel.

"Father," I said, "it will be all right. John is going to be proved right."

He looked almost pityingly at me. "Not without a lot of help, he isn't," he said. "They've banded together against us. You need to read what Lieutenant W. H. Emory has been posting about in the eastern papers."

"Who has banded together?" I asked in confusion. "Who's Emory?"

"Kearny's aide-de-camp," John supplied. "He hates me too." Emory's account, it seemed to me when I read it, was typical of regular army officers who looked down on explorers and others not trained at West Point. It was, according to John, inaccurate and, according to me, inflammatory, but I wasn't as aroused as Father. "What did you say to the president?" I asked.

"He said he understood there had been 'some difficulty among the officers,'" Father said, his tone mocking, "and that he hoped it would not come to court-martial"—just what Polk had said to me when I took Kit Carson to him, I thought— "but I told him I'd demand a full Senate investigation of the entire affair."

I took a deep breath. "A Senate investigation? Even when the court-martial isn't called yet?"

"Can't let them think they've got the upper hand," Father said, and I looked at John, who had turned decidedly pale. "We will have vengeance," Father swore.

The court-martial was called for November, and Father soon enlisted the help of Liza's new husband, William Carey Jones.

"He's an unemployed lawyer," I exploded to John, who silenced me with a finger to my lips.

"He's a lawyer," he said, "and your father has confidence in him. I have confidence in my own case. The trial will be my third report." Fuming, I realized that matters were out of my hands. I had dreamed of writing the third report, but now the men had taken over. We had been in Washington a long time, or so it seemed to me, before John ever turned to me in the night. When we were first together after his return, I attributed his distance to fatigue and worry. He would kiss me ever so gently, as though I might disintegrate in his arms, and then turn his back to sleep. At first I understood, but as the days passed, celibacy began to wear on me. It was not only physical. Somehow I translated his distance into something more specific than a lack of appetite. I saw it as a personal rejection.

A time or two I reached a tentative hand out to him in the night, touching him in ways that I knew had always aroused him. Wordlessly, he would take my hand gently in his own, touch it to his lips, and then place it firmly on my own chest. My frustration grew.

No woman of my generation would discuss such a matter with her husband. It was unthinkable . . . and for all I knew, it was unheard of that a husband ignored his wife in this way. Who would I have asked? Certainly neither of my parents. Liza flitted through my mind, but my pride was too great. I could, I supposed, have asked Sally McDowell if she were nearby—I suspected she would have had worse stories to tell about Francis Thomas—but she was in Virginia, and I would not commit my problem to paper.

When I could consider John objectively, or at least in some degree so, I realized that he was a man in the process of a slow recovery. During the day I could see it in his expression, his bearing, his very response when spoken to. But it was difficult for me to translate that into our intimate relationship.

He had been home four weeks before he ever made love to me. I had dozed off one night when I felt his hand creep under my nightdress, up along my thigh, then across my stomach, raising goose bumps as it went and sending a shiver through my soul. I lay very still, fearful that if I moved he would withdraw. But his hand continued its progress, and soon the other hand joined it. As I turned toward him, his mouth met mine in a long, searching kiss, as though he were asking if I could still love him in disgrace.

With every bit of pent-up passion in me, I tried that night to convince him of the depth of my love, of its independence from his status with the United States

Army or government. When at last we lay spent next to each other, he whispered, "Ah, Jessie, I have missed you so."

"And I, you," I replied, whispering into his chest where my face lay buried. "I . . . I was worried. . . ."

"Don't say it," he begged, "don't talk about it. I know, I know." After that we were once again passionate lovers. And sometime during that interlude our second child was conceived, though it was November—and a desperate time—before I realized that I was *enceinte*.

—◆—

A few weeks before the court-martial was to begin, John received word that his mother was seriously ill. As he prepared to leave immediately for South Carolina, it struck me with renewed force that I had never met his mother—we had enjoyed a cordial correspondence in the last few years, and she had sent me the daguerreotype that hung over my bed. But I had never met the woman about whom I had much curiosity. I knew only that she, a widow, pinned all her hopes on her only son, and it seemed to me there was no doubt that her current collapse was precipitated by news of his arrest.

When I offered—almost insisted—that I should accompany him, John said merely that this was a trip he must make alone. I was left with the feeling that he was, one last time, protecting the woman whose passions had brought disgrace on herself and who had passed that disgrace on to her only son.

"Can you be gone with the trial so close upon us?" I asked anxiously.

"I have no choice," he said, and would brook no further talk about the matter.

To my horror John arrived in Aiken, South Carolina—where his mother summered—just hours after her death—too late to hug her one more time, to assure her of his well-being and to tell her for the last time of his love of her. Knowing of her love for her son from our correspondence, I was terribly saddened at the thought of her dying alone, with John only hours away. I thought of my own mother, so surrounded by love in her illness, and the comparison made me weep.

While John was away, word was published that General Kearny would be sent immediately to fight against Mexico, taking with him two of his top officers, who had been heavily involved in his negotiations with John. To my mind it was clear that these men, just back from duty and deserving of a rest, were being hustled away before the court-martial . . . or else the court-martial would be delayed, which neither John nor I could tolerate. Yet if Kearny were not there, all the evidence would come from dry and distant military reports—the conflict of personalities, the emotional aspect, would be missing, and this case hinged on personalities more than anything.

Once more I took John's fate into my hands. "Dear Mr. President," I wrote, "I ask of you that Mr. Frémont be permitted to make his accusers stand the trial as well as himself. Do not suppose, Sir, that I lightly interfere in a matter properly belonging to men, but in the absence of Mr. Frémont I attend to his affairs at his request."

It must have occurred to me that Father could have made this request rather than me, for I never told him about the letter. Nor did I tell John later. But General Kearny was at the trial. I was not sure whether to take credit for that or not, and so I mentioned it to no one.

I expected John's newly returned self-confidence to be undermined by his mother's death. To my surprise—and concern—he seemed unaffected when he returned. He did not wish to talk about her death or his journey with her coffin from Aiken back to Charleston for burial. He was so matter-of-fact and so seemingly unaffected by what surely was one of life's major moments of grief—the death of one's mother—that I was somewhat alarmed.

"A certain stage of my life, long since over with, is now completely gone," he told me unemotionally; while I prayed silently that Lily might never feel so detached from me.

"I have," John continued, "requested a speedy court-martial. I do not wish this thing to drag out all winter and take us down. And I wish the details of what I did in California made public."

"But the report?" I stammered. "If you would write a report, they would become known. I know it would sell better than the others." This was true, for everywhere John went these days he was met with cheers and congratulations. Everyone knew of his quarrel with Kearny—and no one sided with the general.

"Jessie, Jessie," he said patiently, folding his arms around me, "I know this is hard for you to believe, but I am a subordinate now, not a commanding officer. I wasn't in charge of my own expedition any longer—regardless of whether it was Stockton or Kearny I should have reported to—and as such I cannot write a report. I told you before: the trial will be my report."

I could not help turning away to hide the tears in my eyes. I had so counted on turning the brilliant conquest of California into yet another masterpiece, as we had done with the first two expeditions. "Someday," I promised in a whisper, "someday we will write that story."

He tilted my chin up and planted a firm kiss on my mouth. "If you say so, Jessie, I have no doubt of it."

Father had been busy during John's absence in South Carolina, campaigning for John's acquittal, trying, with a desperation that almost frightened me, to sway public opinion. It was as though Father didn't realize that the public was already cheering for John and totally uninterested in Kearny, who appeared lackluster and boring next to the famous Lieutenant Colonel Frémont.

I knew that Father was trying, in his own none-too-subtle way, to put pressure on the president, though he rarely talked of it, and Mr. Polk remained circumspect in his public statements, wishing simply that the matter could be solved.

Afterward I thought it was Randolph who turned everything sour; Randolph, my uncontrollable, drunken, nineteen-year-old brother, newly returned from Virginia.

"Jessie? You best come to the library and talk with me." Father had that terribly solemn look that I had seen only a few times in my life, on such occasions as Mother's illnesses.

"Yes, Father?" There was alarm in my voice, and I was grateful that John was out for the evening, conferring with friends. "Randolph," he said, drawing a deep breath, "has been to see the president."

"To see the president?" I echoed, my voice rising with amazement. "Whatever for?"

"To tell him," Father said dryly, "that he wants to fight in the war with Mexico. And to bully the president into giving him an appointment as an officer."

I was speechless, fluttering my hands in anxiety, wondering what could come next. The idea of Randolph fighting anyone's war—save maybe his own for survival—was ridiculous. Finally I managed to ask weakly, "What happened?"

"It seems he barged into the president's outer office—literally barged, Jessie— and told him he wanted a commission in the army.

"The president, rightly so, told him such things usually went by seniority and experience."

I held my breath. "And?"

"And Randolph was, and I quote: 'rude and impudent.' Some say there was alcohol on his breath." Father bowed his head and looked for all the world like a beaten man.

I rose and went to his side, putting my arm around his shoulders, but there was not a thing in the world I could say to comfort him. I could not lightly brush the episode away, for we both knew it was too serious—and too typical of Randolph's behavior in the last year or two. The only comforting words I could think of were, "At least you have John as a son," but that would have been cold comfort to a man whose only son was such a terrible disappointment.

"I just hope," Father said, "that Randolph has not soured the president on the whole Benton family."

Those words would haunt me later.

"I'm sure the president understood," I said as calmly as I could.

"I'm afraid," Father said, "that what he understood is that the Bentons and their relatives are a pack of trouble. Just when we're trying to make John look good, first there was Sally McDowell's scandalous divorce, and now Randolph takes his drunkenness public. . . . I fear for it, Jessie, I really do."

I could not bear to see Father, usually so full of belligerent optimism, depressed and fearful. It scared me, for if Father faltered, what would happen to the rest of us?

When John came in that night, I never mentioned Randolph's transgression.

The trial began in November. By the opening day Father, John, and I had spent hours and hours preparing the defense, seeking precedents in British law, tracking down this rumor and that, verifying a calendar of events that had taken place a continent away from us. Liza's husband, William, joined John's defense team, while I was the secretary and copyist, writing document after document as the three men dictated. In a court-martial the entire proceeding is conducted in writing, which was a boon in that it gave the defendant—John, in this case—time for consideration before cross-examination. But the burden of the copying fell on me, and I found it irksome.

It seemed to me that John's case was clear and righteous and that a court-martial could do nothing but exonerate him and censure those who had charged him. I prepared with confidence that was, I told myself, fully independent of my love for my husband. I would have believed in him if he had been a stranger . . . or so I thought.

"John, are you ready?"

He turned the corner from the bedroom and stood before me in the hall, looking splendid, crisp, and dignified in his army uniform. "Ah," I said, "you could melt a girl's heart."

"I'm glad," he replied, almost abstractly. Then, with a sudden directness, "Are you going to a funeral?"

Lightly, I laughed. "Well, almost so, I suppose."

"I mean it, Jessie. You are dressed for a funeral. I want you to look happy, not as though you were in mourning."

I looked down at the black bombazine dress I wore. "I thought . . . not to look frivolous."

He burst into laughter. "Believe me, Jessie, you don't look frivolous. You look, as a matter of fact, as though you were about to bury your husband."

Torn between joining him in laughter and drawing myself up in indignation, I hardly knew how to respond. "You don't . . . you don't like my dress?"

He kissed the tip of my nose. "Had you been with me in South Carolina, it would have been perfectly appropriate, my darling. But, please, wear something brighter . . . to cheer me on through this long day."

I ran to the bedroom, where I literally tore the bombazine off—I never wore it again, I recall—and chose a deep-green taffeta moire that complemented my eyes—well, anyway, John said it did. On my head I wore a black felt with green and brown pheasant feathers.

John seemed to approve, for he held his arm out for me proudly. And that was how we walked into the courtroom, heads high, me on his arm, and Father, looking disheveled and carrying an armload of papers, trailing behind us.

All of Washington, it seemed to me, had turned out for the court-martial. Oh, of course President Polk was not there—it would not have been seemly for him to attend. But Mr. Buchanan was there, and I suspected he would carry every word back to the president nightly, and George Bancroft was there, though I knew from the beginning he would turn traitor to John. When he greeted me, my acknowledgment was cool, so cool that John later twitted me about it and suggested I'd best keep my personal emotions in better control. "Those who think they are winning can always afford to be gracious," he said, "and those who think they might lose had damn well better be gracious, so they look like winners."

I was beginning to see that appearance was much, if not all, to John.

General Kearny had a coterie of officers about him, including Lieutenants Emory and Cooke, who had both written falsehoods about John. In spite of all John's words about graciousness, I refused to look Kearny in the eye or to acknowledge the slight bow he directed my way as we walked in. Old family friend, my foot! He had turned into the worst kind of an enemy.

But John had his supporters in the crowd, mostly men who had been with him on the trip to California: there was his scout, Alexander Godey, and his aide, Dick Owens, and the trapper Thomas Williams. Missing on John's side was Archibald Gillespie, the lieutenant who had met with John in the wilds of Oregon on a secret mission. Kearny had managed to detain Gillespie by official order in California, but we had recently had word that he was on his way east, and we held our breath for his arrival.

Since Congress was about to take up its session, many legislators were in Washington, and apparently lacking anything better to do, they attended the opening session of the court-martial, undoubtedly because it had attracted such publicity. I nodded to this one and that, and it struck me as more than passing strange that so many men whom I had known all my life had now come to sit in judgment on the man I married, whether or not their judgment would have any influence on the outcome of the military court-martial.

I managed to greet them all civilly and to avoid any passing conversation, except when it came to Stephen Douglas of Illinois. The "little giant," as they called him, stopped me just when John had been called aside by someone else.

"Jessie," he said earnestly, "you must do something about your father."

"Pardon me?" I said. I knew my voice reflected the cool distance such a statement aroused.

"Your father," he repeated. "If he had not made of this such a challenge, there would have been no court-martial. It could have been settled behind the scenes. But he forced the president's hand with his excess of zeal."

What if it was Father and not Randolph who had jeopardized the entire family with the president? What if even my letter requesting—almost demanding—that Kearny not be sent to Mexico had contributed to Polk's feelings about us? No, it was a thought not to be borne.

"Senator Douglas," I replied firmly, "I do not know what you can possibly mean. This court-martial is essential to clear my husband's name. We welcome it." Well, that was a white lie, but not too bad.

He shrugged his shoulders as though to indicate he gave up, and I walked swiftly away. I would never, I vowed, tell either John or Father about that particular encounter.

The opening of the court-martial was full of ceremonial formalities that left me wanting to cry out, "Let's get to the business of things." Thirteen career officers sat as judge and jury on John's fate, and the proceedings began with a formal reading of the charges—John was accused of mutiny, disobedience of a superior officer, and conduct prejudicial to the good of the order and of military discipline. Mutiny! Even though I also knew the nature of the charges in advance, I stifled a gasp of horror, for I well knew that the punishment for mutiny could be execution. Even though that punishment had not been used in recent years, the very possibility struck cold terror into me.

I looked at John, but he sat immovable as the charges were read, head high, eyes fixed directly on the officer in charge. When he rose to respond, his voice seemed to ring through the air: "I plead not guilty." Then, almost deliberately, he turned toward me—as though he had sensed my fear—and, outrageously, he winked. The entire courtroom must have seen him, I thought, but there was no ripple of sound in reaction. Right at that moment I felt comforted. John and Father were both right—the court-martial would be his vindication.

Sometimes, listening to those ponderous army officials making their way through tedious and insignificant details, I felt that I would burst, that I would no longer be able to contain my pent-up emotions and I would scream aloud. But at those moments I would look at John, and his confidence would once again anchor me in the world of reality.

As the trial unfolded, what I had always known became clear, so crystal clear that I could not believe there was a person in the country who did not understand it. John was being tried for acts that grew out of his appointment as governor by Commodore Stockton. Doing what he perceived as his duty, he had become caught between two warring officers—Stockton of the navy, who originally had responsibility for the territory of California, and General Kearny, who had taken responsibility in December of 1846 when he arrived overland with his troops from Santa Fe. John, having been ordered to report to Stockton, had considered it his duty to continue to do so until given further orders. Kearny, who had taken charge, considered it military treason and insubordination that John had not reported to him and followed his orders. The crux of the matter, as far as I in my muddleheaded simplicity could see it, was that Kearny had received orders from Washington placing him in charge, but he had failed—deliberately?—to show those orders to John. Therefore John had continued to take his orders from Stockton. To me it was clear-cut—the fault lay with Kearny and not with John. Certainly, at least, the trial should be of Stockton and Kearny, not an officer subordinate to both of them and caught between them.

But that basic issue of command fanned out into a thousand smaller issues—the letters between Kearny and John, a disastrous meeting between the two after John had ridden a night and a day to "help" General Kearny. A new phrase crept into my vocabulary during the trial—the "Capitulation of Couenga," an agreement that John, in his temporary status as civilian governor, had made with the native Californians. From John's point of view it was a conciliatory arrangement, which left the Californians some of their pride and all of their property; according to Kearny it was a lax and ineffective document, which he at once countermanded.

I remembered the words, "Live safe, sleep safe." General Kearny might never have that comfort in California.

The trial dragged us wearily toward Christmas, with no seeming end in sight. Every day the four of us—John, Father, William, and I—went solemnly out the door after breakfast, and every evening we came home exhausted. Court met from ten o'clock until three, and we rushed home only to prepare for the next day, like rats on a treadmill. Many mornings I forced breakfast down, in spite of a queasy stomach, and many evenings I found myself too tired to eat supper, too disheartened and angry to be loving or patient with poor Lily, who was left with Mother, Sophie, and Mathilde for comfort. I was not raising my own child, and I was too numb to care.

As is the way of such military tribunals, the proceedings were often lost in details and the principals—particularly General Kearny and his lackeys, Lieutenant Emory and Lieutenant Philip St. George Cooke, seemed pompous and stern. Cooke, under oath, modified his extravagant charges against John considerably, and I learned for the first time that John had nearly fought a duel with a Colonel Mason, who had specified double-barreled shotguns loaded with buckshot, instead of the usual weapons. I cringed at the thought and was grateful that Colonel Mason had claimed military orders prevented him from giving John satisfaction.

During the prosecution's testimony Kearny testified that John had come to him with a bargain: "Make me governor of California, and I'll report to you instead of Stockton." The words were no more out of Kearny's mouth than I stiffened in horror and leaned forward as though I would reach across to the defense table and restrain John. Even Father looked confounded, as though he could not believe such a charge would be made.

John stiffened noticeably, and a great red spread up his neck and across his face. But he remained seated, fists clenched on the arm of his chair, the knuckles as white as his face was red. When Father first tried to talk to him, John sat staring ahead as though deaf and oblivious to Father's whispers, though they were loud enough that I could hear them in the gallery without discerning the sense. After a minute John turned to Father and they conferred in whispers, though I sensed that John suggested Father lower his voice even further.

During his defense John said with terrible deliberation, "I have never bargained for an office in my life, and I never will." Each word rang out clearly in the courtroom, and General Kearny looked at the floor. Father suggested to John that indeed General Kearny may have offered such a bargain himself, only to be turned down because John had been named governor by Stockton. Fortunately, John never made that speculation public, and Father, not being an officer of the military, was forbidden to speak to the court. John conducted his own defense.

The newspapers ran riot with the controversy, with headlines that read "Frémont Accuses Kearny" and "Did Kearny Offer a Bargain?" Clearly public opinion was on John's side—he was still hailed as the Conqueror of California, the Lewis and Clark of our day—but public opinion stopped at the door of the courtroom.

John did, however, accuse General Kearny of seeking the glory of conquering California, even though it had already been conquered when he arrived there. The courtroom gasped, Kearny harrumphed, and the judge advocate reminded John that the general was not on trial. Ah, but he was, I thought silently.

Commodore Stockton testified for the defense, but he was a weak witness, unsure of himself and waffling on the truth as John had told it to me. He, who had seemed John's brightest hope, was his greatest disappointment. At the end of two days, which Stockton spent justifying his own conduct, the court cut his testimony short. He had never mentioned John.

"Kearny has struck a deal with Stockton," John said late one evening as we sat in the library.

Pen poised to copy something for him, I stopped and stared. "How do you know?"

He shrugged. "It's to the advantage of each. If they can patch up their differences, Stockton is back in the good graces of the military, and Kearny has taken away my one strong weapon."

"Why," I demanded, "is General Kearny so determined to ruin you? It's . . . it's a personal vendetta."

"I beat him to California," John said.

"So did Stockton."

"Not as publicly, my darling, not as publicly. He drew no attention . . . and he still doesn't. I do."

Christmas came and went once again without much celebration on our parts—only the small tree for Lily and a roast dinner that I picked at. I thought back to the past few Christmases, all equally glum because John had been away on expeditions. Next year, I vowed, we would have a festive holiday.

On a bitter cold day in late January, John presented a fiery summation of his defense, pointing out the importance of his scientific experiments, the bloodless nature of his military conquests, the good of his civic administration. "I could return to California, after this trial is over, without rank or guards, and without molestation from the people, except to be importuned for the money which the government owes them."

He would, I knew by those words, go back to California, with or without the army.

Father spent all of John's summation—it was almost as lengthy as some of Father's own speeches—staring at Kearny in a way that would have frightened the devil himself. Finally Kearny could stand it no longer.

"Stop it, Senator! Stop making faces at me and trying to intimidate me by staring at me from under those beetle brows of yours!"

"I'll stare at you till your eyes fall on the floor!" thundered Father just before the gavel pounded and order was demanded.

❦

The verdict was guilty on all three charges. John, standing to face the court, never flinched, but I had to grasp the rail in front of me to keep from swaying.

"You are dismissed from the service, Colonel Frémont, but because of the record of your service, this court recommends your case to the leniency of the president."

John bowed his head just a fraction of an inch in acknowledgment.

How we got out of the building, past the clamoring reporters, into a carriage, and finally to our own front door, I do not know. Questions were hurled at John: "What will you do now?" "What do you think the president will do?" "Do you have any comment?" "Will you return to California?"

John took my elbow, bowed his head as though he would use it as a battering ram if necessary, and shouldered me through the crowd without answering a one of their questions. Indeed, he might as well have been deaf.

At last, inside the house, we gathered in the library, where Father poured brandy, even offering me a small glass. In a gesture totally unlike him, he downed his brandy in one gulp and flung the glass against the marble side panel of the fireplace.

"Damn fools!" he said. "The poor, pitiful damn fools! They have made an enemy of Thomas Benton, that's for sure. I'll . . . I'll . . ." All the air seemed to leak out of him, and he collapsed weakly into a chair. "I guess we'll have to wait and see what Polk does."

John rose and went over to put his hand on Father's shoulder. "You have been loyal and steadfast, and I am more grateful than you know. But you must not jeopardize your career for my sake, my good friend."

Father patted his hand absently. "We'll see what happens."

That night in the privacy of our bedroom, I waited for John to display some emotion—anger, frustration, disappointment, anything but the deadly calm that had not yet left him. Knowing him, loving him, I was terribly aware of the inner anguish that he hid beneath a calm exterior. John Charles Frémont, the child who had endured taunts of "bastard" and the adult who had fought his way to a military career without the benefit of West Point, would not take public humiliation and disgrace without deep and lasting inner wounds.

Wearing my gown, I sat at the dressing table to brush my hair and watched him in the mirror.

He stood at the window, looking out into the night, though I knew he saw nothing of interest. "What do you see?" I asked idly.

"California," he said, "and a home by the sea."

"Will you go back there?" I knew the answer already.

"Of course," he said simply, "and so will you."

Finally I could stand it no longer. "What do you think the president will do?" I asked, and then went on boldly, "I think that he was as much as directed to pardon you."

John turned toward me. "It doesn't matter," he said. "I shall resign from the army, no matter what Polk does."

President Polk could have pardoned John, but he didn't. Who knows how much of a part Father or I or even Randolph played in that decision? For whatever reason the president chose to dismiss the conviction on the charge of mutiny, but to uphold the lesser two charges, and then to commute the sentence. John was ordered to "resume his sword and report for duty."

I had told no one, not even Father, that John would resign, but I harbored no hope that he would change his mind. I did not write the letter of resignation, though I wrote everything for John. This one document he wrote in his own hand. I suspect he had it written well before the president's decision was announced.

John's letter said simply that he was innocent and to accept the president's clemency would amount to a confession of guilt. Therefore, he resigned.

Mr. Buchanan—supposedly at the president's request, tried vainly to dissuade John from his resignation, but John, with Father's support, remained firm. He was flattered by other offers—the presidency of a railroad between Cincinnati and Charleston, a faculty position at his own school, Charleston College—but his eyes now remained firmly fixed on California.

Father was stunned, first by the conviction and then by the resignation, and he was angry. He immediately began to plan a campaign to examine the legality of the court-martial. "And I'll fight them tooth and nail on this Mexico business," he vowed. "If James Polk thinks he'll see me in that White House again during his term, he's a bigger fool than I thought."

Rumors swirled through Washington that Father would meet General Kearny in a duel, and though I knew it was but the rumormongering of small minds looking for excitement, I was strangely disturbed by Father's behavior throughout the trial and his rambunctious anger afterward. A suspicion lived in the back of my mind— and occasionally crept forward to confront me—that if Father had held back, the whole affair might have been settled differently, with less damage to John. Father was used to bullying through whatever cause he championed, and he'd entered this fray with no doubt that his power and influence would save John. That they did not amounted to his first major political failure, a stunning blow for him, I was sure, but also one for the daughter who had worshiped his every move. I wished he would stop charging about like the proverbial bull in a china shop.

Besides, all of Father's ranting and raving changed nothing. Still not thirty-five—at least I didn't think he was—John had a brilliant career in the army, but he was now adrift. What, I wondered, would he do? What would we all do? And what of the infant who now clung to life inside me?

The city of Charleston presented John with an inscribed sword that had been purchased by the citizens by subscription, each who cared to, pledging a dollar toward it. John was immensely pleased at this show of confidence from his hometown, where he had once felt so disgraced; but even as he bragged to me of the honor, I knew the difference, to him, between public sympathy and private grief.

"Jessie, the Congress wants several maps and botanical reports from the last expedition. It won't be a report, but . . . well, we must get to it."

"Let them be damned," I said vehemently. "Why should you prepare anything for them after the shabby way you've been treated?"

He eyed me coolly, as though reprimanding me for my outburst. "Jessie," he said patiently, "I am a private citizen with no income. They will pay me for the work."

I was mollified enough to mutter "Oh," but it was two days before we began to work, and even then my anger and frustration raged beneath what I hoped was a calm surface.

Preuss worked on the maps, while John dictated the botanical reports to me. Perhaps it was my disposition at the time and perhaps it was the nature of the material, but the report, as I wrote, lacked all the fire and drama of the previous reports, and I grew increasingly weary as we worked.

One day we worked late into the dark of evening. My head was pounding, and the candle seemed to flicker and grow dim before me. The last I remember was John calling my name in a frantic tone.

"Jessie! Jessie . . ."

CHAPTER TEN

"How long have I been here?" I asked, dimly aware that I was lying in my own bed, in a darkened bedchamber.

"Three weeks, Jessie." John sat by the bed and reached a tender hand to brush the hair from my forehead.

"I . . . I haven't been . . . I knew you were here, John, but . . ." Talking demanded a great effort.

"You have drifted in and out," he said. "I've been here almost the whole time."

"I remember . . ." My words were halting. "I remember the candle. . . . It seemed to grow dimmer and dimmer."

"You fainted, Jessie, three weeks ago, as we worked on the memoir."

"The report!" I tried to sit up, but his insistent hands pushed me back against the pillow. It came back to me in a rush—the botanical reports we had been working on for the Congress. With our precarious circumstances it was important that the documents be supplied promptly.

"I've finished the cursed thing. It's just a geographical account of what I saw. Nothing as grand as what we produced before. It's gone off to Congress." There was that air of disappointment about him as he spoke, almost a nostalgia for the glory of the first two reports.

My heart broke a little, but I was too tired to care deeply. I couldn't have written a lengthy memoir had Congress given us the chance—my body would simply have not responded to my mind. "Will there be another expedition?"

"We don't know yet, Jessie. I doubt it myself, but we'll see." Much as I understood his desire to be gone, I could not bear to think of parting with John again, at least not until my strength returned.

My hand wandered to my belly and found it rounded and swollen. "The baby?"

"The doctor says it will be fine if you continue to rest. You must not fret, Jessie."

How could I not fret? I wondered, as I looked at my husband. He wore civilian clothes, and his beard was closely trimmed—a new look for a new person. But the old look of sadness was in his eyes, and I knew that he too had yet to recover from the court-martial. My collapse may have been more dramatic, but his, simply of a different nature, was probably the more severe.

"Lily?"

"She is fine," he said with a slight smile, "and asking for her mama. Shall I bring her in?"

Lily, now five, entered hesitantly, clutching tightly to her grandpa's finger. He pushed her ahead a little, and she came to stand by the bedside and reach one tentative hand out to grasp mine.

"Mama? You are all right." It was a statement, not a question, though the worried look on her face robbed the words of the positive force she meant for them to have.

"I'm fine, Lily. But I've missed you."

"Papa said you were sick . . . and Grandpa said I must be good and quiet all the time."

Poor child, I thought, having to be good and quiet all the time.

"You did a fine job of it," I told her, "and now you may run and play."

Saying she was glad I was better, she turned and walked out of the room with dignity. "Run and play" were not in the child's vocabulary nor in her nature.

❦

Benton Frémont was born on July 24, 1848. I had hardly been up yet from my fainting sickness when the baby's imminent arrival put me again into that bedchamber, and I felt, unhappily, quite the invalid. Dr. Thurston, who had been Mother's physician for several years now, attended me through what seemed an easy confinement and a relatively short labor.

The minute I heard the baby's first cry, my heart clutched in fear. It was a weak sound, like a kitten mewing for milk rather than the healthy cry of a newborn infant. When Dr. Thurston said heartily, "Here's your son," and laid the baby in my arms, the child was limp.

I remembered a dog we had when I was a child—she had six puppies and one of them disappeared one day. When I wailed to Father about the missing puppy, he said, not without kindness, "It was a limp puppy, Jessie. The mother knew it would not live."

"What did she do with it?" I demanded.

He shrugged. "Probably buried it somewhere."

Was I supposed to bury this child? With a fierceness that surprised me, I hugged the infant to my bosom, willing him to live.

When John came to see us, I still held my new child fast against my chest. "Is he . . . is he all right?" John asked hesitantly.

"He's fine," I replied, "just fine." But I could see by John's face that Dr. Thurston had already told him different.

It was John who suggested we name the child Benton, "to symbolize the unity of the two families." Father beamed with pride at the idea and went off proudly to tell Mother, who hadn't the foggiest notion what he was talking about.

In spite of my fervent wishes and the close attention of Sophie, the nursemaid, little Benton did not thrive. He seemed always hungry yet nursed haltingly and would give up, whether from satiation or fatigue, after the briefest of spells. We tried sugar tits—with a drop of brandy—and we tried oatmeal so thinned with mother's milk that it ran out his little mouth and all down his clothes. Sophie had heard that tea was good for infants, but I forbade her trying it. Benton grew no worse, but he grew no stronger or better.

In August, Kit Carson came again to Washington. He brought government dispatches to the president from California—I thought it a delicious irony that he was now a trusted courier even though General Kearny, during the court-martial, had denied ever seeing him. "And didn't he turn me back from Taos to California, insisting I guide him for months on end?" Carson said wonderingly. No matter, Carson had not been court-martialed and now he was a hero, while John was in disgrace.

John asked his trusted friend to stand as godfather to little Benton, and Carson declared himself honored. The service was held in the Episcopal Church, and Carson held the infant while the priest spoke the holy words. Afterward, as he handed the baby back to me, Carson looked at me solemnly and said, "I fear he won't make it, Mrs. Frémont. This baby is not healthy."

I turned quickly away, hiding my pain, and within a few minutes I was able to block out the fact that he had ever spoken those words to me. I didn't want to hear the truth about Benton.

———

"You can't, Miss Jessie, you can't take that baby off into the wilds. He has a hard enough time of it here at home." Mathilde stood with her hands on her hips, her eyes flashing real anger at me. Behind her stood Sophie, looking concerned but not quite as bold as Mathilde.

"Mathilde, I do what I must. Right now it is important for us to be together as a family, and I am going to accompany Mr. Frémont to Kaw's Landing. The baby must go with me so that I may nurse him."

She turned away muttering about the foolishness of some folk, but as I had with Carson, I turned a deaf ear to her warnings.

John was about to embark on his fourth expedition, though this time it was not funded by the government. Just weeks after Benton was born, the Senate refused to fund a new expedition. He bore this rebuff with the same stoic calm that had carried him all through the court-martial.

"It's better, Jessie," he said. "I'll seek private funding and not be beholden to the government, which, as far as I can tell, has no intention of paying its debts. I'd rather be funded by people who stand by their word."

John was still legally responsible for thousands of dollars of debt incurred in the service of the government while he was in California, but as yet those debts had not been paid.

We spent days talking about this new expedition, and always the talk came back to the railroad.

"It's what we must have, Jessie. I feel as strongly about a transcontinental railroad as your father does about westward expansion. Can't you see what it would mean to be able to go from one coast to the other by train?"

Holding little Benton and coaxing him to suck on a sugar tit, I smiled up at John and told him I could. "But the Senate has voted against funding." To me the whole thing seemed to have run into a blank wall.

"The railroads," John exploded, scaring the infant into a crying spell, "the railroads are more interested in a pass through the Rockies than the government will ever have the sense to be. They'll fund my expedition."

And that's just what happened. John secured private funding for a fourth expedition to find a pass through the Rockies. He planned to leave in the fall, deliberately timing his departure so that the worst of winter would find him in the mountains. "A pass," he said, "is no good if it is not passable during the winter."

I knew that this was no temporary trip to California. John intended to stay there—had he not already told me that Thomas Larkin had purchased land for him, and had he not arranged for a sawmill to be shipped around the Horn? "John, the children. . . ."

Exuberantly, he pulled me to my feet, took the baby gently from me and set him in his crib, then spun me about the room at a dizzying pace. "The children," he said, mimicking my voice, "could not stand a trip across country." Then, dropping to his own dear voice, "And neither, my dear Jessie, could you. You will come by steamer around the Horn."

"By steamer?" My first thought was one of terror as I imagined myself with two children going so far from all I loved and held dear. And yet, if John were at the end of my journey . . .

"Yes, my darling, by steamer. It's a perfectly safe journey these days, and any captain would be honored to have Senator Benton's daughter—and my wife—as his passenger. You can leave in the early spring, when the storms will have died down around the Horn." Then his expression became positively triumphant. "We will have our home by the sea, Jessie, we will have it!"

"Yes, my darling," I said, "we will." I began to let myself dream a little, envisioning, I confess, the proverbial rose-covered cottage, only mine was on a great cliff and commanded a royal view of the ocean. And in that dream John came home for supper every night, and he slept in my bed every night. Suddenly my sense of chronology caught me up short.

"If you leave in August or September . . . to leave Kaw's Landing in October . . . how long will we be apart?"

He laughed aloud. "Not long, Jessie, not long. You're so familiar with Kaw's Landing now, you can bring the children and go that far with me."

And that, in spite of Mathilde's warnings, is just what I did. We took Sophie with us, though she, too, disapproved of taking Benton on this long journey. She was, blessedly, still not as vocal about her feelings as Mathilde. And Benton seemed as content as he could ever be in her care.

In September we took a steamboat—the *Saratoga*—westward toward Buffalo on the first leg of our journey. We traveled as any other family on that steamer, save that people kept recognizing John and coming forward to express their indignation at his conviction, their admiration for his explorations, their wishes for our happy future. John regained some of his old confidence from all this attention and treated each newcomer graciously, explaining that we were going to California as poor ranchers, hoping to be able to make a living and contribute to the new territory.

We reached St. Louis at the end of September, and the early days of October found us on the steamboat *Martha*, headed up the Missouri. John had put together an expedition of thirty-three men, with sufficient horses and pack animals, and was anxious to be off, though he tried to hide his impatience around me.

"The baby?" he asked. "Does he seem to be thriving?"

I shook my head and looked toward Sophie, who sat patiently rocking Benton. "No, he is a little worse yesterday and today. He is . . . limp." I had begun to hate the very word.

John frowned. "Lily?"

"She is delighted with all she sees," I replied with a smile, "and runs about the boat telling everyone who her father is."

That pleased him, so I never told the truth: Lily told everyone she wished she were back home with her grandfather, who was her best friend.

In the middle of the night Sophie pounded frantically on our cabin door. "Mrs. Frémont, Mrs. Frémont, you got to come quick. The baby . . . he's not breathing good."

Whether it was her tone or my own intuition, I knew that I was about to lose Benton. Yet I had the feeling that if I could just make it to him in time, I could will him to live—as I had been doing ever since his summer birth. "John!" I called over my shoulder. "Come! I need you."

"Wha—what's the matter?" He rose foggily from a deep sleep.

"Benton!"

He was still breathing when I ran into the adjoining cabin and scooped him from the large drawer that served as his crib, but it was a labored, difficult breathing, each gasp seemingly a great effort for the tiny body.

"The ship's surgeon," I demanded. "Get him at once."

But before that man arrived—in disheveled nightdress and looking as bleary as though he'd taken a draught too many—little Benton suddenly went totally limp in my arms, limp in a new way from that which I'd hated but grown accustomed to.

Fiercely, I held him to my chest, breathing deeply as though the movement of my chest would inspire life into his. Lily cowered in her bed, watching from under the covers, and Sophie stood silently by, her head bowed.

John and the doctor arrived at the same time, but it was the doctor who said, "He's gone, Mrs. Frémont. I . . . I am terribly sorry."

I only clutched him the tighter.

"Here," the doctor said, "let me take him for you."

At that I stood up, the baby in my arms, and turned my back on the doctor.

"Jessie! For God's sake, the child is . . ."

"Don't you say it, John Frémont, don't you ever say it!" John knew the meaning of my words without asking—if we had not accompanied him on this fool's errand of a journey, Benton would be alive and well in Washington. In my grief I was perfectly willing to overlook the fact that he had never been well in Washington either.

Lily began to sob quietly, and John, one wary eye on me, went to comfort her as best he could. The doctor, after another halfhearted attempt, bowed himself out of the room, with many expressions of sympathy. Only Sophie stood perfectly quiet, never trying to approach me.

I stayed that way the whole night, clutching my baby to me, crooning softly to him. Suddenly, at daybreak, I began to cry as I'd never done in my life. Great wrenching sobs racked my body, and tears flooded down my face, soaking my clothes and those of the baby I held.

Without a word Sophie came and took the infant from me. I relinquished him, without ever realizing that the tiny body had grown cold and a little stiff. John and Lily watched me warily, as people watch a crazed person, but I merely walked out of the room and returned to my own cot. John followed me.

"His body will have to be returned to St. Louis for burial," I said. And then—my crying over, though my grieving not yet begun—I went fast asleep.

John and I never talked of the child's death again on that trip, but I was filled with a great sadness as I watched John and his men make their final preparations at Kaw's Landing. The Indian agent, a Major Cummins, had with gracious hospitality given us quarters in his log house, but during the days Lily and I preferred to be in camp with John and his men. John rigged a tent for us under a tall cottonwood tree, and from there I watched the preparations, dreading with all my soul the day that preparations would be final and they would leave.

The day came in mid-October, and I, ever my father's daughter, rose to the occasion, bidding John a cheerful farewell and waving brightly to the men who had become my fast friends in the week or more we'd been together. Holding hands, Lily and I watched them ride west, and then, forlornly, we returned to the log house. The trees were bare, and winter was in the air. I shuddered with foreboding and wished John had left in August.

I had trouble sleeping that night. Major Cummins had been troubled by a wolf killing his sheep, but he had discovered the wolf's den and killed all its pups. That night the mother came looking for her young ones, and unable to find them, she howled in misery. As though echoing her grief, the wind seemed a shrieking voice as it tore around the flimsy cabin. Those eerie sounds, full of pain and rage and grief, echoed my own misery, and I was nearly driven to go outside to join the wild beast. Instead I lay rigid in my bed, too anguished even to know what would bring me relief.

I thought I had dozed off and was dreaming of wolves, for a great huge beast seemed to be approaching me, as though to smother me. This was no wolf! It was John, come for one last visit. His beard, newly regrown and therefore prickly, scratched my face as he kissed me hard and long. And then, before I had really roused from my half-sleep state, he was in the bed with me, and in a quick few movements our clothes were gone, and the strength of his body was pressed against mine.

His passion was not gentle that evening. His hands were firm, his movements insistent, and I rose to meet him each time, carried away by the power that I felt coming from him. Later I would wonder if his intensity came from the anticipated time apart or was somehow tied to the need to prove himself, a need I prayed this expedition would meet. Or did he want to leave me pregnant, as compensation for little Benton's death? But none of those thoughts were in my mind, as passion, at once painful and pleasant, carried us beyond the confines of that rude log cabin.

When once I cried out in pleasure, he clapped a hand over my mouth and laughingly whispered, "The major will come to rescue you."

"No," I panted, "I don't want him to."

And then we were at it again. Carried away by John's needs and my own, I made no comparisons between this and other leave-takings. Later I would realize the difference: always before we had lain like boards next to each other, I anticipating the agony of parting, and John probably thinking ahead to the fame and glory the expedition would bring him. Never before, as this time, had he been desperate. Now, disgraced and a soldier no more, this expedition was his chance, his only chance, to prove himself. And the desperation of that challenge somehow bred a fierce passion. Perhaps I responded because my own desperation for him was as great.

Daybreak found us sitting decorously in Major Cummins's kitchen, sipping coffee which that good man had risen and made.

"I heard you stirring around," he said apologetically, "and thought you might want a bit of coffee before John has to gallop off."

And how much stirring did you hear? I wanted to ask. I think I only blushed.

His coffee gulped down, a quick and distant kiss planted on my forehead, and John was gone. He looked full of life, alive for all adventures that might come his way, and I, exhausted from the night's activities, marveled at his stamina. "They'll have broken camp and begun to move," he said as I walked outside with him. "I'll have to ride hard to catch them." Then he was mounted and gone, calling over his shoulder, "Give my love to Lily."

"I will," I said to myself, for he was long out of earshot, even if I had yelled. *And I won't,* I thought, *tell Lily that you came back and never even came to her bedside.* But, then, if he had spent a minute with Lily, it would have been one minute less spent in my bed, and I was uncertain I wanted to make that trade.

Lily and I returned to St. Louis to the dismal task of seeing poor little Benton buried in the family plot. I was anxious to be gone and did what little packing was required as quickly as I could.

One morning a knock at the door surprised me. I had not thought any but my relatives knew that I was in the city. "Yes?" I said, opening the door.

A young black boy stood there, dressed as a house servant. "Mrs. Frémont? I brung you a message from General Kearny."

I stiffened as I heard that name. "Yes, what is the message?"

He held forth an envelope. "I'm to wait for yo' answer, ma'am." I ripped open the envelope and read, written in Kearny's own hand, a plea that I come to see him. He was sick—dying, probably—and wanted to make peace with his enemies, particularly, he wrote, "the Benton family, who have meant so much to me in years past."

Quickly I grabbed a sheet of foolscap and a pen, while the young boy waited.

"I cannot come," I wrote. "A tiny grave stands between us, and there is no forgiveness in my heart."

I gave the message to the boy, and he, having no idea of its contents, went happily on his way. Afterward I was bothered with fits of guilt—should I have gone to a dying man? But then Lily's presence made me realize again how precious children were, and how much Kearny had to do with Benton's weak entrance into the world and early departure from it. No, I had made the right decision.

General Kearny died shortly after Lily and I left St. Louis.

⁓

Once Lily and I were back in Washington, with my intention to follow John to California clearly announced, I was subject to all kinds of campaigns to keep me from what some called "this bit of folly" and one journalist—I was never sure who—referred to as "Frémont's latest bit of self-centeredness."

Not that I didn't have doubts. I was twenty-three years old, a sheltered young woman more used to being with my family than most. I had read with marvel and disbelief of women leaving all they loved behind to follow their husbands west. How, I wondered, could they go so far, knowing they would never see their mothers and fathers again, never bicker with their sisters and brothers, never set foot in the houses where they had been raised? I was too anchored to the house on C Street and the people who lived there. But I put all that firmly behind me in my determination to start anew with my husband, who was, to my view, a lonely and proud figure who had no one else in the world, save me. And, of course, Lily.

"It is a cruel and selfish experiment on his part," Mr. Buchanan exploded one evening, "to expect you to travel clear around the Horn to join him."

"It will be an easier journey than having gone overland with my husband," I said, mustering all my strength in order to sound tranquil.

"Your place," he said firmly, "is to stay here, raise your child, help your father, and wait for . . . for your husband to return."

I knew he had wanted to add adjectives to the noun "your husband" but had at the last minute thought better of it. "That's just the point, Mr. Buchanan. John will not be returning. We are going to make our home in California."

He threw up his hands in disgust. "I give up, Tom. You talk to her."

Father smiled only slightly. "I have tried," he said, shaking his head. "Her mother needs her. . . . I need her, and she should not set off on a dangerous trip by herself, let alone take Lily with her. But I have made no progress in telling her all these things."

"My mother," I said, "has many others to care for her. My husband has none. And Lily and I will be perfectly safe." I wished I believed it with as much assurance as I said it.

Just before I left Washington I received a letter from John, written at Bent's Fort in November. "The snows are early and deep this year," he wrote, "but I am confident we can find the South Pass, and I am anxious to be off on our adventure."

Damn his adventures! I thought. Had he learned nothing about deep snow from his disastrous passage over the Sierras? Why would he now tempt the fates by crossing the Rockies in a bad winter? Even as I ranted—silently, of course, to myself, alone in the privacy of my chambers—I knew the answer. John Charles Frémont had to do what no other men could do. And, yes, he had learned from the Sierras—he had learned how to survive and, having once done it, had no doubt he could do it again. And there was a practical matter—if he had turned back in November, he would still be at Bent's Fort, and Lily and I would arrive alone in California to survive without his protection for endless months. No, the plan must be followed. I prayed that he was safely in California even as I read the letter.

By March, Lily and I were in New York, prepared to board a mail steamer to Panama. When John left in October, the plan had been for me to take ship around the Horn, but just about then we began to hear rumors of the discovery of gold in California. Within months, as these rumors grew, the government decided to subsidize mail steamers to Panama, from where passengers could make the overland crossing to the Pacific. It was a far shorter trip but one far more rigorous. Still, we decided that was the best way to go.

It seemed to me that New York was overrun with gold seekers. Everywhere—on the streets, in the restaurants, even sometimes sleeping in the lobbies of some poorer hotels—were men who had left their lives behind. I was reminded of the old childhood chant about "Doctor, lawyer, merchant, chief," for they were all there—professional men, farmers, and, I was sure, a thief or two. They talked of gold as passionately as Coronado must once have as he sought the Seven Cities of Gold, and they were as sure of success. Underneath, though, were disturbing rumors—of men dying of disease by the hundreds in Panama and of lawlessness in California, where it was every man for himself.

"I would not let a daughter of mine go off to that there wild place alone," the hotel clerk said to Father, shaking his head at me as though already contemplating my funeral.

Father shrugged and thanked the man for his concern. I saw the worry in his eyes, and it made me only the more anxious to be away. The agony of parting was drawing on too long, and it seemed to me that a clean break would be kinder.

Sophie had positively refused to accompany us on the journey, in spite of Mathilde's threatening orders and our fervent pleas. "Not going off to some wild land among naked savages," she said emphatically, and nothing could change her mind.

So at the last minute Father secured a companion for me, upon the recommendation of a friend in New York. Mrs. Pfeiffer looked to be in her fifties, and they had apparently been fifty hard years. Her face wore a perpetually grim expression, and her eyes were cold as metal. When introduced, she had to make an effort to raise the corners of her mouth in a slight smile. She was dressed all in black, though her gown fitted poorly and her shoes were shabbily in need of shining.

"Father," I said, drawing him into the passageway outside our stateroom in the steamer, "I would rather, much rather, be alone than be accompanied by this woman. She is worse . . . worse than the teachers at Miss English's Seminary."

He smiled a bit at that reference to my youth, but he was firm. "She will protect you," he said.

"I've no doubt of that. Dragons could not get by her," I said. At last the call was given for visitors to leave the steamer, and he hurried down the gangplank. I heard him say to the friend who'd come aboard with him, "It's like leaving her in her grave." Lily and I stood at the rail watching him, me with a cold, hard lump in my throat, and she sobbing uncontrollably. I had no words to comfort her.

As the steamer pulled slowly out into the harbor, I took my first note of those around me. There was not another woman—save the grim Mrs. Pfeiffer—on the boat, but there were men—hundreds of them, it seemed—most dressed as workmen. Red flannel shirts, denim pants, and heavy leather boots seemed the uniform of the day, though here and there one spotted a man in a suit and top hat. I immediately decided they were gamblers, much like those who lived on the riverboats in the middle of the country, there to prey on the hopeful, some of whom would undoubtedly lose all their equipment and what little money they had before they even reached Panama. Men, I decided, were given to folly.

Once out of the harbor, the seas proved rough and the wind high. The captain urged me to retire to my cabin, since it was not safe to walk the decks. With a moment of pity for the men who would be sleeping rolled in blankets on those unsafe decks, I took Lily and went below. The cabin was filled with fruit and flowers, but these tokens from well-wishers just made me all the more sad. Whatever was I doing fleeing from everything and everyone I held dear? And then, of course, I knew—John was more dear than any amount of flowers and fruits, or those who sent them, and I was going to join him. I raised my chin with renewed determination.

Through tears and sobs Lily gulped, "I want Grandfather. He makes me feel safe." And then she collapsed in my arms.

Holding her, I rocked back and forth and spoke as soothingly as I could, telling her how safe we were, how good the captain was to us. But it is hard to be comforting when you don't feel safe yourself. At last I suggested we crawl into our bunk, early though it was, and we lay there together, in our nightclothes, my arms around her, until at last she cried herself to sleep and left me alone with my thoughts.

Sometime later I was still awake when I heard the door open slowly. Some instinct of self-protection made me feign sleep, even when a light shone in my face. Apparently satisfied that I slept soundly, the intruder crossed the room to my trunk and began to paw through its contents.

By the light I could now see that it was Mrs. Pfeiffer, only in one hand she held a wig, which proved to be that iron-gray hair that had added age to her appearance. She was, in truth, light-haired and probably no more than ten years older than I. Lying motionless, I watched through slitted eyes as she helped herself to buttons, jewelry, and a tatted lace collar that was a particular favorite of mine. Finally she left the room.

Instantly I jumped out of bed, locked the door, and began to call for help at the top of my lungs. Mrs. Pfeiffer outside beat on the door, demanding to come in—"I'm here to help you! Let me in!"—but I continued to scream and yell until I heard the captain's voice. Shouting through the door, I explained what happened. Then there were the sounds of running, a scuffle, and the captain returned to tell me that it was perfectly safe for me to open the door.

Through it all Lily cowered under the covers, until I went to comfort her. Then she told me solemnly, "Grandfather should never have hired that woman, but you were brave, Mama."

That gave me great comfort and some small measure of increased self-confidence. Perhaps I really could take care of us on this awful journey; more than that, perhaps Lily now believed in me and regretted the loss of her Grandfather's protection just a little less.

Mrs. Pfeiffer was held in custody the rest of the trip, to be returned to New York on the next boat. She bragged to the captain that she had been masquerading, and that Father's friend had recommended her only in the hopes that getting her away from New York would mend her ways. I, it seemed, had been sacrificed in the experiment.

Once the seas calmed, the captain invited me to walk on the deck, and I found the ocean spellbinding. Somehow, looking out at endless water, I had a sense of how John must have felt as he set out across endless prairies. I experienced—to a lesser degree, to be sure—his stirring sense of exploration. This voyage was my expedition, just as crossing the Rockies was his. That sense of shared adventure roused in me a passion that I could not explain but that made the lonely nights in my bunk seem long and empty. Lily, having overcome her sadness and taken to life on the ship with great happiness, slept peacefully in her own bunk those nights.

Nine days later we neared Chagres, and I saw the tropics for the first time. The whole world was greener than anything I could have imagined. We were to disembark into a tender, so tiny by comparison that it looked a toy boat. Clutching Lily firmly by the hand, I stepped into the tiny vessel and consigned myself to whatever fate awaited me. Lily, by contrast, had not only her spirits back, but her curiosity.

She asked about everything as we proceeded down the river, and so we learned that the bright scarlet flowers and the white ones were passion flowers, and discovered a hundred other plant varieties, which I can no longer name. Tall trees arched over the river and in some spots bent their tops low to the water, and the river banks were matted with creeping flowers of all colors and kinds, so that the effect was of being in a conservatory.

After only eight miles it was decreed that the tender could go no farther because of the shallows. All passengers were to disembark again, this time getting into tiny dugout canoes manned by natives.

Lily clutched my hand tightly at this news, for the natives—few of whom had on much clothing—shouted and waved their boat poles wildly, each trying to attract passengers to his canoe. I had heard rumors—surely they were not true—that these Indians were given to murder if antagonized by their passengers. As I looked fearfully at the scene, wishing desperately for the moment that we were safely back in Washington, the captain of the tender came forward to tell me that the owner of the mail steamers—a Mr. Aspinwall, who also hoped to own the first railroad across the Isthmus of Panama—had offered me the services of the company boat, manned by their own men. I accepted most gratefully.

But even that boat had to be poled along the river, and the currents were stiff in that mountain stream. Sometimes the boat had to pull to shore, and we would all disembark so the crew could hack away at the growth that grew so thickly it blocked passage down the river. The canoes, with the less fortunate passengers, followed in our wake, taking good advantage of the path we made. Still, we managed only a few miles each day, and it took three days to reach Gorgona, where we were to exchange the boat for mules to cross the mountains to Panama.

We traveled in luxury not available to those in the canoes. We spent our nights in clean tents with canvas floors and linen cots, and we ate clean rice and drank tea. At night, fires were burned to keep away troublesome vapors, as well as monkeys and other creatures of the jungle. My less fortunate fellow travelers had to put up with dirty food, filthy huts, and unclean people. I was eternally grateful for the reputation of my father or my husband, whichever had preceded me and entitled me to special treatment. And I had no qualms about accepting that treatment. Still, the mosquitoes could not distinguish between any of us and bit Lily and me as ferociously as the passengers in the canoes, and the sun burned down on all of us equally.

"Mother? Why are there so many tents?" Lily was apprehensive again, and I did not blame her. The hillsides all around us were covered with makeshift tents, and the very earth seemed to swarm with people.

"They're waiting for passage out of Panama, ma'am," the boat captain said. "Some of 'em been here quite a spell, livin' on salt rations and fightin' off the sickness as best they can."

"What sickness?"

"Mostly yellow fever, some cholera, some malaria."

"Why can they not leave Panama?" I asked suspiciously, fear beginning to tug at me.

"No steamers," he said matter-of-factly. "Every one that goes up the coast to California loses its crew. They all jump ship to search for gold, so there's no one to bring the ships back down here for the next load of passengers."

"But I have booked passage!" I said indignantly.

He shook his head sympathetically. "Won't do no good, ma'am. Booked or no, there's no boats goin' to California."

"Mother?"

"Hush, Lily. It will be fine. I'm sure there's some mistake." There was no mistake. The only blessing was that Mr. Aspinwall had also sent word ahead that we were on the boat. Accordingly, we were invited to breakfast with the *alcalde* of Gorgona.

Pulling Lily along behind me, I walked up the hillside, through that tent village, to the *alcalde's* house. On either side of me I saw men with hopelessness written on their faces. Some called out pleasantly, and one or two rudely asked what a fine lady like myself was doing among them. Startled, I realized that I saw only two or three women and almost no children. Like everything else about the gold rush, this was a man's adventure—and in this case, a man's disaster.

"Look, Mother, look at that house."

Before us stood a house mounted on high poles, with a thatched roof and sides woven of mud and sticks. It looked like nothing so much as a giant vegetable crate. "Shh, Lily, we must be polite."

Little did I realize to what test our politeness would be put. When the meal was served, the entree proved to be roasted monkey. It looked like a small child that had been burned to death, and I had to stifle a gasp of horror when it was proudly carried to the table. For a side dish we had iguana. Lily and I both did admirably, taking the requisite three bites for politeness—how many times had the poor child been told that over dishes far more palatable!—and pleading that the tiring journey had robbed us of our appetite.

We left Gorgona with relief, and once safely beyond hearing, Lily and I shared nervous giggles over the meal we had been served. It was good to be able to laugh, and I was most grateful for Lily's company—at six she was young to be considered a companion, but she rose to the challenge with great ease.

There was no road to Panama, only a mule track over the mountains, which had been followed for centuries. On the theory that the shortest distance between two points is a straight line, this track proceeded straight up the highest mountain to the summit, then straight down again on the opposite side. There were no bridges across the streams, so the mules simply gathered their legs under them and jumped—several of our fellow riders got a good soaking this way, and one unfortunate fellow got a broken arm. I cautioned Lily to hold on tightly at all times.

John, I thought, can you see us? Can you imagine what we're experiencing, just so we can all be a family in California? Once, under my breath, I muttered, "It had better indeed be the promised land!"

"What, Mother?"

"Nothing, dear. Hold tight now."

Sometimes the passage between the rocks was so narrow, we were forced into single file. At one such passage, a cow, loaded with trunks and bags, could not proceed straight through—the length of her horns would not allow, but her baggage kept her from twisting to make the passage. Watching her, I thought no one could ever talk to me again about dumb animals, for she simply backed up to the rock wall, rubbed her baggage off her back, and went on, leaving behind smashed trunks and broken luggage. I thanked God that none of it belonged to us.

But there came the moment when we topped the last mountain and there, before me, was spread the mighty Pacific Ocean, the sea about which John talked so incessantly. Once I saw it, I was at one with John again, and I knew that we would have our home by the sea. The hardships of the trip fell away from me, and I was positively enthusiastic.

"Mrs. Frémont," the chief guide said—he was of course an employee of the mail company—"I feared to take you on this trip, feared it was too hard for a lady like you. But you've done right well. I . . . well, ma'am, I want to compliment you on your courage."

I was so moved, I nearly cried when I thanked him. Only the thought that crying would have erased all my courage kept my upper lip stiff.

Panama was even more crowded with Americans than Gorgona had been, and I despaired of finding quarters for us, as it was apparent that we would not be boarding a steamer for California any time soon. Every day boats from New York brought more gold seekers, but no boats left to take them to California. It was as if the small isthmus country would soon be overrun with people. It reminded me, unpleasantly, of pictures one saw of the Middle Ages, where whole cities were overrun with rats.

"Ma'am?" It was the boat captain. "Madame Arcé sends her respects and requests that you and your daughter stay with her."

I did not know who Madame Arcé was except that she seemed a savior sent from heaven. It turned out that her nephew had been an ambassador from Panama, and I had indeed met him, though he was fuzzy in my memory. Nonetheless, we were soon ensconced in luxury, quarters as comfortable as our own back in the house on C Street—what a beloved memory that had become! So far and yet so near! Only this time our luxury had a tropical cast to it—grass hammocks to sleep in, red tiles everywhere throughout the house, and beautiful young women to wait on our every need.

The pet of the household was a yowling monkey, but it frightened poor Lily half to death. I thought she was remembering the roast monkey until she told me that Sophie had taught her that monkeys held the souls of bad people, and had always made her turn her head when they passed an organ grinder with a monkey. One day this pet monkey, having the run of the house on a long chain, sprang at her and wound its tail around her neck, putting its little face right into hers and chattering away, presumably with glee.

Lily took it as anything but glee and began to scream frantically, and for several nights she had nightmares. Still, if that was the worst that would happen to us, we were lucky, for around us the Americans in makeshift tents dropped like flies from the diseases that mosquitoes carried and sometimes from the high humidity itself.

Comfortable or not, we were in Panama for seven long weeks, and I was frantic with worry. Was John equally frantic in California? Had he even made it over the mountains? How would I hear from him? Rumors began to arrive with the weekly mail from New York, rumors that John's expedition had met with disaster. Once I heard that John himself was dead, and another time that he had to have his leg amputated. I lived in daily fear, not knowing if he was alive or dead, whole or broken, yet intuitively believing John would survive anything.

My knowledge of Spanish stood me in good stead during those long weeks, and I blessed Father for insisting that I learn the language. "You must learn the language of our neighbors," he told me long ago, "so that you can talk over the back fence without an interpreter." Always before I had practiced my Spanish by interpreting dull and dry documents, but now I was speaking it daily—and managing to communicate quite nicely. Even Lily began to speak it, after some enforced lessons.

Finally a letter arrived, written in January from Kit Carson's home in Taos. John was indeed alive, although he did not mention his leg, and I knew that if it was gone, he would be too proud to write of it. The party had become lost in blinding snowstorms, unable to find the pass they sought. John blamed the guide he had hired—"a man too old for the job, who had forgotten whatever he knew about the southern Rockies"—and wrote of men lying down to freeze to death, surviving for two weeks on one day's rations, afraid to go forward and unable to turn back. At length the party, divided into two groups for much of the time, reached civilization and were saved. What John didn't mention disturbed me most, for the rumors I heard had included the dread mention of cannibalism. But John, now safely ensconced at Taos with the horror behind him, wrote more of California than the tragedy just behind him. "We shall have our home by the sea," he said, and I wondered that he could put the tragedy of the expedition so easily out of his mind. I could not, and since one always suspects the worst, I carried in my mind a horror too great to mention.

Both Madame Arcé and Lily knew that I was despondent, and the former tried to cheer me with sweet tropical fruits and civilized conversation while the latter held tight to my hand and talked of her grandfather and the house on C Street, as though the familiarity of such things would make me more cheerful. Lily was too young to know that her conversation at that particular time only made me more desperately aware of the awful gamble I had taken by leaving everything familiar behind to journey to a far and distant land.

BOOM! BOOM! The sound of a great gun awoke me, and while I struggled to come to consciousness and make sense of this, I began to hear excited shouts from the street just beyond Madame Arcé's house. At length I realized just what the noise meant, and I threw open the shutters to get a view of the harbor. There was the steamer *Oregon*, long expected from San Francisco. The men in the streets went wild with celebration, and in the midst of it all a second gun boomed. The *Panama* had arrived from around the Horn.

"Lily! Lily! Wake up, child! We're going to California! We're going to meet your father!" All the long months of waiting and fear were as nothing. We were really going to California. For the first time I truly believed I would see John's promised land.

"Mrs. Frémont, Mrs. Frémont!" It was Lieutenant Beale, a young naval officer of our acquaintance who had most recently been in California. When he was admitted to the cool solarium of the house, he began an impassioned plea. "You and the child must return with me to New York. I am going to take this"—he fished in his pocket and brought out a dull rock in which I could see flakes of glitter—"it's gold, true gold!"

"Congratulations," I said wryly, not the least interested in gold, which was, as a matter of fact, the cause of my delayed journey. "But I am going on to meet my husband in California."

"That's just it," he said in the same desperate tone, "rumor has it he's gone back east for treatment of his leg. Injured it when he was stranded in the snow—frostbite, I believe."

I managed to remain cool "I have had a letter from him, and there was no mention of returning east. He did mention the leg, but . . ."

"Ma'am, it's a chance you and your child cannot afford to take. San Francisco is without any kind of civilization—there's no government, no law, men just do what they please. Drinking and gambling seem to be the most favored activities. It is no place for a lady."

"My husband will see to our safety," I said with a confidence that covered growing uncertainty. What if John was not there? What if indeed Lily and I were thrust ashore in that wild land without any money, any way to survive, and no John to take care of us?

"That's just it!" Lieutenant Beale exploded. "He's probably not there. You cannot go. . . . It would be folly!"

I stared long and hard at him. "Sir, I thank you for your concern, but I have promised to meet my husband in San Francisco, and I would not dream of disappointing him. I trust he will feel the same way about our arrangement."

And with all the dignity I could muster, I bid him good-bye and returned to my packing. But anxiety gnawed at me, a deep fear that would, I knew, be my traveling companion until I found John.

We sailed on the *Panama* May 1, 1849.

Chapter Eleven

When the steamer pulled into the harbor on June 4, 1849, San Francisco was anything but the paradise I had painted it in my mind. Like a foolish female, I had ignored Lieutenant Beale's stern warnings about lawlessness and primitive living conditions, preferring to remember John's description of lush green valleys, birds and butterflies, a land of milk and honey. I overlooked, of course, that the two men had told me of totally different parts of California and at totally different times.

The voyage from Panama had been almost a relief, in spite of the crowded conditions. The *Panama*, a mail steamer with accommodations for eighty passengers, carried nearly four hundred men ... along with Lily and me. But the Pacific lived up to its name, its waters almost glass smooth the whole trip and the air balmy and pleasant. Lily and I slept on deck, in a makeshift tent under the boom. We could have had a cabin, but it was airless and hot, and I much preferred the outdoors. The men treated us with every courtesy, and each seemed to know of my anxiety about John. One by one they would stop by to reassure me.

"He'll be just fine, Mrs. Frémont, you wait and see."

"Bet he's pacing the beach at San Francisco right now, watching for this old tub to heave into the harbor."

"Can't keep Colonel Frémont down, ma'am, we know that. We got faith in him. Weren't for him, wouldn't none of us be here."

I wasn't quite sure if that was to John's credit or not, but the man meant well, and I thanked him.

When the men gathered on the deck at night to sing songs and talk of the fortunes they planned to find in the hills of California, I was part of the music, though I kept quiet about the fortunes. One man, a Major Derby who called himself "John Phoenix," kept spirits high by inventing musicals and entertainments that were sometimes so slapstick, I thought they were designed for Lily's amusement alone.

The men were loud, no doubt about it, but they were always considerate, never rude, and, released from the hellhole of Panama, they were filled with an excitement I couldn't help but catch.

"Mother? What are you thinking?" Lily came up next to the rail where I stood staring out at the sea, thinking again that this was my expedition, my version of John's great adventures.

"That your grandmother would be horrified if she could see us," I said, reaching out a hand. "I'm afraid she'd say proper ladies would never sleep on the deck nor talk to all these men."

"It's fun, isn't it?" Lily asked, grinning, and I agreed that it was. Would the Jessie who lived in Washington have done those things? I doubted it, remembering the timidity with which I had embarked on my expedition. In less than two months I had seen a world I never could have imagined . . . and learned an enormous amount about myself.

"Mrs. Frémont! San Diego's in sight. They'll have word about your husband."

I turned in alarm. These long, happy days I'd been able to reassure myself that John was fine, that he would be in California waiting for us. Now that the moment of truth was upon me, the old terror—typical of the Washington Jessie and not the new person—overcame me. As small boats were put over the side for several crew members to row into San Diego, I ran to that airless cabin and hid.

It seemed hours that I stayed there, almost in a trance, but I roused quickly enough when I heard shouting and the pounding of feet. "Mrs. Frémont, Mrs. Frémont! He's in California! He's fine! He'll meet you in San Francisco! He didn't lose a leg— bad frostbite, that's what it was!" The glad words came in a babble of several voices, and when I appeared again on the deck, a loud cheer went up from all the men around. That the words "bad frostbite" didn't alarm me was due only to my ignorance.

With that kind of enthusiasm around me, I waited to sail into the harbor at San Francisco. Instead we found a harbor full of eerie ghost ships swaying in the wind, their sails hanging empty and slack, their decks deserted. They were the ships that never returned to Panama, the ships whose crews had deserted to seek gold.

Beyond, I could see a few low houses and many makeshift tents scattered over windswept, treeless hills, the whole scene covered by fog. We were in San Francisco.

"Mother? Where's my father?" We stood at the rail watching as countless small boats came out to meet us. I peered into the fog as each new boat approached, hoping against hope to see John. But he was not there.

At long last we were shepherded into one of the tiny boats, and when the boats were as close as they could go, we were carried in sailors' arms through the surf to the shore, getting thoroughly muddy and soaking wet in the process. More men lined the shore, staring at us with open curiosity, but John was not among them. I knew that by now, for if he'd been in the city, he'd have been the first out to the steamer. Lily and I were cast on our own in a place not suited, as one man told me, "for decent women."

"Mrs. Frémont? My name's Howard . . . William Howard. Colonel Frémont sent word that I was to look out for you until he arrives."

I nearly sank into this strange man's arms, so grateful was I to see him. "Come, Lily, we will go with Mr. Howard." It never occurred to me that I might be foolish to trust—and follow—the first man who introduced himself. I was too desperate to be cautious.

He led us through a town of dirty canvas tents, makeshift shanties knocked together with odd pieces of wood, even shelters rigged of blankets. Here and there one saw a respectable house, but many of those seemed deserted.

"Decent citizens have mostly left town," Mr. Howard explained with a shrug. "These are all men waiting to go to the interior after gold . . . or else wondering what to do with their lives when they've gone bust without finding it." There were, he told me, some military officers who stuck to their posts and a few merchants like himself "We do very well," he said with a smile.

Mr. Howard had found a small adobe house for us, with veranda, garden, and even a rosewood piano. "A Russian count lived here of late," he said without further explanation, and I wondered what had happened to the count. "Mrs. Anderson will help you," he said, introducing a woman who looked too much like Mrs. Pfeiffer of the journey out of New York for my comfort. She was Mrs. Pfeiffer without the wig—younger, fairer, but still hard of features. Mr. Howard whispered that he had gotten a real bargain, and she would work for $240 a month. I gasped in horror at that sum, but he assured me John would think it reasonable.

I soon learned that an outdated New York newspaper sold for a dollar, and a porter who carried your bags demanded two dollars. Dimes and nickels were unheard of and useless, and quarters frowned upon as too small. Merchants never bargained and didn't seem anxious to make a sale, for they had a captive audience for their overpriced goods.

San Francisco, some said, grew by thirty houses a day, and even the short time I was there, I saw it change—the shanties and tents covered more and more hills, and piers were built out into the ocean, for now ships began to arrive daily. Almost afraid to venture out, I stayed safely in my little house, reading the books left behind by the Russian—fortunately, they were in English—and waited for John.

One evening when the sun was setting over the distant ocean and its glow had softened the harshness of the scene around me, I stood in the doorway enjoying the air. A man on horseback approached, and it was but a minute before I recognized John. Then, with a great burst of joy, I was off down the road at a run, arriving with such abandon that I could barely wait for him to dismount, neatly leaping into his arms once his feet were on the ground.

His first words were not romantic. "Careful," he said, laughing, "this leg doesn't work quite right yet."

Blast the leg! I had the whole man in front of me, and I was overjoyed. Holding tight to his arm, I nearly dragged him toward the house, calling, "Lily! Lily! Your father is here!"

She came hesitantly, walking shyly toward him, needing as she always did after his absences the period of reacquaintance, whereas for me, the world instantly went back into its proper order when John arrived.

John bent to her and held out one gentle hand, which she took with a certain shyness. Looking up at him, she asked clearly, "Are you going to stay with us now? We needed you in Panama."

John winced. "Yes, Lily, I plan to stay with you always from now on."

I squeezed his arm tightly. There were no words I wanted more to hear than those he had just uttered.

Late that night John said, "There was a time that I doubted I'd ever see you again, Jessie. We had been led into mountains so snowbound that we couldn't go forward, and we couldn't go back . . . and there was nothing for it."

"Tell me about the expedition," I said. "Not for a report. Just tell me so I'll know what happened." And thus John described the winter crossing of the fourth expedition.

—❦—

"You know, Jessie, that I left with thirty-three men, and since I couldn't get Carson, I took 'Old Bill' Williams as a guide. That was my biggest mistake—but more about that in a minute.

"We reached the Rockies on November 26. I remember Alexander Godey looking up at those icy slopes and saying to me, 'Friend, I don't want my bones to bleach upon those mountains.' We all seemed to have a premonition of disaster, and perhaps I should have turned back—but turning back is not in my nature.

"The first few days were hard enough—the cold was intense, and the rocky ground was treacherous. Sometimes the sleet came so directly at us that we could not—I repeat, we could not make the mules face into it. And the mules were driven to the last of their strength—they had shelled corn and water, but nothing else. One by one they began to drop and die. The men suffered too—with their breath congealed on their faces, and their beards standing out stiff and white, they could hardly speak. Every step upward the temperature got colder, until it would no longer register on our thermometers.

"At last, though, we crossed the Sangre de Cristo range and came down into the San Luis Valley. From there we pushed on to the headwaters of the Rio Grande.

By December 11 we were at the foot of the San Juan Range. This was the critical moment—we had to decide which pass to aim for. Williams insisted on Wagon Wheel Gap, which has an altitude of eighty-three hundred and ninety feet, but I thought another one, though higher, more passable. But we made the decision to follow Williams—he was, after all, the scout, and a man who I'd been told knew the mountains better than anyone, except perhaps Bridger.

"I don't know that I can begin to describe the country we entered, Jessie. The track went through deep gorges with precipices and crags towering above. We inched along slopes so steep that time and again a mule lost its footing and went crashing to the bottom of a ravine. When we crossed the streams, the water rushed down the slope so fast that it terrified the mules and they would bunch in the middle. Then we had to wade in and shove them to shore.

"The corn was gone now, of course, all one hundred thirty bushels of it, and the mules went crazy with hunger. They ate their rawhide lariats by which they were tied and the blankets we threw over them at night. Finally they even chewed on each other's tails and manes.

"At last we crossed the Great Divide—twelve thousand feet above sea level. But the western slopes were buried in snow. We couldn't go back, and we couldn't go forward. We were overtaken by sudden and irretrievable ruin. I decided we must retreat, and on December 22 we began to move. The mules were almost all gone now, and we were reduced to lugging our baggage ourselves, so it took a week to recross the divide. At that altitude the least task seemed impossible, and any effort could cause severe nosebleed.

"We spent Christmas Day in deep depression, and I could not help but remember, Jessie, the joy of the previous Christmas, with all the comforts of your father's home. We were now eating bacon, macaroni, and sugar, but our provisions would not last two weeks.

"In desperation I separated the party and sent four men, including Williams, to the nearest settlement for help. They were to bring mules and supplies to a point on the Rio Grande, while the rest of us struggled the equipment back down the mountains. We averaged only a mile a day, but at last we reached the meeting point. By then we were out of provisions and boiling rawhide ropes to make a sort of gluey soup. One of the men lay down beside the trail and froze to death, almost before our eyes. We dared not stop long enough to bury him.

"By then it had been over sixteen days since Williams and his men had left, and they should have been back with help. I decided I simply had to set out myself, so I took three of my best men, including Godey, and started down the river, leaving orders for the men to push after me as best they could. I told them to hurry if they wished to see me, for I'd be going on to California. I thought it would give them heart.

"On the sixth day after I left, a friendly Ute Indian led me to Williams and two of the three men I'd sent with him—the fourth had starved to death, and, Jessie . . . I can barely tell you this, but they had . . . they had . . . eaten . . . You know what I'm trying to say. Carson later said to me, 'In starving rimes no man who knew him ever walked in front of Bill Williams.'

"Just a minute . . . I'll get my composure back. . . . Anyway, the others were nothing but skeletons. The Ute gave us horses, and I put the men on them and made for the settlement of Taos, reaching it ten days after leaving camp. I immediately sent help back for the men I'd left behind, but, oh, Jessie! We lost ten of them—ten men—in the mountains. And the others were wrecks, hardly men at all. Some of them had to be lifted on mules to be taken to Taos.

"It was Williams's fault, of course. I should never have listened to him about that pass. Carson even suggested that he may have deliberately led us astray so that we would leave baggage behind, which he could retrieve in the spring. And to this day I have no idea why he missed the trail back down the river.

"I recovered at Carson's home. This one leg was badly frostbitten, and they tell me I was nearly snow-blind, but I have no recollection of that. I know I tried to join the relief party, but Carson held me back. But once I was able to travel, it was time to head for California. Most of the surviving men came with me—Godey and the others. They had not lost their courage, I'm glad to say."

I bowed my head, unable to comprehend the horror of what he told me. That was the closest he ever came to mentioning the cannibalism of which I'd heard, and I would not ask more.

Trying to lighten the tension I felt in John, I recounted our adventures crossing Panama. Now, safely in his arms, I could describe them with a slight amount of humor. Still, John vowed that I would never again undergo such an ordeal alone, and I basked in his protection.

"Jessie? You remember the land Larkin bought?"

"The Butterflies?" I murmured. "Yes. Have you gotten your money back? Can we get the land by the sea?"

He smiled ruefully. "Larkin has that himself now. But, Jessie, there's never going to be gold by the sea. It's in the mountains . . . and it's all over Las Mariposas. The mother lode runs through there. And I've found twenty-nine ore-bearing veins."

It was more than I could comprehend.

"We're rich, Jessie, richer than you ever thought of being."

Rich, to me, meant the comforts of Cherry Grove in Virginia. "As rich as the McDowells?" I asked.

He laughed aloud, a sound to delight my ears. "Richer by far, Jessie, by so much we can't count it."

The habits of a lifetime die hard, and I certainly did not begin to act like a rich lady—nor to feel like one.

Within days we moved to Monterrey, which was closer to Las Mariposas. "It's still too dangerous for you and Lily to go there," John said, "but from Monterrey I can come and go without being away from you too long." And while he was away, John had hired a large group of Sonoran men to work the mines, collecting all the surface gold they could.

The governor's house in Monterrey was occupied by the governor's widow—Madame Castro—except for the ballroom, which was storage for crops. But the house had two long arms that reached back toward the enclosed patio and gardens, and we were soon ensconced in one of them. The entire place was of smooth soft-colored adobe, with tile floors inside, and hedges of rose of Castile lining the garden walls and walks and giving the air a fragrance sweeter than I'd ever imagined.

It was my first house of my very own, and my first experience at housekeeping, but hardly a fair trial. We had no meat, fowl, eggs, butter, potatoes, greens, or herbs. What we had was whatever could be put up in tins and glass—lots of potted meat—and more rice than I ever thought I'd eat.

"I shall," I told John, "write a cookbook entitled *How to Do Without*."

"But," he murmured, "you do so well."

We ate squirrel and dove, brought to us cooked on a campfire by Juan and Gregorio, two Indians who worked for us. We ate *guisado* that they made, a combination of bird, squirrel, red pepper, and rice that inevitably cost the dish in which it was made.

"The dish, *señora*, it broke itself," they would say in Spanish, and I would groan again. John had sent French and Chinese china of great value from San Francisco, but it meant little to my two helpers, who stood, sombreros on their heads, and handed me the broken pieces without any sense of guilt.

"I sent extra pieces to allow for their destruction," John told me with a laugh when I complained.

Madame Castro always provided a daily cup of milk for Lily, from the cow she'd kept to feed her own children. Once, thinking to return the kindness, I gave a coin to her youngest daughter. The child came back shortly, saying in Spanish, "My mama says if it is a present, *sí*; if it is payment for the milk, *no!*"

As John returned from various trips to Las Mariposas, we began to accumulate gold in inconvenient quantities—lumps, dust, rich bits of rock, all of it in hundred-pound sacks worth about twenty-five thousand dollars each. "Where will we put it?" I asked, amazed at the quantity and slightly bewildered by its value.

"In the trunks," he said calmly.

"The trunks? Where will our clothes go?"

"On shelves."

And that is just what happened. Juan and Gregorio built shelves, none too stable, for our clothes, and the trunks became our depositories.

We also began to accumulate household goods. From his various trips to San Francisco John shipped Chinese satins, French damask stuffs for drapings and hangings, and wonderful inlaid Chinese furniture, richer than anything I had ever lived with in the house on C Street. We covered the matted floors with bearskin rugs, and I marveled at the blend of cultures represented in the richness of my new home.

Returning from one trip to San Francisco, John dragged with him a man who looked for all my mind like a frontiersman. "Jessie, this is Mr. Johnson. He has a proposition for you." John's eyes glinted with amusement, and I knew that I was in for some kind of trouble.

"I'm pleased to meet you," I said evenly to our guest, waiting to hear his proposition.

"I got this mulatto," he said, his very voice giving away his crudeness. "I'll sell her to you cheap."

Controlling my temper, I asked, "Is she a good worker?"

"The best," he swore. "Clean, honest, good cook. Sure would take a load off you having to do all this." He glanced around, and it was plain he thought it beneath me to be caring for my own house.

"I will pay her wages," I said firmly, "but I will not buy her." John sat back in his chair, watching in silent amusement, and I sent him a look that said, I hoped, I would get my revenge for this.

"Naw," the man said, "I got to sell her. Don't do me no good to let her work for wages."

"Mr. Johnson," I said clearly, "I do not believe in owning people."

"And you a Virginia woman," he said wonderingly as he departed.

When I turned to John in fury, he held up his hands. "I wanted him to hear it for himself, Jessie, and I wanted him to take the message back to San Francisco. Besides," he added, "you're so convincing."

I chased him with a skillet until he caught me and threw the skillet away so that my arms were free. Then, kissing me passionately, he said, "I don't think there's another woman in the world quite like you, Jessie. Surely not one that would suit me as well."

I'd have given up the Seven Wonders of the World for that. Shortly after that our china was saved from Juan and Gregorio.

An Englishwoman appeared, through the machinations of Madame Castro. Sailing from Australia, she was on a ship where there was a mutiny, and the captain was forced to put in at Monterrey. She and her husband were stranded, and while he went to work for John at Las Mariposas, she needed a place to stay.

"I'll keep your house clean and neat for you," she promised earnestly, "if me and my baby can stay here."

If nothing else, the healthy baby convinced me of Mrs. Maclarty's honesty, and she became a part of our household. Juan and Gregorio went back to the horses, where they were much more comfortable.

"Mrs. Frémont, Mrs. Frémont." Juan came running from the stables. "The colonel's horse is down with colic." From his description I soon learned that it was one of the California horses that John prized highly.

Colic? In horses I knew it was even more serious than in children. "What can you do?" I asked, John being away at Las Mariposas.

"Smoke it out," he said in his halting English. "Need linen to burn."

Linen? I wanted to ask if cotton would not do as well, but I saw from Juan's intense expression that he was serious. "You really need linen?"

He nodded.

"Wait just a moment." Inside I went to the shelves that held our clothes and took two linen petticoats, pieces that had been embroidered for me back in Washington. With a loving last pat I thrust them at Juan, who went triumphantly away, calling to Gregorio and waving his treasure high in the air. I thought he could have been a bit more subtle.

The horse lived, but I doubt John ever knew the extent of my sacrifice—and embarrassment.

Mrs. Maclarty didn't last long with us. One day she came to me to say, "Missus, there's a party in town tonight. I thought I'd as like to wear that green silk gown."

"The green silk?" I echoed. It was a new and very expensive gown that John had sent from San Francisco, and I'd had no occasion to wear it. It had occurred to me that I might never have occasion until I returned to Washington, but I surely didn't want my housekeeper to inaugurate the dress for me.

"Yes, ma'am, the very one."

"I am not ready to part with it, Mrs. Maclarty. It's . . . it's a new gown."

"Oh, I'm not asking ye to give it to me," she intoned in her deep British accent, "just give me leave to wear it the one night."

When I refused, as tactfully as I could, she left in high dudgeon, and from there our relationship went downhill. It was as much my fault as hers, I admit, for I was offended with her familiarity, and she was angry at what she saw as my superiority. Within a week she announced that she would leave for San Francisco, after all, and I wished her well with relief.

While most Californians went about the countryside in heavy carretas—clumsy oxen-driven vehicles with heavy wooden wheels—I went about in a wonderful carriage that John had ordered and had sent around the Horn for me. Because of business concerning Las Mariposas, he determined that we should go from Monterrey to San Francisco, and that I should ride in my carriage. Lily and I, he said, would sleep in the boot, and the men of the party could sling hammocks between trees or, in the absence of trees, sleep in their blankets on the ground.

"I won't go unless the carriage is pulled by a reliable horse," I said practically.

"Jessie! I wouldn't think of anything else," he protested. "A fellow has brought me a mare from Oregon—gentle as a lamb, he says. I know those Oregon horses—they can't be beat."

The mare, hitched up to the wagon, proved anything but lamblike. She rose on her hind legs when she felt the drag of the carriage, then trembled violently and shied in every direction. I praised the saints that John was testing her and I was not in the carriage.

"Oregon horses . . ." I began.

"I know, Jessie, I know. She's not gentle enough." Then, drawing himself up a little, "She's not like any Oregon horse I ever saw."

A few days later a man brought a California gelding, no longer young but guaranteed gentle. John hitched up the horse, and they started gaily off down the road. All of a sudden the creature began to buck wildly, then came to a dead standstill. At a loss, John finally unhitched it, only to have the animal nearly collapse on the spot, probably from exertion too great for its age.

"Did you check its teeth to see how old it is?" I asked from my safe point on the sidelines.

He gave me a withering look but said nothing. "John? I want a pair of mules."

"Mules! What kind of a man lets his wife go about the country in a carriage drawn by mules?"

"A man who cares for her safety," I replied serenely.

And that's how I went. Two Indians tied *riatas* to a pair of mules and guided them while they pulled the wagon. A second pair waited their turn, and we traded them off at least once a day.

In this fashion we meandered like nomads from Monterrey to San Francisco, through the valleys of the coastal range, where wild oats were turning yellow and live oaks grew so thick as to look like an orchard. We started early each morning, as the sun peeked over the mountains to the east, then stopped for breakfast about ten and came to a halt for the day in midafternoon.

Our food came from local ranches. Sometimes it was a leg of mutton, but on less plentiful days we often secured a handful of soup herbs or a small sack of pears. Once our messenger came roaring back from a ranch, waving his arms to indicate a great prize, only to have his horse trip in a gopher hole. The three precious eggs he had brought shattered on the ground, and I could not help but laugh at the tragedy.

Occasionally we stopped at the ranches, and I found the women always wanted to meet me and thank me for John's kindness. They seemed to feel that he alone was responsible for the peaceful takeover of California, for the fact that their men had not been killed and they themselves had not been violated. I will always remember one dignified matriarch, ninety-five if she was a day, who gathered four generations of daughters about her to meet me. The little ones bowed most formally, and the middle-aged ones were diffident, but she, the grande dame, was regal, even in her gratitude. "We felt," she said in Spanish, "that we were safe because of him." And when I answered in Spanish, she positively beamed.

"Jessie, you're a different woman from the one I married."

We sat on the ground, apart from our entourage, at the end of a blissful day. "In what way?"

"You're . . . you're more game than I knew you would be. I . . ." He looked with studied thought at his pipe, as though avoiding me. Then, finally, "I worried a great deal about bringing you out here. I wasn't sure you'd survive without your father."

"And I have," I said.

"It's not just that," he said, reaching for my hand. "You . . . you've left your mother's manners behind." He said it haltingly, as though the words didn't quite express what he meant.

"My mother," I said with laughter, "would not have crossed Panama nor ever have kept house in an adobe without servants or what she considered real food. I did what I had to so that I could be with you."

"Why?" He was not being coy. There was an intensity behind the question that almost frightened me.

"Because, John Charles Frémont, I love you, I believe in you, and you are the most important thing in my life."

"Did you ever . . ." He paused, considered, then rushed on. "Did you ever think of asking me to do something else—something that would hold me in Washington so that your life could go on the way it always had?"

"Yes. Father and I even talked about the other jobs you could have had. But it would not have been you, and I would not have wanted half the man."

I thought, then, that he would gather me in his arms, oblivious of the men around us and of Lily, who sat some distance away, watching us with undeniable curiosity.

Instead he gazed out toward the sea. We were camped on the crest of a foothill from which a valley spread below us and then the blue expanse of the ocean. "And if you had, we would not be here in God's country," he said. Turning solemnly to me, he said, "Thank you, Jessie." And then he jumped up and began to organize everyone so that we could move on.

Sometimes he was a frustrating lover.

There was no suitable hotel in California, none that John believed safe for Lily and me. So he bought a ready-made Chinese-built house. It fitted together like a puzzle, the doors and walls sliding into grooves. Inside, Lily and I slept in hammocks, while outside, John took over the carriage that had been my bed all up the coast.

"John? Do you not . . ." My voice trailed off. I was not good at speaking frankly of the intimacies of marriage, and yet I knew that such intimacies had been missing in our marriage of late. For all that, we'd had an idyllic time, but we were rarely together as husband and wife. "Could you not share my hammock?"

"Doesn't sound very comfortable to me," he said brusquely, and then, softening, "but you could share my carriage."

The logistics of it amused me. I could see that a hammock would not be convenient for connubial relationships, but neither was the process of waiting until everyone was asleep and then sneaking out to the carriage. Yet that is just what I did, night after night. I was rewarded with a passion so intense that I wondered that John had not been more insistent on our privacy while we traveled. It was not, however, for a wife to question her husband—or so I thought—and I said nothing.

"You must not," he once said to me, "become the aggressor."

I puzzled long over that.

While we were in San Francisco, some of the Sonorans came down from Las Mariposas and announced, with some embarrassment, that they needed their share of the gold. They had to return to their families. The gold was in those trunks back in Monterrey.

"John, it will be such a long ride for you, there and back," I complained.

"I'm not going," he said. "I shall send a message to Madame Castro to allow them access to the trunks, and they can measure out their half of the gold."

I was astounded. "You can't . . ."

"They are perfectly trustworthy," he said. "You'll see."

And I did. They were meticulous in their parceling out of the spoils, and when we returned to Monterrey, our share of the gold was neatly bagged and returned to the trunks.

"That tells you something about California," I said. "I think maybe thirty years ago you might have been able to do something similar in St. Louis . . . but no more."

For all our lollygagging along the road to San Francisco and back, serious business awaited in Monterrey. In September a convention framed a constitution so that application could be made for statehood. California had no intention of becoming a territory.

Both of us knew that John's name had been mentioned frequently as a candidate for senator from the new state. It was an honor that I determined must come to John.

He deserved it—and he needed the glory, after his court-martial and the failure of the last expedition.

"John, if they named you, would you be senator?"

"If they named me, yes. But I will not campaign for the nomination," he said firmly.

I thought he sounded firmer than he really was, but from that moment on my ambition for him rose again.

Although not a delegate, John was in the thick of the constitutional meeting, and so was the issue of slavery. "California must not enter the Union as a slave state," John said over and over again, and we devoted all our efforts to avoiding that. I encouraged John to bring visitors by the score to our adobe home—soldiers he had marched with earlier, men who came from the East for gold, anyone with a part in the new government.

"You could be the richest woman in the world, Mrs. Frémont," said one man. "All you have to do is convince that husband of yours to use slaves to mine all that gold up there."

"I don't need to be the richest woman in the world," I said calmly, having at last learned the lesson Father never learned—it does no good to argue with a person whose mind is made up.

A Mr. Lippincott from Philadelphia brought several people to the house one evening. "Wanted them to hear you say you wouldn't own a slave," he explained.

"I would not," I said firmly. "No one in my family would. My father never has, and my mother freed her family slaves."

One man eyed me with real interest. "If a Virginia woman like yourself can get along keeping her own house, so can my wife, who's always telling me she needs 'suh-vents.' We'll keep this place clean of slave labor."

I smiled gratefully at him.

But my favorite comment about the issue came from a gold seeker, an old man who had been with John at the Bear Flag Revolt and was now at Las Mariposas, panning for gold. "In a country where every man makes a slave of himself, ain't no use in owning another slave."

The constitution declared California an antislavery state.

———◦◦———

By December the rainy season had come, and Lily and I were often alone in Monterrey, John being at Las Mariposas to check on things or off in San Francisco on business or, increasingly, in San Jose, where the legislature was meeting. Lily and I occupied ourselves by watching the ocean from one big window in our salon, reading borrowed books—I was even lent a set of the *Illustrated London News*—and sewing.

I was a particular failure at the latter, having cut up one good dress to use it for a pattern for the silks John had sent. My "new" dress fit oddly in several places, and I seldom wore it—but its making whiled away the time.

Late one stormy night as I sat reading, Lily long since in bed, I heard hoofbeats. No, I told myself, it cannot be. He would not come this late at night.

But then I heard the familiar step and a shouted "Jessie?" I threw open the door and was immediately enveloped in the wettest embrace I've ever had. John, though, was oblivious of his wet clothes and dripping hair.

"They did it, they did it! I'm elected as senator!" The triumph in his voice was beyond description, and I knew he felt more strongly about this honor than all the praise ever heaped on the first three expeditions.

Pretending amazement, I kissed him heartily, but in seconds he pulled away to say, "We leave for Washington January first."

The wheel had come full circle. We had left Washington at the lowest point, and now we would return at the highest. It was, I thought, justice at last, and I could not wait to write to Father.

"I am so very, very proud of you," I told him, and he looked a little like Lily when I complimented her attempts at cursive writing.

He had ridden seventy-five miles from San Jose to tell me the news, and in the morning he would turn around and ride back. It was, he said, worth the trip to see my expression. Only later, in the night, did he remember to tell me that he and the other senator, William Gwin, had drawn straws, and John had drawn the short term. He would have to stand for reelection again in six months.

It was storming again the night we boarded a steamer for Panama, and John carried me through the muddy streets of Monterrey in his arms. Gregorio bore Lily behind us, though both he and Juan refused our suggestion that they come to Washington with us.

"We meant to stay seven years in peace and quiet," John reminded me. "Are you sad to be leaving?"

"Yes and no," I said. "I will miss much of our life here . . . and I fully count on coming back. But I am so very glad to be going home—and for the reason we are going."

"And, Jessie, we're going home rich, richer than our wildest dreams."

That, too, was part of the joy, but for me it was overshadowed by the emotional side of our triumph.

I thought that crossing the isthmus, not intolerable before, would be sheer adventure because John was by my side and because we were going home, but I hadn't counted on a raging illness that struck all three of us and delayed us for weeks in the home of the blessed Madame Arcé. Lily and I both suffered from intense fever, Lily's so high that at one point her head was shaved in hopes of making it easier to cool her brain. John, meanwhile, suffered severe pain from inflammatory rheumatism in the leg that bad been frostbitten. Madame Arcé lined up three cots in her large ballroom, making it an infirmary, and her servants cared for us day and night, though I remember little of that time.

John later told me he had no worry about either Lily or me until we left Madame Arcé's and headed over the mountains for Gorgona. John's fellow explorer John Stephens, who was living in Panama, had the clever idea that I should be carried over the isthmus in a hammock, my strength being entirely gone after the fever. Stephens rigged a hammock between two poles and enlisted four Indians to carry me—two rested, while two carried. A small crowd gathered as I was being carried out of Madame Arcé's, deathly pale from my illness, and one woman said in Spanish, "*Pobrecita!* Such a shame to die so far from home."

John cried out, "No, Jessie, don't die! Not now! Not when we're at the high point!"

"Would you have let me die after the court-martial, at the low point?" I asked.

He shook his head. "Never. Up or down, I need you, Jessie."

"Without you . . ." He shook his head, and his words trailed off, but he had said enough for me.

It seemed months before we reached Washington, though in truth it was but a matter of weeks. We were home by early March. The trip still blurs in my memory, though I remember that all the men aboard the boat from Panama to New York were taken with sympathy for Lily. She looked so pitiful with her shaved head and her pinched white face—though her color did return during the voyage, simply because of the bracing sea air, I thought. But the returning gold miners gave her all kinds of trinkets and rings and things made of gold and begged me to allow her to keep these gifts.

I did, and she burst through the door of the house on C Street calling, "Grandfather, Grandfather, look what I have!"

"My goodness, Lily," he said, catching her in his arms, "you're a rich lady. You've a wealth of gold."

"It's very valuable," she informed him solemnly.

And then he turned to me, and I saw that he had aged. The court-martial, the ongoing fight over slavery, all had taken their toll on my father, and he was no longer the invincible man I had grown up adoring. Now I almost felt a need to protect him.

"Jessie," he said, his voice husky, "it is good to have you home."

"It's wonderful to be here," I said, my voice betraying the strength of my emotion.

Father and John clapped each other on the back and came as close to hugging as they ever would, and it was no time before Father drew John into his library. "You've got to be aware of what's going on in the Senate, John. This slavery thing's going to wreck this nation."

It was good to be home, and I was glad to be back in the middle of politics. I left the two of them to talk, though curiosity burned through me, and took Lily up to see my mother. She too had failed, but the change was not as dramatic as with Father.

We arrived, though, to find turmoil in the Senate. At issue was whether California should come in as a free or a slave state, and the debate had gotten so hot at one point that Senator Henry Foote of Mississippi had drawn a pistol on Father in the Senate chambers.

"What did you do?" John asked.

"Told them to let him fire," Father roared. "Tore open my shirt and told him to fire on an unarmed man . . . damned assassin! Thinks he can prevail by terror. Well, I showed him I wasn't afraid."

"Obviously," I said, "he did not take you at your word and shoot you."

"Would have," Father grumped, "but too many others got in the way, and then someone took the gun and locked it up. Foote's not a rational man, I tell you."

"He feels strongly about slavery," John said.

"And I feel strongly against it," Father countered. "Besides, the man's already fought three or four duels."

"How are things otherwise?" I asked.

"Hmph! I have to stand for reelection in the fall, you know, and I'm in for a fight. Southerners in Missouri perceive me as an abolitionist . . . and they're right!"

"You're never better than when you're in a fight," I said reassuringly. Father had been in the Senate for thirty years; I could not fathom the idea of his defeat.

I resumed my chores in Father's study, now working for both my husband and my father, which meant long hours at the desk copying speeches and preparing background notes for them. Lily was once again relegated to the care of Sophie and Mathilde, where she flourished.

The summer of 1850 went by in a flurry of parties, gala teas, and simmering tempers. I always enjoyed the world of men, and in California I had often relished being the only woman in a group of men, but now I was glad to be in the company of sociable women. Zachary Taylor was in the White House, and his daughter, a Mrs. Bliss, was acting as hostess, because of the illness of her mother. Whereas Mrs. Polk had made the presidential mansion a formal and serious place, Mrs. Bliss was open and hospitable, and there were many receptions. A steady stream of Californians came to the capital to be presented to the president, and it was our good fortune to take them to the White House.

And there were other parties—the senator from New York, a talented artist named General Dix, entertained often, and we were invited by Baron Von Geralt from Germany and many others. Best of all, I saw the friends of my youth. I frequently saw Count Bodisco and his wife, my schoolmate Harriet. I could not help but cry out her name when I first saw her, and then I nearly had to bite my tongue to keep from adding, "You've grown fat!" She had indeed become a plump matron at an early age, but she was obviously a wealthy matron, lavishly gowned and expensively jeweled.

"Jessie! I've worried about you out there in that wild land. . . ."

"It's not a wild land," I protested, "it's paradise. But I am glad to be back in Washington."

We traded news, and she told me not once but a dozen times what a wonderful man the count was. To my eye he was still the same little ugly man he had always been, but Harriet truly worshiped him, and I was happy for her.

Everywhere we went—and we were celebrities, invited to every party given— talk was of the admission of California and the debate over abolition. John was courted for his opinion, flattered on his accomplishments, and treated as a hero. Every memory of the court-martial seemed to have vanished, and we were, as I'd told him, riding high on the wheel of fortune.

In September, California was admitted as a free-soil state, and I watched from the gallery as John and William Gwin were sworn in as California's first senators. I was also in the Senate when John introduced several important bills necessary for the running of California as a state. I was appalled that the Senate seemed ready to admit the state but to forget about such necessities as establishing courts and postal routes, providing for the recording of land titles and surveys of public lands, setting up land offices, and the like. Without John the Senate would have left California in worse chaos than before.

Trouble came, however, over a bill that had nothing to do with California. John felt strongly against the use of flogging as punishment in the navy and introduced a bill to abolish the practice. Senator Foote, of all people, misunderstood and thought it a bill having to do with California land titles—a bill that had been tabled until the next session.

Speaking against the naval appropriations bill, which John had presented and in which he included the measure to abolish flogging as punishment, an intoxicated Senator Foote said John's bill would "disgrace the country" and implied that the bill sprang from private corrupt motives. It was the last night of the session.

When John heard this, he immediately left the Senate and went to an anteroom. From there he sent a page to demand that Foote be brought to him.

"What did you say?" I asked.

"Told him his language was unwarranted and that no gentleman would have so committed himself," John said. "And then"—he paused dramatically—"the old ruffian tried to assault me."

"Assault you?"

"Absolutely right." John drew himself up indignantly as he paced about the library. "Took three men to pull him off." He shrugged. "I guess I'm lucky he didn't pull that same pistol on me."

"And then?" I was having to drag this story out of him, and I did it with my heart in my mouth, for I knew what the next step would be for any southern gentleman such as John.

"I demanded an apology or satisfaction with the weapons of his choice," John said matter-of-factly, as though it were taken for granted.

To me it was a very real possibility that John would be the loser should a duel actually come about. After all, Foote was practiced at these things, and John, for a certainty, was not. Still, I knew enough to be aware that I could not say that. I could not diminish John by doubting him.

Foote, fortunately, was prevailed upon to apologize in writing to John, and I was left in the happy position of congratulating John on his victory—and silently thanking the Lord for his continued health and well-being.

John was a senator for a little more than three weeks, between the time of his swearing in and the adjournment of the session. Unwisely, I had put to the back of my mind the fact that he had drawn the short term.

On a day in September when I was planning a tea to visit with Harriet Bodisco, John announced, "I must return to California to campaign. I didn't know how satisfying Senate service would be; I want to be reelected."

"Of course," I said absently, my mind busy with thoughts of sweetmeats and tea flavored with mint. "When shall you go?" The delights of California had faded in my mind, replaced by the more immediate pleasures of being in Washington, and I remembered now only the hardships, particularly the physical hardship of crossing the isthmus.

"We," he said, "must go together, Jessie. I cannot do this without you. And we'll leave in five days."

I dropped my pen on the floor and then dived to find it, giving myself time to recover. Still, when I spoke, it was with a gasp. "Five days?"

"There's simply no time to waste," he said firmly.

Every ounce of my common sense knew that it wasn't necessary to hurry back to California, but I was once again forced to let John make the decisions, lest I be accused of usurping the man's role. Who would have accused me? Probably no one in stronger terms than my own, but I still remembered that accusation leveled at me by my father when I was very young. There was, however, one thing I had to say, and then he could draw his own conclusions.

"John, we will have another child in about six months."

He grabbed me from my chair, pulled me into his arms, and said triumphantly, "And he'll be born in California! A true native."

It was not the response I hoped for, but now there was nothing for it. I began to pack that evening.

Chapter Twelve

"Fire! Fire!" Even as the words penetrated my consciousness, I was aware of the clanging of bells and, worse, the acrid smell of fire—not a clean wood fire but that which destroys everything in its path.

San Francisco was ablaze! With my new infant son, John Charles II, in my arms, I rushed to the windows and saw a scene of horror. From the hilltop on which our house sat, I looked down on a layer of smoke with flames leaping through it from time to time, reaching as high as the heavens. And the border of those flames, even as I watched, crept closer and closer to our house, inching its way up the hill.

I was home alone with Lily, little Charley, and the servants. John was away at Las Mariposas, and I was in charge. Paralyzed, I sat and watched the fire come toward me in the dark of night.

We had been back in California nearly six months, having landed in November after yet another difficult crossing of the isthmus. I have deliberately wiped out the memory of that crossing and remember only that none of us were deathly ill and that the baby I carried apparently suffered no harm.

We arrived to find San Francisco a far different city from the one we had left less than a year ago. For one thing, it spread like a blight into the hills and showed no sign of stopping, its border daily pushed out by influxes of newcomers. Many of those newcomers were what John, with studied understatement, called "a rough lot." Convicts and ne'er-do-wells from Australia "escaped" to San Francisco, other British penal colonies allowed men to come to California, and the French sent a large number of the Guarde Mobile—Napoleon had found these men useful, but they since had proved far too troublesome to keep in Paris. These rough men mixed with Chinese, Mexicans, and, of course, the large number of Americans who arrived daily in tattered covered wagons and took up residence in flimsy shacks. Meantime, those who had struck it rich on gold—not a large population—lived grandly in houses filled with French furniture and draped in red velvet. There was no middle ground between the two ways of life, and antagonism was inevitable. Greed seemed everywhere—

I was so grateful that John seemed to have escaped that disease—and the city was dangerous: the word "thug" entered my vocabulary, and I read with increasing horror of muggings and murders on the street.

John spent much of his time at Las Mariposas, where Indian troubles threatened constantly. Gold miners had overrun the hills and valleys of northern California, pushing the Indians ever farther from their land, and it seemed there was no way to prevent an uprising. I worried a great deal about John going into the midst of such circumstances, but as if to show me my foolishness, he undertook a contract to supply beef to the Indians.

I stayed in our house, kept the servants close by and Lily inside, and prayed for the best.

Word of a major upset in my life made its way to me in December. My father had been defeated in the race for the Senate seat from Missouri, a defeat that he had almost himself predicted, but that I had refused to believe. It only underscored to me the desperate straits into which the slavery issue had thrown our country, and I blamed myself some for not being available to help Father with his campaign. "What would you have done?" John demanded on one of his visits. "He's a seasoned campaigner. He surely did what was necessary. The times were just against him."

"But I could have helped prepare his speeches, found statistics and information for him, all the things I've always done."

"Jessie, you are my wife now, and that job takes precedence over being your father's assistant." The words were said kindly, not harshly, but I shivered as I heard them.

"What will he do?" I asked, not really meaning to voice the question.

"He can always come to California," John said. "He would find plenty of government work out here." And with that he turned and left the room, having done nothing to ease the pain I felt for my father.

John himself campaigned for the Senate seat off and on all that winter, but the legislature was hopelessly deadlocked. Vote after vote got them nowhere nearer to results, and John, impatiently, announced that he had better things to do with his time. I knew, but didn't say, that the problem was that he represented the initial wave of settlers from the United States, those who had become landowners of some privilege and who were mightily resented by the thugs and their fellows who had come late and landless. And his antislavery declarations, vociferously made, alienated the proslavery and moderate members of his own party. John, never a true politician, had stacked the deck against himself.

All that winter I worried about the baby I carried, though he seemed active enough to indicate good health. Still, I remembered—who could forget?—little Benton, his health ruined by that court-martial that I'd endured while pregnant. Had this baby been similarly scarred by the last isthmus crossing? I mentioned my fears to no one, but from time to time I would find Lily standing by me, her hand reaching out to hold mine.

"Mother? Are you all right?"

"Yes, Lily, I'm fine, thank you."

"And is our baby all right?"

I could never resist smiling and giving my voice a strong note of confidence as I told her, "He's just fine." It never occurred to either John or me that the baby would be anything but a boy.

He was just fine. Born April 19, 1851, he entered the world with a lusty cry and an enormous appetite. He was his father in all things, and I had nothing but joy in him.

Circumstances, however, did not go as well for the baby's father, and he was not returned to the Senate. His staunch antislavery stand worked against him. "Politics," he told me, "is too costly, anyway. I am glad to be rid of it."

Now both my husband and my father were out of office, effectively removing me from the Washington political scene. The wheel, I felt, was headed downhill.

———— ⌣ ————

But now, with Charley not yet three weeks old, I held him in my arms and faced a holocaust.

"Lily? Come quickly!"

"I smell it," she said with her great practicality as she padded into the room, rubbing her eyes after having been awakened from a sound sleep. "The city is on fire, isn't it?" Then her practicality deserted her as she looked out the window. "Mother! My hens! Give me ribbons to tie on their legs so that I can take them with us."

"Hens?" How could she think of fowl at a moment like this?

"Let them go, Lily. They'll survive. Go to your father's library and gather the papers from his drawers into one big stack."

She hurried away to follow my bidding while I sat with my mind whirling. There was silver to be saved, and Oriental rugs that I would not lose if I could possibly avoid it, correspondence of no lasting value but dear to me . . . and no end of things.

The servants came at a run. Juan and Gregorio, who had returned to our help, burst into the room, shouting in their half-Spanish, half-English patois that I must leave immediately.

"Wait!" I held up a hand. "We must plan carefully. We must gather the things to take."

They nodded solemnly and, under my direction, accumulated a pile of things to be transported. Then they hung wet carpets—not the good Orientals—on the side of the house nearest the fire.

All night the fire burned, coming ever closer, and I sat, clutching my baby, listening to the roar of the flames, the clanging of the bells, the shouting of the firefighters who from time to time rushed in to reassure me.

In the end Juan and Gregorio took the legal papers and silver to a safer spot, the home of friends on Russian Hill, but Lily, Charley, and I remained in the house. And it was spared, though the paint blistered and the grass in front of it all withered and died.

I was so relieved that I was not even angry when it was declared that the fire was of "incendiary" origin—deliberately set. It was the fifth such fire in two months, though none of the others had grown so out of control.

Not long afterward, standing in the front yard, I bent to pick up a paper that had blown against the fence. Thinking it trash, I was about to crumple it in my hand when my eye caught the headline:

"BEWARE! ALL OF SAN FRANCISCO WILL BURN!" The handbill went on to give particulars about revenge for the actions of the Committee of Vigilance—which had recently lynched four persons, to my horror—and to repeat the threat that the entire city would be burned. No one would be spared.

That literally murdered sleep for me. I sat most nights in the windows facing the city, watching for the first flame, the first slight spark. The papers and silver were still on Russian Hill. All that remained to be rescued were the people, but I felt a desperation to save my house.

The fire started not at night but on a Sunday morning, when even Juan and Gregorio had gone to church. The flames this time began so close to our home that I grabbed the baby, wet from his bath, and wrapped him in my dressing gown. With Lily following, we hurried to Russian Hill, where we found ourselves not the only refugees. The house was full of women and children, all sobbing and wailing over the loss of their possessions.

Fanned by summer winds, the flames jumped and leaped from building to building. The woman whose house was next to mine—a Frenchwoman who had been very ill—laughed hysterically as she watched her home disappear into ashes. Then she turned to me with a dramatic, "C'est votre tour!—Your house is next!"

And it was. As I watched, my home and all my possessions went up in flames.

A house was found for me the next day—a lonesome, forlorn barracks out in the sand hills. I cannot tell you my feelings as I walked into that barren building, knowing that I had not a possession in the world with which to turn it into a home. All the fine Orientals, the inlaid furniture, the rich damasks John had bought—all were gone.

Lily had cried silently almost since the first bell clanged, and now I held her close to me, trying to comfort her. She wept, of course, for her hens. As I whispered soothing words to her, she fixed her eyes beyond me, and I feared that she was not hearing a thing I said. Suddenly she stiffened, and I reacted with alarm.

"Mother? Who are those people?"

People? What people would be at this godforsaken place? But my eyes followed where her finger pointed, and I saw a strange procession making its way over the rutted sand road to our new home. A string of people pushed along the road, their hands full of parcels and bundles. A few led small carts over the bumps. When I went to the door, my puzzlement no doubt plain on my face, a middle-aged man with large, heavy features and hands bigger than I could imagine stepped forward.

They were, he said, the English tenants on land that John owned.

When the fire started, they hurried to our house to see if they could be of help. Finding me gone, they proceeded to save everything—mirrors, china and glass, hundreds of books, furniture, even kitchen utensils and all our clothing. I had a household again!

Slowly it came to me—the English tenants. They rented cottages from John and had built a brewery, though many so-called civic leaders had warned John against renting to these people . . . and while he had no trouble with them, he himself had resisted deeding them their land as they wished.

"Missus," said the woman who stood next to the spokesman, "I hope you don't mind that I laundered your clothes. I thought you might be so put about with the changing, the clothes would have a long wait."

Then the man put down a parcel tied in a red handkerchief "We knew the master was from home, and there was a young baby in the house," he said, "and so we brought a quarter's rent in advance, in case you be needing it." He untied the bundle to reveal heaps of silver and gold. Perhaps best of all, they had caught and crated all but one of Lily's hens, and they returned them, squawking indignantly, to a delighted child.

I could do nothing but cry. These people had been chilled by public ill will, and yet they had shown true greatness of spirit, goodness of heart. I did not need the money, but I took it lest I insult them, and I was as profuse as I knew how in my thanks, assuring them that as soon as Colonel Frémont returned, he, too, would thank them in person.

John came days later, striding through the desolation to our house, to find only a chimney standing. "You cannot imagine," he told me, "what horror went through my mind. I was frantic with terror and then to be told only, in the vaguest terms, that you'd taken a home near Grace Church!"

We were, indeed, within a stone's throw of the small church, and John's method of finding us was to stand on the stoop of the church and survey the houses in sight.

"When I found one with muslin curtains in the windows and pink ribbons, I knew I'd found you."

"Why?" I asked.

"Because you love the fresh breeze and would have the curtains tied back to allow ventilation." He smiled at me as he said it, as though I were the most transparent, predictable person alive.

"Father taught me it was healthy!" I said a trifle indignantly.

He laughed aloud and grabbed me in his arms. "I am so relieved to find you well. . . . What would I have done if . . ."

I put a finger to his lips to silence the very thought. "The children are fine," I said, though he hadn't yet asked. "Lily has been weeping, but the tenants' arrival with our goods cheered her up, and little Charley has slept through the whole thing."

"Good," he said, but as he led me toward the bedroom, I knew that his mind was not one bit on the children.

He went the next day to tell the English tenants that they could purchase their land. "That'll make my wife a happy woman," the spokesman told him.

———

In spite of the wealth of Las Mariposas, John was always in financial trouble. "The title isn't clear," he told me. "The government, in its infinite wisdom, hasn't decided what it wants to do. . . . Sometimes I think I'll just sell the blasted place and be free of it!"

I was startled. Las Mariposas meant the wealth of gold, but more than that, it meant ownership to John, a place where he was the master, where he ruled his own kingdom.

"Would you really want to do that?" I asked, my bewilderment showing in my voice. For some reason it bothered me that he would sell Las Mariposas before I ever saw it, but I didn't say that aloud. "No," he said, shaking his head, "I don't really want to do that. But I am fed up with it."

Father, meanwhile, wrote from Washington that it was his opinion—unasked—that John should sell "that damn mountain place" and return us all to civilization. I was left to reply that John did not want to sell—and to add staunchly that I did not want him to either.

Meanwhile Indian troubles continued to brew in California. Miners had displaced the Indians from their usual hunting grounds, driving them back into the mountains, where they had no food. To feed themselves, they simply killed horses and cattle belonging to the intruders. The whites soon retaliated, and a full-scale Indian war threatened. John was instrumental in working out a treaty, part of which required that the Indians be given cattle to slaughter. He then contracted to supply the cattle and drove them from northern California himself with a team of helpers.

The government, as governments will, dallied and refused to pay the bill because the treaties had not been ratified. Then they refused to ratify the treaties, which meant that all arrangements specified under them fell through, including John's contract to supply beef. He had, it appeared, supplied it at his own cost—and considerable cost it was, at $240,000.

Disgusted with the government and with the general lawlessness in California, John announced one day that we would leave for England. "There are Mariposas investors there," he said, "and it's the right place to raise more capital."

"John," I demanded, "do we own Mariposas or not? Are we wealthy, are we poor—what are we?"

He was offended that I would presume to intrude upon men's business—specifically his men's business—although he had known me long enough and well enough to realize that I was not liable to sit back quietly without questions. Especially not when what I heard seemed contradictory.

"It's not as simple as you seem to think, Jessie," he said, his stilted tone telling me that he was posturing for my sake.

Don't, John, I wanted to shout. *Tell me the truth.* But I saw that would do me no good, and I turned away. In my heart I knew that Las Mariposas was a paper empire. Beneath the ground it may have hidden a fortune in gold, but as it stood now, it was almost a liability. And we were in financial trouble, just as Father had been off and on for years. In too many ways my marriage began to echo my childhood.

Still, I persisted in hearing firebells clang in my sleep, and I was grateful to be away from San Francisco. I went to England gladly, hiding my doubts.

———

You'd never have known we were anything but the king and queen of England from the way we traveled. We intended to sail directly from Chagres, taking the eastern route, but our steamer had burned in the Bay of Biscay. Once again it was an isthmus crossing for us. Each time the crossing grew a little better, and this time Charley was old enough that I didn't worry too much—though he was out of my sight for an entire day, carried by Indians.

Then it was on to New York. When we walked into our hotel room, I got my first real look at myself in months and was appalled at my dowdy appearance. Pale I could understand, but shabby and out of fashion were not beyond my control, and I went on an immediate shopping spree. I would not, I vowed, arrive in London looking like someone's poor relative.

"Can we not have a visit with Father?" I asked, even though I sensed, through my correspondence, that a rift had grown between them. Father had expected John to be easily guided, and John had proved to be headstrong, not always swayed by the advice of his father-in-law. I was caught in the middle.

"We cannot wait for him to come to New York," John said impatiently, "and we have no time to go to Washington."

And so we rushed off to sea, at the worst possible season of the year—March, when the Atlantic was beset with storms. The seas were so rough that two-year-old Charley was firmly tied by a rope to the railing of the mainmast—he had about a four-foot radius of freedom and, as Lily gleefully pointed out, spent more time on his head than his feet because of the vessel's pitching and tossing. Those rough seas had scared most other passengers away, and I was the only woman onboard. That worked to our advantage, because we had the ladies' stateroom to ourselves. The captain took almost every meal with us, and the children were fussed over by the crew until they became quite spoiled. I put all thoughts of paper empires out of my mind and thoroughly enjoyed the luxury.

In London we had a suite at the Clarendon, made cheerful by fires and lights and plants and flowers. It was a vast leap to go from being burned out of your home and living in makeshift squalor—well, nearly—to a life of luxury at the Clarendon. From time to time I had to pinch myself.

Shortly after we arrived, there began a social whirl the likes of which I'd never known in my life, not even in the busiest season in Washington. The United States minister to England, Abbott Lawrence of Massachusetts, was indebted to my father in many ways, mostly political, and he and his wife went out of their way to introduce us around. We went to a ball at Buckingham Palace, sat in the Peabody box at the opera, and attended a party at the home of Sir Roderick Murchison of the Royal Geographical Society—John was a medalist of that society. We dined at the home of the lord mayor of London, took tea with the duchess of Bedford, and were invited to the countess of Derby's assembly. We were entertained in buildings with lions over the entrances, and courtyards and gardens that made me catch my breath, and we met all manner of famous and interesting people.

I was constantly introduced as being from North America, a turn of words that rather made me feel like an Indian squaw newly come from those vast plains that John had explored. The British preconceptions about John, however, were even more distorted.

"Your husband is so . . . so charming," said one lady, looking at me through a lorgnette. "I had expected . . ." Her voice trailed off.

"Expected a ruffian?" I wanted to ask, but I forbore. Everywhere I found that the English people were surprised by John, his preference for the refined, his appreciation of classical knowledge. He had been preceded by his reputation as a fearless explorer who had endured terrible physical hardships, and I suspect the British thought anyone who could survive such ordeals must necessarily be uncultured and uncouth. But then there was John, always properly dressed, more willing to talk of Milton and Shakespeare than cross-continental railroad routes and the ever-present slavery question. The British were very interested in our opinions on slavery, and we were never hesitant to declare ourselves.

But the most breathtaking, unforgettable moment of our English stay came when I was presented to Queen Victoria. Being considered a diplomat of some standing—due, I'm sure, to my father's influence and not the rank of my husband— I was presented at the Easter drawing room and, more significantly, invited to remain in the throne room during all the presentations. I wore a pink silk with a pink moire train, with artful roses of all hues appliqued onto it, so that I was, I told Lily, a harmony of roses. It surprised me to see that Queen Victoria was not a great deal older than myself.

I stood in line with the ladies of the diplomatic corps and watched the stately procession of English noblemen. There was Mr. Gladstone, the chancellor of the exchequer, in gown and wig . . . and there the Duke of Wellington. . . . That I stood in close proximity to such men thrilled me more than I was later able to tell, though I sat and wrote a long letter to Father, knowing he of all people would understand my emotion. I felt that day that I was among the fortunate people who lived on the Fortunate Island. John pronounced the whole affair rather like a wedding.

"A wedding?" I asked curiously.

"Yes," he replied solemnly. "The men were of no importance at all."

Our visit to England was a miniature of the pattern of our lives—it started high and ended low, very low. On April 7 John was arrested just as we entered a carriage for a night out. Not one, but four policemen came forward to seize him.

"Wait a minute, men! Take your hands off me!" he declared indignantly, while I screamed aloud, thinking we were beset by thugs. "Police, sir. You best come quietly with us." They were indistinguishable, and I could not tell which one had spoken. "Police?" I echoed.

"You're under arrest, Mr. Frémont, for debt."

Debt? The Mariposas had paid our debts and put us up in the Clarendon—how could this be? "John?"

"Blasted if I know." He shrugged. "I'll just go gently with these fellows"—he nodded at the four—"and you see what you can do to get me out quickly."

Knowing when to give up was not something my father had taught me—had he not tilted at windmills for so many years that he lost his Senate seat?—and yet I sensed now that I could do nothing more than raise a useless scene. And that would embarrass both John and me. I simply nodded at him, and the four bobbies removed him before I could even reach out for a last grasp of the hand.

It was as though the first expedition had started all over again. Once more my husband had to trust me—and I had to live up to that trust. I had to find the money to free him.

I went immediately to the home of his London agent, Mr. David Hoffman.

At first I feared no one was at home, for the house was dark, and my repeated rings of the bell brought no answer. At long last, when I was nearly livid with impatience, a servant came to the door.

"Mr. Hoffman," he informed me, when he'd heard the nature of my visit, "is in bed—ill."

"I don't care if he has the black plague," I said distinctly, "I want to see him now."

The man looked alarmed but finally managed to mutter, "Very well, madam. Wait here."

At length—long length—Hoffman shuffled in, wearing bed slippers and a brocade smoking jacket. When I immediately lashed out with the nature of my visit and my immediate need—four thousand dollars for bail—he began to backpedal.

"I have no such sum," he said, and then added shrewdly, "and I doubt I should give it to you if I did. Mr. Frémont and I have not seen eye to eye on the management of Las Mariposas lately."

"It is his to manage, and yours to finance," I said hotly. But then, quickly, I realized that temper would get me nowhere, and that this man did not intend to help me.

"You, sir," I said in my sweeping departure, "are a scoundrel, and I shall tell my husband of your behavior."

"You do that," he muttered at my retreating back.

John was released the next day, thanks to the intervention—and money—of an American speculator. But he was bitter and angry at being detained.

"This is not about Las Mariposas, is it?" I asked.

"No!" he said angrily. "These are vouchers that I signed for provisions for the California Battalion. The United States government should have made good on them long ago. And there's no reason I should be a scapegoat."

There was no reason, either, that we should stay in a country where he was liable to be arrested again and again for the same debt. It was a monstrous sum we could not begin to pay, and our government showed no signs of interest in the matter. After John's arrest it became clear the matter was deadly serious. It was William Gwin who finally forced the government to settle the debts. "I should have thought," John said, "that your father would be my spokesman."

"So should I," I said shortly, but I knew what John did not realize—the two men in my life were growing apart politically. What neither of us realized was that Father had been pulled into personal grief that no doubt kept him from worrying about our affairs in England, even when he heard belatedly about them. And worse than that, my father was losing his political power.

Just before we left for Paris came word that my only brother, Randolph, had died suddenly of a fever the very day we landed in England. It pained me more than I can yet repeat to realize that I had been writing blithely happy letters back to a family who were grieving. Though their minds would understand that I could not have known, their hearts must have found me insensitive.

I had not been close to Randolph for years. Indeed, I had been angry at him, for he was a continual concern to Father. The infamous confrontation in President Polk's office was but one of many—Randolph had kept Father continually on the alert with episodes of drunkenness, rumors of womanizing, all manner of debauchery. It puzzled me to understand how the boy I remembered as a sweet child could turn so sour . . . and how a son of Father's could grow up so profligate. I, who held Father's example supreme, supposed that his only son should also have felt that way, and so I tended to blame Randolph for his own problems. But I knew that both my parents would be hard hit by his death, and I grieved for them, if not for Randolph.

England had turned bitter for us, and we fled—literally—to Paris. With the help of an acquaintance we located a charming small house—a hotel, the French called it—on the Champs-Élysées, from which we could look down that long avenue one way to the Arc de Triomphe and the other to the Tuileries. Behind our house was a small garden, where the ground fell away toward the Seine. The courtyard walls were covered with ivy, and at the edge of the property stood a cedar of Lebanon, so magnificent that John became obsessed with its green layered boughs and wanted always to sleep under the tree, though he did so but once or twice.

Inside, the house was even more exquisite than out. It belonged to an English-woman who had worried herself into illness over a debt—I could truly understand that after our experience in England—but who had left it furnished as it was for her own use. So we surrounded ourselves with silk hangings, fine China, and many servants. Soon pregnant, I sank into the laziest period of my life and relished it. With each passing day my ambition seemed to disappear and my contentment to grow.

We had a year of rest, rest so complete that it was six months before we even presented our cards at the various legations. The children had a governess, and John took up long-abandoned interests such as mineralogical and astronomical research. He took fencing lessons, went for long horseback rides, and sometimes went for walks in the rain to prove to himself that he was not growing soft. Occasionally, he went to England on business for Las Mariposas—though I never inquired as to the outcome—and we all went on short trips to the galleries at Versailles and other nearby attractions. Once we prepared for a longer jaunt to Italy and Switzerland, then abandoned our plans suddenly when the trip seemed too troublesome.

Anne Beverly—named for John's mother—was born on February 1, 1853, a charming baby in seeming good health who looked to me as though she were part French. Perhaps it was because I thought her part coquette. Her brother and sister adored her, and I, still lost in indolence, thought myself the luckiest woman alive with a complete and very happy family.

"Jessie, I must get back to the States."

I rose from the fainting couch on which I rested—so typical of my approach to life in those days. "Why?" I could not immediately fathom any burning issue, save perhaps the health of my parents, that would pull us from Paris back into the quagmire of politics and financial troubles that awaited us in the United States. And I knew my parents' health had not worsened considerably.

"There are to be expeditions sent west by the government . . . railroad surveys, looking for the best place to cross the Rockies."

"Father mentioned that," I said vaguely.

"Jessie! You've become lazy here! The old Jessie would have already been scheming to secure one of those expeditions for her husband."

His words cut through me as a knife cleaves meat from the bone. I sat straight up. "I shall write Father. . . ."

"No need," he said dryly. "I have this communiqué from your father"—he waved it in the air—"and he says that I am to head one of the expeditions. I must be there yesterday."

"I can be ready to go . . . in a week." I thought that remarkably heroic of me, with three children and a household to consider.

"Jessie," he said quietly, "I sail tomorrow. You and the children will have to follow."

I was angry—furious!—that all this had been decided without consulting me, and I wanted badly to remind John that when he needed me—when he was, for instance, arrested in England—he expected me to solve his problems. In such instances I was an equal partner. But when things arranged themselves to his satisfaction, without his having to worry much or do much manipulating, I was consigned to the role of wife and mother. Not that I hadn't confined myself to those roles in recent months, but, still . . .

When I calmed down—after John had left—and made myself think about the turn our lives had taken, I knew that John saw this as one more chance to redeem himself, to regain that glory we'd known briefly when John was a senator. The court-martial, his defeat for reelection, and more recently, his arrest, could not be glossed over by a life of astronomical study and fencing lessons. The restless streak in John's spirit demanded justification, and the railroad surveys offered an unparalleled opportunity.

As quickly as possible I packed up our household, dismissed the governess and the servants, and with my children—Lily now old enough to be a good help and companion, but Charley still a toddler and Anne an infant in arms—I sailed home.

On that long voyage one thought kept recurring to me: I mistakenly had thought we were through with expeditions, through with the dangers of starvation and frostbite and Indian trouble. John, it seemed to me, had proved himself in those arenas and could now become . . . well, an elder statesman. The trouble was, John had not proved himself to himself.

When at last I reached Washington in late June, it was only to be greeted by bad news.

"I was not given one of the expeditions." His chin was high in the air, and his voice vibrated with defiance.

"It's that Davis, our new secretary of war," Father fumed. "He is determined to push a southern route, in the interests of the cotton growers."

"And you," I said wearily to John, "have made it plain that you favor the route through Santa Fe."

"Of course," he said indignantly. "I'll not change my judgment just to placate a martinet."

It was no use saying to him that he might have placated that particular martinet in order to secure the expedition and then gone ahead and proved what he wanted.

John and Father, it turned out, had already raised the money to fund an expedition privately, and John would leave in August. The expedition would cross the Rockies in the dead of winter.

Why, I wanted to shout, must you tempt the fates again? Why go in winter? But I knew the answer: If John could not make it through in winter, neither could a locomotive.

Washington was muggy and hot that summer, more so than usual, and I worried greatly about Mother, who continued to grow weaker and frailer. My worry, it seemed, was misplaced, for suddenly one day little Anne became ill with fever and had difficulty breathing. All the cool cloths I could find and the gentle care I could give accomplished nothing, as I watched her grow weaker and weaker before my eyes.

"Bring her to Silver Spring," came a terse message, sent by courier, from Francis Blair at his Virginia estate. "The air is cooler and fresher, and she will revive." Francis's daughter, Lizzie, a childhood friend, was there, and I would be grateful for the companionship of a woman.

Like a robot, blindly believing, I bundled up my child and departed for Silver Spring, leaving behind two other terrified children and a husband who busied himself in plans for the expedition in order not to have to think about his child's illness.

John kissed me lightly with a quick "I'm sure she will recover," but it was my father who saw us safely seated in the carriage and who reached out a hand for mine just before we left. He said only, "My thoughts will be with you," but the look on his face plainly told me that he felt himself too old to suffer any more grief. And I, I wanted to shout, am too young for this!

Anne did not revive. She worsened steadily, in spite of the care of the physician hastily sent for. On the night of July 10, Lizzie and I sat together all night. I held my daughter and watched as her breathing grew shallower. Occasionally Lizzie and I talked—of our childhood dreams, what had happened to us, our hopes for the future—but such talk made me all the weepier, for I saw that my daughter had no future, no time for childhood hopes. Just before day broke, little Anne gave one last sigh and lay limp in my arms.

"She is gone, Jessie," Lizzie said at length, her hand resting on the baby's forehead.

"She is only five months old," I said irrationally. "She has had no life. She hasn't had time to know how I love her. . . ."

"She has been loved all her life," Lizzie said, "and I promise you she knew that."

Once again I sat clutching my dead infant to my bosom, and this time I wondered how many times God could cause a person to suffer such unbearable grief. There seemed no answer.

John appeared as devastated as I at the simple graveside ceremony, but afterward he was immediately back to planning his expedition, and I envied him the occupation. I, who had spent my days caring for an infant, found them now heavy on my hands.

His leave-taking in August was once again painful. "Jessie, I want you to promise me something."

"Of course," I answered, wondering.

"If I don't come back from this expedition . . ."

I put my finger to his lips, not willing to hear such talk. I could not bear the loss of anyone else close to me, let alone he who made the sun rise and shine for me.

"No," he protested, "I must tell you this. If I don't, I want you to promise that you and your father will make the government pay the money due me for providing cattle for the Indians. I prevented an Indian war, and it is only right that they should pay. Besides, it . . . it is the only insurance I can leave you."

Feeling that someone had walked across his grave, I promised. "You are up to this?" I asked. "Your leg?"

He shook the offending leg. "Fine, fine," he assured me. Then he laughed. "I suspect I'll have a little trouble adjusting to a wet saddle for a pillow. The last year or so has softened me. But yes, Jessie, I am up to it . . . and I want badly to do this."

"It is," I said in stilted tones, "to your credit that you will take up that rough life again, after the way you have lived, and I think you do it not for personal gain but for the national advantage. I shall always make that known publicly."

"Just collect the money from the government," he said with a wry smile, and pulled me toward him.

The leg was not fine. The expedition set out from Westport Landing in late September. By mid-October I received a telegram saying that John was back in St. Louis, his rheumatism having flared up to a degree that it was impossible for him to continue the expedition. His leg was inflamed, and he was suffering shooting pains in his head and chest. Father's house being closed up, he was staying with my cousin, Sarah Benton Brant, widow of the late Colonel J. J. Brant.

With mixed emotions I made a hasty departure for St. Louis, leaving my children behind, my mother ill, my father in need of my support and assistance. John, I told myself, must come first. A part of me was disloyally thankful that he had been forced to give up the expedition—I would be spared the uncertainty of another winter, the wondering if he was alive or dead, well fed or hungry, warm and cared for or lying frozen in some snowdrift. But a stronger part of my mind knew that John could not bear another defeat. Being forced to give up the expedition, even for physical reasons beyond his control, might be the final failure that would . . . well, I didn't know what the effect would be, but I was sure it would be disastrous for him personally, for us as a married couple, and for our children as a family. That seemed the longest, slowest train trip I ever made, though railroads, by replacing the steamboat route, had much shortened the distance between my two home cities.

"John?" I crept into the bedroom where he slept, expecting to see an invalid. Instead, when he opened his eyes, he jumped—literally—out of bed, threw his arms around me, and said, "Jessie! You've no idea how glad I am to see you . . . but what about the children? Your mother?" Then, telltale, he winced as though in pain and sat rather heavily on the bed.

"I left them," I said, "because I thought you needed me."

"Needed you? Jessie, I always need you." He reached for my hand, pulled me beside him, and kissed me hard and long.

"See?" he asked. But then, more seriously, "But do you mean this leg? It's fine. Look."

He got up and did an awkward little hop, like a child showing off for his mother.

"Fine?" I asked skeptically.

"Well, almost," he admitted. "It will be maybe another five days or so before I'm really ready to leave. But Dr. Ebers says I'm making, and I quote, 'remarkable progress.'" Dr. Ebers was the homeopathic physician treating him by keeping him in bed with his legs raised to uproot the inflammation.

"John," I said seriously, "you don't have to go on this expedition. You can come back to Washington, we'll go to California—"

"No!" His exclamation interrupted me. "I have to find that passage for the railroad, Jessie. It's what my career has been about."

"And if the price is too high?" I asked.

He shrugged, and I remembered his conversation about what I should do if he did not return.

Resolutely I spent the week being a cheerful companion, and the nights a good lover—John's leg did not seem to hamper his activities in bed, and his appetite was strong, perhaps fueled by the thought that we now both tried to ignore: He might never come back from this expedition.

Several times as I lay panting in his arms, exhausted by his needs and my own, I prayed to God that I would not emerge from this week-long late honeymoon pregnant again. I was, I think, fearful of bearing another child only to lose it. But I was fearful, too, of losing my husband if I did not respond to his passion. And truth be known—though I'd never have told my mother—the nights meant as much to me as to John.

"Are you not ready for bed yet?" I would ask, far too early in the evening, when I thought no one else could hear me.

"Are you in a hurry, Jessie?" he'd whisper, and when I nodded my head in the affirmative, we would both fall all over ourselves making excuses to my cousin. My standard excuse was that John's leg required rest, but I noticed that she raised one eyebrow the third time I said that, and so I offered it no more as an excuse. By the end of the week we simply excused ourselves from the dining table and headed for our bedchamber. From time to time I thought my behavior shameful for a grown woman, the mother of two, but John's kisses and his insistent hands banished all such thoughts from my mind.

The week ended, as all such idylls must—we could not bear it, I'm sure, if such rare experiences lasted much longer. And perhaps even idylls would become boring. John departed for Westport Landing, from where he would ride hard to catch the group in the Smoky Hills. At least he took Dr. Ebers with him, and I was grateful for both the man's company and his medical expertise.

I returned to Washington—why did the train seem to travel so much faster headed east, and away from John, than it had when I was headed west, toward him? And then began once again a winter of discontent, of waiting and fearing and hoping and praying, while outwardly I busied myself with the children, sharing the care for Mother with Mathilde and Sophie, copying Father's speeches and doing his research.

Ominous dark clouds gathered on the political horizon, and it was not hard for me to become almost totally engrossed in political matters. When we had returned from England, I found that everyone was talking about a new book, *Uncle Tom's Cabin* by a Mrs. Harriet Beecher Stowe. It had been made into a stage play, and together the book and the play converted hundreds to abolitionism. But Father said direly they were "quick converts" who might not have stomach for the battle ahead. Even schoolchildren were quoting the poem penned by Henry Longfellow in his concern over his country, "Thou, too, sail on, O Ship of State!" Everywhere there was concern, anger, and fear.

The controversy over slavery built toward battle like an angry boil working toward eruption. Senator Stephen Douglas of Illinois—"a little man," as Father described him, and I never knew if he meant physical stature or soul—proposed that Kansas and Nebraska be allowed to vote as to whether they would be slave or free states, in spite of the fact that both lay north of the line set by the Missouri Compromise.

Father was indignant. "The little runt just wants to placate the southerners so he can be elected again." When Douglas and the tall, imposing William Seward, an ardent abolitionist, tangled on the floor of the Senate, Father said it was "the long and the short of it." But when President Franklin Pierce, also anxious to placate the South, endorsed the Kansas-Nebraska Act, Father shook his head and said sadly, "The slaveholders are in the ascendancy."

Still Father preached every chance he got that slavery must not be extended into new territories and states. And now he had a new theme: the Union must be protected against shock and disruption.

When Father's old friend, Francis Blair, and some other Free-Soil Whigs began to talk about a new party whose platform would be the opposition of slavery, Father was dismayed. "That's just the kind of divisiveness we can't stand," he told me.

These matters absorbed my waking thoughts as I worked in Father's library, but at night as I lay alone in my bed, I wondered about John. In part, I wanted him near me so that I could pour out all my worry over the nation's crisis. And, of course, I wanted to touch him, to feel him next to me, to have him wake me in the middle of the night with that whispered "Jessie?" followed by kisses at first gentle and then passionate. But most of all, I wanted to know that he was safe and well.

Chapter Thirteen

By midwinter I was convinced that John was starving to death. It was a hard winter in the capital, and reports from the far West were of heavier snows than usual, colder temperatures. To myself I repeated that old refrain—why did John always have to go in the dead of winter? And why did he have an uncanny knack for picking the worst winters? Try as I might, I could not rid myself of the conviction that he was near death, and that he was alone when he needed me. Quite unconsciously I dismissed the small army of men with him, because I knew John needed me.

Father tried to reassure me. John was, he reminded me again and again, the most experienced explorer, the one who had survived impossible situations. Nothing would happen to him.

His comforting words fell on deaf ears. I had told myself the same things a thousand times. Yet I was so sure that John was starving—perhaps already dead— that I could neither eat nor sleep, though I hid these weaknesses from my family as best I could. My desperation seemed to pale before the national turmoil, Father's own political troubles, and Mother's weakened state.

Lily guessed, and she would stare at me with those large, concerned eyes that reminded me of John. Her looks only made me the more sad, but I hastened always to reassure her that I was fine and her father would be home soon. I don't think she believed me, any more than I believed Father.

One blessing that winter was my renewed acquaintance with Susie, my youngest sister. She had been but a young child when I married, and in my early stays at the house on C Street, I had always been preoccupied with John. Now she was grown, and I had time—albeit nervous time—to spend with her. Susie was a great pianist, and Lily loved to hear her play. Sometimes the three of us would share a sing-along.

But it was in the evenings that Susie and I became close again.

She often would come to my chambers late, when everyone else was asleep, and we would talk—of the young men she thought interesting, her hopes for the future, her fears for our parents. She asked about John and about marriage, with the guile-lessness of a young girl. And gradually, we became confidantes.

One cold evening she had been to a party and brought home with her two friends. The three of them crept to my room to report on the evening's festivities. I found their giggling happiness a welcome distraction from my usual nighttime anxieties, though I repeatedly had to hush them lest they wake Mother, who slept fitfully at best and who was always frightened to lie awake at night.

But the night drew on, and the girls showed no signs of tiring. "I'll just put another log on the fire," I said, stepping into the dressing room to fetch it. As I knelt to pick up the log—a hefty one that required some force from me—I could have sworn I felt a gentle touch. Startled, for I knew no one was there, I turned quickly. Nothing. I was alone in the small chamber. But then I heard, plain as day, John's voice, saying my name. Just "Jessie," nothing more. Briefly I fooled myself into thinking John had once again surprised me with his return, as he had from the second expedition. Faintly I asked, "John?" But there was no more. Bewildered, I tried to martial my thoughts. I had always scoffed at the idea of supernatural experiences, yet even though I knew John was thousands of miles away from me, I had just heard him speak my name clearly. There could be no other explanation. John had spoken to me in spirit . . . and I had heard him.

Far from being alarmed, I was comforted. All my fears and anxiety seemed to drain away in an instant, because I knew that John was alive and would be home safely.

As I knelt there, clutching that piece of wood, with tears of relief running down my cheeks, the disembodied voice spoke again: "Just let me surprise Susie." Susie had long been smitten with John, in the way of young girls, and he had often loved to frighten her just to hear her prolonged, high-pitched scream. The next thing I knew, I heard that scream.

Dropping the wood, I ran back into the room to find Susie rolling on the floor, screaming hysterically. "John! John!" she cried. I finally had to take a robe and put it over her head to stop the screaming, lest she wake the entire household.

"She's overwrought," I said solemnly to her guests. "Too much excitement at the party, I guess."

At length I got them all settled into beds. Susie had calmed down, though she was still somewhat shaky. As I tucked her into her bed, however, she said, "John is all right, isn't he?"

"Yes," I said, "he is." I was too weary with relief to try to explain supernatural experiences to Susie.

The next day I told Lily the whole story. Some may say it was too frightening an experience to share with a child her age, but she had lived through much fear, and I felt she had a right to the reassurance. After that, whenever anyone expressed concern for John or curiosity about his return, Lily would give me a knowing look as though to say that we shared a secret.

John did not return until early summer, and we had no direct word from him until then. He had sent a telegram from New York, but as sometimes happened, it was delayed, and he was his own messenger.

After the joy of reunion, we told each other our stories of the winter past, and then, like lightning, my experience of that February night came crystal clear.

"There was a time, Jessie," he said haltingly, "when I thought I was dying. It was like nothing that has ever happened to me before." It had been from the beginning a journey more perilous than the others. To catch up with his men after he was delayed by the inflammation in his leg, he had ridden over forty miles of burned and burning prairie, the effects of a wild prairie fire. The expedition had been encircled by fire, gradually retreating to a river, by the side of which they piled their supplies, ready to submerge them. Yet they would not leave the area, for fear John would have no way of finding them.

After John finally found the group, some of the animals were stolen by marauding Cheyenne, though thankfully recovered shortly thereafter. "If we hadn't gotten them back," he said, "we'd have been afoot in Comanche and Paiute country—not good for anyone's scalp." He gave a bitter laugh.

Finally reaching Bent's Fort—John's oasis before the Rockies—they discovered that it had been looted and burned by Indians. Mr. Bent had saved very few supplies, so they were unable to replenish sugar, flour, coffee—all these essentials. Without adequate supplies they headed into the mountains, to be met by snow so deep that forage was impossible to find.

"One day," John recounted, "I was going up a slope, breaking my way through the snow, when suddenly I felt the life leaving me. I could not move, and I could not cry out—no sound came. A curious sense of vacancy overcame me, and I thought, 'So this is death!' I truly believed I would die, Jessie, right there on that spot."

I could scarcely breathe, listening to this tale of horror. "And?" I gasped.

"It passed." He shrugged. "I was able to get up and go on in a bit, and no one seemed the wiser . . . except me."

"That's it," I said excitedly. "That's why I began to worry so!"

He looked curiously at me.

"In late January or early February," I explained, "I could not shake the notion that you were dying. I was convinced . . . and I could not talk myself out of it. When . . . when did you know you were safe?"

"When we reached Parawon, the Mormon settlement," he said. "We got there on the ninth of February, and, Jessie, they treated me like a hero. . . ."

"The ninth of February?" I nearly shouted. "That was it, that was the night you spoke to me." My voice was shrill with excitement.

"Jessie! For heaven's sake, what are you talking about?"

I recounted the story of Susie's visit to my room and his ghostly visit to both of us. Suddenly John's face paled.

"What time of night was it?"

I told him, and he began to sob silently, his shoulders shaking. "I wrote to you that night. Once all my men had been warmed and fed, my next thought was that I must let you know that I was alive and well. I never expected the message to reach you for months. But if I wrote at eleven or so, and it was after one in the morning when you thought you heard me . . ."

"I know I heard you," I said firmly. "There was an instant communication."

Stunned, we simply sat and stared at each other, unsure how to digest this amazing happening. What it meant to me was that there was a bond strong as life itself between John and me, and whatever happened to us, we would always be together. More than our marriage or the birth of our children, this was the most spiritual moment of my life.

John, however, was almost embarrassed. "We best go to bed," he said somewhat gruffly.

He was a shy, uncertain lover that night, almost as if that mystical experience had given me some power he didn't understand, something that frightened him. John never liked to feel out of control, and this incident, so reassuring to me, was terrifying to him, though it took me some time to figure that out.

There was to be no written report of this expedition, and so I did not relive it with him as I had the earlier ones. In bits and pieces I heard of his adventures, but they never came glowingly alive like the others. Over and over John repeated that he had found the way to build the railroad. He had gone to the spot where the fourth expedition had gone astray, and, determining that there was no pass near, he had turned south, following the information given him by trappers and Indians. He had found good passes all the way, in a straight line between thirty-eight and thirty-nine degrees latitude. "The railroad must go that way," he said with passion. "It will make the United States the link between Europe and Asia. It must be built!"

By August, John was ready to leave again for California. "I must go," he said. "I . . . I have to return to you, Jessie, to refresh myself. But I cannot stay here. . . ."

"Here?" I asked. "You cannot stay with me . . . or the children . . . or is it this city?"

"It's this city," he cried vehemently. "I've known too many changes in fortune here. My life is in California. . . . I must see to Las Mariposas so that we can have our home there. I would take you and the children . . ."

I shook my head regretfully. "I cannot leave my mother," I said, and though I hated having him go off alone again, I would have made no other decision. Women sometimes have to choose between the old life and the new. I recognized the conflict and accepted it.

"You are my wife," he said, his voice just ever so slightly petulant. "You should be with me."

"John," I began, only to be interrupted by his laughter.

"I know, I know. I am only feeling sorry for myself. Your trouble, Jessie, is that you are my strength . . . and you are your father's strength. We both need you desperately." All laughter was gone as he added, "But my need is physical as well as emotional, you must never forget that."

I did not forget it the two months that John was home that summer, for he refreshed himself physically as well as mentally. It crossed my mind that John gained some kind of strength from our physical union, for he was tireless and—it pained me to admit it—demanding. It was as though my physical response gave him some needed reassurance.

I responded with all my heart, because I desperately loved this man, with his strange mix of strength and weakness. But my body, sometimes less eager to respond, betrayed my fear of another pregnancy. Some nights I willed myself to be passionate, moving my hands over his body in ways that I thought would please him, moaning when I thought it expected . . . but always playacting.

"Jessie," he whispered one night, "you are not with me. What troubles you? Is it your mother?"

How could I blame my coldness on that poor woman, whose burdens were already too heavy? Or on my father, or even on concern for the children? "No, John," I said, "I am afraid of another pregnancy. I don't think I could bear to lose another child."

Silent, he withdrew from me and turned his back, and then I was consumed by guilt, for I had rejected the man who could least stand rejection. I reached a tentative hand for him, only to have him shake it off.

"No," he said.

"I . . . I only told the truth. It has nothing to do with my love for you," I said.

"It has everything to do," he muttered.

"John, I would risk anything for you . . . and for your love. I will quiet my fears." My hands began to stroke the length of his back, wandering down onto his thighs, and finally pressing between his legs. He stirred, then his entire body stiffened as though determined to ignore me. I kept up my gentle campaign until at last, with a groan, he turned to me.

My response was apparently ardent enough to convince him. As he lay panting next to me, John said the only words I ever wanted to hear from him: "Jessie, I love you."

"And I, you, John," I answered, wishing I could tend to myself immediately, as though that somehow would prevent another pregnancy. But I never refused John, and I became an artful deceiver.

John, who generally let me run the household while he was off on his travels, turned strangely stubborn just before he left. He insisted we rent a small house not three doors from Father's house.

"John! The children and I can live with Father much more economically," I said, totally unprepared to consider this wild idea. "Susie is gone now, and Father will need me all the more."

To our great surprise Susie had quietly married one of her suitors, a French nobleman, and they had taken up residence in India after a small wedding. "Mother's condition," Susie said, when asked if she did not want a formal ceremony. Perhaps sudden and small wedding ceremonies ran in the family.

"I want to see my family in their own home," he said, his voice every bit as determined as mine. "We have lived off your father long enough."

In a way, this was like making love. John, once again, had to prove himself.

"It will just be inconvenient for me, having to run down the street to care for Mother," I said.

"It will also give you a place of peace to which you can retreat," he countered, "and I have hired a maid so that you will not have to run the household. Jessie, I mean this as a help to you." His voice took on a certain pleading tone, as though he wanted me to applaud what he had done.

"Thank you, John, I know that you do. And you're probably right—it will turn out for the better." As it was, it turned out much for the better, though none of us could have known that at the time.

The house was partly furnished, so it was a simple matter to transfer our personal belongings down the street. We had carted the Oriental rugs and the inlaid furniture around the country so much that I wondered they were still intact—the damask draperies had long since gone to other uses, including a gown for me. Father was puzzled—and a little hurt—but I assured him I would spend most of my time in his house and this was just a move designed to keep the children from under his feet or from bothering their grandmother. He nodded silently, but his expression told me that he did not accept my halting excuse.

"John thinks it best?" he asked.

"Yes," I said, and he simply nodded again.

John left in August, and by September I knew that I was pregnant again, but there were other things on my mind. Father, having been defeated for the legislature, set out for Missouri to repair whatever political fences he could. It worried me to see him troubled with chronic headache, and it saddened me to see a political career that had once bloomed so brightly fade as the slavery issue overtook the country. But nothing could persuade Father that he should retire from politics nor that he should change his antislavery stand, not that I would have wanted him to.

Meantime, at home, there was Mother. "Mother, can you not take a little broth?" "Not now, Jessie," she whispered. Even her voice had grown weaker in recent days, and I knew—though I wouldn't admit it to myself—that the end was near. Had he been home, Father would have paced the hall outside her room and entered to stroke her hair and stare at her with a love so strong that it would break your heart. But he was gone, and I was all Mother had—my presence was slight compensation for a life lost for the sake of the man she loved. Even as I nursed her, cajoling her into eating, I wondered if I would sacrifice that much for John—and then, with a shock, I realized I probably would, for I had long let my love for John dominate my life. As a result there lay behind me a string of disasters: expeditions that failed, a court-martial, and—worst of all—two of our children, dead. Instinctively, I clutched my rounding belly.

On the evening of September 9—how that date burns in my memory!—Mother sat up in her bed and, her voice stronger than usual, announced, "I want to go downstairs."

With my arm to lean upon, she ventured down the stairs, into parts of the house where she had not been for months. With a strength of purpose that both frightened and amazed me, she headed for Father's library. There, throwing off my arm, she stood at his chair, stroking it as though she were stroking the head of the man who normally sat there. With great care she touched the stacks of foolscap, the penholders that lay there, an old pipe that had been tossed to one side.

Then, weeping, she turned to me. "He is a very good man, your father. You must take care of him, Jessie. I have never been able to." Then, still leaning on me, she walked through the downstairs rooms of the house, pausing to stare at the matching oil portraits of her parents, running a loving hand over the high polish of the sideboard that had come from Cherry Grove, stopping to sit for a moment in the wingback chair that had by tradition been hers in years gone by, when she'd spent evenings in companionable silence with my father.

I grew increasingly nervous, fearing that she was getting too tired, and yet reluctant to hurry her along. Finally she said, "I am ready now," and I thought she meant to go upstairs. But no sooner were the words out of her mouth than she collapsed onto the floor in a small heap, and I, my heart in my mouth, leaped to her side. She had, for all I could tell, merely fainted. I called for Mathilde and with her help was able to get Mother back up the stairs and into her bed, though all the while we struggled with her inert weight, I said prayers of appeasement to the unborn child in my womb.

My mother died on September 10, without ever regaining consciousness. I decided she had died at peace, and that was what she meant when she said, "I am ready," though I pondered long in the following days about the meaning of her life.

Father returned from Missouri a broken man, all thought of the next election banished from his mind. His terrible grief brought home to me in unexpected ways the importance a woman plays in her husband's life. There I had it—two examples, both of which confused me utterly. My mother had sacrificed all for my father and had seemingly done so without regret; my father, that strong, outspoken, garrulous man, was apparently so dependent on a frail, invalid wife who rarely left her room that without her presence he was reduced to helplessness. Where, I wondered, did John and I fit into such patterns?

John wrote impassioned letters of condolence from California, regretting more than I could know that he was not in Washington to support me when I needed him. Even as I replied, assuring him I felt his support across the continent, a glimmer of thought raced through my brain that this crisis was more easily gotten through without John.

And then I banished the thought as disloyal.

And so we passed another holiday season, this time in mourning, John gone as usual, the house deadly quiet. Father could not be drawn into a celebration, so what festivity there was occurred at my little house. "John," I whispered aloud late one night, "how wise you were to put us in this little house." Lily and Charley sat around the evergreen tree on Christmas morning and opened modest gifts that brought joyous gasps far out of proportion to the contents. But they were happy. And I was gleeful to see them so.

Father came for dinner and, despite his best efforts, put a pall on things. Late that night as I tucked the covers up around her, Lily asked, "Will Grandfather ever be himself again?"

"I don't know," I sighed, "I really don't know." But deep in my heart I did know, and that was a burden to be borne. My father had lost his strength. I nearly had to run from Lily's room to hide my tears. Once I was safely closeted in my own chambers, the tears came in unchecked torrents as I cried for all that Father had lost, for the great things he had accomplished and the even greater things that he had been prevented from doing, for a political career in ruins and a man heartbroken. I cried, too, for myself, for the reflected glory I had lost. Raised as Senator Benton's daughter, I had been used to privilege, and it had come to me gradually over recent years that my heritage no longer brought the privilege it once had. Oh, I was still Senator Benton's daughter, but it was a tarnished crown I wore.

If privilege in our nation's capital mattered to me—and I wasn't sure if it did or not—then I looked to John to provide. And he was off in California, running from the center of power as though it had burned him. And perhaps it had.

In February another tragedy blotted out all other thought.

"Mama, Mama, Grandfather's house . . ." Lily came running in the front door, screaming in a way unlike that usually placid child.

"Lily!" I had been about to scold her when her words penetrated my thinking. "What about Grandfather's house?" I asked.

"It's burning!" she cried.

I was out the door and into the cold air without a wrap or a thought, running the short distance between the two houses. But even as I sprinted down the steps of my own house, I saw smoke rising in the sky high above, and flames pouring from the windows of the first floor of Father's house—my house, the home I had grown up in, the place that had always been my refuge.

Gasping from terror, I clasped my hand over my mouth and stood in the street, the horror of the San Francisco fire flooding over me again. Now, even before my very eyes, the flames grew bolder, reaching up to dart out of second-story windows, consuming the roof in great sections.

Mathilde and Sophie soon joined us, having come from the back of the house. They stood in silent horror, staring at the house.

"How?" I asked.

Mathilde shook her head. "Don't suppose we'll ever know. That Joe Mr. Benton done hired a while back, he come runnin' into the kitchen shoutin' 'Fire!' I didn't believe him, till I pushed the swinging door into the dining room and seen the flames eatin' up the whole front of the house." She paused a minute. "It started in the senator's library, Miss Jessie."

Father's library! All the books and maps and the records of a lifetime. He had some time ago finished the first volume of his memoirs—*Thirty Years' View*—and had started the second volume. All his papers, I knew, were in that study.

"Probably the chimney," Mathilde muttered. "Must not've been built right."

But it worked all these years, I wanted to shout!

The fire company had arrived, amid clanging bells and much shouting, with their horse-drawn wagon and the hand pump it carried. It took two men to work the thing, and they pumped furiously, but the supply of water in that small wagon was soon exhausted. I saw one man holding a great, tall ladder and staring at the house, as though baffled as to what he should do. His duty, I supposed, was to put it up to the second floor and rescue people, but there could be no one inside that inferno now. Then he laid the ladder down and joined the bucket brigade, men throwing ineffectual buckets of water from the cistern. They reminded me of gnats fighting an elephant.

A great anguished cry escaped my throat, and I staggered drunkenly. Lily, by my side, grabbed my arm and said, "Mama, it's all right."

I wrapped my arms about her and held tight. "Your grandfather," I said, "I don't know where he is. . . ."

"There," Lily said, pointing down the street, where Father came half running along in that awkward gait that an elderly man takes on when trying to hurry.

Even as I rushed toward him, he waved me away, as though he wanted to witness this tragedy in solitude. He stood, feet planted apart, thumbs hooked in his belt, watching the destruction of all that he had held dear.

"All of Elizabeth's things," Father said under his breath.

"Your memoirs!" I shouted, as though I thought I had to remind him that they were more important than Mother's possessions.

Father just shook his head hopelessly, and together we watched the final destruction of the house on C Street. Within minutes there was nothing left except a blackened shell of bricks and a fireplace chimney extending crookedly beyond a roof that was no longer there. One wall had fallen partway in, but the bricks mostly stood firm, a sort of grim reminder of the shape of the house. The fire had taken all record of us as a family . . . and much of the record of Father as a legislator.

That night we sat late and silent before a small but warming fire in my parlor. The children were in bed, and Father and I sat together without talking. Finally I ventured, "I had not thought I would want to see flames again so soon." I nodded at the fire.

He just looked at me, and then finally he said, "I have lost everything that matters to me. Everything. It makes the idea of dying so much easier, there is so much less to leave."

My shoulders convulsed as I tried to hide my sobs, and Father—he who had been my rock—reached over to comfort me.

At last I raised my face, trying to smile. "I'll help you rewrite the memoir."

"We'll see, Jess, we'll see," he said wearily.

One thing about Father: He was not easily defeated, by political enemies or natural disasters. Within a month he presented me with plans to rebuild the house and announced that work would begin the next week. And his memoirs? "I've started again," he said. "I think the manuscript will be better this time."

At that moment I hoped and prayed that I had inherited more of Father's strength than Mother's weakness.

～ ～

John did not return until early May, just in time for the birth of Francis Preston Blair on May 17. He was my fifth child, a special blessing, though he took a long time coming into this world and exhausted me. I was thirty-three years old—too old, I decided, for childbearing.

John disappeared during those long hours that I labored, and sometimes, through a haze of pain, I longed for him, wanted his comforting touch, wanted the renewal that he had found in me. But he was gone, only to reappear when the baby was safely born. I would not say healthily, for the infant was weak enough to strike terror into my heart.

John was there, though, almost immediately, holding my hand, telling me he loved me.

"John, I want to name him after Francis Blair . . . Father's friend." Francis Blair was also the father of the Blair brothers, who were lawyers in St. Louis and friends to both John and me.

"Fitting," John said, "but can we call him Frank?"

We could and did.

Chapter Fourteen

The presidency! I had not dared to think of John as presidential material. If I had thought about it, I would have said that he was too young and untried, too green and unknown. Presidents, I would have said, were my father's contemporaries—Franklin Pierce, James Polk, Zachary Taylor. There were never men of John's age.

And yet when I first heard his name mentioned for president, I shook with a thrill so strong that for a moment it terrified me. Could I want something that badly? And if I did, why? What did the presidency mean to me? In sane moments I would say that it meant a chance for John and me to advance the causes we believed important—even crucial—to the country's future: abolition and westward expansion. Caught late at night or in an unguarded moment, I might have confessed that having grown up in Washington, the White House represented the ultimate in achievement and power to me. I wanted it badly for John—and for myself. I never denied being ambitious.

Even before John returned from California that spring, I was hearing rumors of his possible candidacy for the presidency. The Democrats wanted to run an antislavery man.

"Jessie, he'd be perfect," my cousin William Preston of Kentucky said. "He's antislavery, he wants to win . . . and we're going to win."

"He'll not compromise on the slavery issue," I warned.

Francis Blair, who had come with William to our meeting, just looked skeptically at me, as though he were telling me that every man had his price. Not John Charles Frémont, I wanted to tell him, but I kept my counsel. It was for John to say such things.

What John said was that the Native American party—a southern outgrowth of the Democrats—appealed to him tremendously. He heartily agreed with their belief that we should close the borders to immigration before the New World became as overcrowded as the Old World. Advocating a twenty-year residency requirement for voting, the Native Americans believed land should be held only by those willing to take responsibility. "A dissatisfied citizen of the Old World will never become a useful citizen of the United States," John told me, echoing political sentiments he heard from supporters among the Native Americans. It seemed to me all counter to the principles of our country and, certainly, to the teachings of my father. I kept my counsel, though.

"Ah, Jessie, can't you see us in the White House?"

Then I let myself dream a bit, doubts or no. "I've been there so often, John, and I know just what we would do differently . . . how we would conduct things. . . . Oh, yes! It would be wonderful."

John was perhaps taken aback by my enthusiasm. The look on his face suggested he wanted to remind me that the presidency was occupied by a lone man, not a man and his wife, but it mattered not to me. We were partners.

I hoped all along that a presidential bid would come from the Democrats and not the rump Native Americans. By the time John attended a meeting of the southern Democrats in New York, it was late summer and the children and I had left the city for the quiet coolness of Nantucket. Frank was a good baby, healthier than I had at first expected, and Lily took wonderful care of Charley, walking him along the beach for hours on end, so that I was left free to rest.

But my mind was never at rest, no matter that the world thought Mrs. Frémont was recuperating from the birth of her last child. My imagination ran to presidential balls and receptions at the White House and presidential policy and a thousand matters of state—the things on which I'd cut my teeth as my father's assistant. I waited impatiently for John.

And yet, when he arrived, late one night, I saw defeat in the slump of his shoulders. My eyes asked the question my voice did not dare.

"We'll talk later," he said. "Let me see the children."

And so he spent an hour or two watching his children play on the beach. John was never good about playing with them, always remaining more of a spectator. Frank lay on a blanket at our feet, and occasionally John would waggle a finger at him. Lily from time to time came to stand by her father, and once I heard her say shyly, "I'm glad you' re home." He thanked her formally, and she, after an awkward moment, went back to Charley, who played at the water's edge. Charley was, I had decided, the least inhibited of my children, frankly enjoying every minute of life with a zest that I envied.

As we sat on a blanket on the beach, I itched with impatience to hear John's story, and he, I suspected, knowing my curiosity, drew out the suspense. At length the children were bedded down, with Sophie to watch over them.

"Shall we walk along the beach?" he asked, offering his hand.

I took the hand silently and went with him, waiting for him to speak. He stopped to remove his shoes and roll his pant legs so that he could walk in the water. Since I was still shod, it meant that we sometimes walked far enough apart that he had to raise his voice to make me hear. I found the distance between us awkward and disconcerting.

"I cannot do it, Jessie," he said at length. "The Democrats expect to win . . . and I think they may."

"Did they . . ." My voice faltered because so much seemed to ride on the moment. "Did they offer you the nomination?"

He gave me a long dark look, and in that moment I was intensely aware of the water lapping against the beach, the moon shining on the sand. *Here we are* I thought, *discussing things so weighty I can hardly bear to talk about them and yet we are in an idyllic setting where all cares should be banished.*

"They can't afford to lose the South," he said. "Whoever is the nominee will have to support the extension of slavery into Kansas and Nebraska."

I stifled a gasp. "You . . . you cannot do that?" I made it a question, but in my heart I knew it was a statement.

"No," he said, "I cannot. It is the choice between a wreck of dishonor or a kindly light that will go on its mission of doing good." There was a bitter taste in my mouth as I agreed with him. Badly as I wanted the presidency, I could not conscience the extension of slavery into new territories. Father would support me, I knew.

What Father didn't support was John's leanings toward the new Republican party. "We don't need another party," he had fumed months ago to me. "It will split the country beyond repair."

When the first tentative Republicans approached John about running on their abolitionist ticket, he said to me, "This will anger all your southern relatives. You'll no longer be welcome at Cherry Grove."

"Nor you among your family and all those you grew up with," I said. "And Father will never accept it." I was going to be forced to make a choice between the two men in my life—my father and my husband. John, I knew, would go whichever way I went. If I asked it, he would reject any hope of the presidency for the sake of family unity; Father was never so flexible. He would see things one way, and one way only. But I could not counsel John against what I was sure was the best policy for us personally, and for the country. "We must work to get the Republican nomination," I said.

"I had intended to take all of you to California this fall," John replied, "but I've been advised not to go. Your father's friend Francis Blair, among others, wants me to be available as they gather support for my nomination."

I measured my words carefully, trying to still the excitement that must have crept into my voice. "Is it worth staying? Worth leaving the Mariposas to others? Worth leaving behind all our relatives and friends?" What, I wondered, would I have said if he had decided the risk was not worth the prize at the end of it all?

But he didn't. "Jessie, I want this," he said. "I want it more than I can tell you."

"And so do I," I whispered. Our fate was sealed then, and the past left behind us. We moved to New York City in September and took up residence at the Clarendon Hotel. I tackled the problem of making John live up to his image.

"John, you need new clothes. Yours are all outdated, relics of the years before you went to California. If you are to be about making a good impression, you must have new clothes." I looked at him, remembering the beauty of him in army uniform and wishing he could wear that.

"I don't want fancy clothes, Jessie—no velvet on the coat."

I laughed aloud. "All right, no velvet, but a new greatcoat. You must always look a bit the westerner."

He looked startled. "Why?"

"Because the country will want to elect a new man, not someone who is part of the same old group. And what they know you best for is western exploration."

Doing a small dance around me, he demanded, "Do you want me to go abroad in buckskins?"

"No, not quite," I answered, "but maybe nankeen trousers and a linsey waistcoat."

"I will not, Jessie! Linsey is for poor farmers. I'll wear wool coats and linen shirts and satin waistcoats." He pronounced this with a slightly defiant air.

And so we ordered him new clothes—coats of black, with sparkling white linen shirts and black bow ties to be worn at the neck. His hair had turned fully gray now, and he wore it cut just below his ears, with a full beard and mustache. When properly dressed, I thought him dashingly handsome . . . and told him so.

"You're prejudiced," he said, grabbing me to waltz around our bedroom, a waltz that ended with both of us tumbled on the bed.

"I am prejudiced," I whispered. "You'll be the handsomest president of the country yet."

"Ah, Jessie," he murmured as his hands loosened the buttons of my dress, "never without your ambition."

Within seconds he had entered me with a ferocity that told me my ambition was no threat to our marriage. It may well have been the bulwark upon which it was built.

Father did not come to New York to see us. I had harbored a small secret hope that he would throw himself into John's campaign and thereby find a relief from his grief over Mother's death and the loss of the house on C Street, but my dream was only wishful thinking.

I heard from Francis Blair, who had two lengthy visits with Father, that his work on the second volume of *Thirty Years' View* was progressing, but that he was staunchly opposed to the Republican party and to John as a candidate. "Your father fears he lacks political experience," Mr. Blair wrote. I wanted to suggest that very lack was the factor that made him appealing to a large portion of the country, but I was learning to hold my tongue. Mr. Blair surely could figure that out for himself.

If Father did not come to us, I should, I thought, have gone to him . . . and yet I was reluctant. He no doubt needed me more than anyone else, and yet to go would be to diminish my husband. Torn, I often walked the floor trying to puzzle my way out of the trap in which I saw myself. But there were no easy solutions.

I sent Lily to Washington, at the cost of missing her schooling, but she returned sooner than expected and announced that Grandfather was not himself. "He works all day at his desk," she said. "The only thing that breaks his day is a horseback ride . . . and he wouldn't let me ride with him."

"Wasn't he glad to see you?" I asked.

"I guess so," she said reluctantly, "but he never talked to me. The only thing he said, over and over, was for me to tell my father not to run for president. Papa? Are you going to?"

John looked positively helpless, but I, my heart breaking for my father, said, "Yes, Lily, he probably will."

She smiled as though it were a personal triumph. "I'm glad. I hope Grandfather can learn to be glad too."

There was, I knew, not much chance. All that winter I wrote bright and happy letters to Father, but he never replied, and my news came from Liza, who, with her husband, William Carey Jones, was now living in the rebuilt house with Father. Long after John's military trial William had developed an unfortunate dependence on alcohol, and Liza's thoughts were so occupied with her own troubles that she had little understanding of Father—or of my separation from him. Father, meantime, spoke out more and more actively among the Free-Staters urging compromise on the Kansas issue to preserve the Union.

Sally McDowell remained my confidante. I could and did spill out all my fears and hopes to her with frequency. We wrote about the latest fashions—I could never wear my skirts as short as hers—and our children—little Frank was growing roly-poly and thoroughly healthy and happy—and about deeper issues—my father's unhappiness. I confessed my dissatisfaction with New York society—"I have been to two parties. The women were dressed within an inch of their lives and stupid as sheep—some of the men had sense but not many. I feel like a dancing doll, dressed up to perform."

That whole long winter John and I played "almost pretend" with each other. Each of us knew that the presidential nomination was the most important thing, and yet we feigned casualness. John worked at the affairs of the Mariposas, in which I took little interest, and I busied myself running a full household with three children and several servants. As was the fashion, we let others campaign for us, though there was a constant stream of visitors at the house we had rented on Second Avenue, after we decided the Clarendon Hotel was too confining.

The Republican party strengthened its organization, and almost as a direct result, enthusiasm for John's candidacy grew. Newspapers began to take notice of him, calling him "Pathfinder" in reference to his work as an explorer. When the proslavery element won the government in Kansas—Pierce's terrible mistake!—and the antislavery faction set up an opposition government, John wrote an eloquent letter in defense of abolition to "Governor" Charles Robinson that earned him newspaper space throughout the nation. Matters escalated in May when Congressman Preston Brooks of South Carolina attacked and caned Senator Charles Sumner on the Senate floor in retaliation for Sumner's long speech, three days earlier, against slavery in Kansas. Then antislavery fanatic John Brown and his followers raided in Kansas, murdering five men.

"I feel it is my destiny," John whispered one night as we lay in bed, "to lead this country against slavery. Someone's got to do it."

The Democrats, meeting in Cleveland in late May, nominated my old escort, James Buchanan, of whom I had heard Father say, "He has middling talents." Yet Father attended the convention and began immediately to campaign for Mr. Buchanan. Then the Native Americans met in early June. They had been invited to join ranks with the Republicans, and John thought—he privately confessed—that they would nominate him. But the majority of that party nominated N. P. Banks of North Carolina, while a rump group bolted and chose Commodore Stockton of New Jersey. Thus, by the time the Republicans met, there were three candidates—two of them all but unknown—in the presidential field. As it turned out, the Native American party had little influence on the election, nor did the dying Whig party, which ran Millard Fillmore, whose lackluster presidency had guided the country in the first two years of the decade.

The first Republican National Convention was held in mid-June of 1856 in Philadelphia. John and I, waiting in New York, did not hear the news until Francis Blair arrived in triumph after the convention. While we waited, John wrote to Frank Blair in St. Louis that he felt as if there had been a preliminary shock, presaging an earthquake. "I feel as men do who are momentarily expecting a great shock . . . but my nerves are tranquil." I, meantime, was a nervous wreck, pacing the floor, peering out the window for two days, until at last I saw Mr. Blair.

"You're the candidate, my lad," he said. "First ballot, and to tremendous acclaim, I might add. There was some sentiment for John McLean of Ohio—especially among delegates from Ohio and Pennsylvania—but not enough to make it, and we made a plea for unanimity. You got all but thirty-eight votes."

I held my breath until, slightly dizzy, I had to grasp a chair to support myself.

"Jessie?" John asked.

"I'm fine. I'm just overcome . . . and proud of you, John. We must think about your nomination speech."

Even Francis Blair laughed. "Leave us a day to savor the moment, Jessie. We'll get to work soon enough."

But I was already planning the speech in my mind—short, straightforward, and firm on the subject of slavery.

Two weeks later, speaking in New York, John said strongly, "The extension of slavery across the continent is the object of power which now rules the government, and from this spirit have sprung those kindred wrongs of Kansas. . . . A practical remedy is the admission of Kansas into the Union as a free state. . . . It would vindicate the good faith of the South."

The crowd went wild, shouting "Three cheers for Frémont!" And then, to my astonishment, I heard "Three cheers for Jessie! Mrs. Frémont!" They all took up the cry, yelling, "Give us Jessie!" No candidate's wife had ever appeared publicly—I had to insist that John let me attend his speech, sitting unobtrusively in the audience, accompanied by Francis Blair. But now the crowd kept up its demand, calling my name.

"Francis?" I asked, knowing what I myself longed to do.

"Why not?" He shrugged. "Nothing else will quiet them." Rising and offering his arm, Francis Blair escorted me to the podium, amid cheering so strong it nearly made me burst. I stood next to John and reveled in the moment—a crowd of thousands, giving John the support and approval he had so long needed and earned, and too often been denied. That they cheered for me only meant that they recognized my support of John, that I was part of their cause.

Father, I said to myself, *I wish you could see this.*

Father, of course, never acknowledged the moment. He was now running for governor of Missouri, campaigning hard for the Democratic ticket and Buchanan.

"Doesn't it strike you as odd," John asked one evening, "that your father is supporting a ticket that advocates compromise with slavery—a position he has vociferously denounced—while he is condemning me, though I am running on a ticket that supports his own stated position on slavery?"

I could not answer. Tears blinded my eyes and choked my voice.

—◦—

"John," I asked one night as we sat alone before a dying fire, the rest of the household long since asleep, "do you realize we have been married not quite fifteen years?" To me he still looked the young explorer. I suppose I refused to see a certain sadness in the eyes, a tiredness around his mouth, and the very obvious graying of his hair.

He reached to put an arm around and draw me close. "It's been quite a fifteen years," he said thoughtfully.

"Well," I responded indignantly, thinking he was making light of it, "it has! Fifteen years ago no one knew who you were. Now you're a presidential candidate, the hero of the nation, the man they call Pathfinder."

He laughed. "I had the sense to marry Senator Benton's brightest and smartest daughter."

I drew away. "Is that why you married me?"

Instantly he was on the floor at my feet. "Of course not, Jess. You must never think that. I married you because I love you . . . and because you are the best thing that could ever happen to me."

Still suspicious, I pushed the point. "To you . . . or to your career?" I was plunging into deep waters, for I well knew that I wanted his national fame as much—maybe even more—than he did. I was accusing him of my own sins.

Now he jumped to his feet to pace. "Jessie, if you even begin to think that. . . . If what we have shared—the triumphs of the explorations, the grief over lost babies—means nothing to you . . . I will resign the candidacy now. We'll go to California and live quietly as private citizens. I'll run the mine, you raise the children, and—"

"No!" I said, rising to meet him. "I am just tired. I don't know what got into me. I want you to continue. . . . I want the presidency for you."

"And the White House for you?" he asked with a slight smile.

"That too," I admitted, adding, "even Lily is excited about living there."

"Poor Lily. I hope she is not disappointed."

"She won't be," I said fiercely.

I didn't want to live as private citizens in a remote mining camp in the Sierras.

———

"Frémont and Jessie" became the rallying cry of the campaign, to my outward embarrassment and secret pleasure. Crowds chanted our names and called for us, though we never again appeared nor did John speak in public. Following custom—better than I had by going to the podium!—he remained at home while his party campaigned for him.

It was, John said ruefully, a women's campaign. Though I never again was so bold as to appear, crowds called for me, and men and women alike wore buttons that read "Frémont and Jessie" or "Jessie's Choice." There was even a song—"Oh Jessie Is a Sweet, Bright Lady," sung to the tune of "Comin' Through the Rye." Abraham Lincoln, a young Congressman from Illinois who was making quite a name for himself as a speaker, reported over a hundred women with nursing babies in the crowd when he spoke for John at an Illinois rally, and abolitionist Elizabeth Cady Stanton spoke out on John's behalf.

Of course, the opposition used women's support of John against him, the most blatant example being a cartoon that portrayed a cigar-smoking, pantaloon-wearing woman declaring herself for Frémont. It was another thing from the papers that I did not show John, but I was torn by guilt. Had this popularity, which I could not deny enjoying, hurt John? I would have died a thousand deaths before I would hurt his campaign. And yet a secret corner of me relished the vision of myself as the headstrong and independent yet romantic lady who had the good sense at the age of seventeen to elope with this man. I was glad neither John nor Father was privy to that thought!

Ours was a busy house, as callers and letters flooded in. Francis Blair and I decided that the newspapers and letters should be screened before John saw them, lest innuendo and outright accusation upset him. He agreed readily to this. In addition, I also took on the chore of answering the personal and private correspondence. It galled me to think that public statements on political matters were issued by two hired minions of the new party, when I should rightfully have been taking care of such. But I kept my peace and worked away every morning in the downstairs of our house, while upstairs John and a partner practiced their fencing, their stamping feet making the hall ring to the roof.

The bitterest personal correspondence came from friends and acquaintances in the South. One man, a schoolmate of John's after whom he had named a river in the West, wrote that their correspondence was now painful to him and he wished never to hear from John again. I hid that letter.

When callers came to the house, John was quiet, almost shy, while I did the talking. One day Mr. Horace Greeley was announced. I was anxious to meet the editor of the *New York Tribune,* whose various causes—vegetarianism to phrenology to women's rights—were nationally famous. He was an ardent abolitionist, and his paper was supporting John strongly. I entered the parlor expecting to meet a man of dignity and was instead greeted almost awkwardly by a tall, gangly man in baggy clothes, various papers trying to escape the pockets of his jacket.

"We do appreciate your support," John said formally, while I cut to the chase.

"What are our chances?" I asked.

Greeley looked out the window so long that I thought perhaps he hadn't heard my question—or was embarrassed by not knowing how to answer. Then, at length, he spoke in slow, measured tones: "I think they are good, if you can carry Pennsylvania. That's going to be the most important state."

"Pennsylvania was for McLean at the convention," I said quickly. He looked appraisingly at me. "You have a good head for politics, Mrs. Frémont. So I've heard. You're right, Pennsylvania was for McLean. That's not our problem. Businessmen who aren't interested in alienating the South, if it means losing their business, are the enemy . . . in Pennsylvania and anyplace else."

"But that's not the point," I said, probably too loudly. "The whole election is about freedom and independence, the principles of our constitution."

"Ah," he answered, "I only wish it were. No, ma'am, it's like everything else . . . it's about practical matters. When it comes right down to it, men will vote their pocketbook and not their ideals."

Angrily I turned to John, expecting him to leap to my defense, but he said nothing, and I was left with a bitter taste in my mouth. Mr. Greeley may have looked awkward, but he was forthright and honest, when the truth was what I least wanted to hear.

I was more determined to be practical when it was publicly charged in newspaper after newspaper that John was a Catholic. Even the *Tribune* printed the charge, though at least it made light of it, and I silently thanked the forthright Mr. Greeley. The proof offered was so obviously false as to be ridiculous to my mind: John had carved a cross on Rock Independence on his first expedition, we had been married by a priest, he had seen to it that a niece attended Catholic school.

"John," I pleaded, "you must deny the charge. You must make it public that you have been an Episcopalian all your life."

He shook his head. "I can't do that, Jessie. If this election is about freedom, it is about all kinds of freedom, religious among them. If following Catholicism, which is a lawful religion, disqualifies me from holding office, then I will seek no man's vote. I will not encourage the religious fanaticism that has brought ruin to the Old World." There it was again, John's comparison of the ills of the Old World and the bright possibilities of the new, possibilities that depended on freedom.

I wanted to retort that this was no time for high-minded idealism, with the presidency within our grasp. We could not, we simply could not, lose it now. But then I remembered my anger at Mr. Greeley's practicality, and I was quiet.

The Republican party had a conference to deal with the matter and urge John to make a public declaration. He remained firm and, on Greeley's advice, followed his convictions.

The most devastating charge—and the one that I could not keep from John— was that he was a bastard. At Francis Blair's suggestion I had written a campaign biography for publication. In it I had glossed over the circumstances of John's family background. I should have known better, for the papers pounced on my deliberately vague rhetoric.

"There!" John said one Sunday morning, flinging across the room a Virginia newspaper that referred to him as a Frenchman's bastard. "That's the end of it! I will withdraw tomorrow. I will not have you exposed to such gossip."

"The gossip is not about me, John," I said as calmly as I could, bending to retrieve the papers. "It's about you, and it's well founded."

He looked sideways at me. "It is and it isn't," he said softly. "You know that . . . I told you the whole story before we married."

"You told me," I said, steeling myself to be cold and hard on him, "that you had been called a bastard as a child and that it had hurt you deeply."

He looked about to cry, and I wondered if all those memories had come flooding back to him. "Yes," he said so low I could hardly hear it.

"And now you've been called a bastard again. Are you going to let that defeat you? Are you going to turn tail and run?" The words hurt me as I spoke them, and I felt like a gambler, staking my whole pot on one throw of the dice.

He was instantly defensive, almost a whine in his voice. "How can I defend myself?"

"By refusing to dignify the charge," I said. "Certainly not by withdrawing from the race." And by standing straight and talking firm, I wanted to add.

He paced the floor, hands locked behind his back, head down for so long a time that I held my breath, convinced that I'd been too harsh on him. At length he raised his head and asked, "You do not mind being married to a bastard?"

"I am not married to a bastard," I said. "I am married to John Charles Frémont, a great explorer, a national hero, a presidential candidate."

He came across the room to me, his arms open, tears on his face. "Jessie," he murmured as he enveloped me in a hug, "where would I be without you?"

It was not a question that needed an answer.

— ~ —

In the end Greeley proved right. It was not Catholicism nor his parents' illegal union that cost John the election, not even the Republicans' poor choice of a vice-presidential candidate, though John always blamed poor William Dayton and claimed that Abraham Lincoln should have been the candidate. "Lincoln gave the best speeches on my behalf of anyone in the campaign," John would muse, and I would reply that it was because Lincoln, like himself, was so committed to abolition that he refused to muddy the waters with other issues.

But practicality defeated John: New York businessmen subscribed funds that were given to support other parties in other states beyond New York's borders. In short, Pennsylvania was controlled by New York money, and it went against John. Had he won that state, he would have been president.

Urged to contest the vote, he refused. "No defeated candidate has ever done that," he said, "and I will not stoop to it."

I was schooled enough in politics and tradition to recognize the truth of what he said. It would have been no good to have won the election by default, after contesting the vote. John would have lost all.

We sat late into the night, neither of us talking for long periods, each of us taking comfort in the presence of the other. At length John said, "I could have kept the

Union together, Jessie. I would have instituted the gradual abolishment of slavery . . . not overnight but over time, and I would have proposed a program of government payment to owners. Now . . . now I think it will be war. Your father has gotten the candidate he wants, but I think he'll get the very result he doesn't want."

I drew closer to him, resolved that I would not let my own grief intensify his. "It was a good show for a new party," I ventured.

"That," he said wryly, "makes me the sacrificial lamb for the Republican party."

I sighed. "Maybe you were, and maybe the next candidate they offer will win. Will it be you?"

"Never in a thousand years," he said firmly.

Next morning at breakfast we were greeted by a sobbing Lily. "Child, what is the matter with you?" I asked in concern, feeling her forehead.

"I want . . . I want to live . . . in the White House." She was crying and hiccuping at once, so that the words were barely distinguishable.

"So that's it," I said, pulling her from her chair. "You come with me."

"Where?" she asked plaintively.

"You're going for a walk," I said briskly, "until you can control yourself. Here . . ." I gathered a woolen coat, hat, muffler, and gloves from the hall tree and began dressing her, as though she were a three-year-old going out to play in the snow. As a finishing touch I wrapped a thick veil over her face. "There, that will hide your swollen eyes. Now, walk around Washington Square until you can come home in charge of yourself."

"Fourteen years old and so bitterly disappointed," John said when I returned to the table. "Maybe she is just more honest about her emotions than we are."

"No," I said firmly, "she has to learn to control them. She is not concerned about the future of the country or of the Republican party and all it stands for . . . she's simply selfishly disappointed."

"Jessie," he said, "you are a hard taskmaster."

⚊ ⚊

Charley soon distracted me from politics and presidential defeats by developing a raging case of scarlet fever. For ten days I stayed at his bedside, sponging down that little five-year-old body every hour, praying that the Lord would not take another of my babies.

John frequently stuck his head into the nursery to inquire about Charley. Then he would nod sagely, say, "Call me if you need me," and leave. And what, I wondered, would happen if I did call?

Toward the end of his illness, when I could tell that Charley would recover, I began to sneak away for a few hours each night to sleep in my own bed rather than scrunched in a rocking chair. I left Sophie to care for Charley, but he would wake and call out for me, so I got precious little sleep.

"You lookin' very tired, Mrs. Frémont," Sophie said, with the familiarity that longtime servants often assume. "I were you, I'd do something 'bout how I looked."

Startled, I turned to look in the mirror. Staring back at me was a thin, haggard woman, her eyes dark with fatigue, her hair stringy and lifeless, her face lined. She looked to be at least forty-five instead of thirty-three.

"I married to a man handsome as the colonel," Sophie continued, "I'd sure keep up my appearance."

"I have had other things on my mind," I snapped, peevish because I knew she spoke the truth.

"Yes, ma'am," she said politely, removing Charley's soup tray. Charley was well enough that night that I was very firm with him, telling him I needed my rest and that I would come to him once during the night to make sure he was fine, but that I would sleep in my own bed.

"Can I call if I need you?" he asked, his voice quavering.

I softened. "If you really need me, and it's something Sophie can't do for you." How could one say no to a child who looked at you with such adoring eyes?

When had John last looked at me with adoration and not need? I brushed that thought from my mind.

As I left his room, Charley called out softly, "I think I am going to really need you."

"You try and let me rest," I answered.

I began my evening with a long soak in a hot tub and a thorough shampoo and brushing of my hair. Soaking in that hot, relaxing water, I let my mind wander back to Sophie's words. There had been accusations, of course, that John's attentions had strayed while he was in California—one newspaper even printed that he had kept a virtual harem of California women, but it was one of the articles I never showed him. I thought it so far-fetched as to be ridiculous. But now I wondered . . . and there was Priscilla, a young maid who had left our employ suddenly and without explanation, just before the election. When I'd asked why she had to leave, she had simply shrugged and said it was personal, but as she left the room, I thought I heard her mutter, "Ask Mr. Frémont." Once one begins to "read signs," as John so often spoke of doing on his explorations, significant signs seem to be everywhere . . . or was I imagining things?

With such doubts whirling around in my mind, my uninterrupted night of sleep was not too restful. John worked late in his study, as was now his custom, and was not there much of the night to witness my restless tossing and turning. I did check on Charley once, only to find he slept almost as soundly as Sophie did in the chair. I tiptoed out without wakening either of them.

In spite of slight sleep I felt and looked better the next morning, my hair clean, my complexion freshened with a milk bath, a smile lightening my face. This, I resolved, was the first day of the rest of my life.

But Sophie had planted a kernel that grew like trumpet vine. Try as I might, I could not stamp it out, and that tiny doubt tangled itself like a tendril around my heart.

John spent most of his time in his study—working on his memoir, he told me. Nursing his wounds was more like it to me. Whereas I wanted people around me in defeat—the support and comfort of those I loved—John tended to withdraw. I could not call him inattentive nor ever accuse him of looking at another woman—he was simply hidden, physically and emotionally.

Still, I kept my resolve, saw to it that I had plenty of rest, took care of my appearance, and tried to put on a game front. Sophie complimented me one day, saying, "I glad you listened to me, Mrs. Frémont. You sure made a difference in yourself."

I thanked her.

Still, Inauguration Day was particularly hard for me. I envisioned in painful detail James Buchanan—now almost elderly—taking the oath of office, placing his hand on the Bible and swearing to lead the country to the best of his ability. It won't be good enough, I thought bitterly, convinced that John could have done so much more. And then I envisioned that niece of Buchanan's, welcoming guests into the White House, playing the hostess in the role I should have had. They already were calling Buchanan "the bachelor president," but his niece had quickly made it plain that she would see to the social graces.

To banish all these thoughts from my mind, I took a walk so long that even John was alarmed when I returned.

"Where have you been?" he asked, greeting me at the door.

"Everywhere," I answered, "and nowhere. Just walking."

"You've been gone three hours!"

"I know," I said, "and Buchanan is now officially the president." I longed for John to take me in his arms and comfort me, but he simply turned away and said, "Yes, he is, isn't he?"

———

Father came to visit soon after. Having been forewarned of his arrival by Liza, I watched him walk down the street. I'd not seen him since the beginning of the campaign—last spring—and the change, even from a distance, distressed me. His walk was slow, like an old man, not the vigorous, strong man he'd been even in recent years.

Up close the change was even more alarming. He had lost weight, a lot of it, and his face wore the pallor of illness.

"Are you all right?" I asked, once the flurry of greetings was over.

"As all right as you are," he replied. "We are all dead politically, so I thought we should be alive as a family."

"I would like that very much, Father," I said, going to his side. He put one arm around my shoulders roughly and drew me to him, then asked for his grandchildren. Lily greeted him happily, though her eyes told me she saw the physical difference in him. But the boys, too little to remember him, stood back bashfully, and it took all of Father's gruff charm to win them over.

By the time John entered the parlor, Charley sat on the floor at Father's knee and little Frank was in his lap. "Sir," John said formally in greeting.

Father set the boys aside and rose to greet John, holding out his hand in a gesture of friendship. John took the hand reluctantly, and that awkward greeting set the tone between them for Father's visit.

"I'm waiting for him to apologize," John said that night in the privacy of our room. "Don't you think I'm entitled? He not only didn't defend me, he sometimes led the accusers. He's fortunate I even let him in my house or near my family."

The idea that John thought he could banish Father startled me. My father would always be welcome in my home, no matter what he did. I soothed John as best I could, but I knew Father would never apologize.

"He looks awful," John finally said.

"I'm really worried about his health," I told him. "But he brushed the subject aside when I inquired. Said he had a little constipation."

Father stayed only three days, and they were tense days. He and John never mended their fences, though I had not really expected them to. What distressed me more was that Father and I had lost our old camaraderie and did not now seem destined to recover it. We were no longer conspirators in the political games, for neither of us could forget that we had been opponents.

"I'm tired of it, Jessie, tired of politics," he said the morning he left.

"You'll never tire of politics," I told him. "Wait until you get back home."

He just shook his head. "If I had it to do over, I wouldn't do anything else . . . or different."

And then he was gone.

⚘

The burning question for me was what John would do next. Now in his early forties, he had known great triumphs as an explorer, as a leader in opening California to United States settlement, and now as a presidential candidate. But in my honest moments with myself I had to admit that each of those triumphs had ended in disaster—near death in the mountains, court-martial, political defeat.

Now when John spoke of the election, he talked only of his pride in being chosen for what he called "a true uprising of a great people." But I knew that underneath he was not so easily consoled, and I was not surprised when he announced that he had to return to California. "The Mariposas needs me. I have been too long away, too long trying to conduct the mining business in absentia." He stood, his back toward me, looking out the window. "You may do whatever you want, Jessie—California, New York, Washington."

"None of those appeal to me," I said. I didn't tell him that I dreaded the rural life in California, for I feared I would end there one day no matter what, and I didn't need to tell him that I would never return to Washington. To do so would have been like a prisoner choosing torture over freedom. And New York? There was little left there for me.

In the end John departed for California, and I took the children to Paris. Susie's husband had been appointed French consul to India and they would be leaving Paris for that country. A last visit was my excuse to cross the ocean again. But I was restless in Paris and almost relieved, in one sense, when I was called back to Washington by the news that Father had suffered a severe intestinal attack.

After an anxious trip back across the Atlantic, willing the ship to move faster with every breath, I found Father at work in his library.

"You what?" he asked. "Who told you I was ill?"

"Liza, and she was right to do so."

"Nonsense. It was just a brief episode. I'm fine."

"Are you?" He did not look fine at all. His eyes, more than anything else, spoke of chronic pain.

He shrugged. "That same old problem—constipation. There's a small fistula. It is no matter." He bent to his desk as though he would return to work and close the subject.

Chapter Fifteen

I went to California because I could not bear to be apart from John again. That was the lesson I learned in Paris. But I went as an exile. Nothing there interested me—I remembered rural life in California all too well—and everything that made life fascinating for me was missing, except John and the children. There, as the poet said, was the rub.

In Paris I had missed John desperately. At first I thought it was the frantic pace of the campaign that I longed for, the expectation that any minute glory would be ours. But it slowly dawned on me that John himself was what I really wanted, that if he had come to Paris and wrapped me in his arms, I would ask nothing more and would live there contentedly. And a corner of my mind remembered ever after Sophie's warning about a handsome husband. In the dark of the night, with an ocean and a continent between us, I could—and did—give in to black fantasies about John's private life in California—the women who must, I thought, be surrounding him. In those minutes I forgot all that I knew about the masculine nature of rural California . . . and the lack of women.

John did not, of course, come to Paris to get me, and the news of Father's intestinal attack, offering a clear excuse for returning to the States, came as a mixed blessing. I worried for Father, of course, desperately, with a fear that lodged in my heart as a lump, right next to the lump caused by worrying about what John was doing. But I welcomed any excuse to be back in the States and that much closer to California.

The only true regret I had when I finally left Washington for California was leaving Father, for I saw in his eyes that we would not be together again.

"Jessie, I have drawn a will—"

"I cannot talk about that," I said shortly.

He looked long and hard at me. "It's nothing. Just in case. I might be knocked down by a runaway carriage tomorrow, the way these drivers are. I have put it on record."

"Fine," I said. "I assume William knows where it is."

"It is not for William," he said. "It is for you to know and take care of." Seeing how his words distressed me, he said lightly, "Pray you will have nothing to do for twenty years."

"Yes, pray," I whispered.

The very day of parting was even more difficult. Father felt compelled to leave nothing unsaid, and I was flatly ungracious about not wanting to hear it. We stood awkwardly in the entryway of the house on C Street, the new house with new furniture, a house that held none of my memories—a fact that made it only barely easier to leave. "Jessie," he said, looking at me with those tired eyes in a face puffed and pale with illness, "you have been everything to me, everything that your mother could not be. Next to her, you have been my greatest treasure."

"Father, I . . ." My voice cracked, and I could say no more. Father plowed determinedly ahead. "We've had our disagreements, and your marriage is one of them . . . but I've kept my peace privately and have publicly done what I believed I had to for the country. But you must know that through it all my feelings for you have never changed."

"Nor mine for you," I lied, thinking of my resentment of him during the campaign, my futile wish that he would leap to John's defense.

The old war horse saw through me. "I hope that's not true. I'd expect more loyalty to your husband from you. But I . . . well, I've said what I wanted to say."

"Thank you, Father," I replied, walking into his embrace and hiding my tears on his shoulder.

"There, now," he said, wiping awkwardly at my face, "you mustn't cry. We've had the best of everything together."

"We almost caught the brass ring," I said, and managed to smile just a bit as I said it.

"Everyone has his own brass ring, Jessie. Who knows? Maybe we have caught ours."

With those words ringing in my ears, I left him. As the carriage pulled away, I leaned far out the window—so far that Lily tugged on my coat as though to keep me from falling out—watching that old man standing on the stairs, his hand raised in farewell. I would never see him again, of that I was sure. Once again I had chosen John but it was never an easy choice for me.

John met us in San Francisco and whisked us off to Bear Valley and the Mariposas with little more than an overnight stop in San Francisco. No shopping, no investigating who were the dignitaries now—though I doubted I knew them—none of the taste of civilization I'd expected at the end of my long journey.

The children were excited beyond measure at the prospect of life in the country, clamoring to ride a horse immediately and demanding to know if there were really bears in Bear Valley—there were!—and would they have to go to school? My head grew tired from listening to them all chatter at once, and I was more peevish than usual.

"You'll grow to love it, Jessie," John said quietly, reading my mind. "It's not New York or Paris. . . ."

"I would have chosen either," I said shortly, "but for you."

He chuckled. "I'm flattered. We shall stay here three years, make our fortune, and then you may make your choice."

An empty promise? One offered with good intentions but no surety? One that I could hold out as a beacon through long and hot California summers? I had no way of knowing.

"Look, Mother, there are flowers everywhere! And there's our house . . . it is our house, isn't it, Father?" Lily's voice rose in excitement.

"Yes," John said, "it's our house."

It was a whitewashed cottage, set in a valley with the pasture around it bordered by a grove of white oaks, thick with undergrowth—later I would learn that the Indians, unaware of the terrible irony involved, called it the "White House." It never failed to grate on my nerves to hear a simple Indian woman refer to my humble home as the White House. Pictures of Mr. Buchanan and his hostess-niece flashed before my mind, and, briefly, I felt that old resentment. But I tried to put it behind me.

As we approached in the carriage, I saw that mountains rose on either side of the house, shutting it in until I felt claustrophobic in anticipation.

"Are there really bears?" Charley demanded again.

"Yes, there are," John said solemnly. "They eat at the hog ranch down the valley . . . and sometimes they wander in here when they're hungry."

"May I feed them?"

"No!" I shouted. "If you see a bear, you run for home—"

"If you see a bear," John interrupted, "stand very still and wait for it to go away. Don't listen to your mother in this particular case. She knows little of bears and country life." He offered me a reassuring smile, but I was not comforted.

It took all my energy to turn the cottage into a livable home. In the town of Mariposas, some thirteen miles away, I made an unbelievable find—French wallpaper. I used it to brighten the main room of the cottage, where John had installed fine brick chimneys at either end of the room. The rest of the house I brightened by putting cotton over the planked walls and adding my Oriental rugs to the floor. Once again our few good things had followed us across the country.

"It is," Lily pronounced one day, "a fine home!"

About a month after we arrived, some neighbors—a man and his wife—rode up. The man left his wife on horseback by the gate while he dismounted and, with a nod to me as I worked in the garden by the stoop, went in to see John. I thought it rude of him to leave his wife thus and reasoned that the least I could do was go to the gate and be gracious.

"Good morning," I called as I approached.

"Good morning," she replied. "And how are you, Mrs. Frémont?"

"Why, I'm just fine, thank you," I said, "working in my garden and enjoying this fair weather."

"I'm so glad to hear that you've recovered from your father's death," she said in all sincerity.

My world spun, whirling around me in a great vortex, and I reached for the gate as all threatened to turn to blackness. Just as I finally managed to ask, with a wail in my voice, "Is my father dead?" her husband ran out of the house, leaped the fence without bothering with the gate, and began angrily to lead her horse away.

I turned, only to run right into John, who had come up behind me. Now his arms went around me and he held my head to his shoulder, stroking my hair and murmuring comforting words as one would to a child.

"My father is dead," I whispered.

"Yes, Jessie, I know. He died while we were en route."

"Did you . . . did you know?" I could not believe he would keep that secret from me, even with thoughts of protecting me.

"No, by the heavens above, I did not know until two minutes ago. I . . . I am as shocked as you are."

"I should . . ." A sob stifled my voice, and I had to start over. "I should have been with him. He shouldn't have died alone."

"He had Liza and William," John reminded me gently.

"That's not the same," I muttered. "He knew when I left that we wouldn't be together again."

"He would not have had you stay," John said. "That wasn't his way."

I knew he was right, but that didn't lessen my guilt.

Dry-eyed, I left his arms and turned toward the house. "We must tell the children," I said, practicality being all that kept me from collapsing.

"I'll tell them, Jessie." He reached an arm to steady me as I stumbled on the first step.

"No," I said in a tinny voice. "I'll tell them."

And tell them I did, my voice absolutely calm and without emotion. Only Lily sensed the enormity of this tragedy for me and came to put a loving arm around my shoulders.

"Is Mother all right, Lily?" Charley asked. At nine he was old enough to comprehend that something awful had happened, but not old enough to be sure how to deal with it. Three-year-old Frank merely watched me, his eyes wide.

"She will be fine," Lily said reassuringly. "Run and play, boys, and see you tend to my chickens."

John took my arm and, with Lily trailing close behind, helped me to the bedroom. Once in the privacy of my room, I collapsed onto the bed, all my starch and strength washed away, great sobs racking my body as I cried for the man who had made me what I was, without whom I might have been another person—less driven, happier, but never the same.

"Father?" Dimly I was aware of Lily and John.

"Let her cry," he said. "It's good for her, and I will stay with her."

And so he stayed, sitting on the edge of the bed, waiting until my wails had subsided into an occasional deep sob. And then he rubbed my back, gently, lovingly, until at long last I slept. And did not wake for twenty-four hours.

My family tiptoed around me for days. "Can I bring you a cup of tea, Mother?" "Jessie, would you care to walk out this evening?" "Mother, I'll see to the boys. You go and rest." At first I relished their care and concern. But then I began to tire of being a fragile porcelain doll, and I began to assert myself, taking over my responsibilities, trying to start conversations that did not deal with Father's death.

The sadness, of course, did not disappear in a fortnight or a month. I carried it around with me—a sodden lump, a black cloud over my head, whatever form it took—for weeks and months. But each day it lessened a little, and each day I told myself to remember that Father really believed he had caught his own brass ring in his time. I learned to dwell on the successes of his career and the closeness of our early relationship rather than on his more recent defeats and our political differences.

Summer came on with unbearable heat. Since we had not arrived in time to plant a garden, we had at first no vegetables and subsisted on a diet of canned vegetables and rice.

"I cannot feed my family this way," I fumed.

"There's a new farmer down the valley," John said one day. "I can offer him sluice water for his garden, in return for vegetables."

"Do that," I demanded, and soon we had a plentiful supply of vegetables.

Once again Lily kept a poultry yard, with chickens, turkeys, and ducks, so we soon had fresh meat on our table.

"See," I told John one evening with triumph, "we shall live in a civilized manner in the wilderness!"

"I never doubted it, Jessie," he said, taking another bite of chicken, "never for a minute."

Our laundry was done by Indian women, whom we had been told never to trust. Yet I found they took not a thing without permission, not even discarded tin cans, which they used for cooking over their open fires. We saved scraps for them and found, to my absolute amazement, that their favorite food was a mixture of turnip peelings and suet put between two pieces of bread. The Earl of Sandwich would have been as amazed as I to see to what uses his invention had been put.

One day they arrived with a large crop of mushrooms and toadstools, which they proudly offered to me. "For family," said the spokeswoman.

"No!" I said, my voice rising sharper than I meant. I softened it immediately and tried to think how to tell them about poisonous toadstools. "Some bad," I said, falling into the trap of thinking they would understand pidgin English or baby talk. "Make you sick."

The three women in front of me laughed heartily, showing blackened and missing teeth. "No sick," said the spokeswoman.

"Wait!" I cried, and dashed into the house for a silver coin and a dish of water. Back in front of them, I put some of the toadstools—the ones so obvious even I could tell the difference—into the water and then tossed the coin in. "Watch," I said, "black." Sure enough, the coin turned black almost instantly. "Poison," I repeated.

The spokeswoman laughed heartily again, reached into the dish, and popped a toadstool into her mouth. As I cried out in alarm, she chewed once or twice, swallowed, and smiled broadly again.

"Come tomorrow," she said.

And sure enough, she did, apparently none the worse for the toadstools. They never again, however, offered me toadstools for the family, and I was grateful.

In midsummer I had another example of the lack of civilization in that place— only it was a terrifying example that truly threatened my family.

There was always trouble over the ownership of mines. John had carved Las Mariposas into a shape that included several of the richest veins, and when the matter was before the court and legal title was granted him, there was much resentment. I understood that and dismissed it, figuring that he who was smart enough to succeed always aroused some enmity. My pride in John and my naiveté blinded me to the dangers.

Soon after I arrived in California, a group of Frenchmen seized the Guadalupe mine, and John had to seek a court order to evict them from his property. When the sheriff, running for reelection and afraid to jeopardize his standing, refused to serve the warrant, John himself presented it. He went unarmed, though Jake, the black man who helped us around the place, had secretly come to our cottage and, with Lily's help, armed himself to follow John. Still, John was so successful that the Frenchmen not only agreed to vacate the mine but asked him to bring us all to supper, especially, they said, "the little boy who can speak French." They meant Charley, who was fluent in the Gallic tongue. When we accepted some time later, we dined on sweet omelettes, a real treat, as eggs were scarce.

But then the California legislature, in a move I would never understand to my dying day, decreed that any untended mine was fair game. Anyone who came across an untended mine could simply claim it and begin to mine the gold. John therefore kept his mines occupied at all times—but even this did not work. The guard at the Black Drift was bribed to leave the mine, making it thus empty and legal prey for a group of men who felt they had been cheated when John had laid out the boundaries of the Mariposas. They called themselves the Hornitos League, and they were backed by a rival mining company, the Merced.

In midsummer the Hornitos bullies seized the Black Drift and laid siege to the Pine Tree and the Josephina, where men were at work. Their plan was to starve the men out, so that the mine would be untended and they could jump it. But the plan backfired: our men refused to leave their mines and, instead, barricaded themselves behind rocks, prepared to fight if necessary.

I knew nothing of all this until the early morning hours of a night so hot I had been unable to sleep. A rider approached the house, shouting for John. "The Black Drift! It's been jumped."

John, who slept soundly in heat or cold, awoke suddenly and was pulling on his pants before I could even react. "Go back to sleep, Jessie," he said. "It's nothing—just some mine business I must tend to."

But I had heard the anger and panic in the man's voice, and I knew it was more than "just some mine business." I raised my head for a kiss and then sank back into the hot bed, where I tossed and turned until early daylight, then escaped to sit on the front stoop and catch what cool I could.

Before long the children were up and our day into its usual full swing. I kept them busy with games and chores, but all the while my eyes were on the road, watching for John to come home. It was a good three miles to the mines, over a perilous and skinny mountain trail known as Hell's Hollow, so I could expect neither speed nor sound to give me a clue. When he arrived at noon, I rushed to meet him.

"Jessie!" he said. "What's the matter?"

"I . . . I was worried about your safety."

"Nonsense. It's simply a dispute among men," he said reassuringly, but I was not comforted.

Jake—he who had taken guns to defend John against the Frenchmen—told me the whole of it later that day. "You've a right to know, Mrs. Frémont," he said, telling how the men in the Pine Tree had barricaded themselves with fused powder kegs, which they threatened to ignite if anyone tried to enter. "They have plenty of fresh air and water," he told me, "but no food. And the Hornitos, they won't let anyone go near with food. Mr. Frémont, he went to talk to the Hornitos, not armed or nothing, though he tells me he had a derringer in his shirt pocket."

"Small comfort that," I murmured.

Gleefully he chuckled. "You're right, missus. Derringer wouldn't do no good against all them rifles that was pointed at him." My heart leaped in fear, but he went on, "But he was quiet and fair, and there weren't no trouble. . . . Course, there weren't no solution either."

I watched the road openly then, no longer pretending to the children that things were normal. At nightfall John appeared, looking tired but at least in one piece.

"That Mrs. Ketton," he said as soon as he dismounted and gave the horse to Jake to be put up, "she's a prize. Arrived at the mine tonight with a basket of food"—her husband was the foreman of the men in the Pine Tree—"and when they tried to turn her aside, she said she was going in, no matter what. 'It's a pretty name you'll leave behind you—shooting a woman for carrying supper to her husband,' she told them. And then she marched right into the mine. I suspect she had guns under the food in that basket."

"Don't you worry for her?" I asked, credulous at what this woman would do for her man. It didn't occur to me that I did and had done as much—but in other ways, ways that didn't require such bald courage.

"Yes," John said, "I worry a great deal. But I think those men are reluctant to shoot a woman . . . and I think they also know they're dead men if they do."

"You must send someone for help. The governor—he can't let this happen," I said.

He shook his head tiredly. "The roads are blocked, Jessie. There must be well over a hundred men involved in this, and they say they'll shoot anyone who tries to ride out of this valley."

We were captives, surrounded! I could not believe that such could happen in modern times.

"What are you going to do?"

"Whatever occurs to me," he said.

Things got worse the next day, much worse. John had been at home for the night, and he, Jake, and Jake's "assistant," Isaac, had been armed to the teeth—thirty-two bullets among them, I'd counted, wondering how long they would last. But not an hour after John left to return to the mine, a rider came by the house at a fast gallop and threw a rock that barely missed a window, instead making a nice dent in the front door. Attached to it was a note warning that the children and I had twenty-four hours to leave the valley or "suffer the consequences." The note, which demanded a reply by sundown, said the house would be burned.

"Mother?" Lily asked, for she had found the note and brought it to me.

"Have Jake bring the buggy around," I said, "and put on your best town dress."

I, too, dressed for town—not as I would have in Washington but plenty good enough for Bear Valley, and not the mourning for my father that I'd been wearing—and we went directly to the saloon where the Hornitos had their headquarters.

"Wait here, Jake," I said as he helped me out of the buggy.

"Mrs. Frémont, you can't go in there."

"Yes, I can," I said determinedly, marching through the swinging doors. Once inside, I found myself confronted by speechless men, all of whom seemed to freeze in mid-gesture as they stared at me.

"Your note," I said scornfully, throwing the piece of paper, still tied around its rock, onto the floor, "has been received. There will be no reply. You may come and kill us—women and children—but there will be no victory in it." With that I swept out of the saloon and back into the carriage.

"Home, Jake," I said, an order so imperious that it set Lily to giggling.

"Are you not afraid?" she asked as we drove away.

"Yes," I confessed, "I'm afraid of a bullet in the back at this very moment. But if Mrs. Ketton can be that brave for her husband, so can I."

Lily's look of admiration was more than enough thanks for me. "We've got to get word out to the governor," she said.

"Lily," I cautioned, "don't even think of it. You cannot ride out of here, good horsewoman that you are."

In the end, though, it was Lily who saved us. While I kept vigil in the bedroom window—watching to see that John's horse was ridden home and never led, which would have meant he was tied across the saddle—Lily developed a plan and put it into effect. She used her mountain horse, Ayah, and without my knowledge, at night, rode along a mountain valley, guided only by the stars, until she reached Coulterville some ten miles away, from where she was able to send for help.

The governor sent immediate word that the Hornitos did not have a prayer. There was no way they could force men to abandon a mine and then claim it was unworked. When he threatened to send in the militia, the siege was over.

Afterward we were occasionally troubled in the night by a bomb of powder in a tin can, but other than frightening the wits out of Lily and me, these were harmless.

"Jessie," John stormed, "you should never have gone into town. I don't want to think about what could have happened."

"If Mrs. Ketton could feed her husband," I said serenely, "I could do my part too. And they were cowards . . . they wouldn't have done a thing to a woman." Then, turning the tables on him, I accused, "You should not have gone before them unarmed."

"A man does what he has to," he said, shrugging, and I knew he did not see the similarities in our arguments. I never told him that I had been so frightened that I'd penned my will—an astonishing forty pages, as though I had many possessions to leave!

A week or so after everything had calmed down, a delegation of women from the valley came to see me. They rode sidesaddle, dressed in their best finery, and accepted shyly when I invited them into the house for tea.

"Had you given up and left, our valley would have run red with blood," one woman said. "We're grateful to you."

My spirits were high to know that I had not only helped John, but also helped a group of women who saw themselves as helpless.

We stayed at Las Mariposas two years, or three summers, but the summer of 1860 proved so unbearably hot—we found we could roast eggs in the dust of the road in eighteen minutes—that John announced one day we were going to San Francisco.

"Oh, John, it's too hot. I cannot get myself together for a trip." The thought of dressing in city clothes and putting on my public face was more than I wanted to deal with. But he was insistent.

"It is cooler by the ocean," he said, "and you'll be glad you've come with me." He had just returned from a business trip to the city, and I was frankly baffled by his eagerness to return.

Things had been going well for John. For a while the Mariposas was under a gray, if not black, financial cloud—John's former partners, who had been in charge during the presidential campaign, sued for their share, and taxes and legal fees seemed to take everything, so that we had a principality but no cash for groceries. But then the lawsuit against the Merced Company, those who had been behind the Hornitos fiasco, was settled in John's favor, and he put in a new crushing mill, which accelerated operations greatly. But his biggest triumph was the building of a railroad on the property. With John acting as his own superintendent, Chinese workers—the first to work on railroads in this country—built four miles of track winding up the steep faces of Hell's Hollow. John was triumphant, and I could not help pointing out that he'd gotten his railroad one way or another. "Not quite the transcontinental route I dreamed of," he admitted, "but I'm satisfied with it."

I told myself that this trip to San Francisco was probably a celebration that things were going so well at the mine, and it behooved me, heat or no, to show some enthusiasm. So soon enough we were off in the carriage, the boys left behind in Lily's care, with the one-eyed supervision of a cook I'd recently hired. John dubbed her "Irish Rose," though not to her round and florid face.

John drove not to any of the places I'd expect—the hotel or stores—but straight on to a point of land that jutted out into the ocean. There he pulled up at a modest but charming house.

"John! We cannot arrive to pay a call unbidden," I protested. "We're not 'paying a call,'" he said. "This is our new home—your new home. I bought it in your name."

"My name!" The very idea of owning property overwhelmed me. Hesitantly, I stepped from the carriage into his waiting arms.

"Come!" he said. "Don't you want to explore?"

The house had windows and French doors in abundance, so that almost every room had a view. To one side we could see the entrance to the bay—John had named it the Golden Gate on an expedition years before—and directly ahead, Alcatraz Island. Beyond, across miles of water, the Costra Contra Mountains. Looking back landward, I stared at the city.

"It is mine?" Then irrational fear struck at my heart. Was he getting rid of me, putting me somewhere out of the way? "You you won't live here with me?"

He laughed heartily and put his arms around me. "Of course not. I'll be back and forth. I can't leave the mine . . . you know that, Jessie." His voice took on an earnest, pleading tone. "But I want you to be in the city. You don't have to live like an exile anymore."

I jumped a little. Had he known how I'd felt all along in Bear Valley? I'd thought I'd hidden my feelings better than that.

"John . . ." I could say no more. Tears streamed down my cheeks, and I walked into his arms. We stood there together, silent, in our new home for a long time.

We called it Black Point because of the laurel trees that surrounded it and, from a distance, made it all appear dark as coal. I furnished the house with all the things I'd had in my father's house and had missed so terribly. Outside we made curving walks through beds of roses and fuchsia and little patios, where I could sit and marvel at the view in any direction. We were close enough to the water that I heard the flapping of the schooners' sails as they rounded the point, and the wooden paddles of the steamers. When the children arrived, we had horses and Lily's eternal poultry yard, and in no time Black Point was the home of my heart.

"I have no need to go back east ever," I told John. "With Father dead the East holds nothing for me. It is dead to me. We shall live our lives out here." I should have known that fate never works that way.

⌒

A young Unitarian preacher named Thomas Starr King was making a name for himself speaking on behalf of abolition and Abraham Lincoln, now the Republican candidate for president. I went to hear him one day and was so impressed that I introduced myself afterward. "Mrs. Frémont! This is indeed an honor." He was taller than John, though not nearly as robust, and he had those same intense blue eyes that looked directly at you without wavering. Still, there was almost an air of frailty about him until he spoke, and then his vitality overwhelmed the listener, drawing you along with him to heights of glory—sometimes for rationality, always for abolition, and often in Mr. Lincoln's name.

"I admired very much what you said," I told him, suddenly at a loss for words before those eyes, "and the way you said it."

"That is high praise, coming from you," he replied, never taking his eyes from mine. "I should like to call at your home, if I may. I know I can benefit from your knowledge and experience with politics."

"Of course," I assented, and left hurriedly, lest he see the blush that had begun to creep from my neck to my cheeks.

Within weeks Starr King was a regular caller at Black Point, and I, a lifelong Episcopalian, had purchased a pew in the Unitarian Church. I had also learned a great deal about the minister. Among other things he was precisely my age. Like John, he had been raised in the South and had been desperately poor, so that now he was both ambitious and proud of how far he'd come.

His wife, Julia, accompanied him to Black Point only once. She spoke with a Bostonian accent, sat very straight in her chair, and seemed unable to smile.

"How are you liking our California weather?" I asked amiably as I served tea.

"Not at all," she replied without hesitation. "Nor the city. I am simply waiting for the day Thomas comes to his senses and returns to Boston."

Taken aback, I made no more small talk about Boston—nor did I inquire about children, of which I knew they had none. In minutes Starr and I were deep into a discussion of Mr. Lincoln's political possibilities and the mistakes we both thought he was making in his campaign. Julia sat silent and martyred for the better part of an hour while we chattered like magpies.

Shortly thereafter, the poor Julia broke her foot on a flimsy wooden sidewalk—"It never would have happened in Boston!" she told Starr—and was confined to her house for many months.

"Seeing quite a bit of that new Unitarian minister, I hear," John said on one of his visits.

"Mr. King comes often to discuss politics with Mother," Lily said helpfully. "We like him."

John shot me a look over her head. "So I hear, so I hear." When our daughter was out of earshot, he added, "Watch, lest I get jealous, Jessie."

That blush began to rise again, for I feared that John, having read my discontent at Bear Valley in spite of my best pretenses, could now pierce through my acting to discover my strong attraction to Starr King.

It was, I told myself repeatedly, foolish even to think of King as anything but a friend. He was not as handsome as John, nor as bold and courageous. But then the other side of my mind would remind me of his intellect, the long and passionate discussions we shared . . . and, yes, his attentiveness. To Starr King I was new and wonderful. John and I had not been lovers for some time; we were companions and business partners and parents together, and occasionally we shared a bed and went through the motions of love, but the passion that had sparked our early marriage had dwindled to nothing. The bloom, as they say, fades from the rose with familiarity. Starr King offered the kind of sensuousness, the drowning in pleasure, that comes with a new relationship.

"I am unhappy, Mrs. Frémont, and I must confess it to someone," Starr said one day. Though I called him Starr in my mind—fascinated by all that such a name implied—we had never in conversation let ourselves get beyond the formality of addressing each other as mister and missus.

"Perhaps," I said teasingly, "you should find a priest to whom you can confess."

"Sometimes I wish I could," he said ruefully. "Catholicism makes things easier in that sense." Then, without another second's hesitation, he plunged into his unhappiness. "It's Julia. She is so bitter all the time that we . . . we have no marriage left at all. We cannot talk . . . we . . ." He hesitated, and I knew he was thinking of the privacies of marriage, which a well-bred man would not discuss with anyone, let alone a happily married woman. "We are strangers to each other," he finished lamely.

"Every marriage goes through dismal periods," I said primly. And then, striving for more honesty, added, "My relationship with Mr. Frémont has been anything but even over the years. The presidential campaign took a great toll . . . but I am happy now to say that we are enjoying the fullness of marriage as it should be." I still sounded prim, and besides, I was lying. Our relationship was good and strong and solid, but it lacked the very element Starr was hinting at.

"I am happy for you," he said, but his eyes told me that was not what he meant. "I wish," he continued boldly, "that I had a wife like you. I hope"—and here his voice faltered just a minute—"that Mr. Frémont is fully aware of his good fortune."

My heart beating furiously, I murmured, "I believe he is . . . and I of mine." The message that I hoped I was somehow sending was that one of those rare and unpredictable mixes of chemistry drew me to him but that I was not going to allow myself to stray.

I had been tempted and survived, and I hoped desperately that the same had been true of John—and always would be.

Starr continued to call frequently, and our discussions once again centered on politics—ultimately, he was the one who saved California for the Union.

One night he brought with him a young man who looked to me a gambler—shiny black suit, curly dark hair, a sort of dramatic mustache—but had none of the personality to go with his appearance. Whereas Starr's appearance was so bland as to distract and animated only by the force of his personality, this man's appearance hid a painfully shy soul.

"This," Starr announced dramatically, "is Bret Harte, the newspaperman." He added the qualifier as though I would immediately recognize Mr. Harte. I didn't but managed to welcome him heartily. "Harte writes short stories," Starr continued, as proud as though he'd just invented the man himself.

"Really?" I asked with genuine interest. "You must read them to us." There were some five or six people assembled in the parlor, each of whom nodded encouragingly.

"Oh, I could never . . . I could not read my work aloud," he protested quietly, and I saw that he was not simply being modest and waiting for us to urge him on. He was genuinely shy.

"Perhaps later," I said, and drew him toward the group, where he sat for hours, listening to the conversation but offering not one word himself.

It was weeks before he finally ventured to read, and then it was a story about a baby born in a rough mining camp. We applauded heartily when the reading was finished and demanded the title of the story. "The Luck of Roaring Camp," he replied.

Bret Harte joined us every Sunday night for dinner thereafter, but he never wore out his welcome. Charley and little Frank hung on the tales he read aloud and pronounced him their favorite author.

I took the position of critic, one that I was glad to fill. John had been supposed to work on his memoirs with me, and I'd looked forward to being his amanuensis once again, but the Mariposas kept him too busy. I sensed, anyway, a reluctance on his part to begin the project, as though to write one's memoirs signaled the end of one's accomplishments. John, I knew, still had adventure in his soul. Meanwhile, I could be Mr. Harte's amanuensis. I worked with him, suggesting a word here, a phrase there, never being as bold as I would have with John but still leaving my mark on his writing.

"Mr. Harte," I said one evening, "we have a visitor who will no doubt interest you. Mr. Melville from the East . . . you know his books, I am sure."

Harte's old shyness returned, and he managed only to mumble when I introduced him to Mr. Melville, who was then fleeing from the failure of his two latest books, *Moby-Dick* and *Pierre*. "I thoroughly enjoyed *Moby-Dick,*" Harte told him in his soft voice.

"You're about the only one," Melville said. He had a pitiful air of defeat and sadness. Fleetingly, I wondered if I could take him on as a project, too, but I quickly dismissed the idea. Melville spent the evening discouraging Harte from trying to be a writer. "They'll kill you," he said. "Go find yourself a safe job somewhere. I'm going back to work in the customs house. I'll never write again."

Harte was aghast and managed to mutter, "I work for a newspaper, but I . . . I can't stop writing." Silently, I applauded.

⌒⌒

In the spring of 1861 John announced that he was sailing for France to negotiate the sale of half of the Mariposas. "They cheated me," he said, his calm manner hiding a great anger.

"'They'?" I asked, though I knew the answer.

"The men I was fool enough to trust the property with while I went off to run for president," he said bitterly. "I shall have to sell to recuperate and pay their suit." He was convinced he would find a buyer more quickly in France than in either our own country or England.

I was invited, but the implication was plain that he would be busy and I would be adrift on my own. The idea of being purely selfish in Paris had strong appeal, but ultimately I decided to stay at Black Point. I was like a nesting hen—too comfortable to move, too protective of my brood and my new life.

Starr and John met one evening at dinner at Black Point just before John left. They were always easily friendly with each other, though obviously held together chiefly by my presence. Left on their own, they would have been political acquaintances but never friends.

"I have been in touch with the president," Starr said. Lincoln had, of course, been elected and inaugurated, though the new president hadn't eased the country's woes. His election had only made the South openly rebellious, and talk everywhere was of war. John, of course, took this as a doubly bitter blow, for he was convinced he could have avoided war if he'd been elected. I was still a passionate advocate of the Union—my father's face rose before my eyes, and I heard his voice saying, "The Union must be preserved at all costs." But passionate or not, it all seemed remote to me. There would be no war fought at Black Point.

"I was just telling Mr. Frémont," Starr repeated, drawing my attention back to him, "that I have been in touch with the president. He has authorized me to speak for him in offering you a post. . . ." In spite of myself my heart beat quicker, and I glanced at John. John remained outwardly calm. "A post?" he inquired, as though totally uninterested.

"Ambassador to France," Starr said quietly.

John considered for a long minute before he spoke, and then his words were slow and deliberate. "Were our country not about to be plunged into war, sir, I would be most honored and would humbly accept. But I feel the winds of war . . . and I must take a more active role to preserve the Union."

There they were again, those words: "preserve the Union."

"You will think on it, though?" Starr asked.

"Yes and no," John replied. "I am, as you know, leaving for France the day after tomorrow. If there is any service I can do the government while I'm gone, I would be pleased to be of help."

"I'll be in touch," Starr said, and that was the last I heard of the conversation.

"John?" I asked that night. "You will not accept the ambassadorship, will you?"

"No, Jessie, I won't. But when war comes, I'll go in one capacity or another to serve the North."

And I thought, will wait at Black Point—another separation in a marriage that was as apart as it was together.

John left for France in March, and Fort Sumter was fired upon on April 12, 1861. My idyll at Black Point was over, though I didn't yet know it.

Chapter Sixteen

"Ten thousand rifles from France," John said, strutting about our hotel room, "and another seventy-five thousand dollars' worth of arms and ammunition from England." He was obviously pleased with himself. "This will be a long war, Jessie, hard on both sides, and we must be prepared."

"And how did you guarantee payment for all this?" I asked. It was not a naive question. I knew John too well. "On my personal signature," he said grandly.

"John! You who had to sell half the Mariposas? You who have property aplenty but can't raise any cash? How could you?" I was aghast . . . and frightened. "Why didn't you get the minister to England to guarantee government payment?"

"Adams?" His voice turned scornful as he whirled to look at me from the small sofa that provided the only seating in the room besides the bed. "He refused. But don't worry, Jessie, the minister to France ultimately signed for it all. We're free and clear."

But he had taken the risk—that thought wouldn't leave my mind. There was no sense, however, dwelling on a gamble that had worked. "You were right, then, and I congratulate you. The war is going to be a glorious experience for you, John. It will wipe out memories of the campaign."

He smiled happily and leaned over to kiss my forehead. "For both of us," he said. "It's time our fortunes were in the ascendancy again."

And that was the way we sailed into the Civil War, expecting another Frémont triumph.

—◆—

The children and I had met John in New York, after a hasty packing and dismantling of Black Point. In five days after receiving his wire, our clothes were thrown into trunks, the furniture was covered with sheets, and the house closed up. I wandered through it for a last look, lingering over the view on each side, running my finger over the piano I had played, the table where Herman Melville had talked with Bret Harte, the chair by the fireplace where Starr King habitually sat. No house, except perhaps the one on C Street in Washington, would ever hold such memories for me. I hoped the war would be brief, and we would be back at Black Point for Christmas.

We sailed from San Francisco to the Isthmus of Panama with calm weather and good spirits, but everything changed once we boarded the train to cross the isthmus. The guard was heavy, and we were told that the cargo included arms, ammunition, and gold, all of which the Confederacy desperately needed.

Once we boarded a ship in the Gulf of Mexico, the situation became even more tense.

"We are in danger of being boarded by a southern pirateer," said the captain, a man ironically named South. "I will work for the Confederacy once this trip is over, for I am a southerner—from North Carolina—but I promised Mr. Vanderbilt I'd bring his ship in safely . . . and I'll do it." He went on to say that he usually stopped for mail at a tiny island in the West Indies, but he feared an ambush there by the *Sumter* and would not this time be stopping. I bit my tongue in disappointment, for I'd hoped the mail would bring word from John.

We were allowed no lights onboard, so we ate an early dinner and retired at sunset to a darkness so total that it frightened me. I had all I could do to comfort Frank and Charley, who begged for light that they might have me read to them. I sat in the dark and sang soft songs in my own off-key manner until they finally slept. The darkness was made worse by the total silence, for the captain cut the engines at night. "Sound carries across the water," he said.

Needless to say, he had a pack of terrified women on his hands. The sailors did their best to cheer us. One kept whistling "Dixie," and when I finally could not restrain myself from frowning at him, he shrugged and said, "It's a good marching tune. I know I cannot even think of it on shore, so I'm just going to whistle it to my heart's content while we're at sea."

Our worst fears came true on a sparkling cold and windy day just after we passed Hatteras off the Carolinas. "A sail," came the cry, all need for silence gone once a pursuing ship was sighted. We ran to the rail and saw a long, low ship, with every sail set, rapidly closing the distance between us.

"It's the *Jeff Davis*," cried the lookout, having read the name through his spyglass.

The captain had previously told me that the *Jeff Davis* was the swiftest slaver afloat, and his steamer was no match for it. Now he ordered his crew, "Save the steamer, or I'll sink her. No man gets this treasure." He posted men around the engine and by the magazine, and I knew that his intent—and his threat—were serious.

There ensued a daylong chase. Sometimes the Atlantic winds helped us, dying down so that the *Jeff Davis* had no power and we were able to steam away. Then the winds would rise again and help the enemy. Finally, toward dark, the winds died and we pulled away, leaving the pursuer far behind us.

Lily was pale but calm and quiet. The boys, however, thought it a great adventure. "Like Jean Lafitte, isn't it, Mother?" Charley exclaimed, and I agreed with him, for I had the weird sensation that I was living a century earlier and was on a boat about to be boarded by pirates. With a shudder I remembered how pirates often treated their captives and gratefully brought my imagination back to the nineteenth century.

We sailed into the Bay of New York with no further incident. When we landed, we learned that the *Sumter* had waited three days off the island we had avoided.

John was in the crowd at the wharf, whisking us away to the hotel. "I've been put in charge of the Department of the West," he whispered as the carriage pushed through crowded streets to the hotel, "one of four major generals given significant appointments. I had my choice, but I insisted on the West. It's my country."

The West would consist of Illinois and all states and territories between the Mississippi River and the Rocky Mountains, with headquarters in my sometime hometown of St. Louis. And John would be in charge. Later we would talk about breaking old ties—what few southern roots the presidential campaign had left us—but for now it was enough to enjoy John's triumph.

Writing to Starr King in California, I confessed to a lack of humility about my husband's future. "I see his future looming brightly. It is, I know, a time for bold men of action, men who are willing to write their own rules as they go. John is such a man."

St. Louis was no longer the city of my childhood. I expected the usual bustling activity, the kind of raucous frontier air, with people and animals going everywhere in cheerful confusion, sailors whistling and singing while they loaded barges on the wharves. And, yes, I'd hoped for some kind of reception for John, some modest but encouraging welcome, with a few cheers.

Disembarking from the train, we rode by carriage through a city so silent that the clip-clop of the horses' hooves echoed mercilessly through the night.

"Where is everyone?" Charley whispered, apparently afraid to talk in a normal voice.

"This is spooky," Frank said in agreement.

Neither carriages nor pedestrians were to be seen, curtains were drawn in the shops, and homes seemed barricaded behind pulled draperies and closed shutters. From far too many homes fluttered the flag of the Confederacy. We even passed a building that was being used as a Confederate recruitment office.

"John?" I grasped his arm, pointing to the offending building.

"You knew this was a southern city, Jessie. Surely you didn't expect a welcome. I'll take care of that office."

I would not be so foolish as to admit that I'd hoped for a welcome.

We moved immediately into the stately home of my cousin, Sarah Brant, with whom John had stayed when his leg had forced him back to St. Louis at the start of the 1853 expedition. Sarah was glad of the rent we paid, and we were glad of a building spacious enough to house all of John's officers and operations in one place. The basement became an arsenal, with arms and ammunition stored for emergency use. The ground floor housed staff offices, and on the second floor John had his own office, complete with a large table where he could spread out maps and diagrams. We had modest living quarters also on the second floor, while Cousin Sarah went to stay with other relatives. "We must post sentinels immediately," John said. "No telling what lengths some people would go to for the ammunition we have here." I thought it a wise decision.

Then he sat with his maps. "We will clear Missouri of all rebels and then march to Mississippi, clearing as we go."

"The president?" I asked.

"I met with Lincoln just before you arrived in New York," he said. "He gave me *carte blanche*—that was his term—and said he had complete confidence in me."

My optimism knew no bounds. For once John was fully supported by the administration in charge. He could exercise his tactical skills without fear of redress. He worked from before sunrise until midnight every day, trying to get munitions and supplies for an army that was, as he put it, "understaffed and unequipped—the men are untrained, they have no horses, no arms, no ammunition." Authorized by Lincoln to take five thousand muskets from the St. Louis arsenal, he found the arsenal had less than thirteen hundred. On paper John had twenty-five thousand men; in reality, less than fifteen thousand. He communicated these problems to Mr. Lincoln through Montgomery Blair, the oldest of the Blair brothers, who was now postmaster general and John's liaison to the president. Blair's reply was that the president had full confidence in Major General Frémont and that the major general was to proceed as he thought best.

The major general did just that, bringing in Major Charles Zagonyi, once a Hungarian officer and a man in whom John had the greatest confidence. Zagonyi brought his Garibaldian officers, men who wore proud uniforms of dark blue with white plumes in their hats. "We have to show the West what an army should look like," John said as he installed the Garibaldian officers as guards around the house. When he went abroad in the city, a phalanx of them rode about him. "No telling where an ambush shot might come from," John said, articulating a fear that I had tried to quiet. I was grateful for the Garibaldians, with their polished sabers and deadly revolvers.

Francis Blair, the man who had been John's major supporter in the presidential campaign, now became a supplicant, writing to John to request an appointment as major general for his younger son, Frank, now a congressman from Missouri. John replied as tactfully as he could, pointing out that he had discussed such an appointment with Frank when in Washington, and Frank had indicated that he thought his services more valuable if he were to remain in the Congress. Privately, to me, John said, "He has an unfortunate temper and bad habits." I dismissed Frank from my thoughts, sure that we had a strong ally in his brother, Montgomery.

What John soon found out was that all official concern was focused on Virginia, where the Union forces had just suffered the devastating defeat of Bull Run. Nobody thought the war was being fought in the West—nobody, that is, except John and me. Montgomery Blair wrote that the authorities would pay no attention to the problems of the Department of the West. "Do the best you can," he advised.

"We need a victory, Jessie, something that can give the entire Union heart."

"General Lyon has been begging for troops and assistance in the southern part of the state," I said. "If he could hold out . . ."

"I've told him to retreat," John replied. "I've not enough men to send him, and what men I have are safeguarding Cairo, at the president's request. He feels, rightly, that we must preserve barge traffic. If we lose the rivers, we lose the West. I've sent an untried general there—fellow by the name of Grant—Ulysses Grant—isn't that an odd first name? Anyway, I feel he'll do the job."

And so we pored over maps, moving troops here and there on large boards, as though we were playing with miniatures. We plotted strategies against rebels who were wrecking railway trains, cutting telegraph wires, raiding farms, and terrifying northern sympathizers.

Writing to Starr King, ever my confidante, I described it as "the most wearing and welcome work of my life. As I bend over maps with John and write and rewrite reports, the glorious days of the early expeditions return. I am at my best aiding John as he forges new greatness for himself and for the country." Putting my pen aside, I felt a momentary sadness that Father could not see what John was doing. But then I remembered the bitterness between them toward the end, and I was grateful to have Starr as my listening post.

One part of my job was the same as it had been during the presidential campaign: to keep away from John those people who would upset him. I arranged all appointments and generally chose who saw him. "He must not be bothered, when he is so busy, by people with this petty request and that," I explained to an aide. "He must save his time for the major issues." It became difficult, nearly impossible, for the St. Louis citizenry to gain access to the commander of the Department of the

West, but I kept their many problems and complaints from distracting John from the business of planning the war.

Such power made me seem arrogant, I knew, and there was no way I could explain to anyone—did I have to?—that I did what I did at John's request, even insistence. "You must help me," he begged. "I cannot do this without you." And then he was very specific about what I must do: "Keep the damn nuisances away!" If one weighed the balance, as I did, it was worth being called arrogant to serve John, and in so doing, to serve the Union. I had no regrets.

Of course, it was not long before we heard the rumors. Some, jealous perhaps of John's authority and strictly enforced regulations, began to call me "General Jessie." One newspaper, from southern Missouri, wrote that I had "stepped beyond the bounds of a wife," and another claimed that I had "a man's education, a man's power." Yet they did not see me at work with John, nor did they know that I made it always a point to defer to him, to make it plain it was John who made the decisions, John who commanded the Western Department.

Criticism of John himself began in earnest when General Lyon refused to retreat. Lyon had a reputation as a hero, having saved the St. Louis arsenal from rebels and then having put the rebels to flight at Booneville, a town on the Missouri River. But all this had happened in June, before we arrived in St. Louis. By summer Lyon was in southern Missouri near Springfield and was virtually abandoned—no communication with headquarters and an army that was shrinking as ninety-day volunteers came to the end of their stint. His army was unpaid and virtually unequipped—no tents, poor food, and ragged clothing. John ordered him to retreat because there were no fresh troops to send him and because Springfield was not as vital as Cairo. "It is the key to southern Missouri—lead mines, farm resources, and volunteers," John said sadly, "but I cannot countermand the president's order to save Cairo first."

In early August, John sent two regiments toward Lyon, but he expected the general to retire to meet them. Instead Lyon moved to attack Confederate forces under General McCullough. In the battle of Wilson's Creek, one of the war's most fierce encounters, Lyon repulsed attack after attack, slowly gaining ground and driving the rebels back. But then he was hit, a minié ball piercing his breast. Firsthand reports told us that he instantly fell dead from his horse. After that Federal troops retreated.

"Too late," John moaned, "too late. He was an outstanding officer—but intemperate, given to disobeying orders. Always thought he knew more than whoever was giving the orders."

There was outrage, of course. Lyon's body was taken from city to city, from Missouri to his home in New England, and the northern press cried out in anger and dismay. John should have sent reinforcements, he should have done this, that, or the other.

"But none of them sit where you sit," I consoled. "None of them are faced with the decisions you are, nor do they have your knowledge of actual conditions."

"Thank you, Jessie," he said quietly, but I could see that the criticism bothered him. He never made a case of his orders to General Lyon nor the reason for them, and only I understood most of it. Sometimes I wanted to shout it from the balcony of our headquarters, explaining John's position to a hostile world. But I could not do that, any more than I could tell the rabble that I didn't deserve to be mockingly called "General Jessie."

In September, Dorothea Dix came to St. Louis to tour the hospitals, and I accompanied her to Jefferson Barracks. I was curious about her, especially in light of the "General Jessie" rumors.

"Do you not," I asked, "face criticism for taking women into men's hospitals, for caring for wounded and dying men?"

"Every day," she replied, "but my work is too important to worry about that." Tall and beautiful, with black hair swept back from her face, she was always in control, whether she was facing John across a desk—as she often did, though she had his full support—or mopping up a floor after an amputation, a sight I once saw, much to my horror.

"Your nurses—" I began.

"Must be over thirty, plain, and wear only black or brown," she said crisply, moving through rows of beds where young men, too ill to feed themselves, lay with mugs of coffee and pieces of salt pork on their chests. The theory was that the food would be handy should they gather the strength to eat it.

"The sun blazes on them," I said, looking at dying men who lay in sunlight so bright it made them use what little energy they had left to squint.

"There are no funds for curtains," Dorothea said. "I have asked. I shall have to think about how to handle that."

"I'll handle it," I said quietly. "I'll see that General Frémont's office provides the funds." And I did. Blue shades were hung on the windows the next day, and bedside tables put in place so that food need not be set on patients' chests.

"They deserve civilization," I stormed at John, "not to die like barbarians when they've given their lives for their country."

Once again he said only, "Thank you, Jessie." Then he added, "I cannot be everywhere at once and see everything. You are my eyes and my ears."

Frank Blair came to see John when he first returned to St. Louis from Washington and seemed full of support. "I told them," he said, "that Lyon died of red tape." Then he got to the real business of his call. "I've got a friend, a businessman—he can provide clothing and equipment for forty thousand men. Here, Frémont, I've saved you some trouble and brought along a contract, already drawn up."

John, as he told me later, took the document and read it carefully before pushing it back across the desk to Frank. "I've let several smaller contracts to a variety of people," he explained. "If I gave all the business to one firm and it proved unable to perform, the department would be crippled. I would certainly agree to a smaller contract with your associates. Take this to the quartermaster and see what can be worked out."

Frank apparently did just that, and the quartermaster found such irregularities in the contract that he rejected the entire notion.

"I'm afraid you've made an enemy of Frank," I said when John told me all this.

He looked contrite. "His father is already leery of us, over that business of giving Frank an appointment. I'm sorry, Jessie. Francis Blair was a major supporter of mine, and I always thought it was because of your family ties. I know how important that family has been all your life, and I would not—"

"Shhhh!" I put a finger to his lips to silence him. "You must do what is right for the department, not what is right for me or my old friends. I support you wholeheartedly."

John and I were lovers again, as though the challenges of the war had energized us, taken us back to earlier days when we were more than parents, more than people struggling with an indebted mine. Now we were young—in spirit, at least—and fighting together for something we believed in. The effect in our bedroom was remarkable.

John, who got very little sleep anyway, would wake me gently in the middle of the night, stroking my head, running his hand lightly over my face, then lifting my gown to rub my back, his hand reaching ever lower until I began to moan a little. Then he would withdraw, to make a great show of removing his clothes, while I lay in the bed, my desire mounting the longer he delayed. When we finally came together, it was with a frantic urgency that I had not thought possible in midlife, a passion that surprised and amazed me. The idea of pregnancy still frightened me, but I had learned before how important it was to respond to John. The ups and downs of our marriage, the absences and the low periods, had taught me that caution was not always best, that sometimes passion had to take precedent over reason.

And a corner of me was almost grateful that John still found me that desirable, a woman nearing forty with a body thickened by childbirth. I welcomed him almost every night, with an eagerness that surprised and pleased him. Each morning we greeted each other formally in the office, our eyes twinkling as though we shared a great secret that no one else could suspect.

Two weeks after he had asked John to sign his friends' contract, Frank Blair appeared unannounced on the second floor of our headquarters.

"Frank! I wasn't expecting you. I . . . didn't think you had an appointment with John," I said, being as tactful as I could.

"I don't have an appointment," he said angrily, "and I near had to fight my way through all those aides and whatever-you-call-'em downstairs. But I'm going to see John now!"

One look at his face told me this was no time to argue. "Of course," I said. "Just let me tell him you're here."

"I'll tell him myself," Frank said, storming through the door into John's office, with me at his heels.

"Frémont, we've got to talk," he said to John, and then, turning to see me, added, "and we don't need you, Jessie."

Quietly, controlling his temper, John said, "Jessie stays. She is my closest adviser."

Frank opened his mouth to protest, then closed it suddenly and threw himself into a chair. I wondered if he had been about to say something mean about "General Jessie."

"I'm hearin' all kinds of things I don't like, John."

John stared at him without saying a word, almost daring him to go on.

"You know," Frank said, "that Lincoln walks around the streets of the capital by himself? Anybody who wants to can come up and shake his hand, talk to him. But what do I hear about you? No one can see you, can't get an appointment. I damn near didn't get in here myself today."

I opened my mouth to protest, but John silenced me with a look. "And those blasted foreigners you got around you—the Garibaldians or whatever, with their feathers in their hats and all. Don't you think that's a bit pretentious, John?"

"I think it's practical," John said. "The atmosphere is hostile in this city. I cannot help how they dress—they are an excellently trained troop."

Frank began to repeat himself, and John, instead of talking openly with the man who had once been his strong supporter, became more close-lipped and imperious—there was no other word for it—as the minutes ticked by. After an hour they were open enemies, all hope of peaceful solution shattered as far as I could tell.

John brooded for days afterward. Then one night, some four or five days after his visit with Frank Blair, he rushed into the bedroom where I lay sleeping. "That's it, Jessie! I've got it!"

"What's it?" I murmured sleepily. Since we'd been in St. Louis—with my energies at a pitch all day every day, and my passions at an equal pitch many nights—I slept more deeply than I ever had in California.

He shook me, not even very gently, to make sure he had my attention. "I know how to turn things in our favor. What we've got to do is unite the Union element, keep them from fleeing. Listen to what I've written."

And so he read a proclamation that established martial law in the state. "How else can we unscramble Missouri, Jessie?" His document prescribed court-martial and the firing squad for unauthorized persons found bearing arms in the district, which he extended to cover all of Missouri and parts of Kansas, and it provided for the confiscation of all property belonging to rebel sympathizers, including their slaves who were "declared freedmen."

Fully awake now, I gasped at the last clause. "John, you would free the slaves?"

"Yes, I would."

"That . . . that changes the nature of the war," I said. "It makes it a war about slavery, not one to preserve the Union."

"That's what it has always been," John said quietly.

"I know," I whispered, "but no one else has dared say it before." I remembered my father's determination to preserve the Union at all costs, the cost for him being a backhanded support of slavery. "John," I said, tears in my eyes, "you have done a truly great thing." This, I thought, would make him the next president.

There was a small printing press in our headquarters, and copies of the proclamation were immediately made upon it and released to various newspapers. It was printed in its entirety throughout the West. Union people rejoiced, and recruitments rose, while rebels became cautious.

President Lincoln was also cautious. His reply, dated September 2 and supposedly sent by special messenger so that it might reach John speedily, was not received for six days, though it was but a journey of less than two days from Washington to St. Louis by train.

Lincoln was concerned—greatly concerned, he wrote—that John's proposed confiscation of slaves would alarm "our southern friends" unduly and turn them against us. There it was again—the preservation of the Union taking precedent over the fair and humane treatment of all men. "Allow me, therefore, to ask that you will, as of your own motion, modify that paragraph. . . . This letter is written in a spirit of caution, and not of censure."

"I will not modify it," John announced. "To do so would indicate that I myself thought the proclamation wrong. If Lincoln thinks I'm wrong, he'll have to ask me directly to rescind the order."

John wrote the president to that effect and received a carefully worded reply, which still insisted that the confiscation of property and the liberation of slaves was in contradiction to the last act of Congress upon the subject. Lincoln again suggested, strongly, that he modify the proclamation.

"I must reply immediately," John said, while I stared out the window, lost in my own thoughts.

Suddenly I whirled. "John! I will take your message to the president myself. Look at the length of time it took you to receive his first response. I suspect you have enemies in the president's closest advisers, and that they might delay your response—or even see that it never reaches him. I think a personal reply would be best."

"You would go all the way to Washington?" he asked incredulously.

"I would," I said firmly, "and I will."

"You will be well received," John said thoughtfully. "After all, Jessie, Lincoln knows of your work with your father and with me. He must know that you understand these matters as well as I do."

"I would hope so," I agreed.

I took the next train east, riding for two days in a dusty hot car that was as crowded as a streetcar in New York. Arriving in Washington late at night, I was met by John's good friend Judge Coles of New York, who escorted me to the Willard Hotel.

"I must send a message to Mr. Lincoln immediately," I said, only to be met with laughing protests that it was late in the evening and surely my message could wait until morning.

"No," I replied, tired as I was, "I must at least get word to the president." And so by messenger I sent a brief note, simply telling the president that I carried a confidential letter from John and would like to see him at his earliest convenience.

The messenger returned within the hour, bearing a card on which was written, "Now, at once. A. Lincoln."

"Now?" expostulated Judge Coles. "He cannot mean it. . . . It is nearly ten o'clock at night."

"I must go now," I said, terribly conscious that I still wore the dusty dress in which I had traveled for two days. Because of Father's death, I was in mourning, and the black dress showed the wear much more than any other color might have.

Judge Coles escorted me to the White House, and as we entered, I had a gripping attack of nostalgia, remembering the times that I had come there with Father as a child, when President Jackson used to brighten from his depression if I sat by his side, and then the triumphal visit that John and I had made at the reception celebrating President Tyler's inauguration. To hurry in, late at night and almost secretively, seemed almost a sacrilege to me.

Once announced, we were shown into the Red Room, there to cool our heels for quite some time. "His message said 'Now' as though it were urgent," I whispered to Coles, the room seeming to inspire a need for low tones.

"No excuse for this," Coles said emphatically.

At length the president entered from the other end of the room. He was taller than I expected, and every bit as gangly as I'd heard, his arms dangling almost helplessly at his sides and ending in hands too big for his body. But it was his manner that impressed me most—there was a sadness about him, a heaviness that

I could not imagine bearing in any circumstances. Thinking what energy the war gave to John, I could not believe the war alone was responsible for Mr. Lincoln's sadness—or that he would have been a cheerful person were the war won tomorrow. He nodded at me but neither spoke nor offered his hand.

I introduced Judge Coles, who then retired discreetly behind a door.

"You have a message?" the president asked.

"Yes," I said, holding it out to him.

He did not sit but walked over to stand directly under a chandelier and read John's reply. More weary than I ever remembered being before, I pulled out a chair and sank into it, conscious once again that I was middle-aged and tired.

"I thought I might answer any points about which you required more information," I said haltingly, for once completely undone by the coldness of the man I faced. "I come as General Frémont's trusted adviser."

"I know who you are," he said with a smile that was not at all pleasant. "You're quite a politician—for a woman. Nonetheless, I have written the general, and he knows what I want done."

I knew instantly that he not only dismissed me because I was a woman meddling in men's business, but that he was offended that I had come.

"The general," I said, feeling obligated to press John's case in spite of the obvious prejudice against me, "feels that he is at the great disadvantage of being opposed by people in whom you have great confidence."

He appeared surprised and demanded to know who I meant, but I too could fence. At length, his patience apparently exhausted, Lincoln said, "He should have listened to Frank Blair. . . . I sent him there to advise the general. . . . He should never have dragged the Negro into the war."

Appalled, I could only reply, "We were not aware that Frank Blair represented you. He did not say so."

My protest brought only a glower, and it was soon apparent that the interview was at an end . . . and was a failure, as far as John was concerned. Lincoln said I would have his reply soon, and when I pressed, asking if it might be the next day, as I needed to return to St. Louis, he said that he was very busy with many things but he would see that the reply was sent to my hotel within two days. I could ask for no more and turned to leave. He did not bid me farewell.

Walking back to the Willard, Judge Coles, who had listened at the door, said, "This ends Frémont's part in the war. He will no longer be effective."

"Of course he will," I replied, aghast at the thought. "John has much left to do. I was the problem."

Coles shook his head discouragingly.

At the hotel I insisted on sending a wire to John, telling him of the outcome of my meeting.

"Is that wise?" the judge asked. "There are apparently spies everywhere." He glanced around the lobby, as though expecting to see someone watching us.

I smiled grimly. "John and I have a cipher by which we can communicate without fear of discovery." And I sent my message.

Francis Blair Sr. came to see me at the Willard the next day. "Jessie," he said, in a voice that had once been strong but now quavered with age, "I have been fond of you since your childhood, and your father . . . he was one of the best men I ever met . . . and I supported your husband for the presidency. But now, Jessie, my heart is sick. How could you go before our president and find fault with him?"

Find fault with the president? I laughed aloud—my first reaction—and then saw that Francis Blair was not amused. Sobering quickly, I said, "I did not find fault. Indeed, if anything, he found fault with me . . . and treated me rudely."

Mr. Blair stayed two hours, haranguing me all the while about John's sins, until he finally got to a discussion of my own faults. "You should have stayed in Washington as I told you. It is not fitting for a woman to go with the army."

"It is fitting," I replied coldly, "for a woman to accompany her husband and to support him. That is all I have done." The fact of my being a woman seemed to keep coming up to slap me in the face, and I had little idea how to deal with such criticism. Longingly, I thought of Father, who had seen me as the editor of his political wisdom and thought—and had treated me like a son.

Mr. Blair, so wrought up that I feared he would have an attack right before me, finally blurted out that Frank had written to Montgomery that he feared John was intemperate and not in firm control of the situation. "Montgomery showed the letter to Lincoln," Blair said vindictively, "and the president now knows the truth about your husband . . . and about you."

"Me?" I could barely speak, as the connection between things came clear to me.

"You . . . the cunning you learned from your father, the secretiveness."

And I had just been thinking I had learned political wisdom from Father!

"Mr. Blair," I said, keeping my voice as calm as I could, "I think you best go now."

And go he did, taking all his anger with him, and leaving me behind, an emotional wreck.

Suddenly impatient to be out of the capital, I sent two requests to Mr. Lincoln, asking that he reply as quickly as possible so that I might depart. In the second I also asked for a copy of Frank Blair's letter to Montgomery, explaining that I did not think it fair to ask my husband to fight a shadow enemy. Finally I received an answer: The president had sent his reply to General Frémont by messenger. As for the other letter to which I alluded, he did not feel free to release a copy without the authorization of both the author and the recipient.

Angrily, I threw my few belongings into my valise and checked out of the Willard in time to catch the afternoon train west. But before I caught the train, I sent John another message, in cipher, telling him of the latest developments. I did not want him to receive Lincoln's reply without advance warning.

It so happened that Governor Curtin of Pennsylvania, with whom I was previously acquainted, was on the train, and he and his wife invited me to join them in their coach car. I did so with relief, thinking that congenial company might relieve my mind a bit. But the very first thing he said to me, once we were settled, nearly threw me into a frenzy.

"So Lincoln refused to approve your husband's proclamation, did he?"

I managed to laugh lightly and say, "That is business between men, Governor. I know nothing of it, though I'd hope it is not true." I'm sure my blush gave me away.

"Come now, Mrs. Frémont. We know you are privy to your husband's business," he said, his tone also light and laughing.

"But not," I said calmly, "to the president's business." Inside I was wondering desperately how the governor came by this bit of information, when Lincoln had refused to disclose the contents of his letter even to me.

We went on to talk of other things—all connected to the war, of course—but it was with relief that I saw them off the train in Pennsylvania some hours later. Hiding my concern and anger had become a terrible chore in their presence.

But then, the next day, a couple traveling to Illinois spoke to me of their dismay that John's proclamation would not stand. Before I could respond, the woman broke out into great, loud sobs. "My son," she managed to gasp, "I gave him willingly for the Union . . . but now it means nothing. If we cannot free the slaves, he died for nothing."

I had such compassion for her that I could do nothing but put an arm around her and murmur comforting words, while her husband patted her hand helplessly and muttered, "There, there . . ."

At our headquarters I found that the president's special messenger had beaten me only by a little more than an hour—and he turned out to be none other than Montgomery Blair himself. When an aide told me who was inside with John, I put aside all decorum and burst into the office.

"Jessie!" John rose from his desk and held his arms out to me, obviously relieved to see me. "I did not dare expect you so soon." He welcomed me with a warm embrace, throwing a glance at Montgomery, as though to warn me.

"I'm sure," I said archly, "that Montgomery did not either. And are you, Montgomery, the one who is publicizing Mr. Lincoln's private correspondence to John?"

Montgomery, who had risen when I entered the room, shifted his weight from one foot to the other and back again. "I'm sure I don't know what you're talking about, Jessie." But he couldn't look me in the eye.

"Jessie," John said, "do sit down. We were just discussing Mr. Lincoln's reaction to my letter." This time his glance toward Montgomery was one of pure anger. "The president," John went on, "has named General Hunter to replace me. . . ."

"Replace you?" I know my voice screeched like a hoot owl.

"Calm down, Jessie," Montgomery drawled. "To replace him only if John refuses to rescind his order."

I looked at John, begging for an answer. He stood behind his desk, straight and full of dignity, his head held high. But he said nothing for a long moment.

Finally, when he spoke, his voice was a whisper. "I will rescind the order."

I clasped my hand over my mouth and left the room hurriedly, without a word to either man. Behind me there was a great silence. "How could you?" I demanded when at last we were alone. "How could you give up the most important part of the proclamation?"

"Because if I am replaced, I can do nothing. But if I am in command, even with my hands tied to some extent, I can still do some good, still make this war go the way I know it should."

In my mind I heard again the words of Judge Coles: "This ends Frémont's part in the war." Ill at ease in my presence and knowing that he had let me down, John made an excuse to leave the room, and once he was gone, I gave in to great and bitter sobs.

There began our war with the Blair family. Rescinding the order was not enough for the Blairs, father and sons. John and I had placed ourselves in political opposition to them. John had knuckled under—how I hated the phrase that sprang to my mind!—not to the Blairs, but to Lincoln, and the Blairs knew it. He had not given in to the Blairs, and they knew they could not be sure of him in the future.

I remembered something my father had once told me was commonly said about the Blairs: "When they go in for a fight, they go in for a funeral." Father had declared that he never wanted Francis Blair Sr. for an enemy—and now we had as enemies both him and his sons, one of them, Frank, quick of temper and intemperate in his use of alcohol, a deadly combination.

The rumors that soon flew made anything about "General Jessie" look pale. John had ordered, for his private use, a half ton of ice—he did order it, for use in hospitals and hospital ships on the river. He was incapable of command because of his addiction to opium. He—and this was the most damning—was determined to establish an independent empire in the West as he had once tried to establish one in California. Since we knew that Frank wanted to be king of Missouri, I thought this a case of the pot calling the kettle black, to put it mildly.

"I had Frank Blair arrested today," John informed me two days later, "for insidious and dishonorable efforts to bring my authority into contempt with the government."

All I could do was repeat the appalling word. "Arrested?"

John's firm nod was confirmation.

I had no feeling left for the Blairs. They had proved themselves less than friends—and Frank had proved himself a scoundrel. But for John to arrest a congressman stepped beyond some boundary I had not yet defined in my mind.

"They say." John continued in a deliberate and slow fashion, "that it is your doing." Guiltily, he looked away from me.

"My doing?" Amazement had replaced my vague sense of anxiety. How could I have had Frank Blair arrested?

"They say that you are hungry for revenge, because they are my enemies and you are sworn to protect me." He emphasized the word "protect" in a way that sent me a message of caution.

"I did not know you needed protection," I said guardedly, feeling like the loser in a fencing match.

"You are always my strongest support, Jessie, and I am grateful. But I would not want the word to get abroad that I need your protection."

"Nor would I," I murmured, keeping the rest of my tumultuous thoughts to myself.

Frank Blair was released the next day.

Meanwhile, with a vigor that delighted me, the northern press hailed John as a hero, calling his proclamation the most important document of the war, his courage unquestionable, his leadership abilities the highest in the Union army. President Lincoln was strangely silent, his few messages to John tactfully worded and equivocal in nature. He neither defended nor condemned—he vacillated.

"He cannot dismiss me," John said, "because I have such a strong following."

He reminded me of a young boy walking across a frozen pond on thin ice and hoping that it would not break with his next step.

In October, John said again those words he had pronounced before General Lyon's death: "We need a victory, Jessie." The previous month the Western Department forces had suffered a disastrous defeat near Kansas City—men and supplies seized in numbers that astounded. Now, in spite of the Blairs' ardent campaign and Lincoln's indecision, John took to the field himself, moving southward with forty thousand troops. "I won't just drive the rebels from Missouri," he told me as he left. "I plan to go straight on all the way to New Orleans. The Mississippi River shall be ours!"

My mind flashed back to all those earlier leave-takings, when he'd set off on long expeditions and I'd not known if I'd ever see him again. "You will come safely home to me?" I asked.

His manner softened from the stern pose of leadership. "I'll certainly try, Jessie, but you know, if I have to, I am ready to die for the Union . . . and for abolition."

I hugged him fiercely. I believed in those causes every bit as much as he did, but I wasn't ready to lose him to them.

Back at headquarters I settled into a routine that would, I hoped, numb my nervous heart. Lily was my helper and sustainer, as I dealt with John's desperate requests for more arms, more transport, more supplies. In odd moments, when my attention wasn't demanded by a thousand details of running John's command, I worried about Lily. She favored me rather than John, but at nineteen her figure resembled mine in middle age—square, even a little stocky. Her hair was a dark brown, like mine, but she tended to draw it back severely, and I didn't see a smile gracing her face too often. She had no beaux courting her and, indeed, had shown no interest in the young officers who surrounded her daily.

"Lily," I said, "if I were your age, I'd be smiling at the young lieutenant who brings dispatches from your father, and maybe trying to talk to him about the war or the weather . . . or whatever." A vision of John as I'd first seen him flashed through my mind with an intensity that was almost physical.

"But you are not my age," she said practically, "and I am not interested in him."

"Is there . . ." I hesitated. "Is there anyone in whom you are interested?" I could tell that she felt no physical symptoms of attraction to a man, and that bothered me. I wanted for her the happiness I knew with John.

"No, Mother, there's not. I'm perfectly content to help you with Father's affairs and to care for Charley and Frank."

It was not the time to point out to her that none of those things were lifelong callings. In time neither her father nor her brothers would need her, and what would she do then? But I had other things on my mind, pressing things, and the problem of Lily was pushed to the back, where it lingered in my subconscious.

"Mother," Lily said one day, "they say in the city that you can run the department as well as Father, and that you like taking a man's role." There was a question in her eyes that went beyond her words. "Lily," I said, going to wrap my arms about her, "don't believe everything you hear. When a man is as bold and courageous as your father, men are bound to be jealous and to start all manner of rumors."

"And when," she said, "your mother is a bold and courageous woman. . . ."

I looked quickly at her to see the intent behind her words, but I found her smiling as though in pride, and again I hugged her.

John had named his encampment Camp Lily, and this pleased her greatly. I could tell only by the smile on her face, for she never said anything.

From Camp Lily, John wrote that his men's battle cry was "New Orleans and home by Christmas!" and that he felt extremely optimistic about the campaign, eager for battle. He planned to chase the Confederate army south until the Confederate leaders turned to fight. "We have twice the men," he wrote, "and all the ammunition and rifle power an army could want." Major Zagonyi and his Garibaldians, only 150 of them, scored major victories against the rebels, clearing the way for the advancement of John's troops. Hearing such word in St. Louis, I waited breathlessly for news of John's great victory.

"He has great ability and a foolproof military plan," I wrote to Starr King, "but it is frustrating to me to see him so hampered by a lack of supplies, his abilities held in check by a lack of administrative support." As always, I could be honest in my correspondence with Starr.

Then in early November the bits and pieces of news turned sour—John had been replaced by General Hunter, his troops had mutinied, Hunter had retreated. I kept vigil through the long nights, afraid to sleep for fear I'd miss the next rumor or—worse, yet—John's arrival.

He arrived late the night of November 8, the most dejected I had ever seen him. Plied with coffee and brandy, he spun out a tale that it taxed my mind to believe.

"The night of the second of November," he began, "I got word a messenger had arrived. We were ready to attack the next morning. There had been some word that General Hunter would arrive to supersede me, but then we'd heard nothing for days, and the men were impatient to be about it. So I told them that evening that if he had not arrived by midnight, I would lead them in the charge.

"Jessie, you've never heard such a reaction. Men cheered, throwing their hats in the air, and the various regimental bands began to play. It was the grandest celebration I've ever seen." He shook his head, as though trying to clear his brain, and I reached for his hand, only to have him withdraw it angrily and begin to march about the room.

"Toward midnight I received word that a messenger had arrived. The man was brought to me—a nervous man, who suddenly ripped the lining from his coat and took from it the message he brought from Lincoln. It was . . ." His voice fell, as though words were difficult for him. "It was my dismissal."

I could not speak. The injustice of it, the affront to his honor, the sheer wrongness of such an order stilled my tongue and numbed my brain.

"Hunter arrived about an hour later to take command. He had, I suppose, been deliberately dallying behind the messenger, as though the thing were a staged performance. I did what any officer should—shared my plans and strategies with him.

But he would have none of it. Said Lincoln thought it useless to pursue the rebels all the way south."

"The men?" I managed to ask.

"They were near rebellion. They threw down their guns, and the officers said they would serve no one but me. I begged for calmness, and they listened. But, Jessie, all Hunter did was lead them in retreat."

"Retreat? They outnumbered the enemy and . . ."

"I know," John said sadly. "It must have been the strangest sight in the world. They went from the sublime to the ridiculous, forty thousand men retreating from half that number, running as for dear life. I hear the rebels captured some men and wagons at the rear. Lincoln has paid his price."

"Yes," I said sadly, "he has." I knew enough of John's strategies to believe that he would have won a glorious victory, one that would have compensated for the Union losses at Bull Run. He could have cut the Confederacy in half and opened the Mississippi to Union shipping clear to its mouth in the Gulf. The possibilities that were lost were enormous, and I wondered that the president had not seen them.

"You told Lyon to retreat, and he wouldn't. Now Lincoln orders you to retreat . . . and loses."

"Because he ordered it from half a country away," John said. "He knew nothing of the particular situation. It was a blind judgment." "John," I said, "you have done a work so noble for your country that I don't know how to tell you. That the country . . . and the president . . . did not recognize it is folly so great that it will go down in history as a major blunder. But you must always know that you were outstanding."

I rose to meet him, and he held me in his arms. After a minute I was aware that his shoulders were shaking, and John—the unconquerable explorer and fearless general—was sobbing. His tears dampened the neck of my dress.

The next day word had spread abroad that John had been dismissed and was back at our headquarters. By midmorning the streets were crowded with people chanting his name, shouting hurrahs for him, and calling for a speech. At our arrival months before, I had wanted a celebration, but the streets were empty; now they were full of northern sympathizers who had before been afraid to make themselves known in this southern city.

"Who are they?" John asked incredulously.

"Unionists," I said. "Many Germans who have always supported you. Others who believe your proclamation was the only fair thing for the North." And then I dared a prediction. "There will be a great outcry from northerners who feel that an injustice has been done them. You watch and see."

John greeted the crowds below by waving from the balcony on the second floor, but he did not attempt to speak. I stood at his side, waving as strongly and proudly as he. It was one of our finest moments, and I never gave a thought to the propriety of a woman appearing with her husband—or following him to war.

Within days we received a copy of a poem that John Greenleaf Whittier, the New Englander, had written in John's honor. "Listen," I said. "It begins thus: 'Thy error, Frémont, simply was to act / The brave man's part without the statesman's tact.'"

Chapter Seventeen

My hair turned gray in St. Louis. Overnight, as they say. When John left the city to chase the rebels out of Missouri and all the way to New Orleans, my hair was dark brown, chestnut, gleaming and alive. It was, as I grew older and thicker about the middle, the one physical feature of which I could still be proud. But then when John, dismissed from his command, had been home but two days, I glanced in the mirror one morning before rushing to his study to work and was astounded to see great streaks of gray coursing through the brown. And the brown ... it was no longer vital and alive, but somehow a dead color. How, I wondered, could that have happened? How could hair, already grown from the head, change colors? I was afraid to ask John if he noted the change in my appearance and said nothing, keeping this latest disappointment my small secret.

My King George's mark, that red blotch at the corner of my mouth, had appeared instantly upon word of John's dismissal. In truth, it had been lingering around the corner of my mouth for two months, but it never came to full fruition until he arrived back in St. Louis. And then I wore it, like a stigmata, for two long months. That and gray hair.

For two weeks after John returned to St. Louis, we worked feverishly, for John wanted to collect every bit of documentation he could before we left the headquarters. "I shall have to defend myself someday," he said, "if I am ever to have another command. And I need ammunition. You must help me sort through this mountain of paperwork, Jessie."

And sort I did. But I also had another chore. Where once I had turned angry citizens of the city away, now I welcomed them into John's presence, interrupting him so regularly throughout the day that he claimed to feel lonely if left in his office without interruption longer than half an hour.

They came singly and in groups to tell him how important he was to them, how much they admired his stand on slavery, how his proclamation was the only thing that made sense of this war for which they were losing their sons and their homes. Many of them were German citizens, a group particularly appalled by slavery, but others were simply northern sympathizers who found themselves, uncomfortably, in southern Missouri . . . and in a land of southern sympathies.

"Mrs. Frémont, I do not wish to bother the general. My name is Schmidt, Franz Schmidt, and I have here . . ." The caller gestured at a long, thin parcel, wrapped in butcher paper.

"For the general?" I asked.

"Ja, for the general. From the people of St. Louis."

"He will see you immediately," I said, striding toward John's door.

The parcel proved to be a sword, a gleaming silver sword that had been made by a local silversmith and enclosed in a fine leather case embossed by a St. Louis saddlemaker.

After it was presented, John weighed the sword in one hand and then the other, commenting on its fine balance and weight, then examining in detail the careful workmanship on the case. At last he spoke to Herr Schmidt, who had been silently standing and watching him.

"It is the finest sword and case a man could hope to own, sir. I am uncertain how to thank you."

"We want no thanks," Schmidt said in his accented English. "You have done a great deal for us, for northerners, for those against the slavery. But if you could . . ." He let his sentence dangle away.

"Could what, man?" John demanded. "If it's in my power, I'll do it."

"Before you leave, on Sunday, if you could appear on your balcony, the people— my people—would like to bid you farewell."

"Agreed," John said, reaching to shake his hand.

And so we stood, John and I, once again on the balcony of the Brant mansion, this time on a Sunday afternoon. Before us was a cheering throng. Two weeks earlier the Garibaldians would have kept these people at a distance, but now they were close—and they were John's friends. I hoped that the eastern papers—especially the Washington papers—would take note.

"The sword," they cried, "the sword!"

And John raised the sword high in the air, shouting his thanks over their tumultuous cries. He never did make a speech that afternoon—the crowd was too exuberant—and after thirty minutes or more we retired, their cries echoing behind us.

"They like me, Jessie," he said.

"Of course they do, John. You have been a great inspiration for them. You've given them faith that they are right."

"I wish . . . I didn't have to leave them." Suddenly he was the little boy again.

I took his arm. "You'll have another command, and you'll do much more good for the northern cause. And, John, these people will know, and they'll be proud you carry their sword with you in that cause."

"I will carry it," he said, clasping the sword as he spoke.

That night he fell asleep in my arms like a child who needed to be cradled and cuddled and reassured.

He never mentioned my gray hair, and two weeks after he returned from Camp Lily, we left for New York.

—⁓—

"The public is behind us," I wrote to Starr King, "but the powers that be—the president, the cabinet—are all against us. I asked John if we should not just return to Black Point, but he is not ready to give up. He will seek another command, and with the public outcry that we are hearing, I do not think Mr. Lincoln can deny him."

In New York, John was a celebrity, and this time it was not just the everyday citizen who praised him. Men of influence spoke on his behalf before public audiences. When Wendell Phillips, the abolitionist orator, praised John's boldness and condemned what he called Lincoln's "pious caution," audiences went wild.

Still, when Henry Ward Beecher begged us to attend his Sunday service in Brooklyn—"There is something I want you to hear"—I had to drag John there. To an overflowing congregation Beecher called John a hero and, turning to him, said, "Your name will live and be remembered by a nation of Freemen!" We could leave the church only by passing through a corridor of men and women anxious to grasp John's hand, touch his coat, sing out their praise and thanks.

I heard a rumor that Lincoln was baffled by John's continuing popularity. Had he asked me directly, I could have explained it: John had made the war meaningful for northerners. He had courageously said what everyone whispered: It was a war to free the slaves. That was why northern women sent their sons and husbands to war, and that was why those men were willing to fight and die. John became a symbol for all of them.

In spite of public support John remained almost lethargic, sunk into a depression that frustrated and frightened me. The quieter he got, the angrier I became—not at him, but at the world, the system, whatever, that had not allowed his full talents to shine. While John sulked in his study—there is no other way to describe it—I settled the family into our new house with a flurry of activity, spurred on by the energy that anger often gives a person.

"I know!" I said to him one night late, as we sat over a glass of sherry before the fire. "I will write a book about Zagonyi's guard." John looked startled. "Why would you do that?"

I swirled the sweet liquid in my glass for a moment, thinking about how to phrase my answer. Finally I said, "It's the best way to tell the story. The guard was criticized as much as you were—and they were part of the criticism against you. I can tell your story through theirs."

"Jessie, that's an outlandish idea! You can't write a book!"

Stung to the core, I was silent a minute, quieting the instant responses that rose within me, the urge to fling at him the fact that I'd written all his expedition reports and many of my father's speeches and reports. Of course I could write a book!

"Do you mean," I asked cautiously, "that it's not fitting for me to write a book?"

He looked sideways at me, then quickly said, "No, no. That's not it at all. I just thought. . . . Don't you have enough to do with the children and the house and . . . ?" His voice trailed off, because he knew the answer to that question and was sorry he had ever raised it.

I wrote as though the avenging furies sat at my shoulder, at a pace I myself would never have thought possible. The truth is that once I began to tell the story, the words poured out so that my hand was hard put to keep up with my brain.

"I write only the truth," I told Starr King in a letter, "but I am telling it in a gentle manner so that none can take offense." In recounting the story of the guards' superb victory at Springfield, I wove in the details of John's planned rout of the rebels and how it was thwarted by governmental order, of why the Garibaldians were the key to John's success and not, as charged, an ostentatious show of power.

Ever aware of that old charge of "General Jessie," I begged readers, in an after-word, not to think me unwomanly for having written. It was, I told them, a strange time in our national history, a time that sometimes made women step beyond their normal bounds, and I did so ever conscious of my duties as a woman and a wife. Indeed, it was for that reason I wrote. As I reread that passage, I thought with some satisfaction that no wife who valued her husband could read it with a dry eye nor condemn me for having written.

The editors at Ticknor and Fields, a major New York publishing house, were very interested in the manuscript, pressing me for delivery of the completed version. But then they grew a pair of cold feet, which I ascribed to political fear. When at last they offered a contract—in December of 1861—I then withheld the manuscript, to their everlasting confusion.

But I knew why. John had said to me, in his careful and measured tones, "Jessie, I want another command. I want it badly . . . and your book . . ."

"Might turn the administration forever against you?"

He shook his head sadly. "I know why you wrote it, and . . . I could never ask you to bury it."

I rushed to put my arms around him. "I wrote it for you, John, to tell the world your story. And if publishing it would hurt you, then I won't publish it."

Even then I did not see him as selfish nor myself as martyred. I had done what a woman should—put my husband's interests first.

———

When the Congress, distressed by the North's lack of success in the war, established a Committee on the Conduct of the War, John was given notice that he would be asked to testify. All those records he had so carefully collected before St. Louis were now invaluable, for they would provide the basis of his testimony and, if needed, the proof.

We moved the household to Washington to prepare, and I became—without his asking or my suggesting—John's legal counsel, his sounding board, once again his amanuensis. We worked for long days and nights, and as I sat at his side, I was drawn back to the days of the court-martial, thinking how many who had been with us were now gone—some through death, like Father, and others through alienation, like Liza's husband, William Carey Jones, or all the Blairs—and the McDowells, whose southern loyalties separated them from us. The poet was right who wrote about the cruelty of war on those who do not fight.

"Jessie! President and Mrs. Lincoln are giving a gala at the White House, two weeks from now, February fifth."

Without turning from my papers to look at him, I remarked dryly, "Well, we won't be invited."

"Ah," he said, coming toward me to wave a paper under my nose, "but we have been. Here is the invitation!"

I read it carefully, even examined the envelope to make sure it was addressed to Major General and Mrs. John Frémont. I could not imagine that the president would want us present . . . but neither could I imagine that he would throw a festive party in the midst of war.

"Why is he doing that, John?"

He shrugged. "Who can read his ways? Perhaps he wants to consolidate his forces. We won't go, of course."

"Of course not," I agreed, my mind lingering on the balls I'd attended at the White House and the hopes I'd had of being hostess at some myself. But John was right this time: We would not be present. Besides, I would have had to attend wearing mourning, and if I went to a ball—even with my gray hair—I wanted to go as light and laughing.

On February 3 a messenger brought us a thick white envelope.

Scrawled in the upper left-hand corner was the signature "A. Lincoln." And after the address, underlined, the words "By hand," signifying the importance of the document. I deferred to John to read it. "He asks particularly that we attend the gala, in spite of our earlier regrets," John said wonderingly. "Says it would be a special favor to him. . . . Jessie, if I want a command, I think we should be there."

Feeling like a ship that was blown first this way and then that, I agreed, and two days later found myself, dressed in my best black, being greeted by the president and his wife. Mr. Lincoln greeted me civilly, giving no hint of our last meeting, and Mrs. Lincoln, overdressed and obviously nervous, fluttered over me, making silly remarks about my famous husband. I was grateful when we were forced to move on so that others could greet them. I whispered to John that the president looked more forlorn and sad than he had when I'd had my late-night meeting with him.

"You would too if you were losing a war," John said grimly taking my arm and steering me toward Dorothea Dix, whom he'd spotted across the great expanse of the Red Room.

I greeted her enthusiastically, but her mood was solemn. "I spent the morning here," she said. "The president asked me to take charge of the care of his ten-year-old son, Willie. He has diphtheria."

I caught my breath in horror. "And?"

"And there's not much I can do or anyone. I fear the boy will die, and the president knows it."

"No wonder he looks so sad," I said, feeling myself undergo a change of heart for the man. As a parent I knew too well the panic that descends when one of your children is ill—in fact, Frank at the age of three had suffered from diphtheria, and I had lived by his bedside for two weeks. He, fortunately, had recovered, but the pain . . . ah, I knew the pain! I watched the president the rest of the evening with great care and concern.

A public announcement was made that there would be no dancing because of young Willie's illness. But the Marine Band played loudly, and I thought it terrible that it would play while the boy lay dying. The irony of it tore at my heart, and I was in a hurry to be away from that place.

Perhaps it was little Willie's illness, but something made people ill at ease with the Lincolns, and few lingered to talk after once greeting them. By contrast a great knot of people gathered around John at the opposite end of the room, some anxious to praise his work in Missouri, others curious about his future plans, some just standing and listening.

Finally, making his way toward me, he said, "This is not good. The president can't help but remark all these people. We must make our excuses and be gone."

And we did, only to be summoned back by a messenger who said that Mr. Lincoln particularly wanted General Frémont to meet General McClellan.

"One does not," John said, "deny one's president, especially not when it comes to meeting one's commanding officer."

So back we went, where we were introduced to General and Mrs. McClellan. I had to stifle a gasp and pretend a coughing fit when I was introduced to Mrs. McClellan, for she wore secessionist colors—a band of scarlet velvet across her chest and scarlet and white feathers in her hair. For the wife of the commander of the Union army to wear such colors astounded me. I could not believe it was accidental. But how would she dare do such a thing deliberately?

"And sometimes you worry that I will embarrass you," I said to John in the carriage on the way home.

He only laughed and hugged me. "You never embarrass me, Jessie. I am always proud of you."

I was about to ask, "Even with gray hair and a thick waist?" but I didn't. I remembered my father saying you never give ammunition to the enemy.

After his appearance before the committee, popular demand gave John another command. His testimony was clear and to the point, all the problems we'd had in Missouri, the plans he'd made, the way they'd been thwarted. Frank Blair rose on the floor of Congress to denounce his testimony as "an apology for a disaster," but the congressmen stood by John.

In March 1862 he was given command of the Mountain Department, newly created by Lincoln. With headquarters in Wheeling, West Virginia, the department included the mountain country of western Virginia, eastern Kentucky, and parts of Tennessee, a 350-mile line of defense against an enemy who was continually reinforced with troops, supplies, and ammunition. There were tunnels and bridges to protect and river transportation routes to keep open. John was credited by the War Department with officers and staff he never once saw, and in some ways it was Missouri all over again. His troops were apparently never intended to fight. They were better disciplined than the Missouri troops and better armed, but they had no food and no clothes.

Specifically, they had no shoes. "I refuse to ask them to fight barefoot," John stormed. "A government that can provide full supplies to other commands can surely put shoes on the feet of my men and food in their bellies."

A testy correspondence ensued between my husband and the president. John wrote asking for the thirty-five thousand men he had been promised. Lincoln replied that he had given John easily that many at first and that was all he had the power to give. In return he asked why John had not retaken Knoxville as he'd been directed. "I know that you have done the best you can, under the circumstances, but I would suggest you go more on the offensive," the president wrote.

John's army had been living without shelter for forty rainy spring days. To march to Knoxville, as the president requested, required supplies, transport, and reinforcements. John refused to risk his troops, although he worded his message more carefully than he had when he exclaimed to me that he would not send them to fight barefoot. In spite of their condition John's men nearly cut off the retreat of General Stonewall Jackson, the "rebel Napoleon." But the clever Confederate general escaped. "If the others had supported me, I'd have gotten him," John raged. "The others" were other Union generals in the region.

When General Carl Schurz, sent by the president to assess conditions in the department, affirmed that it would be impossible to carry out Lincoln's orders with the present troops in their existing condition, Lincoln decided—rightly—that he had too many generals but no organization among them. Accordingly, he put General John Pope in charge of the several commands in the area, which meant Pope—an old enemy from Missouri—was now John's superior.

"Dear Jessie," John wrote, "I have resigned my command and am coming home to New York. General Pope has been appointed my commander, and I cannot, with a just regard for the safety of my troops and what was rightfully due my honor, suffer myself to pass under his command."

John was the second-ranking general in the Union army, and Pope was clearly his junior. The president had delivered John another terrible slap, and I was left to sit in New York and wonder if it would be fatal.

My mind whirled. Was John set up to fail? Was it some clever plan of the president, to make him fail so that his dismissal in Missouri would be justified? I remembered the man so grieved about the death of his son, the man so obviously moved by the wholesale deaths of his soldiers, and I could not believe that. The most I could accuse the president of was a lack of good judgment—but I was firm in that conclusion.

John was weary when he came home to me—an old man before his time. The Civil War—and the Mountain Department—had been the chance on which he had pinned his hopes for the future, the crisis that would reinstate him in governmental favor. He did not need public favor—he already had that—but he was constantly defeated and turned aside by the government he chose to serve. The war was over for John long before Appomattox.

"We have lost our personal life," I told him. "Everything about us has been consumed by this war. It is time for us to take back our own lives. Let's go to Black Point, John. We can be happy there."

He stared at me, his eyes almost glazed with disappointment.

"We can't go to Black Point," he said haltingly. "The government has taken it over for military purposes."

"The government . . ." Visions of my beloved house danced before my eyes, and I felt faint. "They can't just take property that is ours."

He spoke slowly, with great reluctance. "It wasn't exactly ours. It seems we never had clear title." Then, almost desperately, "I'm trying, Jessie. I've started a petition in the courts to have it returned, but those things move slowly." He shook his head reluctantly. But then he rose and came to me, wrapped his arms around me. "Jessie, publish that damn book. We've worried about the government long enough. Let them worry about us now."

The Story of the Guard was published in time for Christmas in the year 1862.

"He is weary of all the strife, and I worry about him," I wrote Starr King. "It is hard to believe that a man with such vision has been so continually thwarted by the administration, but I have hopes that he will respond by taking his interests in a different direction. Meantime, the continual failure of the northern army is bitter justification for John. We would both rather it were not so." I never told Starr that Black Point was no longer ours—I couldn't bear writing the words, and for months I carried on the pretense that we would return soon.

Frank and Charley came to me one day after we were settled again in New York. They rarely saw their father. He rode horseback in Central Park, he took fencing lessons, and he closeted himself in his library, though even I did not know what he was doing. And if I was curious, the boys were even more so.

"Mother," Charley said formally, as though reciting a speech he had rehearsed, "Father is home from the war for good, isn't he?"

"Yes, dear, he is," I answered, looking from one earnest face to the other.

"Is he a hero?" Frank asked intently.

Suddenly I knew what this was about. They'd heard rumors about their father at school from playmates—maybe they'd even overheard careless adults—rumors that said John had failed at two commands in the war. I put an arm around each pair of thin shoulders and drew the boys to me.

"Of course he is a hero. His name stands for freedom to many, many people, and he has been a loyal soldier—and a courageous one."

"Didn't he lose a battle?" Charley pressed.

"Well, he didn't defeat Stonewall Jackson, if that's what you mean. But he was the only Union officer to chase Jackson and to make him turn and run. That's quite an accomplishment."

"What else?" Frank asked impatiently.

"He was the first to make people realize what this war is about, boys. He had the courage to say that we're fighting to free slaves. That was very brave."

"Did it get him in trouble?" Charley seemed to have a need for placing blame.

"In a sense," I said. "Your father lost a lot in this war, and we must all understand that. He and I both have family and friends who are committed to the Confederate cause, and now they no longer speak to us. Your father used his private funds, and his army pay, to care for the wounded, to order supplies, to do those things the government couldn't—"

"Or wouldn't," Charley interrupted, and I wondered just how much adult business this child was privy to.

"We cannot know what goes on in the government," I said, "and so we can't criticize." I prayed silently that God would forgive me for telling my children something that I myself did not believe.

"We still have our gold mine, though," Frank said confidently. "We're rich!"

"We have it, Frank, but it's much smaller, and I don't think we should consider ourselves rich. We have . . ." My voice faltered. "We don't have Black Point anymore." Tears began to well up in my eyes, despite my best efforts.

Frank began to howl, while Charley said indignantly, "Nobody can take Black Point from us. It's ours! It's our home!"

I hugged them closer and, bowing my head, began to cry in earnest, while Frank continued to howl and Charley patted me awkwardly on the shoulder, saying, "It'll be all right, Mother. It will be." With that talk it came home to me how much the war had cost us—and I did not think only of friends and property and money.

The war went from bad to worse for the North. We grew used to seeing hollow-eyed men, sometimes missing a leg or an arm, on the streets of the city. But we never grew used to the daily casualty lists, which seemed to grow longer and longer. The Union defeat at Gettysburg in 1863 seemed to demoralize many, and the cry was for peace at any cost.

John came to me one night as I was making my toilette, preparing to retire. He startled me, for he seldom entered my bedroom those days, keeping to himself in his library until long after I had retired, and usually sleeping on a daybed in his dressing room. Now he put his hands on my shoulders, ran them gently down my arms, and bent to kiss the top of my head, burying his face in my hair as he used to do when we were younger. I said nothing but simply waited.

At length he raised his head and spoke. "There is a movement afoot to nominate me for president again."

The elections of 1864 were but months away, as I well knew, but I had thought John through with politics, a finality that gave me both relief and an ever-present sense of loss. Now that little glimmer of hope sparked in me again. Could the White House, would it ever really, be ours? Just as quickly reality took over, and I knew that John could not survive another campaign.

"And?"

He shook his head wearily. "I don't know. The war is a massacre. It makes no sense to use our boys as so much cannon fodder, and Lincoln can't come up with a general he trusts or a plan he'll follow for more than a week. There's no organization behind this war."

I was thoughtful for a long time, weighing the possibilities—and the consequences. Ultimately, I did not think John was the one to run: He had been defeated too many times, and it had taken the spirit from him. The very droop of his shoulders now as he talked with me testified to that. "I think," I said slowly, "that you should step aside . . . as long as Lincoln is not the choice of the party."

He stiffened a little, and I saw that some deep part of him, like that hidden spark in me, still longed for the presidency. Ah, John, I thought, let us be practical now that life has shown us so many times that we are its pawns.

"I must think about it more." He turned to leave and then changed his mind. "Jessie, if I did go for it, would I . . . have your support?" He stood like a forlorn child, asking to be loved.

I rose to go to him, my arms open. "Of course, my darling. You know that I will fight whatever battle I have to for you."

"Ah, Jessie," he said, wrapping his arms around me. "Why am I so lucky?"

John stayed in my room that night, and we lay close together, holding each other like two frightened children. But there was no passion between us—we were both too world-weary, a feeling that goes far beyond tired, and I was aware that we had not yet left politics and the national good behind us in favor of finding our own personal lives. I could not help the tears that ran silently down my cheeks.

—◦—

Over the next days it came to me that a presidential campaign was not at all what I wanted. Nor in truth was the presidency appealing. More than anything I wanted back my life at Black Point.

As though fate had been waiting for me to reach that decision, it dealt me a blow so severe that I almost gave way under it. Word came from San Francisco that Starr King had died of diphtheria complicated by pneumonia.

I sat in the parlor, motionless, the cursed letter dangling from my hand, my face frozen. John, coming downstairs for his midday meal, found me there.

"Jessie." I could only nod toward the letter.

He came and took the letter, then straightened to read it, glancing at me once or twice as he read. "I'm sorry," he said softly, putting the letter back in my lap. "I know that he was very important to you."

I nodded but could not speak.

After a long silence, during which John stood rather awkwardly in front of me, he asked, "Jessie? Were you . . . in love with him?"

I shook my head. "No," I finally managed to mutter, "but I could have been, had it not been for you." I paused. "You and I," I said slowly, "have had our ups and downs . . . and there are times I am desperately lonely for the companionship of a man—even the adoration. But beyond that, I know that I love you."

"You mean, in a way, that, yes, you were in love with him, but you refused to acknowledge it . . . or act upon it?"

"I guess so," I said.

He knelt by me. "Jessie, I am always telling you how lucky I am. Now I'm telling you that I will try to live up to the loyalty you've shown me. Come, let's go to the table. The children are waiting for us."

"You go without me," I said, and he did. Once he was gone, great, silent sobs rose in my throat. I had lost not the man who loved me but perhaps the man who understood me best and who, unlike either Father or John, treasured me for myself and not for what I did for him. With Starr King I had been Jessie—not Senator Benton's daughter or General Frémont's wife.

John did not run for president. "The Democrats will put up McClellan," he told me one night at dinner while Lily listened intently. These days she knew almost as much about politics as I and was almost as ardent.

"McClellan!" I said scornfully. "His wife wears the Confederate colors!" I never could forget her outfit at the Lincolns' disastrous gala.

"That's not the worst of it," John said dryly. "McClellan will end the war without abolishing slavery."

"Father," Lily said righteously, "you must run. We can't let that happen."

My heart sank. I saw no alternative, no way that would work either for us or for the country. John should not run—I was more and more convinced of that—but we could not let the country elect a "peace at any price" president like McClellan. That left Lincoln—and I could not stomach the idea of another four years of his administration.

Lincoln was the Republican nominee. It was widely rumored that he had promised John another command—a promise made out of guilt, I thought—in turn for his withdrawal from the election. It was a question so potentially explosive that I never asked John, though in my heart I wanted to believe it was not true. Once he did say to me, "I did what I had to do for the safety of the Republican party. I could not put personal or political considerations before the supreme object of crushing the Confederacy." He looked at me earnestly. "Jessie, we must win this war."

I could not argue that point at all.

Montgomery Blair was dismissed from the Cabinet within days of Lincoln's renomination—the Missouri delegates to the convention had pressed for a reorganization of the Cabinet. And a pro-Blair faction, sent to the convention, was excluded by the Credentials Committee. The House of Blair had come tumbling down. Could that have been part of John's bargain with Lincoln? The thought gnawed at me, but I never asked.

We waited in New York almost a year for the new command, which never came. John still worked in his study and still spent long hours fencing. He and Lily had taken to going for frequent horseback rides through Central Park, and I rejoiced to see them become companions. I busied myself with charities and longed for Starr King and his reassuring words. Life went on, though I had the feeling always of living in suspended animation.

When Lincoln issued his own Emancipation Proclamation, it was a bitter blow for John, made more so by Lincoln's telling a group of his supporters that "the pioneer in any movement is not generally the best man to carry that movement to a successful issue." John was, of course, the pioneer to whom he referred.

In April of 1865 events happened with such rapidity that none of us could absorb their impact. On the third, Richmond fell to Union troops; on the ninth Lee surrendered at Appomattox, rendering us all speechless not with joy but with relief that the long contest and misery had been ended without loss of principle. And then, on the night of the fifteenth, came the tragedy that sent the nation reeling—Lincoln was shot as he watched a play at the Ford Theater. "I cannot believe it," I murmured to John as we sat staring at a dying fire in his library. The word had been telegraphed to us, and we sat praying for the slim chance of survival, though we knew in our hearts that it was not to be.

"It is harder," John said, "to have been his enemy now than his supporter. I would have defeated him a thousand ways ... but never this way."

I reached for his hand. "The worst of it," I said, "and this is self-serving, is that I believe the truth will now never be told. There are facts about your assignments ... and your dismissal ... that will go to the grave with Lincoln."

"Jessie, that doesn't matter. What matters is that a man who sincerely loved his country has been cut down by a fool. Lincoln's name will be written large in history. It will stand for freedom—you mark my words."

To myself I said, *But it is your name, John, that should be written that large in history, that should stand for freedom.* I felt petty for my lingering resentment of a dying president—but that did not diminish my resentment.

We moved to a home on the Hudson River, a vast and magnificent estate that I called Pocaho. The house was of rough gray stone and commanded a view of the Catskills in one direction and Haverstraw Bay in the other. There were woods and acres of lawns, stables and boat docks. Inside the house we put all our treasures from California and some new things—Albert Bierstadt's painting of the Golden Gate, my piano, John's vast library, and, newly acquired, the library of the recently deceased geographer Humboldt.

John rode his Irish hunter, Don Totoi, daily, usually accompanied by Lily on her thoroughbred. The boys, when they were not at school, spent their time sailing—Charley had a yacht—and I busied myself with charities, principally getting relief supplies to children in the South, and with entertaining. Life was sort of a perpetual vacation after the intensity of the presidential campaign and the war years. I, who had for years lived by my father's prescription of the active life, involved in politics and governmental affairs and the world of men, suddenly found myself living the life my mother had dreamed of—Pocaho reminded me of Cherry Grove, but without all that southernness.

When Elizabeth Cady Stanton asked me to support women's suffrage, I refused, telling her that I did not believe in her cause. "Women," I wrote, "get slapped when they step beyond themselves, and I am weary of being slapped." I would never again give the world a chance to call me General Jessie. And when Susan B. Anthony wrote for support, I sent a generous check and my regrets that I could do no more. When they dedicated a statue to Father in St. Louis, I was there to pull the curtain off and wish that he could know in what esteem his city held him in, but I made no speech. I had retired.

Not that John was retired. Various legal entanglements—he had judged poorly when he'd entrusted shares in Las Mariposas to associates—kept him in court far too much of the time and cost him both legal fees and, eventually, most of his shares of the mine. He was gone a lot, spending almost more time in New York City and Washington than he did at Pocaho.

Just as the 1850s had been the years of gold in California, the 1860s were the years of railroad expansion, and John saw that his long-held dream of a railroad from one coast to the other was about to materialize. He immediately plunged into the railroad business, ultimately investing heavily in the Memphis and El Paso Railroad.

I watched all this from a distance. John and I were like two ships on a parallel course—always in sight of each other but never quite touching. His interests were railroads and money; mine were maternal. "Lily, you haven't been off these grounds all week, except to ride with your father. Are you not a little lonely?"

She had grown into a substantial but—I hated to say it—plain young woman, and she did little to improve her appearance. Try as I might, I could not interest her in fashionable clothes, let alone the hairdo of the day. And she did not have the bright-chestnut hair that had once made me so proud—hers was simply plain brown.

Now she faced me across some sewing she held in her lap. "I am perfectly content to stay at home, Mother. I prefer it. Parties and visiting and the like . . . they make me uncomfortable."

"But you will never meet a young man staying here!" I exclaimed, the words unfortunately out of my mouth before I thought of their effect.

"I do not need to meet a young man, Mother. I have no interest in it. Besides, you fill the house with people." Expressionless, she turned back to her sewing.

I shrugged. There were always people at Pocaho, always an extra place set at the table for whoever should drop in, but they were not interesting people in the sense that my visitors at Black Point had been. I still longed for Starr King and Bret Harte but had to make do mostly with people who had too much money and too much time and knew not what to do with either. I didn't tell Lily that, if forced to honesty, I would admit I would not want her to marry any of the men who came to Pocaho those days. Instead I asked, "But don't you want to marry and have a family?" It was unthinkable to me that she did not.

"No," she said simply, "I don't."

"Lily," I said almost desperately, my hands twisting in my lap, "I cannot imagine life without your father. I cannot imagine going through life alone. He has been everything to me."

"I know that," she said, and I thought I detected a note of bitterness. "And what has it brought you?"

"Happiness," I replied instantly, "and comfort." I waved my hands vaguely around the sumptuous parlor in which we sat, its furniture of English mahogany, its draperies of fine cut velvet, its rugs the rarest of Orientals.

"Comfort," she said, "but I don't know about the happiness, Mother. Anyway, it's not the kind of happiness I want for myself." And with that she put an effective end to the conversation by excusing herself and leaving the room.

I sat stunned.

By happenstance John came into the parlor, looking for a book he had misplaced, and found me sitting there like a statue. "Jessie? Are you all right? You look . . . well, like lightning has hit you."

I wanted to cry out and ask him, "Aren't we happy? Tell me that we are!" But instead I said quietly, "John, I'm going to take the children to Europe. Lily must broaden her horizons."

Most men would have asked what prompted this sudden decision, why I was so adamant, and a thousand other questions. To his everlasting credit John simply said, "Fine. I need to go on business; we'll all go together."

CHAPTER EIGHTEEN

WE SAILED IN THE LATE SPRING OF 1869, JOHN BOUND FOR PARIS, AND LILY, FRANK, and I determined to see the Alps in Switzerland, after a stay in London to do some shopping. Poor Charley had been left behind, on a naval cruise as part of his training at the academy. But we had not been long in England when an irresistible invitation reached us: we were invited to Copenhagen for the wedding of the crown prince of Denmark and the princess of Sweden.

"The Alps," I told Lily, "have been there for a very long time and no doubt will still be there when we get around to them. But a royal wedding . . ."

Lily agreed placidly, showing neither hesitation nor enthusiasm. I hoped that the romance of a wedding might wear off on her and change her mind a little, though I might as well have wished for a sudden shift in personality.

Frank elected to stay with his father, and so Lily and I left for Copenhagen. Our first hint of the elaborate festivities came as our carriage drove into the city—flags flew everywhere, the blue and straw of Sweden, the cherry and white of Denmark. People thronged the streets, all in a festive mood. It was clear that this wedding was to be proclaimed a national holiday.

Soon after our arrival we attended a royal reception at which Danish nobility gathered from across the small country to welcome the bride. At special notice from the queen, I was given the honor of an escort by the minister of war and also had the privilege of visiting briefly with the king. When he asked how I liked the climate in Copenhagen, I forgot momentarily both my manners and the fact that he was king and so should not hear any criticism of his country.

"You have no climate, sir, you have weather!" Fortunately, he laughed heartily.

As a married lady of some international respect, I was privileged to stand near the king and queen as people paraded past them—first the nobility and then the people of the country. The rule was that "any person of decent appearance" could pass through the gallery in which the reception was held; by so doing, the people themselves became part of the ceremony. I thought it a custom that would have been well suited to our own democratic company, until I remembered with a shudder the stories about President Jackson's open reception in the White House when he was inaugurated. Somehow Denmark had more mannerly citizens.

At length we passed from that gallery into another, where musicians played. This hall was lit by wax candles in Venetian glass holders; unfortunately, the wax ran over the holders and collected in small puddles on the floor. At the opening quadrille of honor, a portly middle-aged gentleman slipped and fell, knocking his head so badly that he was stunned and had to be carried out.

I danced cautiously with several noblemen who sought my hand and felt much like a queen myself, though I watched always for those small puddles of wax. In the midst of one dance, however, I was startled when the music came abruptly to a halt, and then, after a second's hesitation, the musicians broke into the national anthem.

The crowd parted as a little old woman, a fairy godmother sort in yellow-and-white silk, made her way to the thrones. Her white hair was held by an ordinary cap, upon which sat a coronet of diamonds. Around her neck were strings and strings of necklaces—diamonds, rubies, pearls—so many that one could barely see the fabric of her dress. At least as many bracelets jangled on her arm, so that I thought she should have been quite weighted down by all that jewelry. She proceeded slowly forward, however, the crowd bowing in her honor, until the king came forward to greet her and escort her to a chair. She was, of course, the dowager queen, and I was most impressed with the respect shown her. I intended to tell John that our country could take strong lessons in manners from the Old World, if the Copenhagen court was any example.

Lily, being an unmarried woman, was not afforded the freedom at the reception that I was and had to stand with the young girls her age who were strictly chaperoned. Afterward I asked if she had enjoyed it, and she nodded vaguely and then, with more life than usual, recounted that one of the chaperons asked her to point out the American lady.

Lily nodded toward me.

"The one in the violet and white, with white hair?" the woman asked.

I winced as Lily told me this, to think that my hair was now totally white, though I was but forty-five years of age.

"She told me," Lily continued, "that you could not be the American. You were an English lady. When I asked how she knew, she replied, 'Her hair is fixed to fit her face, rather than to the latest style.' I told her," Lily said emphatically, "that I knew you were American because you were my mother."

I laughed aloud! "And what did she say then?"

"She said," Lily answered, almost shyly, "that my hair was not dressed in the latest fashion, either. . . . She seemed to consider that a great compliment." Lily was apparently uncertain whether or not to take it in that spirit.

"Ah, Lily," I said, "we have been given a great treat—an inside look at royalty, at the lives they lead, the life . . ." My voice trailed off, for I wanted to say that it was the life we should be leading. Had John been elected to the White House, I would have brought just such grandeur, such formality to the presidency. It would, I knew, be something the country needed—something, I thought somewhat spitefully, better than the Lincolns' ill-fated gala.

"It was all a bit much, don't you think?" Lily asked, drawing me back to the present.

A few nights after the wedding—which surpassed the reception in grandeur but does not linger in my mind in the same way—we were invited to a dinner with the great storyteller, Hans Christian Andersen. I had expected someone rather magical and wonderful and met, instead, a man whose peculiarities made him seem like a spoiled child. It hurt his feelings if you smiled when he spoke or read, and he would not talk if you wore a color displeasing to him—pink, in particular, for he disliked "clothes the color of skin." At dinner, if he did not like his position or seatmates, he simply refused to speak at all.

But he was most interested in talking to us—fortunately, my gown was of a deep blue that evening—and hearing of his reputation in America. As long as I flattered him, he was extremely cordial.

After dinner he read to us from an unpublished story, "A Tale of a Thistle." Though he read in Danish, we had been provided an English translation and could follow easily enough. Afterward he gave me a small statuette of the match girl, and I told him, through a translator, that I would add it to my treasures at Pocaho.

From Denmark we made our way back through the Alps, but I had been away from John and Frank too long and was itchy to be with them again. John had hired a governess for Frank and then sent him off with friends to row on a picturesque lake, so his letters didn't mention Frank at all, and I gathered that father and son were not spending too much time together.

John's letters did mention more than once a young sculptress whom he'd met in Paris. "What do you think of this Vinnie Ream?" I asked Lily, who had also read the letters. It was, I thought with a twinge of regret, a sign of what our relationship had come to, that John's letters were addressed to "Dear Jessie and Lily," but I dutifully shared them.

"I think," she said, her eyes fixed out the window of the carriage, "that she is too young for Father to be so enthusiastic about. She is my age."

"Two years younger," I answered far too quickly, giving away just how much thought and attention I had devoted to Vinnie Ream.

"Here comes another village," she said, as though to distract me. Almost immediately I heard the postilion on our carriage blowing on his brass horn. I had not figured out whether the horn was to warn away pedestrians and stray sheep—which would have made sense—or to announce our passage in some grand manner—which, I admitted only to myself, appealed to the same part of me that had been thrilled by the ceremonial approach to life in the Danish court.

On first greeting John my inclination was to demand right off, "Tell me about Vinnie Ream!" but instead I asked about the sale of stock in the Memphis and El Paso.

"Slowly," he said, "slowly. But I have a good agent, a Monsieur Probst, working on it for me. Your brother-in-law put me onto him." My brother-in-law was, of course, Susie's husband, Gauldreau Bouilleau, who had taken Susie first to India and then to Paris, where he was American consul. Now he was in France, doing I knew not what. "I barely have to worry about the railroad," John finished.

A little alarm sounded in my head, but John rushed on so quickly I had no time to listen to the warning. "Let me tell you about Vinnie Ream," he said. "She is a wonderful sculptor, just twenty-two years old, here in Paris with her parents to work on a bust of Lincoln—she was awarded the commission after his assassination. You must sit for her, Jessie. I've told her you would."

I wanted to hold up my hand and ask him to pause for breath.

Inside I was thinking, *Twenty-two? John, you are fifty-six!* But I knew that a young girl like Vinnie Ream would see him as worldly, famous, and wealthy; she would not know the John that I did. Aloud, I asked, "Have you sat for her, John?"

"Hours and hours," he answered guilelessly. "I am intrigued with her, absolutely intrigued. You will be too."

I went and put my arms around that dear white head. "Of course I will, John," I said. John was not having an affair with Vinnie Ream—I was as sure of that as I was of the sun and moon in the sky. He may well have, over the years, dallied with other women—the suspicion had often occurred to me, but I had never wanted to know and still didn't. But he had never been so open about another woman before, and that very openness gave me relief. John and I were only occasional lovers, but we were friends—and both relationships were intact, in spite of Vinnie Ream.

She was, as John said, a remarkable young woman with a great deal of talent. The late president had sat for her half an hour a day for over five months, she told me.

"With his busy schedule!" I murmured, feeling myself catty without intent.

She was as guileless as John. "Exactly what Mrs. Lincoln said," she replied, "but there was no changing the president's mind. I . . ." Her voice faltered. "I had almost finished the sculpture when he died. Now I must change it to make it appropriate—not a man at one time in his life, but the sum of that life."

I posed one afternoon and days later received by post a small and none-too-flattering bust. It would not go with the match girl among my treasures.

John was abruptly called back to America, and on but a few days' notice I left with him. Perhaps I was thinking it best not to leave him too long alone again and chose, therefore, leaving my children behind as the lesser of two evils. Lily was to supervise young Frank's education in the European manner, but that lasted only until war was declared between France and Prussia. Then, with great prudence, she saw to it that she and Frank were on the last passenger train out of Dresden and safely onboard the last German passenger steamer that crossed the Atlantic before the Franco-Prussian War.

We assembled again at Pocaho, a family reunited and, at least on my part, glad to be home again.

It was not long before John's railroad empire began to unravel like a frayed sweater when a thread is pulled. I had kept myself ignorant of his business affairs, yet his tragedies came as no surprise to me. Without looking I had seen the signs but refused to acknowledge them.

He entered my bedchamber one midmorning looking shaken. I was still abed, having adopted the habit of having a breakfast tray sent to me while I read the paper and then taking a short nap before facing the day.

"Jessie?" His very look startled me.

"Yes?" I swept the papers aside and made room for him to sit on the bed.

"Monsieur Probst has been arrested in Paris . . . and so has Susie's husband."

"Arrested? For what?" I had sensed in Paris that things were not right.

"They . . . misrepresented the whole thing. They claimed the railroad was transcontinental."

"Transcontinental!" I interrupted. "Couldn't anyone with a sense of geography know that the very name—Memphis and El Paso—indicated it covered but a small portion of the southern route?"

John withdrew, looking offended. At length he said, "If you'll let me finish. . . . It was to be transcontinental one day—you know that as well as I do. But Probst and Bouilleau didn't wait on the facts . . . and they let people assume that the government had guaranteed subsidies and backed the bonds."

"John!" I was truly horrified at the magnitude of this deception. "You . . . you didn't know."

"Of course not." His eyes, focused out the window, refused to meet mine. "I was preoccupied in Paris, and I trusted them—foolishly."

The thoughts that tumbled through my mind were not appropriate to utter at the moment. I couldn't accuse him, beaten as he was, of not having learned the lesson at Las Mariposas of trusting the wrong men again—particularly when one of them was his brother-in-law. Nor could I suggest, much as I longed to, that he should have paid less attention to Vinnie Ream and more to his business.

"There is a French warrant for my arrest too," he said.

"Well, if you don't go to France, they can't arrest you." Practicality seemed to me the first place to start. "What about the railroad itself?"

"We have laid only three miles of track . . . and graded twenty-five more." He whispered the words, as though reluctant to admit the magnitude of this mistake.

"When will more track be laid?" I asked.

"There is no money to lay more track," he whispered, still avoiding my eyes.

I was seeing my husband disintegrate before my very eyes, and the scene became so painful that I thought I should scream aloud—anything to make it end. When I spoke, the calmness of my voice surprised me. "Not unless, I assume, you invest more of our money in it."

Now he sank his head into his hands, and his voice was so low that I could hardly make out the sense of it. "We have no more money, Jessie. We can't pay our taxes . . . and the railroad is bankrupt."

My world tilted before me, and the safe walls of Pocaho seemed about to crumble before my eyes. "John, tell me . . . tell me that you have just misspoken. We cannot be penniless."

John had never been extravagant—he neither drank spirits nor smoked tobacco, he preferred a quiet evening at home with friends to gala parties, and he was inclined to wear the same clothes year after year unless I nagged him into buying himself new ones. But his simple habits were by choice, never necessity, and when I lived extravagantly—I had to admit that I had done so—he had seemed pleased, never worried nor critical. With a wrench I thought of our recent trip to Paris, my carefree shopping and the lavishness of the festivities in Copenhagen, which I had enjoyed so much.

For the first time in all the years of our marriage I did not go to him with my arms outstretched to comfort him. I simply could not do it. I would not censure aloud, but my heart knew that John had brought this catastrophe on us. In our previous defeats I had often thought him a victim. This time he could have averted tragedy.

Through that long morning the rest of the story came out—a sordid tale of misplaced trust and carelessness. An investor had purchased the Memphis and El Paso in bankruptcy court and was forcing John out, as he had already been forced out of Las Mariposas. He had not only lost a fortune, he had no prospects of an income.

"Pocaho?" I asked.

"The tax collector was here yesterday, while you were out visiting. He has made a list of everything—from the Bierstadt to the stables and horses—and we cannot sell anything without accounting for it to him."

"The land in California?"

"We can sell that, and I have set it in motion."

"I want to go over those records with you," I said, rising from my bed. "And we must petition the government for payment for Black Point." After a ten-year hiatus I was ready to do battle again.

"It's not all my fault," he said. "There has been a panic in this country, you know." His tone was defensive.

I wanted to tell him not to whine. I knew that the collapse of Jay Cooke's banking firm had sent thousands of other firms—including a lot of railroads—into financial ruin. But that didn't excuse John . . . I couldn't even define what John had done as wrong, and I didn't want to. But I would not see us as yet another victim of the Great Panic of 1873.

Within the next months it all disappeared—first the land in California, then Charley's yacht and the horses, next the Humboldt book collection, and after that—tearing my heart out as it went—the Bierstadt painting of the Golden Gate. And, finally, Pocaho. We moved to a small rental house on Madison Avenue in the city, a dark and cheerless place, which under other circumstances I could have brightened with our personal things. Now I had none of those things left.

We had been the richest of the rich, and now we were paupers.

———

"What is this?" John's voice was cold, calm. Only his waving hand revealed his anger. In that hand he held a copy of the *New York Ledger*.

With a sinking heart I knew what it was, but I played the fool. "What do you mean?"

"This article." He spread the paper out on the table where I sat, a writing pad before me.

"Oh, John, it's just a little piece I did when the editor—you know, Robert Bonner—asked me if I wouldn't write something. I've done several of those sketches . . . about famous people I've known."

"Famous people," he said with some irony. The sketch was of Starr King. Then, "Why must you do that and reveal to the world how desperate our circumstances are?"

None of this came as a surprise to me. If I'd thought he would respond differently, I would have told him about the articles when I agreed to write them—or, as truth would have it, when I asked Robert Bonner if the interest he had shown some years earlier still held. He had said it did, and he agreed to pay me one hundred dollars a sketch for a series on the distinguished persons I had known. So within two weeks I'd earned four hundred dollars by writing about Starr, Kit Carson, Andrew

Jackson, and Hans Christian Andersen. I wondered if it would be too obvious if I next wrote about Thomas Hart Benton.

Lily and Frank had been in on the secret. When their father was hidden in the small closet he now had for a library—John always had to have his private place!—I had read my sketches aloud to them and had been gratified by their approving response. Lily had been almost effusive.

"You've pictured Mr. King just right," she told me. "Mother, you're really a great writer."

Lily's praise, which gave me no end of pleasure, was followed by the thrill of seeing my work in print, with my name above it. Always before—except *The Story of the Guard*—I had written so that first Father, and then John, might have the credit. I'd done it gladly, and would again, but it gave me no end of happiness to write in my own name.

But I knew that John would be unhappy ... no, "embarrassed" was the right word. And I remembered my words to Elizabeth Cady Stanton some time earlier: "Women always get slapped when they move out of their sphere." I had moved out of mine.

Now I had to defend myself. "John, no one thinks that is why I wrote that piece, least of all me. I need to pass the time these days. You are always busy in your study, and I no longer have the entertaining and charity work that I did at Pocaho. What am I to do all day, every day? Writing is a pastime for me, nothing more." I took a deep breath and added, "There are three more sketches, and there may be others."

"Jessie, you cannot do this!" His words were firmer than his voice.

"I am paid one hundred dollars for each one," I said, hastily adding, "though that is not why I write."

"That," he said "makes it worse." And he turned and left me sitting at the table. All my pride, all my happiness, could have crumbled before his disapproval ... but I knew I had to stiffen my spine. I could no longer give in to John, though I could still worry about his frailty. I wanted to wrap my arms around him and tell him to stop worrying about what others thought—now in his old age, and in our unhappiness, he ought to rest on the glory of all he'd done in his life. But the gulf between us widened—and I dared say no such thing to John Charles Frémont.

John never again mentioned my writing, though I longed for his praise. After the *Ledger* pieces were well received, the editors of *Harper's Weekly* approached me, and I did a series of pieces on the gold rush in California, even describing those early frightening trips across the Isthmus of Panama. As I wrote, I could feel my skills improving, my writing getting better. Each bit of improvement, each new assignment only spurred me to work harder, and I spent long days at my table while

Lily kept the house running. By 1878 I had collected enough related pieces to be published, and my first book came out—I never did count the one about Zagonyi as my own. This one was called *A Year of American Travel*.

I was asked from time to time by reporters about my husband and the tragedy— their word, not mine—that had befallen us, and my response was always that General Frémont had long dedicated his talents and his fortune to the good of his country. He had, I hinted, perhaps been too trusting, as it was the nature of a good and decent man to assume all other men are honorable, and as a result he had been the victim of unscrupulous businessmen. Too, he had the courage to take a strong antislavery stand when such was not popular, and he should now, I always said, be recognized for his bravery.

When quotes from my standard response appeared in print, John was unfailingly grateful, thanking me for my support.

John, I wanted to cry out, *don't you understand that I love you? Don't you know that I would suffer again all that we have suffered just for your sake?* I knew him as a man who had experienced failure after failure, but that did not change the fact that I loved him. The only difference now was that I had to be the strong one; all pretense that John was the leader had to go by the boards.

We remained cool and polite to each other, distant strangers living together in a tiny house with two grown children. It broke my heart, and I cried myself to sleep more nights than not.

When I dreamed aloud with Lily of bringing back the good times, she listened indulgently, but once she said to me, "Mother, your geese are always swans!" Perhaps I was indeed the eternal optimist.

When Rutherford B. Hayes took the office of president in 1878, we had a friend in power. Hayes, as a young lawyer, had been a strong supporter of John's candidacy for president, and I thought him the perfect person to remind of the government's long-forgotten promise to John of another appointment.

"I hesitate to bring this to your attention," I wrote, without John's knowledge, "but it seems a waste to me that a man of General Frémont's tremendous knowledge and proven capabilities is not serving his country actively, when nothing would please him better than to be of service ... I must ask that you keep this letter in confidence, as General Frémont's natural modesty would be offended by my having written. Yet I think it is the right thing to do."

President Hayes responded by offering John the governorship of the Idaho Territory—which John promptly refused.

"You were offered it and you refused?" I asked incredulously.

"Yes," he said carelessly, "they will also need a governor in Arizona, and I am interested in some silver mines there. I'll hold out for that."

I wanted to scream . . . or throttle him, I wasn't sure which.

With my knowledge of our financial situation I was convinced he should have taken whatever was offered him. But I dared not speak.

The gods had not always looked favorably on John, but they did this time. Hayes did indeed offer him Arizona, and he accepted. The salary would be only two thousand dollars a year, but that was certainly more than he was earning at the time. And despite myself I felt my hopes rising: Once again John had a last chance to prove himself, and with every fiber of my being I willed him to do it.

"Jessie," he said formally one day as I sat sharing a morning cup of coffee with Lily, "we shall have to pack."

"How soon do we leave?" I was in my appropriate wifely role as a helpmate, determined to see him succeed.

"Only a few days," he said. "We depart by train for California, then to Yuma, and finally by ambulance to Prescott. It will be a wearying journey." He paused and looked at me. "You are up to it?"

Did he want me to remain behind? No, that was unthinkable. "We are all up to it, John, and we shall make you proud."

He nodded and left the room.

In late summer we went by Union Pacific to California, the first time an "iron horse" had taken us cross-country. The seven-day trip was one of celebration. John's new appointment was publicly known and so was his travel schedule. At cities across the nation—Chicago, Omaha, and others—he was honored with receptions when the train stopped, hailed as the man who had opened the West. "You had the vision of a transcontinental railroad," said one speaker, "and it is only fit that you ride that railroad to your new post."

It would, I thought to myself with some bitterness, have been more fit if he owned the railroad.

As the train labored westward, the man in the seat behind John, a New York banker, complained mightily of the discomforts of the trip, the long time it took.

Finally John turned to me and said loudly enough for the man to hear, "It required a great deal more than seven days to make this trip in my time, and a great part of it was made on foot. There were also a few discomforts along the line of march—hunger, for instance, and cold!"

I smiled and reached for his hand. For an instant there my old John was back.

The fast and luxurious train took us to San Francisco, where the Pioneer Association of California held a dinner in John's honor, and then we took the Southern Pacific to Los Angeles, where another enthusiastic crowd greeted him. John stood visibly straighter, and his step became more confident at each reception. In California, he was still a hero. But we were not to stay in California, and I viewed Arizona with some measure of uncertainty.

We went by train to Yuma, but that was the last of civilization we saw. From there we traveled for seven days in army ambulances, each pulled by six good mules. Just out of Yuma, we crossed the bottom lands of the Gila River, a monotonous landscape broken only by tall cactus plants.

At the Castle Dime Mine, eighteen miles beyond the Colorado River, we were welcomed into the home of the supervisor—an adobe structure with an earthen floor and a roof of cactus. I eyed it askance—would we live in similar quarters? But there were irresistible touches of civilization in that small home—a pair of opera glasses hung on a nail, and a delicate woman's slipper served as a watch pocket.

"I would not bring the owner here—not until better quarters are prepared," the supervisor said when questioned about the slipper.

When we camped at night, I slept in an ambulance—a privilege I jokingly demanded because of my age, leaving out my fear of snakes and scorpions and other creatures. Lily slept in the tent prepared for both of us, and John and Frank slept on the ground with the men.

We crossed dry beds of stony creeks, where bits of blooming jimsonweed provided only a faint bit of color. The landscape and the almost unbearable heat gave me further uncertainty about the land we were going to. I conjured up visions of the beautiful view from any room at Black Point and the lush greenness of Pocaho, trying to tell myself that I had lived in some of the world's most wonderful spots and I could surely endure one not so beautiful.

But then we met a Captain Woodruff, headed the other way from Prescott, and he called out cheerily, "New York for two years!" His joy was so great that I nearly called after him to wait for me.

John and Frank, meanwhile, saw it all as a great adventure. Frank caught a jackrabbit, and John lectured to any who would listen—and some who would not—about rock formations and geography and the importance of a transcontinental railroad—all topics he somehow related to the land we were crossing. Lily and I exchanged looks but said nothing. We had no need—we could read each other's minds.

The desert offered us only one boon—the most glorious sunsets I had ever seen, eclipsing even those of Black Point. Here intense purples faded into blues, and then the whole was enveloped in crimson, and while we sat about a fire waiting, the sky turned black and was punctuated by thousands of the brightest stars I'd ever seen. Nights in Arizona were definitely better than days.

Gradually we passed into mountains, their sides covered with flowers of pale blue and scarlet, and then through beautiful grass country. We were nearing civilization, for we began to see here and there a farm and the house that went with it, often a house so primitive that I wondered that people could live there.

"This is Skull Valley," John said to me, waving his arm at the farmland we were passing.

I shuddered. "It's an awful name."

"Awful story, too," he said. "There was a battle here, and the white men who died were just left on the field—you know, Indians always carry away their dead and wounded. Well, several years after the battle the Indians came back and piled up the skulls of the white men, as though they were rubbing in their victory."

"Maybe they were," I said, "but who would fight them for this land?"

"A lot of people, Jessie, a lot of people. Including me."

Two miles outside Prescott we were met by the outgoing governor, a man named Hoyt, and a welcoming party, which included Mrs. Hoyt. I was immediately given over to her companionship, but not before I noticed John openly staring at a beautiful woman who wore a leghorn hat trimmed with dark-red silk and bunches of poppies.

"I hope," I heard him say to Governor Hoyt, "that all the women of Prescott are as beautiful." The governor laughed appreciatively, and I for a moment—dusty and dirty, old and tired—hated John for bringing me here, hated him for eyeing another woman, just plain hated him. But it was a passing moment, and I turned my attention to Mrs. Hoyt, who was telling me how much I would enjoy the sociability of Prescott.

"I'm sure," I murmured.

In Prescott there was no house immediately available, and we had to make do by borrowing a home from a lawyer whose family obligingly moved into his office. But then one of the leading merchants announced that he was "going inside"—their term for going to California—and would lease his house for ninety dollars a month.

"John! We cannot afford that!" We were already paying forty dollars a month for a Chinese cook and servant that one of John's friends insisted we must take with us, and John's annual salary of two thousand dollars would not stretch much further.

"We cannot afford not to take it," John said. "Would you rather live in a tent?"

The house, situated on a hilltop, had bare plank walls covered with sheeting and a heavy infestation of household pests. The sheeting had to be removed and the planks repeatedly scrubbed with boiling lye before we could live there. I wondered about the merchant and his family.

I was a housewife again, and I did my best to brighten our new home—small it was, too—with curtains and drapings. I found my mind going back to earlier days at the California White House when I'd been a housewife—no campaigns, no reports, nothing about the world of power to distract me. Then we had to make do with what we could get. This was the same, though I had less energy for it— and even less money. Life in Arizona was expensive: twenty-five cents for a can of tomatoes, thirty cents for a pound of sugar, nearly ten dollars for a cord of wood for the cookstove. Beef and game were plentiful, but, as I wrote to Liza, we were "four days' travel from a lemon."

John was busy from first light until well past dark, but I knew little or nothing of his business. Sometimes he dropped hints about gold and silver mines along the Colorado River, and he seemed to be forever riding out to inspect this mine and that, but he never shared his business with me. I heard rumors—mostly from Lily—that he was particularly interested in the Silver Prince Mine and was seeking financing for it, and that he also was promoting the Sonora Cattle Ranch . . . and then there was a railroad from Tucson to the Gulf of California that needed congressional support. For once poverty was a blessing—we had no money for John to invest in these schemes and therefore no money to lose. But I was always aware, with a terrible mixture of relief and pain, that he did not talk to me about his latest wild dreams. Shut out, I would have been bitter . . . except that when he was away I let the housekeeping go and kept to my desk, writing furiously. Among other things, I had begun a project I called "Great Events in the Life of General John Charles Frémont and Jessie Benton Frémont." I intended to write about the conquest of California, the Republican nomination for the presidency, the Civil War, and the governorship of Arizona.

"I hear you are teaching," he said to me one day. "For pay?"

Indignantly I replied, "Of course not for pay, John! I am teaching the history of this country because I know much more about it than the schoolteacher, and the students like to hear me talk about people I've known. Some of the townspeople come to listen too."

"I suppose," he said bitterly, "that you'll turn it all into articles and sell them."

I fell silent and did not rise to his bait, but he was not far off the mark. I talked at the school once a week and was absolutely amazed to find myself a celebrity. "You mean you really knew Andrew Jackson?" "What can you tell us about President Lincoln?" "What was Queen Victoria like?" In answering those questions I made history and its figures come alive for my listeners, but I was also, as John suspected, sharpening the material of my sketches.

"Jessie, you'll have to abandon your writing for a bit," he said one night when he'd just returned from a two-week absence—surveying the mining prospects of the state, he said.

John knew I was writing, but we had an unspoken agreement to ignore it. Now, needing my help, he brought my work out in the open, using it, I thought, as a tool with which to manipulate me.

"What do you need, John?" There was no sense debating the writing issue with him, and I would willingly help him.

"Your help," he answered. "I have a territorial report due next week, and I've been so busy . . . away so much . . . I haven't had time to work on it."

"Of course, let's start now." I gathered foolscap and pens and arranged the table so that we had room to work. "Tell me what you want to say."

So I found myself writing about all the things that were John's causes—mining recommendations and railroad routes and irrigation reservoirs. (John believed that the Colorado River could be used to flood the southern region of the state, the Salton Sink, and thereby improve the climate and vegetation of America.) Once again we were in harness. The report went in on time and was well written, if I do say so.

But once the report was finished, the distance between us opened again. John sensed my doubts, no matter how I tried to hide them. And the harder I tried to be warm and loving, to put our relationship back on its old footing, the more he withdrew—to his library when he was home, but more often by simply leaving Prescott "on business."

Oh, Prescott society thought we were a fine couple, for we made our way together through dinners and dances, opera performances and recitals. It was a busy place, with citizens who were well educated (and much more comfortable financially than we) so that there was always refined entertainment of some sort. In some ways it put me in mind of the Washington of my youth, and I enjoyed the life. I liked being "Mrs. Governor," a big fish in a small pond.

But it was not working. After nearly a year I was miserable—wanting John's love and earning only distance, wanting to trust him and unable to.

"John, I think I'll go back to New York." We were at the dinner table, the three of us—John, Lily, and myself, Frank having gone off to attend the Army War College. Lily's eyes widened, but she said nothing.

"I'm sure," John said, "that you are lonely for the city . . . and your friends."

Was there a barb there? Was he referring to my editors?

"But," he continued, "I'm surprised you would risk that awful trip to Yuma and back, just for a change of scenery and people."

"I . . . had not intended coming back. I thought to stay in New York." I could have added "for my writing," but prudence silenced my tongue. I put down my fork and folded my hands in my lap, twisting them anxiously under the tablecloth where no one could see.

"Not coming back?" His voice rose in amazement, the most reaction I'd gotten from him in some time. "What would my constituents think if you left me?" His knife clattered out of his hand onto the table, and Lily tactfully reached over to place it on his plate.

"I am not leaving you," I said. "You will return to New York eventually, and I will simply wait for you there. You can tell people that I've gone east to look after your business interests."

He scoffed. "You look after my business interests? Likely they'd all fall to ruin if I listened to your advice, Jessie." Then he added more kindly, "Not that I haven't always valued your advice . . . I just think the world of finance and investment is for men, not women." My appetite for dinner gone, I took a sip of the claret in my glass and found it like vinegar.

"Besides," he continued, "I intend to keep this post for a long time. It . . . al . . . it allows me to develop new investment interests while drawing a government salary."

And, I thought, drawing popular criticism for not paying enough attention to your government duties because you're so interested in your own business.

Lily spoke up now. She had been silently watching us, her head turning each time one of us spoke, her face almost expressionless, though I knew this talk must raise deep conflicts in her. "We can simply tell people that the climate here has been too hard on you, and you are returning to New York for your health."

Had I taught her to dissemble so? "If you wish," I said, "though I've truly never felt better or stronger."

"What shall I do?" she asked, her voice showing just a hint of her bewilderment.

"You," I said firmly, "will stay and take care of your father."

I left Prescott two days later. John and Lily saw me off in the ambulance, with much hugging and loud good wishes. But I think John was secretly relieved that I was going . . . and I knew that I was.

Epilogue

My life began again in 1879 when I returned to New York City. It was, I decided, my third existence: I had been Senator Benton's daughter, and then General Frémont's wife, and now I was Jessie Frémont, author, an identity I took on with joy.

I found a small house in the city and fitted it to my tastes, never once mourning for the fine furnishings I had once known. Silk scarves and swatches of paisley were now my decorating materials, and serviceable plain furniture was sparsely scattered about the house. I needed little more than a table and chairs and a bed.

But my desk sat squarely in the middle of the parlor, dominating the house, just as my writing dominated my life. I arose early each morning and was at my desk within an hour to spend the day working on this article and that. Assignments came from several magazines, and I wrote about life in California, a set of tales set in France and Nassau, more sketches of famous people I had known, recollections of my childhood and my travels. The income was not great, but I supported myself and occasionally sent a small amount to Lily, who wrote uncomplaining from Arizona that her father expected to "be rich again any moment . . . meanwhile I am darning his socks and patching my own petticoats!"

Mine was a solitary existence—I rarely went out and seldom invited visitors in, for my writing absorbed all my time and energy. Once or twice Liza came up from Washington—she had divorced William Carey for his drunkenness—and we had a good visit, reliving old times—times that we both knew, without regret, were gone forever. Susie wrote bitterly from France, where her husband was still in jail, and I replied as kindly as I could—but I had no help to offer and little sympathy to give, even to my favorite sister. I had lost contact with Sarah totally and assumed she was deep in the bosom of the southern branch of the family, where they preferred to act as though I had died during the war. Charley and Frank, both now married, came for quick visits when they could get leave. They were strong and honorable young men, and I was proud of them, overjoyed to see them arrive and always a little relieved to see them leave.

Those who knew me before—in those other lives—wondered that I could be content living so quietly, out of the public eye—indeed, my neighbors thought me just another widow woman, and I did not correct them. Had I been dependent still on John and Lily for companionship or charitable works to give my life meaning, I could not have borne it. But I had my writing. It was almost like having another child.

John and Lily stayed another year in Prescott and then, for reasons I never understood, moved to Tucson, where they spent yet one more year. But by 1881 Hayes had been replaced as president by Chester Arthur, who was not a supporter of John's and was under pressure to replace him because he paid so little attention to his duties as governor. There was no secret about it, no inner knowledge given me by friendly politicians—the charges were published in the newspapers. Under pressure John resigned as governor in October 1881. It was his last great event, and it too had ended in failure.

I welcomed them with open arms, made a place in my small house for John to work at his everlasting projects, and life went on. I had lost my solitude, but not the sense of myself that the period of aloneness had brought. Now, with John and Lily about me, I continued to write, ignoring John's frowns and displeasure. Lily tended the house, while John went back and forth to Washington, seeking a military pension, demanding recompense for Black Point, trying to raise congressional support for a railroad from Tucson to the Gulf of California or financial backing for the Silver Prince Mine, always looking for the miracle that would restore us to the wealth and power we had known.

In 1887, because of John's poor health—he was now seventy-four years old—we moved to California, but he still spent much of his time on the East Coast. He was in New York in July 1890 when he was taken ill—ptomaine poisoning, the doctor said—and died within three days.

Charley reached John's bedside in time to be with him at the end and then to send me a telegram, which said simply, "Father is dead." Devastated by grief, poor Charley failed to realize that I had no warning, no preparation for such shattering news.

I was alone in the parlor when I read the telegram, and I simply sat in stunned silence. I could not imagine a world without John. No matter our differences and our disappointments, he was a part of—no, he was central to—my world. All that I had done in my adult life had been for John—or, of late, in reaction to him. With him gone I was adrift, a ship without an anchor.

At first I was too shocked, too surprised, for tears. When Lily found me staring into space, she asked in concern, "Mother?" And then, only then, did I burst into sobs. Unable to speak, I could only hold out the telegram in a shaking hand.

Lily, ever the stoic, read in silence and then sat with her arm around my heaving shoulders for more than an hour, until I had calmed some.

It grieved me even more that John was alone when he died. It was good that Charley had been there, but it was not the same. I should have been with him, and I was torn with guilt and grief.

As the days passed, I began to feel a great sense of relief. And that plagued me as much as the grief and the guilt. The great events were really over—the power and the glory gone, but gone also the wild financial schemes, the poverty, the accusations and innuendos from friend and foe. John was at last at peace . . . and so was I.

Publicly I always laid his failures at the door of unscrupulous business partners, unfortunate circumstances, and bad luck. I breathed to no one, not even Lily, my own conviction that John had brought about his own luck, that his vision had exceeded his grasp, that perhaps Mr. Lincoln was right when he said the person who introduces a reform is not necessarily the best one to see it brought to fruition. If John could only be remembered for all his greatness—but I feared the failures would live longer.

I tried to write John's biography—ghostwrite his autobiography, really—but *Memoirs of My Life—A Retrospect of Fifty Years* was a commercial failure. My heart was not in it. I, who had been his most passionate defender all those years, now saw the real man behind the facade all too clearly. Someone else would have to write the biography that would take John's name into history.

Still, there is this manuscript—my own memoir. Lily says I should burn it, but I will leave it guarded with instructions it is not to be published for seventy-five years after my death. By then no one will care about John's failures and triumphs—or mine. But I want to leave a record of a life well lived. If I had it all to do over again, I would change nothing. And I would elope with John Charles Frémont again.

Author's Note

Jessie Benton Frémont is the subject of the novel *Immortal Wife*, by Irving Stone (1944), while her husband, John Charles Frémont, is at the center of the long novel *Dream West*, by David Nevin (1983). Having read both long before I began work on this novel, I deliberately avoided rereading them as part of my research. Each novelist must bring an individual approach to the facts of history.

In her later years Jessie Frémont attempted an autobiography, but ill health and her daughter's displeasure discouraged her from finishing the work. The unfinished manuscript is too often devoted to a biased accounting of John's affairs or secondhand descriptions of his expeditions and adventures. Occasionally, however, Jessie recorded fascinating details of specific periods in their lives—their year in California before he was elected to the US Senate, their trip to Arizona when he was appointed governor. Unfortunately, she rarely recorded information about her own feelings, and the novelist is left to conjecture. This incomplete manuscript and Jessie's other papers are in the Bancroft Library at the University of California, Berkeley. There are, of course, numerous studies—some bad, some good, some sympathetic, others not—of John Charles Frémont, but his only "autobiography" was penned by Jessie, so we are once again unable to look to the written word for insight into his true feelings—or hers.

For this novel I relied heavily on Jessie Frémont's unpublished autobiography, along with other works by her: *A Year of American Travel* (1878), *Souvenirs of My Time* (1887), and *Far West Sketches* (1890). For some parts of Frémont's life the memoirs of her oldest daughter, *Recollections of Elizabeth Benton Frémont* (1912), were extremely valuable and offered a fresh viewpoint. Secondary sources of great help were Pamela Herr's excellent biography, *Jessie Benton Frémont* (1987), and the two-volume biography of John Charles Frémont by Allan Nevins (1928). Also helpful was *The Letters of Jessie Benton Frémont*, edited by Pamela Herr and Mary Lee Spence.

In weaving Jessie's story into fiction, I have taken small liberties with history for the sake of dramatic storytelling and also to simplify what was an unbelievably complex life. I hope, though, that I have not distorted history and that I have been true to the spirit of Jessie Frémont's life. Often caught between two strong men, she ultimately triumphed and proved herself the strongest of all.

About the Author

Judy Alter is the author of over a hundred books, fiction and nonfiction, for both adults and young adults. Her awards include the 2005 Owen Wister Award for Lifetime Achievement, Spur Awards from the Western Writers of America for the novel *Mattie* and the short story "Sue Ellen Learns to Dance," Western Heritage (Wrangler) Awards for "Sue Ellen Learns to Dance" and "Fool Girl," and a Best Juvenile of the Year Award from the Texas Institute of Letters for *Luke and the Van Zandt County War*. She was named one of the Outstanding Women of Fort Worth by Mayor's Commission on the Status of Women in 1989 and was listed by *Dallas Morning News* (March 10, 1999) as one of one hundred women, past and present, who made their mark on Texas. She has been inducted into the Western Writers of America Hall of Fame and the Texas Literary Hall of Fame. Alter continues to write about the history and literature of the American West. Her most recent book is *The Second Battle of the Alamo* (TwoDot, 2020).